continued . . .

Criminal Intent

"In the last two decades we've seen an explosion of the legal thriller. Every other lawyer, it seems, has one under way. The better of the breed is Sheldon Siegel. . . . Siegel writes with style and humor. . . . He's a guy who needs to keep that laptop popping."   —*Houston Chronicle*

"Siegel does a nice job of blending humor and human interest into the mystery. Daley and Fernandez are competent lawyers, not superhuman crime fighters featured in more commonplace legal thrillers. With great characters and realistic dialogue, this book provides enough intrigue and courtroom drama to please any fan of the genre."   —*Library Journal*

"Siegel is . . . adept at detailing the workings of criminal law from the inside."   —*Publishers Weekly*

Incriminating Evidence

"Without a doubt, *Incriminating Evidence* . . . was the most fun to read this summer. For those who love San Francisco, this is a dream of a novel. . . . Siegel is an astute observer of the city and takes wry and witty jabs at lawyers and politicians."   —*USA Today*

"Outstanding. . . . Mike Daley narrates with a kind of genial irony, the pace never slows, and every description of the city is as brightly burnished as the San Francisco sky when the fog lifts."   —*The Newark Star-Ledger*

"Considerable charm. . . . Daley is an original and very appealing character—a gentle soul who can fight hard when he has to."   —*Publishers Weekly*

THE
CONFESSION

Sheldon Siegel

A SIGNET BOOK

SIGNET
Published by New American Library, a division of
Penguin Group (USA) Inc., 375 Hudson Street,
New York, New York 10014, USA
Penguin Group (Canada), 90 Eglinton Avenue East, Suite 700, Toronto,
Ontario M4P 2Y3, Canada (a division of Pearson Penguin Canada Inc.)
Penguin Books Ltd., 80 Strand, London WC2R 0RL, England
Penguin Ireland, 25 St. Stephen's Green, Dublin 2,
Ireland (a division of Penguin Books Ltd.)
Penguin Group (Australia), 250 Camberwell Road, Camberwell, Victoria 3124,
Australia (a division of Pearson Australia Group Pty. Ltd.)
Penguin Books India Pvt. Ltd., 11 Community Centre, Panchsheel Park,
New Delhi - 110 017, India
Penguin Group (NZ), cnr Airborne and Rosedale Roads, Albany,
Auckland 1310, New Zealand (a division of Pearson New Zealand Ltd.)
Penguin Books (South Africa) (Pty.) Ltd., 24 Sturdee Avenue,
Rosebank, Johannesburg 2196, South Africa

Penguin Books Ltd., Registered Offices:
80 Strand, London WC2R 0RL, England

Published by Signet, an imprint of New American Library, a division of Penguin
Group (USA) Inc. Previously published in a G. P. Putnam's Sons edition.

First Signet Printing, August 2005
10 9 8 7 6 5 4 3 2 1

For my friends and colleagues at
Sheppard, Mullin, Richter & Hampton

CHAPTER 1

"A Sliding Scale for Sin"

A high-profile lawsuit against the San Francisco Archdiocese for allegedly covering up a pattern of sexual abuse by a prominent priest was put on hold when the plaintiff's attorney apparently committed suicide.

—*San Francisco Chronicle,* Tuesday, December 9

"**BLESS ME, FATHER,** for I have sinned."

My rote recitation of the traditional catechism is met with a mixture of piety and detached amusement by my friend and seminary classmate Father Ramon Aguirre, who is sitting on the other side of the portal in a musty confessional booth at the back of St. Peter's Catholic Church at eight P.M. on Tuesday, December ninth. The organ is silent and the bells from the tower are being drowned out by the rain that's beating against the vaulted ceiling three stories above us. The modest wooden structure in San Francisco's historic Mission District was erected in the 1880s and survived the 1906 earthquake, but its good fortune ran out almost a hundred years later when it was severely damaged by fire. It was rebuilt a few years ago and looks much the same as it did when my parents brought me here for my baptism a half century ago.

Ramon is fluent in Spanish, but there is no trace of an accent when he asks, "How long has it been since your

last confession, Mike?" Nowadays, relatively few
Catholics—even recovering ones like me—get to confess
their sins to a priest who knows them by name.

"Do we have to go through this ritual every time we
get together?"

"I'm just doing my job."

"Do I get any dispensation for all the Hail Marys I said
when I was a priest?"

"You can't use Hail Marys like frequent-flyer miles.
You know the drill. How long has it been?"

"When was the last time I saw you, Ramon?"

"About a month ago."

"That was the last time I went to confession."

The pews are empty and a few votive candles are
flickering near the altar. St. Peter's is a reminder of simpler times when this area was populated by Irish immigrants. My parents grew up a few blocks from here on
opposite sides of Garfield Square, but that's ancient history. Like many of our neighbors who wanted more room
for their growing families, we moved from our cramped
apartment to a small house in the foggy Sunset District
forty years ago as part of a larger exodus from the inner
city that was taking place in many metropolitan areas at
the time. My old neighborhood has been home to a work-
ing-class Latino community ever since, and the sweet
aroma of burritos, salsa and fresh fruit permeates the
modest commercial strip around the corner on Twenty-
fourth Street. The refurbished church is in pretty good
shape thanks to a substantial infusion of cash from the
archdiocese, but the residents of the community lack the
resources to maintain many of the bungalows and low-

rise apartment buildings that date back to the late nineteenth century. Things are especially grim near the Valencia Gardens Housing Project and the BART station at
Sixteenth and Mission, where drug dealers and prostitutes
outnumber conventional businesses. Parts of the neighborhood gentrified during the dot-com frenzy, but the upgrades went on hold when the NASDAQ crashed.

Ramon is also a throwback to an earlier era. The polit-
ically astute and utterly pragmatic priest is a worthy suc-
cessor to the legacy of the legendary Peter Yorke, who
was born in Galway in 1887 and plied his trade in this
very building in the early part of the last century. Father
Yorke was a labor organizer, newspaper publisher and political gadfly. Ramon understands that he can better tend
to his flock if he has the resources to do so, and he got into
a little trouble a few years ago when he accepted dona-
tions from a produce wholesaler who supplemented his
income with drug and prostitution money. To this day,
Ramon insists he didn't know the funds were dirty. He
used the cash to feed the poor, and neither the DA nor the
archdiocese was inclined to pursue it. He opens his church
to the homeless on Thursdays and there is a dance in the
social hall every Saturday night where he always takes a
turn at the mike. The *Chronicle* dubbed him the "Rock-
and-Roll Reverend."

His tone has the requisite level of priestlike judgment
when he says, "How often do you stop by to chat with
God?"

"Occasionally." My record has been spotty since I left
the priesthood almost twenty years ago. "Is this interrogation necessary?"

"I'm in the business of saving souls, and yours is at the top of my list. You're a test case for the greatest challenge of my career."

"Which is?"

"I'm trying to get my first lawyer into heaven."

Sometimes I miss the good old days when priests were stern taskmasters instead of aspiring stand-up comics. "What are my odds?" I ask.

"Not good. I have to hold you to a higher standard because you used to be one of us."

"There's a sliding scale for sin?"

"Yes."

"That rule wasn't in effect when I was a priest."

"It is now." He chuckles and says, "One of the things I love about this job is that I get a lot of latitude in deciding what constitutes a sin."

It's one of the many reasons I'm no longer in his line of work. I never felt qualified to sit in judgment of people who tortured themselves with guilt for things that didn't seem all that sinful to me. The nice people felt compelled to confess to trivial things while the schmucks were running amok on the streets. I developed a reputation as the "easy priest" at St. Anne's in the Sunset where I worked for three years before I threw in the towel and went to law school. My lackadaisical attitude in meting out punishments was met with greater enthusiasm by the kids in my parish than by my superiors.

"How's Rosie?" he asks.

"She's fine."

His simple question has a more complicated answer. Rosita Fernandez is my law partner, significant other and best friend. She's also my ex-wife. We've covered a lot of territory since we met at the San Francisco Public Defender's Office sixteen years ago. We've managed to get married, have a daughter who just turned twelve, get divorced and start a law practice. I mixed in an unsatisfying stint at a big law firm, and we tried our hand at being law professors at my alma mater, Boalt Hall. That latest experiment came to an end about a year after it started.

Our last high-profile case was eighteen months ago when we represented an indigent man who was accused of stabbing a Silicon Valley hotshot behind a liquor store on Sixth Street. We tried to take a break after the case ended, but we discovered that Rosie was pregnant and we welcomed an energetic baby boy in January. This led to rampant and unsubstantiated speculation that we might get married again. Some people are meant to live together, but Rosie and I aren't, and we decided to continue to live in nonmarital, noncohabitative semi-bliss in our respective places in Marin County. It isn't an ideal arrangement, but life is full of compromises, and over the last eleven months, we've come to appreciate the three-block demilitarized zone that separates her house from my apartment. After reembarking upon parenthood shortly after turning fifty, I've decided to hold off on any additional life-cycle events for the foreseeable future.

"Has there been any recurrence of the cancer?" he asks.

Rosie had a mastectomy three years ago. "She's cancer-free," I report.

"That's great news."

Yes, it is.

"So," he says, "have you given any thought to making her an honest woman?"

He always tries. I wag a finger at him and say, "Priests aren't allowed to do any suggestive selling. You're supposed to sit back and listen while I tell you all the horrible things I've done." I've always loved the fact that the Church has rules for everything.

"I hate doing confessions for ex-priests," he says, "and lawyers are even worse. They argue about everything."

Yes, we do.

He pleads his case. "I wasn't trying to elicit a confession," he insists. "I was simply giving you some helpful postmarital or, best case, premarital counseling."

Priests are even better at parsing than lawyers.

He tees it up again. "Have you and Rosie thought about trying a more conventional relationship? It would make my boss happy and I could check off one more item on my to-do list. I'll put in a good word with God if you think it would help."

"Technically," I say, "what we're doing isn't a sin." We got a civil divorce, but we never got one from the Church. "According to you guys, we're still married, so you have to lay off."

We've covered this territory, and he changes the subject. "How's Grace?"

"Fine." Our daughter is a good kid who is showing her first signs of independence. Things are going to get more interesting when her braces come off and her figure fills out. God help us when her first boyfriend shows up at the door.

"Do you take her to church every once in a while?"

"From time to time." She isn't wildly enthusiastic about it, and I don't push. I'm hoping she'll be able to find a relationship with God on her own terms.

"And Tommy?"

Over the years, the name Tommy has had multiple meanings in our family. Originally, it referred to my father, Thomas James Charles Daley, Sr., who was a San Francisco cop for four decades until he succumbed to lung cancer just after Grace was born. For twenty-two glorious years, it also meant my older brother, Tom Jr., who was a star quarterback at St. Ignatius and Cal before he went to Vietnam and never came back. Nowadays, it means the active eleven-month-old lad with a charming disposition and strong lungs that he exercises at four o'clock every morning. We're hoping he'll sleep through the night sometime before he leaves for college.

"He's been a little colicky," I say, "but he's doing great." Rosie says that any woman who has a baby after she turns forty should hire a stunt mom.

"Give them a hug for me."

"I will." I sound like Grace when I say, "Can we get dinner now? I'm hungry."

"You still haven't confessed to anything. You must have done *something*."

When I was a kid, my brother and I became adept at making up a few sins on our way to church if we hadn't done anything especially egregious during the week. If all else failed, we'd swear at each other, then we'd go inside and confess. "If I admit to something, will you stop bugging me about getting married again?"

"Seems fair."

It strikes me as amusing that I choose to confess my sins to a man who was known as the "Party Priest" at the seminary. We used to go out for a few beers a couple of nights a week while we were studying to become God's emissaries, and we had to cover for each other from time to time. He's toned things down considerably since he became the head honcho at St. Peter's and freely acknowledges that it wouldn't set a good example if they found him passed out on the steps of the rectory with an empty beer can in his hand.

I go with an old standby. "I said a bad word in court today, and I took the Lord's name in vain when Tommy's diaper exploded last night."

"That's the best you can do?"

"I'm afraid so."

His tone turns appropriately judgmental when he says, "You shouldn't swear in front of the children." He lets me off with a light sentence and the usual admonition to set a better example. I promise to play nice, but I'm reasonably sure my ticket to hell was punched the day I was admitted to the California Bar.

I DUTIFULLY SAY my Hail Marys and we adjourn to a religious shrine of a different sort. The Taqueria LaCumbre is a hole in the wall on Valencia, about a mile from St. Peter's. The tiny room isn't long on ambience, but the restaurant has been here forever and many of us think the recipe for the *pollo asada* was handed down directly from God. We're sitting in the corner and I'm devouring my chicken as Ramon takes a long draw on his second beer. He's a lanky man with dark brown eyes, a prominent Roman nose and a full head of silver hair. He still plays basketball a couple of nights a week at the Mission YMCA and looks like he could glide down the court with the USF varsity, where he was once a starting forward. Rosie says he's the sexiest man in the Bay Area. She's always had a thing for priests.

His normally ebullient demeanor turns serious when our conversation turns to Church gossip. "It isn't as much fun as it was when you were still in the business," he says. "You can't pick up a newspaper without reading about some priest who was molesting kids or sleeping with his parishioners. You lawyers are a big part of the problem—the lawsuits never stop."

The tribulations of the Catholic Church in the early twenty-first century have been well documented, and the fact that some attorneys have taken the opportunity to line their pockets with legal fees hasn't gone unnoticed. "Sounds like I got out at the right time," I say.

"You were a good priest."

I was also an unhappy one. I never had a knack for Church politics, and I had no aptitude for raising money. This led to frustration and ultimately depression. Eventually, I went to Ramon for counseling and his steady hand helped me stay the course during a yearlong period that was even darker than the worst moments when Rosie and I were getting divorced.

"I'm more of a politician than a priest," he says. "Our parish is poor, and I spend half my time fund-raising. With the scandals and the economic downturn, people have become terribly cynical." He tells me about a ninety-year-old parishioner whom he visits at a nursing home. "Last time I saw her, she winked at me and said she didn't have time for sex—and she came to church every Sunday. Imagine how the disenfranchised people are feeling. We've become a punch line for David Letterman, and the archbishop thinks we can solve the problems with a public-relations campaign."

Ramon's propensity for expressing views that run counter to the party line has never endeared him to the Church hierarchy, but in all the years I've known him, I've never heard this level of frustration in his voice.

"Are you thinking of getting out?" I ask.

His tone is uncharacteristically sharp when he says, "You did."

It would have consumed me if I hadn't. "I wasn't cut out for the job."

"I'm tired of being a full-time apologist who hears confessions when I'm not beating the bushes for money."

I offer a priestly platitude. "Things will get better."

"I hope Jesus is still listening to you."

I finish my beer and look into the eyes of my old friend. "Why did you call me, Ramon?"

"Have you been following the O'Connell case?"

"A little."

His mentor, Father Patrick O'Connell, started his career at St. Peter's and later moved to St. Boniface in the teeming Tenderloin District. About a year ago, allegations began to surface that Father Pat had been engaging in illicit sexual activities with his female parishioners for two decades. One of his alleged victims filed a lawsuit naming the archdiocese as a co-defendant.

Father Pat died of a heart attack a couple of months ago, but the case against the archdiocese didn't go away. Things were coming to a head last week when jury selection was set to begin, but everything came to a screeching halt when the body of the plaintiff's attorney was found in her Mission District flat, an apparent suicide.

"The plaintiff's lawyer was a member of our parish," he says, "and her mother asked me to officiate at her funeral. I suspect this was viewed with mixed feelings down at archdiocese headquarters."

I'll bet. Maria Concepcion grew up a few blocks from here and graduated at the top of her class at Hastings. She spent the early years of her career taking endless depositions and briefing arcane rules of law on behalf of the tobacco companies that paid her prominent downtown firm millions to defend product-liability lawsuits. She was compensated handsomely for her efforts and became well versed in the minutiae of class-action litigation, but she never saw the inside of a courtroom and grew weary of killing trees to facilitate the uninterrupted flow of nicotine. Coincidentally, her old firm has represented the archdiocese for decades. She had a falling-out with her colleagues and her husband, and she found herself unemployed and divorced.

She set up shop in her Mission District apartment and took on small matters for her neighbors. Her career took an unexpected turn when she filed a lawsuit against the archdiocese as a favor to a friend who was trying to collect a modest judgment in a slip-and-fall case. She played it for all it was worth and got a check and an apology from the archbishop. More important, her photo appeared on page one of the *Chronicle* the next morning.

The timing was fortuitous. Two days later, a priest was accused of propositioning several altar boys. The victims hired the mediagenic Concepcion, who filed a dozen law-suits against the Church for everything from child abuse to sexual improprieties. The players on Cathedral Hill and their highly paid attorneys tried to dismiss her as a publicity-seeking hack, but the evidence proved other-wise. If you believe the *Chronicle,* she had negotiated settlements that ran well into eight figures, and there has been speculation that an adverse result in the O'Connell case could push the archdiocese into bankruptcy.

"I've known Maria since we were kids," he says. "She may have been a hotshot lawyer, but she was still a regu-lar at mass—unlike present company."

"She was suing the archdiocese for millions, yet she kept coming?"

"She still believed in the Church, but not in the people who are running it."

"Did that include you?"

"She wouldn't have come to St. Peter's if she thought I was part of the problem. The fact that she was a member of our parish didn't endear me to my superiors, but you can't throw somebody out of the club just because she's suing the guys who have the keys to the social hall."

The power priests in the cushy offices down the block from St. Mary's Cathedral might see things a little differ-ently. I lower my voice to confession level and say, "The press is saying it was a suicide."

"It's inconceivable to me."

"Is this something we need to talk about?"

"Is this conversation attorney-client privileged?"

"It is now."

He glances around the empty restaurant and says, "The cops have been asking questions."

"That's the usual procedure." Especially if it *wasn't* a suicide.

"They said they might want to talk to me again. I was hoping you'd be available."

"Of course. Do you have any information that might be of interest to them?"

There's a hesitation before he says, "I don't think so."

I pick up on it. "Is there something you haven't told me?"

"I'm probably just being paranoid."

Or hiding something.

"HOW IS RAMON?" Rosie asks.

Her sculpted cheekbones and olive skin have regained the youthful luster that belie forty-six years of mileage, two children and a battle with breast cancer. After Tommy arrived, she went on a torturous exercise regimen to regain the svelteness that had disappeared after Grace was born. The only hints of her age are a few small creases at the corners of her cobalt eyes and my insider knowledge that her long black hair gets a helpful boost every so often from certain over-the-counter products that you can find in your local drugstore.

"He's still having a hard time with Pat O'Connell's death," I tell her.

Once upon a time, Tuesday was our date night, but it became laundry night after Tommy was born. We're watching the eleven o'clock news and folding clothes in the living room of Rosie's rented nine-hundred-square-foot palace across the street from the Little League field in Larkspur, a tidy burg about ten miles north of the Golden Gate Bridge. Tommy is dozing in Rosie's bedroom and Grace is sleeping in her room at the end of the narrow hallway.

Rosie isn't surprised when I tell her that Ramon knew Maria Concepcion. Rosie's family moved into the Mission around the same time that we left. Her mother still lives in a white bungalow around the corner from St. Peter's, and she knows everybody in the neighborhood, including the Concepcion family. Rosie says she'd met Maria on a couple of occasions, but they weren't close. She describes her as pretty and very ambitious.

I ask about her vendetta against the archdiocese.

"It started by accident and snowballed," she says. "The fact that her old law firm represents the Church may have given her some additional incentive."

"Was she a publicity hound?"

"She was a good lawyer."

"Did she strike you as the type who would have committed suicide?"

"I didn't know her that well."

I'm pulling a load of laundry out of the dryer a few minutes later when the phone rings. Rosie gives me an unhappy look and dashes into the kitchen to pick it up. People with little kids generally aren't wildly appreciative of calls in the wee hours, but in our line of work, they're an occupational hazard.

Tommy wakes up and I head into the bedroom. He's

pulled himself up by the posts of his crib and is wailing with an intensity that will serve him well after he passes the bar exam in twenty-five years. I hoist him up on my shoulder and feel the full diaper, then I gently place him on the changing table and sing "To-Ra-Loo-Ra" with the same inflection my mother used when I was a kid. I'm not sure if it's my vocals or the removal of the diaper, but he stops crying. I put him back in his crib and say, "Why don't you give Mommy a break tonight?"

He gives me a bemused look. The son of two lawyers knows better than to make any promises.

I'm sitting in the rocking chair next to the crib when Rosie walks in. There is a troubled look on her face as she hands me the cordless phone. "It's Ramon," she says.

Something's very wrong. I take the phone and whisper, "What's up?"

His voice cracks. "I'm sorry for calling so late. I hope I didn't wake Tommy."

"It's okay."

"I need your help."

"I told you I'd be available if the cops wanted to talk to you."

"They do."

"Fine. When?"

"Right now."

"What?"

"I've been arrested for the murder of Maria Concepcion."

CHAPTER 2

"How Many Lawyers Does It Take?"

Cases involving the clergy are especially troublesome.

—Inspector Roosevelt Johnson, *San Francisco Chronicle*

"**WHERE IS HE?**" Rosie asks.

I'm pulling on my jacket as I say, "The rectory at St. Peter's."

"Who made the arrest?"

"Marcus Banks and Roosevelt Johnson." The SFPD isn't taking any chances. The veteran homicide inspectors have more than eighty years of experience between them. "Johnson was standing next to him, and Ramon couldn't say much. Banks told me to meet them at the Hall of Justice."

This elicits a troubled look and a realistic analysis. "Sounds like the chances of stopping the train before things get out of hand aren't very good."

I need to deal with an important issue up front. I ask, "Do you have the energy for this?" It isn't a purely academic question. Rosie's health problems are largely behind her, but murder cases take on a life of their own and we agreed to steer clear of high-profile matters until Tommy gets out of diapers.

"We know all the reasons why we shouldn't take this case," she says.

I hope there's a "but" coming.

"But it's Ramon," she says. "We have to help him."

When push comes to shove, Rosita Carmela Fernandez is always there. On to another touchy subject. "He's a priest," I say. "He isn't rolling in cash."

"We didn't pay him to mediate our divorce."

No, we didn't. Ramon engaged in six weeks of thankless shuttle diplomacy while Rosie and I negotiated our settlement. We spent more time hammering on him than reviewing the legal documents. He never lost his composure even when the sniping got especially nasty.

"You're prepared to handle his case pro bono?" I say.

"The archdiocese may be willing to pay his legal fees."

"And if not?"

Her sense of obligation trumps her customary dedication to fiscal responsibility. "We owe it to him. I'll take the kids to my mother's, then I'll meet you down at the Hall."

End of discussion.

IN MY HOMETOWN, the wheels of justice grind *ever* so slowly in a massive gray temple we lovingly call the Hall of Justice. The monolithic six-story structure takes up two city blocks adjacent to the 80 freeway and houses the criminal courts, the morgue, the DA's office and the Southern Police Station. The architect who designed the Plexiglas-covered jail wing that was added in the early nineties drew his inspiration from Cold War–era structures in East Berlin. The cops derisively refer to it as the "Glamour Slammer."

The lifeless slab is especially depressing in a driving rainstorm as I pull into a parking space on Bryant Street a few minutes after midnight. The cross-section of San Francisco's underbelly who conduct their business while the sun is still up are absent, and the dimly lit granite hallway echos with an uninviting reverberation. I'm soaked as I pass through the metal detector where the night guard greets me by name. I take the excruciatingly slow elevator to the fourth floor, where Marcus Banks and Roosevelt Johnson are waiting for me outside an airless interrogation room next to the bullpen where the homicide inspectors ply their trade. This area bustles with activity during the day, but is eerily quiet at this hour. Things could be worse. In normal circumstances, we'd be conducting this unpleasant exercise at the intake center in the Glamour Slammer.

Banks is dressed in a custom charcoal suit that exudes cool control as it hugs his ebony skin. In a minor concession to the hour, his Armani tie is loosened. The only hints of his age are the gray eyebrows that form a single line across the top of his wire-rimmed bifocals.

Johnson played linebacker at Cal and was a member of the SFPD's first integrated team when he walked the beat with my father a half century ago. He came out of retirement to keep busy after his wife died earlier this year. His attire is a study in meticulous business casual: khaki slacks and an oxford shirt. His trim mustache is now a distinguished shade of silver, but he looks as if he could still cover a tight end sprinting downfield.

We exchange forced greetings and I address Johnson, whom I've known since I was a kid and who is generally more forthcoming than his partner. "Where is Father Aguirre?" I ask.

He gestures toward the interrogation room and responds in a measured baritone. "His arraignment will be at ten o'clock this morning."

Rosie is making the obligatory calls, but it's unlikely the duty judge will grant bail. The best-case scenario is that Ramon will be here for only one night. Given the circumstances, all I can do is cast a line and start fishing. "What's this all about?" I ask.

The combative Banks grudgingly offers a morsel. "Ms. Concepcion's mother found her daughter's body in the bathtub, wrists slashed."

"The papers said it was a suicide."

"They were wrong. We found a kitchen knife in the bathroom. It was covered with her blood."

"That's still consistent with a suicide," I say.

"Except for the fact that Father Aguirre's fingerprints were on the knife."

Hell. "I'm sure he has an explanation."

"He hasn't shared it with us. A lawyer advised him not to talk."

That would have been me. I'm tempted to explain that Ramon knew Concepcion, but you never offer anything that could be used against you. "I want to see him," I say.

"You'll have to come back during visiting hours."

No way. "I want to see him right now."

"We'll try to work something out as soon as he's done talking to his lawyers."

What? "I'm his lawyer."

"Not according to the two guys inside who say they're representing him."

"Who?"

"F. X. Quinn and John Shanahan."

The archdiocese isn't wasting any time protecting its turf. Father Francis Xavier Quinn is the overbearing chief in-house counsel for the archdiocese, a man who looks like Orson Welles and talks like Donald Rumsfeld. He earned a law degree at night and has worked his way up the bureaucracy at the archdiocese for thirty years. When I was a priest, he oversaw the administration of St. Anne's Parish, and he was less than understanding when I decided to leave. John Shanahan is the eloquent senior partner of the well-connected firm of Shanahan, Gallagher and O'Rourke, where Concepcion started her career. Quinn and Shanahan are the designated SWAT team when a priest gets into trouble. Quinn is the muscle and Shanahan is the mouthpiece.

I give Banks my best Clint Eastwood look and say, "Father Aguirre called me first."

"This isn't a race."

"He asked me to represent him. He's always free to change his mind."

"Evidently, he already has."

"I'll need to hear it from him."

"This is like a bad joke," he says. "How many lawyers does it take to represent a priest who is accused of murder?"

"Just one," I say. "Me."

CHAPTER 3

The Muscle and the Mouthpiece

The moral authority of the archbishop must never be brought into question.

—Father F. X. Quinn, *San Francisco Chronicle*

F. X. QUINN SQUEEZES my hand and feigns civility. "Nice to see you again, Michael," he lies. His tone lands somewhere between condescending and patronizing when he adds, "Thank you for coming down here in the middle of the night, but the situation is under control."

John Shanahan nods emphatically. Smart lawyers don't talk unless they must and always agree with their meal-ticket clients.

We're standing in the empty corridor near the Homicide Division, just out of earshot of Banks and Johnson. They've given us five minutes to decide who gets to be Ramon's lawyer, and the issue does not lend itself to a prompt resolution by a one-potato-two-potato contest.

Quinn towers over me by six inches and outweighs me by a hundred pounds. The onetime defensive tackle at St. Ignatius wears the traditional collar and carries the accoutrements of authority with regal splendor. His bald dome, multitiered chins and basset-hound eyes suggest he's a grandfather type, but his looks are deceiving. He preaches peace and love, but he views every legal claim against the archdiocese as a personal affront to God.

Shanahan is a third-generation USF alum whose father was a member of the Board of Supervisors and whose uncle was a judge. He epitomizes the fading line of lawyers who built their practices by trading on family contacts, political connections and shameless cronyism. Seeking to curry support from the political establishment, the then-reigning archbishop sent a few personal-injury cases over to young Johnny Shanahan's newly minted firm forty years ago. Now in his seventies, the world-class senior squash player and former Marine sergeant has taken on the persona of a silver-haired sage whose practiced eloquence is ideally suited for his role as archdiocese spokesman. It brings prestige and eight figures in fees annually to his once-fledgling firm, which now employs three hundred lawyers. Genteel John's refined demeanor and aristocratic air belie the fact that he's a street fighter who approaches every battle as if it will be his last. Whether it's a multimillion-dollar trial or a squash game, he hates to lose.

Shanahan may be the Church's voice to the public, but Quinn lays down the law. His voice is commanding when he says, "You can go home, Michael. We'll take it from here."

He may as well have added the words, "You're dismissed."

"I need to talk to Father Aguirre," I say.

The Voice of God turns more emphatic. "We have it covered."

It will serve no useful purpose to initiate a shouting

match with the chief legal officer of the archdiocese, but I have an obligation to make sure Ramon is represented by the lawyer he chooses—especially if it's me. "I really have to see my client," I say.

"He isn't your client."

I dislike him intensely, and I'm quite sure the feeling is mutual. "He asked me to represent him, and I intend to do so until he tells me otherwise."

Quinn is a control freak who isn't used to having his authority challenged. His tiny eyes narrow when he says, "I'm telling you otherwise, Michael."

"You aren't my client, Francis."

He detests being called by his given name. "That isn't the way things work at the Church," he says.

"It's the way things work in the real world."

"We're representing Father Aguirre."

"You're representing the archdiocese. I'm representing Father Aguirre."

He slowly enunciates every syllable when he says, "This is a Church matter."

I'm equally dogmatic when I reply, "It's also a personal matter."

"Let us handle this, Michael. I don't want you to get in over your head again."

"What's that supposed to mean?"

"I've seen you in action."

"You've never seen me in court."

"I've seen you in church. You abandoned your parishioners. I have an obligation to make sure you don't do the same to Father Aguirre."

"That was twenty years ago, Francis. The fact that I

decided to leave the priesthood has nothing to do with my capabilities as a lawyer."

"Old habits die hard. I realize that Father Aguirre called you, but I was hoping you'd do the honorable thing and remove yourself from consideration."

"I can't do that."

"You mean you *won't* do it. In good conscience, I'm not going to recommend your firm."

"Look at our track record, Francis. We've handled more than our share of high-profile cases. We know what we're doing, and we get excellent results."

"I can't take that chance."

"It isn't your choice."

"It is when there are ramifications for the archdiocese."

"All the more reason for Father Aguirre to hire someone who is independent."

The unflappable Shanahan interjects a modulated tone. "I know you're trying to help a friend," he says, "but you have to think about what's best for Father Aguirre."

"That's exactly what I'm doing."

"You have to understand that it's our job to protect our people."

"No, it's your job to protect the *archbishop*. It's *my* job to protect Father Aguirre. He needs a defense lawyer."

"We have several in our firm."

"Who specialize in defending civil suits against the archdiocese. You don't have anybody who's handled a murder case, and you have a conflict of interest."

He feigns exasperation. "Are you suggesting we would set up a priest to protect the reputation of the archdiocese?"

Exactly. "I'm suggesting the conflict should be disclosed to Father Aguirre. If he doesn't want me to represent him, I'll go home."

The omnipresent Quinn responds. "I'll ask him about it," he says.

"*I'll* ask him about it."

His jowls work furiously. "Are you saying you don't trust us?"

Precisely. "He called *me* and asked *me* to represent him. I'm not in a position to take instructions from you, and I'm not leaving until I talk to him."

CHAPTER 4

"We're Only Looking Out for Your Best Interests"

The archdiocese must take a proactive role in preventing legal problems.

—Father F. X. Quinn, *San Francisco Chronicle*

THE ONLY SOUND in the stuffy interrogation room is the buzzing from the industrial-strength clock. Ramon looks more like a felon than a priest as he's sitting in one of the two heavy wooden chairs and staring at a Styrofoam cup of water that's resting on the gray metal table. His hair is disheveled, and his denim shirt and cotton pants will be replaced in due course by an orange jumpsuit. Quinn has jammed his ample torso into the other chair, and Shanahan is standing by the door with his arms folded. I'm leaning against the graffiti-covered wall. Rosie hasn't arrived yet, and I'm feeling outnumbered.

Ramon addresses us in a hoarse whisper. "They've made a terrible mistake," he says.

I try to sound reassuring. "We'll get you out of here as soon as we can."

His eyes fill with hope. "When?"

"Probably not until morning."

Not the answer he wanted to hear.

Quinn clears his throat and moves to the top of his agenda. "Ramon," he says, "I was explaining to Michael that we plan to handle your representation."

I interject, "You need an experienced defense attorney right away."

Quinn says, "We'll bring in a lawyer from John's firm if the need arises."

I glance around and say, "The need has arisen." I try to give Ramon some cover by invoking legal misdirection. "A conflict could arise if your interests diverge with those of the archdiocese."

Quinn fires back. "This is a Church matter," he says. "We are trying to find the truth, and we would never turn our backs on a priest. Let us choose lawyers that we know and trust."

And who will bow down and kiss your ring. His analysis might change if the archdiocese would face financial ruin and a public-relations disaster if it didn't offer up Ramon's head on a platter. Not to mention the fact that it would be a career-limiting move if the archdiocese is forced into bankruptcy on his watch.

Quinn adds, "We can always retain separate counsel if an actual conflict arises."

It's a truthful, albeit glib, argument. Getting another attorney up to speed on short notice isn't impossible, but he'd begin the race fifty yards behind the starting line.

"Look," he says to Ramon, "I'm not going to tell you what to do."

He just did.

"We're only looking out for your best interests."

In my long and occasionally illustrious legal career, I

have observed that whenever a lawyer says he's looking out for your best interests, it is frequently the case that he isn't.

Quinn is still pontificating. "If we make a mistake," he says, "God will forgive us. If we lie, He won't."

It was inevitable that somebody was going to play the God card sooner or later.

Ramon can't summarily dismiss the head legal honcho of the archdiocese without significant repercussions, so he searches for a compromise position. "I appreciate everything that you're doing for me," he says, "but I would like Mike to be on my team. He's an excellent lawyer who understands the issues facing priests."

He might have added that he knows me and trusts my judgment.

"There are plenty of good lawyers who never went to the seminary," Quinn says.

"All things being equal," Ramon replies, "I'd prefer one who did."

Quinn tries to fob it off on the bureaucrats. "I'll have to check with our insurance carrier," he says. "They're very picky about the lawyers we use. It's a risk-management and cost-containment issue."

A moment ago, he was only interested in finding the truth, but now it's a risk-management issue. He's starting to sound like the guys who run the HMOs.

Ramon turns to me and says, "I'll find a way to pay you."

I assure him that we're prepared to handle his case pro bono.

Ramon says to Quinn, "That should eliminate your concerns about cost containment."

"I'll still need to check with our carrier," he says.

We'll never see a penny. I try not to sound too sarcastic when I say, "You'll let us know."

"I will."

"Then it's settled," Ramon says.

Quinn responds with a resigned nod, and Shanahan tries to make the best of the situation with a transparently phony attempt at sounding conciliatory. "We will make all of our firm's resources available to you," he says.

He won't do it for free. His gesture will cost the archdiocese upwards of five hundred bucks an hour, depending upon which of his colleagues does the work.

There is nothing to be gained by being ungracious. "I'm glad we'll be working together," I tell him. There will be plenty of time to jettison them down the road.

"I trust you will provide full disclosure of all relevant information?" Shanahan says.

We'll see. "Of course."

"And input on strategy?"

I won't let Quinn and Shanahan tell me how to run this case. "I'll need the final call on all strategic decisions," I tell him.

Ramon says to Quinn, "I can't think of any reason why that shouldn't be acceptable to you, Francis."

I can think of a few.

The response is a grudging "I suppose."

Ramon tries to calm the political waters when he tells Quinn, "I want you and John to participate actively in my representation."

Quinn isn't giving up. "I would be more comfortable

if we resolved this matter within the family," he says. "The archbishop may not look upon this favorably."

The archbishop hasn't been arrested.

"I'd be happy to talk to him if you think it would help," Ramon says.

"So would I," I interject.

Quinn derives much of his power by controlling the lines of communication. "That won't be necessary," he says.

Banks knocks on the door a moment later and lets himself in. "Have you decided which of you will be representing Father Aguirre?" he asks.

"All of us," Quinn says.

Banks's expression makes it clear that it's all the same to him. "We need to take your client down to booking."

Quinn glances at his watch and tells Ramon that he'll return in a couple of hours. "We have to make a few calls," he says.

The archbishop is undoubtedly at the top of his list.

I accompany Ramon as Banks and Johnson escort him to the Glamour Slammer. As he's about to be taken inside for fingerprinting, he turns to me and says, "I need to talk to you as soon as I'm done."

"I'm not going anywhere. I'll make sure Father Quinn and Mr. Shanahan are with me."

For the first time, his voice has the unmistakable sound of abject fear. "No," he whispers. "I want to talk to you alone."

CHAPTER 5

"They Always Have an Agenda"

I have complete confidence in the leadership of our arch-diocese.

—Father Ramon Aguirre, *San Francisco Chronicle*

RAMON IS UNCHARACTERISTICALLY agitated when he returns from booking, where he was finger-printed, showered with disinfectant and given a perfunc-tory medical exam. He tugs at his freshly issued orange jumpsuit and snaps, "You have to get me out of here."

I'm glad his emotions are running high. Guilty people tend to polish their stories, but innocent people get mad. I can't give him the answer that he wants to hear, so I have to revert to a lawyerly cliché. "We're doing every-thing we can," I say.

His expression suggests he's thinking, "Yeah, right."

The consultation room at the intake center in the Glamour Slammer is hardly elegant, but it's a significant upgrade from the wild booking hub in the old Hall that's now used for hardcore prisoners. At two A.M., the tight quarters are deathly silent and smell of cleaning solvent. Quinn and Shanahan will return at any moment, and we need to get right to it.

"What did you want to talk to me about?"

"I just need to be sure there is somebody on my team whose loyalties are unquestioned."

"You can count on me. But what about Quinn and Shanahan?"

"They work for the archbishop. Francis will do anything to avoid conveying bad news, and John doesn't want to jeopardize his firm's relationship with its biggest client. It's no great secret that they've cut deals to avoid embarrassment to the archdiocese."

Which is exactly what I'd been saying before. "But if you have questions about their loyalty, why do you want them to represent you?"

"Because I have no choice. I can't afford to piss them off, and it will look terrible if the archdiocese bails on me."

He's right.

He exhales heavily and says, "I need to get back to work. It's almost Christmas, and the children need me."

"You'll be there."

"Not if I get fired."

"They can't fire you if you're innocent."

"They can send me to another parish or put me on leave. Even if I'm ultimately exonerated, my reputation will be ruined if this isn't resolved in the next couple of weeks."

It may be ruined already. I fully understand the problem, but I can't fix the criminal-justice system by Christmas.

He asks, "What will it take to get the charges dropped at the preliminary hearing?"

A miracle. "Realistically, we'll have to prove that Ms.

Concepcion committed suicide or we'll have to find the real murderer."

"And if we can't?"

There's no way to sugarcoat it. "We'll have to get ready for trial."

The reality is hitting home, and his lips form a tight line across his face. "Working at St. Peter's was the only job I wanted after I got out of the seminary," he says. "You can't let them take it away from me."

His fear is genuine. He's an only child who grew up a few blocks from St. Peter's and was the first member of his family to break out of poverty when he got a scholarship to USF. He decided to go to the seminary after his parents were killed in an auto accident twenty-five years ago. St. Peter's is more than a church—it's his family.

"What are the chances of bail?" he asks.

Not good. "Depends on the charge. It's unlikely if they go with first degree." I don't mention the worst-case scenario—if they ask for the death penalty, there will be no bail. "Do you have access to any money?"

"They don't hand out stock options in my line of work."

"What about the archdiocese?" The willingness—or unwillingness—of the archbishop to post bail will be an early indication of his commitment to Ramon's cause.

"I don't know. I suppose they could mortgage St. Mary's."

Not likely. I tell him I've arranged for him to be housed in "Ad Seg," the so-called Administrative Segregation area of the new jail, which is reserved for prison-

ers who are likely to be harassed or injured. At least he'll
have his own room tonight.

The wheels start to turn. "Where do we start?" he asks.

The conventional wisdom says the police start with
the victim and the defense attorneys start with the accused. "I need you to tell me where you were the night
Ms. Concepcion died." I purposely leave out any mention of the bloody knife with his fingerprints. It's the
only information I've gleaned from the cops, and I don't
want him to start adjusting his story to account for it—
at least not yet.

He hasn't been living in a cloister, and he cuts to the
chase. "Are you asking if I did it?"

Absolutely not. It's always tempting to ask a client
straight up, but that isn't how defense lawyers work. If he
lies to us, we'll have to deal with unpleasant issues relating to California's perjury laws. I want to hear it in his
own words. More important, I want to study his body language. Nonverbal cues and significant omissions often
tell you much more than anything your client says. "They
didn't pull your name out of a hat," I tell him. "I need to
know what happened—and I don't like surprises."

"I didn't do it."

So much for my attempt to elicit a narrative by asking
open-ended questions. "The cops think you did. I need
you to give me enough information to prove that you
weren't in the vicinity of Ms. Concepcion's apartment
last Monday. I'll explain everything to Banks and Johnson, and you can go back to work."

No response.

"Come on, Ramon. You have to be straight with me."
You'd *better* be straight with me.

He clasps his hands together and says, "There's a problem."

Uh-oh. "Which is?"

"I was at Maria's apartment on the night she died."

CHAPTER 6

"Her Personal Life Is Confidential"

Above all, our parishioners expect us to keep their private matters confidential.

—Archbishop Albert Keane, *San Francisco Chronicle*

I START. FIRING questions in rapid succession. "What were you doing there?"

"Counseling."

"For what?"

"That's none of your business."

It is now. "I need to know everything you can tell me about her."

"Her personal life is confidential."

Good priests are obsessive about privacy. "So is this conversation," I say.

"Come on, Mike. You know the rules."

All too well. I get him to reveal grudgingly that she came to him after she broke up with her boyfriend in September. "Who is he?" I ask.

There is a long hesitation before he says, "Eduardo Lopez."

I recognize the name. Concepcion's ex has operated a popular eatery at Twenty-third and Mission for three decades. An astute businessman with political aspirations, he's used the profits from his restaurant to make a killing in real estate. A devout Catholic with time and money on his hands, he's also formed several partnerships with government agencies and nonprofit organizations to build low-income housing in the community.

"Why did they break up?" I ask.

"Maria wanted a commitment, but he didn't."

It's an all-too-typical scenario. Maybe we can get him some couch time with Dr. Phil.

Ramon adds, "The situation was complicated by the fact that he's still married."

Oops. "I take it Ms. Concepcion was aware of that?"

"Yes. He promised to divorce his wife and marry her."

Seems he never got around to it. This may be a little more than Dr. Phil can handle in a one-hour show. I ask if Lopez's wife knew about her husband's infidelities.

"Yes, and she wasn't happy about it."

I want to know where Lopez's wife was last Monday night.

"Maria was forty-two and desperate to have a child," he explains. "She figured Lopez was her best chance—and maybe her last."

When I was a priest, the rules were written in black and white. As I've gotten older, I've come to appreciate the many shades of gray. I think back to our conversation in the confessional and observe, "You've become pretty forgiving of premarital sex and infidelity."

"You shouldn't judge until you've walked in somebody's shoes. She had the best mental health that money could buy, but she was still unhappy."

"Unhappy enough to commit suicide?"

"No."

He gives me the name of her therapist, but isn't forth-coming when I probe for additional details. I change course and ease him into a discussion about the night she died.

"I drove to her apartment at eight o'clock," he says.

It's just a few blocks from St. Peter's. "Why didn't you walk?"

"It was raining." He says he stayed until ten and as-sures me that she was very much alive when he left.

"Was she upset?"

"Yes."

One-word answers are profoundly unenlightening. "Why?"

"The O'Connell case was starting the next day, and her plaintiff was getting cold feet."

I let his answer hang. People often feel compelled to fill the dead air, but Ramon doesn't elaborate. I ask him if he entered her apartment through the front door or the back.

"Front."

"Did you leave the same way?"

"What difference does it make?"

"Maybe none. I want to know if anybody may have seen you."

He tells me he left through the back door because his car was around the corner and it was quicker to go through the alley. He didn't see anybody outside.

"Did you eat anything while you were there?"

"I had an apple and a cup of tea." He holds his palms up

and says, "This would go a lot faster if you just told me what you wanted to know."

I tell him about the bloody knife with his fingerprints. Ramon gets indignant. "You think I killed her?"

"Ramon, you know and I know that an explanation would make my life a lot easier."

He's still mad. "I cut the apple with a knife. It could have been the same one they found in the bathroom."

"How did it get there?"

"How should I know?"

I can do without the sarcasm, but his adamance suggests he's telling the truth. The cards are on the table, and I want to fill in details. "Will the cops find your prints anywhere else in her apartment?"

"I was there for two hours," he says. "My prints are probably all over the place."

Swell. "Did you touch her?"

"I hugged her when I left. It was platonic."

I wasn't going to suggest otherwise. "Where did you go?"

"To St. Peter's. I had a lot on my mind, so I did what priests do—I prayed." He says the church was empty and it's unlikely that anybody saw him. Then he went for a walk around midnight, and he returned to the rectory at one. "I said good night to Father Keyes."

For our purposes, this means that nobody can corroborate his whereabouts between eight and one. We'll have a problem if the medical examiner concludes that the time of death was during that window. I send up a final flare. "Did she say anything else that seemed unusual?"

"Yes. She said that somebody was following her."

What? "A stalker?"

"A private investigator."

Huh? "Why would somebody have hired a PI to follow her?"

"She was looking for witnesses to testify against Father O'Connell, and she figured the attorneys for the archdiocese were keeping an eye on her."

All's fair in love, war and litigation.

He lowers his voice. "You'd better watch your backside," he says. "Francis Quinn and John Shanahan play hardball. They may put somebody on your tail, too."

It's a new and unusual twist to the concept of professional courtesy, but I take his warning seriously. It gives me the creeps if I think I'm being followed.

"There's something else," he says. "She was having issues with her ex-husband. He still works at John's firm and never got over the fact that she filed for divorce."

"Why did they split up?"

"Among other things, he had a different concept of fidelity than she did."

Asshole. "Did he know she'd been seeing Lopez?"

"Yes. She told me that he was jealous and had a temper."

It doesn't prove anything, but it's another possibility. "What's his name?"

"Dennis Peterson."

"Why didn't she ignore him?"

"She couldn't. I thought you knew."

"Knew what?"

"He's the lead attorney for the archdiocese on the O'Connell case."

CHAPTER 7

"Do You Understand the Seriousness of This Matter?"

We are certain that Father Ramon Aguirre will be fully exonerated, and our prayers are with him for a speedy resolution of this matter.

—Father F. X. Quinn, *KGO Radio,*
Wednesday, December 10, 7:00 A.M.

THE CAFFEINE FROM Rosie's second Diet Coke has kicked in as we regroup in my cramped office at the world headquarters of Fernandez and Daley at seventhirty on Wednesday morning. She's already running at full throttle when she asks, "Are you ready to go to war with the DA?"

"Of course."

I've been up all night, and my temples are throbbing. I take a sip of Peet's House Blend and admire our unfinished walls. We run a low-overhead operation on the second floor of a tired walk-up building a half block north of the crumbling Transbay bus terminal in space that's better suited for a garage band than a law firm. Our tenant-improvement budget went to pay for Tommy's diapers, and we put our remodeling plans on indefinite hold when our former partner and my ex-girlfriend, Carolyn O'Malley, was appointed to the Superior Court bench six months ago. Our downstairs neighbor, the El Faro Mexican Restaurant, won't open for another four hours, but the pungent aroma of yesterday's special is still with us. Our staff—such as it is—consists of a receptionist/jack-of-all-trades named Terrence "the Terminator" Love, a former heavyweight boxer and small-time hoodlum who was more successful at stealing than fighting. We've logged more than our share of hours trying to keep him out of jail since our days in the PD's office, and we put him on the payroll to help him comply with his latest parole agreement. So far, it's worked out for everybody—he gets to stay out of jail and we get somebody to answer the phone. He also doubles as my bodyguard when I venture to the earthier parts of town.

"What about the archdiocese?" she asks. "F. X. Quinn couldn't have made it any clearer that he doesn't want us on this case."

"Been there, done that," I say. "We'll deal with him, too."

"He isn't going to make our lives any easier."

"Ramon gets to pick his own lawyer and we've dealt with our share of assholes."

Her eyes narrow when she says, "You can't let it get personal. This case has nothing to do with what happened twenty years ago, and you need to keep your head together if Francis Quinn starts yanking your chain."

"I will. Besides, we're theoretically on the same side."

"For now." She asks me about Concepcion's ex-boyfriend.

"Lopez is no Boy Scout," I say, "but he has a high profile and political aspirations. I find it hard to believe he'd throw it away in a fit of anger."

"And her ex-husband?"

"If he really wanted to get her, he would have tried to embarrass her at trial. That's what lawyers do. In fact, I'll bet he was looking forward to taking her on in court."

"What makes you think so?"

I wink and say, "Ex-husbands know all of their former spouses' weaknesses."

"If I were in your shoes," she says, "I wouldn't try to extrapolate that theory to other situations."

I know better. "The case is over if we can prove it was a suicide," I say.

"It won't be easy to get Rod Beckert to change his mind."

Dr. Roderick Beckert is a walking encyclopedia of forensics who has been our chief medical examiner for almost four decades. "Even if it wasn't a suicide," I say, "the fact that they found Ramon's prints on the knife doesn't prove that he killed her. If he'd had the presence of mind to try to fake a suicide, he would have been smart enough to wipe the prints."

"Then how did the knife find its way to the bathroom?" she asks.

"That's our job to figure out."

Her eyes bore into mine. "Bottom line," she says, "do you think he did it?"

"Ramon isn't capable of murder."

"For what my two cents are worth," she says, "I happen to agree with you."

It doesn't change a thing, but it's nice to know I'm not the only one who thinks so.

JUDGE LOUISE VANDEN HEUVEL'S long blond hair is pulled back into a tight ball as she glides to the bench with commanding elegance at exactly ten A.M. Her courtroom is packed with reporters and Ramon's supportive parishioners, but the veteran judge's stoic demeanor suggests it's just another day at the office. She dons her reading glasses, turns on her computer and studies her docket, then she bangs her gavel once and invokes an even tone that is equally authoritative and seductive as she instructs the gallery to be seated.

My hair is flat and my shave is spotty, but I'm presentable enough in my gray suit. The defense table is crowded. Rosie is to my left and Ramon is to my right, and Quinn and Shanahan are squeezed in at the end. Our show of numbers may appear impressive to the uninitiated, but it's unlikely to have any significant bearing on the outcome of today's proceedings.

Bill McNulty is a veteran ADA with a reputation for aggressive tactics, compulsive attention to detail and a grouchy demeanor. He looks unhappy as he stands by himself on the other side of the aisle. "McNasty," as he's known around the Hall, has put in over thirty years in the trenches and could phone in an arraignment. He knows today's proceedings will be short. Ramon will enter a not-guilty plea, and I'll beg for bail. Then we'll all go outside and plead our respective cases to the cameras.

The lawyers state their names for the record, and

Judge Vanden Heuvel reminds us that we're here for the purpose of listening to Ramon's plea. After we dispense with a formal reading of the charges, she turns to Ramon and says, "Do you understand the seriousness of this matter?"

"Yes, Your Honor," he whispers.

Quinn decides to make a play to the crowd. "Your Honor," he says, "on behalf of the archdiocese, we object in the strongest terms to these unsubstantiated accusations."

Duly noted. His sermon isn't going to change anything, but it elicits a smattering of applause from Ramon's disciples in the gallery.

The judge bangs her gavel. "Father Quinn," she says, "your client will have ample opportunity to present a full defense. For now, we need to hear his plea. If you'd like to discuss any other issues, you'll have to take them up at the appropriate time and in the proper venue."

"But, Your Honor—"

"How does your client plead?"

I'm glad she's taking out her frustrations on him. I turn to Ramon and nod. His voice cracks when he says, "Not guilty, Your Honor."

"Thank you, Father Aguirre." The judge looks at her calendar and says, "I'm setting a preliminary hearing before Judge Tsang a week from Friday at nine A.M."

Not a great draw. Ignatius Tsang is a scholarly jurist who used to be an ADA. I've always gotten a fair shake from him, but he's generally regarded as prosecution-friendly.

"Your Honor," I say, "we would like to schedule the prelim as expeditiously as possible. Father Aguirre hopes to celebrate Christmas Mass at St. Peter's." It's a reach, but I have her attention. I want to pressure McNulty to reveal his evidence. More important, I want the reporters in the gallery to think I have no doubt that Ramon is innocent.

"What did you have in mind, Mr. Daley?"

At least she didn't dismiss me out of hand. By statute, the prelim must be set within ten days after the arraignment, but the judge can speed up the timetable. "We're prepared to begin on Friday," I say.

"Your Honor," McNulty says, "we can't be ready on just two days' notice."

Sure you can. "Your Honor," I say, "my client was forced to spend the night in jail. His parishioners depend on him, and the holidays are approaching."

She throws me a bone. "We'll squeeze you in at nine o'clock on Monday morning."

I keep pushing. "We'll need expedited discovery," I say. "We'd like copies of the police and medical examiner's reports no later than noon on Friday."

"So ordered."

It's more than I thought she would give me.

McNulty starts to speak, and the judge stops him with an upraised hand. "I trust you'll be prepared to move forward on Monday," she says to him, "and I expect you to comply with my discovery order." She closes her calendar and says, "Anything else?"

It's my turn again. "We'd like to discuss bail, Your Honor. Father Aguirre has strong community ties and lacks the resources to flee. We therefore respectfully request that he be released on his own recognizance."

I would never request anything disrespectfully, and it's just an opening bid. She's unlikely to go for it, but she may be willing to consider bail.

McNulty is up again. "It is unheard of to release a murder suspect on O.R.," he says, "and highly unusual to release him on bail. It's a matter of public safety."

It's true. "The judge has discretion to review all of the attendant circumstances and to act in the interest of justice," I say.

Judge Vanden Heuvel gives McNulty the first score. "I'm not going to release the defendant on O.R.," she says.

"Your Honor—" I say.

"I've ruled, Mr. Daley."

I start backtracking. "You didn't rule out the possibility of bail, Your Honor."

"No, I didn't." Her high cheekbones flush, and she gives McNulty the first chance. "Do you have anything to say about it?"

His response is predictable. "The People oppose bail," he says. "The defendant is accused of first-degree murder and is a substantial flight risk. He is an expert at fundraising and would have no trouble finding the means to flee the area or even the country."

"Your Honor," I say, "Father Aguirre has no intention of going anywhere and is prepared to surrender his passport. He simply wishes to clear his name and return to work."

"Your Honor," McNulty says, "the victim was maliciously stabbed six times in a premeditated act. We're considering the possibility of adding special circumstances."

Ramon gives me a desperate look and whispers, "Is that what I think it is?"

I nod. It's the California euphemism for a death-penalty case. I turn to the judge and say, "This isn't a capital case, and Father Aguirre is willing to wear an electronic monitoring device."

The judge ponders for a long moment before she issues her wisdom. "Bail is denied."

There is panic in Ramon's eyes. He turns to me and whispers, "This isn't happening."

I grit my teeth and whisper, "Stay calm." I say to the judge, "Your Honor—"

She stops me. "You can revisit this issue at the prelim, Mr. Daley."

I'm about to accept the fact that there is nothing I can do until Monday when I hear the distinct sound of F. X. Quinn's voice. "May it please the court," he bellows, "we would like to call a witness to testify on behalf of Father Aguirre with respect to the subject of bail."

He never mentioned this to me, and the judge isn't buying it. "I've ruled, Father Quinn," she says.

"If you would hear me out for just a moment."

His request is met with an irritated look and a question. "Whom do you wish to call?"

"The archbishop of San Francisco."

CHAPTER 8

"I Am the Archbishop of San Francisco"

This arrest of Father Aguirre is an unfortunate mistake.

—Archbishop Albert Keane, *KGO Radio,*
Wednesday, December 10, 10:00 A.M.

MCNULTY SHOOTS UP like a Roman candle. "Your honor," he says, "this is highly unusual."

Yes, it is, and it puts Judge Vanden Heuvel in a tough spot by raising the age-old question of whether a Catholic judge who is up for reelection is prepared to tell the archbishop of San Francisco to go to hell. There are a lot of Catholics in this town, and most of them vote.

The judge makes the call. "I will listen to Archbishop Keane's testimony," she says.

I can't look at Rosie. This is as good as it gets.

Quinn asks for a recess and returns a moment later with Archbishop Albert Keane, a charismatic redhead in his late fifties who played football with F. X. Quinn at St. Ignatius and started his career at St. Peter and Paul's in North Beach. He's wearing the traditional collar as he takes the stand with the confidence of a man who could be running a Fortune 500 company.

Quinn stands a respectful distance from the witness

box, and his tone has the appropriate level of reverence when he says, "Would you please state your name for the record?"

"Albert Keane."

"What is your occupation?"

As if we didn't know.

"I am the archbishop of San Francisco." He says he's known Ramon for more than twenty years.

"Could you describe Father Aguirre's character?"

McNulty's head slumps. You don't get training in law school about strategies to rebut the testimony of a sitting archbishop.

Archbishop Keane's demeanor is calm, almost serene. His bearing is erect and his high-pitched voice is soft, yet authoritative. The courtroom is silent as he addresses Judge Vanden Heuvel directly, and there isn't the slightest suggestion in his deferential tone that she will burn in hell for all eternity if she doesn't grant bail. "I appreciate your taking the time to hear me, Your Honor," he says.

Her expression indicates that she approves of his tenor. "Thank you, Archbishop Keane."

His delivery is flawless. "Your Honor," he says, "Father Aguirre is an honest, moral and hardworking priest, and I am sure these unsubstantiated charges will be proven false. We are prepared to offer whatever dispensation as may be necessary to ensure that he is not required to spend time in jail while he is awaiting his opportunity to rectify this egregious error."

Just the way Quinn scripted it for him.

"Your Honor," he continues, "the archdiocese is prepared to post bail and to allow Father Aguirre to stay at our headquarters until his legal proceedings have concluded. I will personally guarantee his appearance at the appointed time."

It's a defense attorney's dream: the archbishop is swearing my client will appear at trial.

Judge Vanden Heuvel turns to McNulty and says, "Do you wish to respond?"

What can he say? All eyes, including those of the archbishop, turn to McNulty, who addresses her in a subdued tone. "We have great respect for Archbishop Keane," he says.

It's a good sign when your opponent acknowledges the moral authority of your witness. McNulty is Catholic and may be reluctant to tweak a guy who has a pipeline to God.

"But," he continues, "it is highly unusual for bail to be granted in a murder case that may involve special circumstances."

It's true. The Penal Code says bail cannot be granted in a capital case if the proof is evident and it is likely the defendant is guilty. Then again, this isn't a capital case— at least not yet—and so far, the proof of Ramon's guilt is hardly evident to me.

Quinn lays it on thicker. "Your Honor," he says, "the purpose of bail is to ensure the defendant will appear at the designated time. The archbishop is willing to vouch for my client's character, provide a verifiable place for him to stay and to post bond."

The judge nods, but doesn't say anything.

McNulty reads her expression and begins damage control. "In the circumstances," he says, "bail should be substantial and conditional upon the defendant being re-manded to the personal custody of the archbishop."

Quinn says, "We're prepared to accept those conditions, Your Honor."

Judge Vanden Heuvel has the opening she needs. "Bail is set at one million dollars," she says, "and the defendant is ordered to remain at the headquarters of the archdio-cese, except when he is required to appear in court. The attorneys will work out the details for implementing an appropriate monitoring regimen." She pounds her gavel and adds, "We're in recess."

Rosie leans over and whispers, "Do you think we could persuade the archbishop to provide similar testimony for some of our other clients?"

CHAPTER 9

"Parlor Tricks Don't Work in Murder Trials"

I don't believe in luck. I believe in preparation.

—William McNulty, *San Francisco Chronicle*

THE GRIMACE ON the face of San Francisco's most cantankerous ADA is more pronounced than usual, and the sarcasm has its customarily pointed edge when Bill McNulty says to me, "Are you planning to call the archbishop to testify at your client's trial?"

Understatement has never been his forte. "Only if it would help our case," I say.

"Parlor tricks don't work in murder trials."

"The truth does."

"The truth is that your client murdered Ms. Concepcion."

"Then you shouldn't have any trouble proving it."

McNulty's boss holds up a delicate hand in a conciliatory gesture. Our mediagenic district attorney, Nicole Ward, is pouring herself a designer water at the wet bar in the corner of her elegant office on the third floor of the Hall. The deep gray carpets, soft leather sofas and dark oak paneling are a lasting testimonial to the uncontrollable ego of her predecessor, Prentice Marshall Gates III, a megalomaniac whose tenure came to an unceremoniously abrupt end a few years ago after he was accused of murdering a male prostitute in a room at the Fairmont. Gates paid for the upgrades on his own nickel, and the city doesn't have the spare cash to tear them out. Not surprisingly, Ward hasn't insisted on returning her office to its former bureaucratic splendor.

She takes a seat behind her desk between the Stars and Stripes and the California state flag. She sips her Perrier and flashes the airbrushed smile that adorns the cover of this month's *San Francisco* magazine. Her lineage is impressive, and her political aspirations have been well documented. She passed up a chance to run for mayor last year to train her sights on a shot at the U.S. Senate. The forty-year-old is more than a pretty face, and the conviction statistics of the DA's office have gone up significantly since she took the job.

Her stated purpose for calling this impromptu summit conference was to set ground rules for the expedient exchange of evidence, but that was an entirely transparent pretext. In reality, she granted us an audience to try to smoke out information. Turnabout being fair play, we'll see what we can get from her. My defense shield is up, and my phasers are set on stun. The chances she'll reveal anything meaningful are slim.

Rosie and I are sitting on the overstuffed couch adjacent to her expansive mahogany desk. Quinn and Shanahan are parked in tall chairs on the other side of the oriental rug. Johnson and Banks are standing as sentries on either side of Ward's leather chair.

Ward's plastic smile is replaced by a practiced sincere

look that plays more convincingly on TV than in person, and she starts by addressing Quinn. "We're sorry that we have to meet again in such trying circumstances," she says. "You have no idea how difficult this is for us."

I can't imagine.

Quinn responds with a tempered nod. "This is difficult for all of us," he says.

Ward darts a glance at McNulty, then she turns to me and says, "That brings us to the murder of Ms. Concepcion."

"Alleged murder," I correct her. "We think it may have been a suicide."

"We don't. Has your client provided you with an explanation of his whereabouts on the night she died?"

I recite the correct legal answer. "You know we're under no obligation to provide information to you about our discussions with our client."

"Yes, we do." She rests her elbows on the polished mahogany and shakes her chestnut locks. "Frankly," she says, "we have no great desire to prosecute another priest."

Except for the fact that you'll be the lead story on the news for the next year.

She tugs at the sleeves of her St. John knit suit and adds, "These cases are difficult, and we were hoping to find common ground to resolve this matter before things get out of hand."

Shanahan's interest is piqued. "What did you have in mind?" he asks.

"If your client is prepared to come clean, we would be willing to negotiate this down to second degree with a recommendation for a reasonable sentence. I' best we can offer."

McNulty interjects, "It's a good deal, and the *Chronicle* will crucify us for offering it. If I were in Nicole's shoes, I wouldn't be doing it."

He isn't in her shoes, and his observation sounds rehearsed. A cynic might suggest Ward is looking to make political capital by trying to elicit a quick confession in a case that could cut against her if things get ugly. That cynic would be me.

Shanahan opts for a tempered response. "We'll take it back to our client and consider all the ramifications before we make a final decision."

It's a rational thought, but it isn't enough for me. "I won't recommend it," I say.

Ward's chiseled features become more animated. "He murdered Ms. Concepcion."

"No, he didn't, and you can't prove it."

"Yes, we can."

I'm not egging her on just to hear the sound of my own voice. Well, maybe a little, but if I can keep her talking, she might reveal some useful information. I lower the volume and say, "How do you figure he did it?"

She measures her words carefully. "He stabbed her and tried to make it look like a suicide. A neighbor saw him exit the victim's apartment at ten o'clock that night."

I could resume the argument about the semantics of whether she should be calling Ramon a murderer, but I'm more interested that she mentioned a witness. "Who's the neighbor?" I ask.

"Her name is Estella Cortez. She lives across the alley."

Banks interjects, "I've talked to her, and she's very reliable."

He's an excellent judge of character, but we'll interview her just the same. I ask Ward if Cortez saw anybody else enter Concepcion's apartment.

"No."

"Was she watching the apartment the entire night?"

"Of course not."

Good answer. "Then it's possible that somebody else went inside without being seen."

"Anything is possible, Mr. Daley."

Precisely.

"We found his fingerprints on the murder weapon," she says.

"Doesn't mean a thing," I say. There's no reason to hide the ball. "Father Aguirre told us he was at Ms. Concepcion's apartment that night for a counseling session. He used a knife to cut an apple."

She stops for a beat. "You don't know that it's the same knife."

"We'll take our chances."

Her seemingly airtight case may have sprung its first leak, and her smug tone has a hint of concern. "You can't prove he's telling the truth."

"I don't have to. You have to prove beyond a reasonable doubt that he murdered Ms. Concepcion. It isn't our job to show that he didn't." It's a tidy legal argument, but juries are good at connecting the dots. "Ms. Concepcion was a distraught woman with serious personal issues whose case against the archdiocese was falling apart. Her wrists were slashed, and there was no evidence of forced entry or a struggle. How can you possibly rule out suicide?"

"Dr. Beckert said it wasn't. He gave us a preview of his report. Ms. Concepcion sustained a blow to the back of her right shoulder that rendered her unconscious. Then the murderer placed her into the bathtub and slit her wrists. She bled to death before she regained consciousness."

Ugh—doesn't sound too good. I feign exasperation. "Come on, Nicole, there isn't a shred of evidence that Father Aguirre had any contact with her."

"Yes, there is." And now she's smiling. She's been waiting to spring this on me ever since I walked in: "Dr. Beckert found your client's thumbprints on the back of her neck."

CHAPTER 10

"It's My Job to Have Faith"

Our priests are God's emissaries. We'll do everything to protect them.

—Father F. X. Quinn, *San Francisco Chronicle*

THEY SAY THE best defense is a good offense, and while I'm trying to figure out how to answer, Shanahan jumps in with an indignant response. "Everybody knows you can't lift fingerprints from human skin," he says.

He's developed his keen expertise in forensic science by watching *CSI* every week.

Banks corrects him. "Yes, you can," he says.

Big John has expressed a widely held view, but it turns out that Banks is right. Before Shanahan can dig himself in deeper, I say to Banks, "Did you use glue fuming?"

"Yes."

Shanahan gives me an incredulous look and says, "What are you talking about?"

I watch *CSI,* too. "It's a process to remove fingerprints off a cadaver," I explain.

For decades, most experts believed it was impossible to lift latent prints from human skin because of its pliability and the fact that it is covered with perspiration and other chemicals. The problem is often exacerbated in homicide cases because the victim's skin is frequently subjected to harsh conditions such as mutilation, weather and decomposition. The FBI recently developed a procedure in which portions of the body are covered by an airtight plastic tent, sprayed with fumes of a chemical known as cynanoacrylate and dusted with special fluorescent fingerprint powder. This so-called glue fuming process is most reliable if the perpetrator grabs the victim tightly and the body is discovered shortly after death.

Shanahan isn't the sort of guy who would ever acknowledge that he may have been wrong, and he continues his misguided onslaught. "It still doesn't prove that Father Aguirre knocked Ms. Concepcion unconscious or slit her wrists."

Ward responds in a sugary tone. "We'd be happy to listen to any explanation your client is willing to provide," she says.

So would we. I ask her if they identified any bruises on Concepcion's shoulders.

"You'll have to ask Dr. Beckert. In the meantime, notwithstanding this damaging evidence, our plea-bargain proposal remains on the table."

This time Quinn responds. "We won't counsel our client to confess to a crime that he didn't commit," he says.

I like the show of fortitude, but it may be nothing more than bluster.

"You have a lot of faith in him," Ward says.

"It's my job to have faith."

"Even so, our offer will remain open only until noon tomorrow."

*   *   *

THE FINGERPRINTS ON Concepcion's neck are a problem," Rosie says. We're driving north on Franklin Street toward archdiocese headquarters in a misty rain at noon.

"They were friends," I say. "Maybe he gave her a back rub?"

"Even if you're right, it was a bad idea. There's a big difference between counseling and massage. As my mother would say, it just doesn't look nice."

I can't disagree with her. We drive in silence as I search for a parking space in the crowded Cathedral Hill area. In the "All's Fair in Love and War" spirit of this endeavor, I cut across three lanes and practically barrel into a van as I pull into a metered space on Gough Street. I ignore the blaring horns and say, "I was surprised Ward was so willing to deal."

"I don't think she wants to prosecute a popular priest, and she'll get political points if she gets a confession— even if she has to cut a deal. The last thing she needs is to put a priest on Death Row."

Perhaps. I search for something positive. "At least the archbishop agreed to post bail."

She has a more benign view. "He had to do it. Ramon's parishioners are inundating him with calls and e-mails. It would have been a PR nightmare if he had turned his back on him."

"You still have questions about their loyalties?"

"Absolutely."

We get out of the car and I'm about to open my umbrella when a dark green Chevy Impala barrels by us and crashes into a puddle, blasting a wall of water toward us.

Rosie jumps out of the way, but I'm not quick enough.
The splash leaves me soaked from the waist down.

"Asshole," Rosie mutters.

"Yeah."

She reads my troubled look and says, "What is it?"

"That Chevy was behind us when we left the Hall.
Somebody is already watching us."

CHAPTER 11

"I Know How This Must Look"

God forgives those who acknowledge their mistakes.

— Father Ramon Aguirre, *San Francisco Chronicle*

RAMON'S RESPONSE TO Ward's plea-bargain proposal is unequivocal. "No deal," he says.

It's the answer I was hoping to hear. "We'll convey your response to the DA," I say.

Our newly constituted legal team has reassembled in a modest conference room in the nondescript building down the street from St. Mary's Cathedral that houses the offices of the archdiocese. A night in jail has drained Ramon's energy, and his complexion is gaunt. His gray slacks hide an ankle bracelet that allows the cops to monitor his whereabouts. The sandwiches on the credenza are untouched.

Quinn is sitting at the end of the oval pine table. His large presence contrasts with the small etching of an emaciated Jesus that's hanging on the wall behind him. Shanahan is nursing a Sprite and writing on a legal pad. He's been up all night, but there isn't a hair out of place.

Ramon's expression doesn't change when I tell him they've found a witness who saw him leave Concepcion's apartment at ten o'clock on the night she died. "I told you I was there," he says. "I'm prepared to admit I handled the knife, but they can't show that I knocked her out."

It's a more lawyerly response than I was hoping for. "They found your thumbprints on the back of her neck," I say. "We need to know how they got there."

He drums his fingers on the table and says, "She had back problems and was very tense. I gave her a massage, that's all."

Quinn's eyes light up, and not with joy. "You know it's against policy for a priest to touch a parishioner," he snaps.

Especially if she's suing the archdiocese.

"I'm well aware of that," Ramon replies, "but it was no different than a platonic hug."

"The newspapers won't see it that way."

Neither will the archbishop. Neither do I, for that matter.

Quinn jabs a finger into Ramon's face. "This is how we get into trouble," he says. "You decide to play fast and loose with the rules and the next thing you know, we're getting sued for sexual harassment. You were putting yourself and the archdiocese at risk."

"It wasn't like that, Francis. It was a gesture of friendship."

"It was a gesture of stupidity that's going to play out in open court. Why didn't you just invite Ms. Concepcion's mother to file a civil suit?"

"You're overreacting."

"It's my job to overreact."

I hold up my hand and say, "Let's try to keep our eye on the ball."

"Easy for you to say," Quinn barks. "I'm going to get an earful from the archbishop."

I won't gain anything by arguing with him. I turn to Ramon and put the cards on the table. "Was there anything going on between you and Ms. Concepcion besides counseling and back rubs?"

"No."

"Was there any hanky-panky of any kind?"

"None." He swallows hard and says, "I know how this must look. I'm not naive—but it's the truth."

I believe him.

Rosie gives him one last chance. "If there's anything else that we should know," she says, "this would be an excellent time for you to tell us."

He flashes a rare sign of anger. "Are you asking me if I slept with her?"

"In a word, yes."

"Then the answer, Rosie—in a word—is *no.*"

CHAPTER 12

"Nobody Is Bigger Than the Church"

Members of the clergy must avoid the slightest appearance of impropriety.

—Father F. X. Quinn, *San Francisco Chronicle*

QUINN'S BLOATED FACE is an unsightly shade of crimson when he says, "Now do you see why this job is so difficult?"

I decide that his question is intended to be a rhetorical one, and I don't respond.

The chief legal officer of the archdiocese is sitting behind an inlaid-cherry-wood desk in a spacious office at Church headquarters. The walls are lined with books that are divided between secular and religious tomes, and a large silver cross hangs behind his chair. A century-old version of the Latin Vulgate Bible is sitting on an antique end table. Except for the religious artifacts and a photo of the massive Quinn towering over the frail pope, the elegant surroundings could pass for a senior partner's office at a major law firm. The door is closed.

Rosie and I are sitting in armchairs opposite the expansive desk. Shanahan muttered something about going back to the office to review motions for the O'Connell case and is nowhere to be found.

Quinn is still expounding. "Do you know how hard it is to keep hundreds of priests from doing stupid things?" He answers his own question. "You give them training, you send them memos and they still screw up."

Guys like Quinn believe they have a God-given right to lay down the law. To the priests in San Francisco, he *is* the law.

I offer a priestly platitude. "They're human," I say.

He won't let them off the hook so easily. "They have no idea how much damage they can inflict. Sometimes I wish I'd gone straight to law school instead of the seminary."

If he thinks it's tough to keep a bunch of priests in line, he ought to meet some of the partners at my old law firm. "You wanted to see us?" I say.

"I did." He opens an envelope with a pearl-studded letter opener, then he takes a sip of tea from a bone-china cup and says, "Father Aguirre's case is very disturbing."

Thanks for bringing it to our attention.

He temples his fingers in front of his face and says, "We're appreciative of your efforts, but we think this matter should be handled internally."

Here we go again. "Who is included in the 'we' that you're referring to?"

"John and myself."

I've never trusted people who refer to themselves as "myself." "We resolved this issue," I say.

He clears his throat and says, "Another member of our hierarchy expressed reservations."

We're getting squeezed. "Who would that be?"

"The archbishop." He clears his throat again. If he keeps doing it, he's going to rupture his larynx. "Let's just say he isn't . . ." He hesitates, cocks his head at an angle and says, "comfortable with you."

The back of my neck is turning red. "Why not?"

His head returns to its upright and locked position when he says, "He didn't say."

"I'd like to talk to him about it."

"That isn't possible. He asked me to inform you that he expects you to resign."

And that's that.

But Rosie's eyes blaze. "We aren't going to back away from our obligations to our client just because the archbishop is *uncomfortable*," she says.

"If you're going to be unreasonable, we're going to have to let you go."

It's my turn for indignant posturing. "You can't let us go, Francis. We don't work for you. Ramon is our client, and only he can fire us."

"Then that's what we'll persuade him to do."

The hell you will. "We'll file a grievance with the State Bar."

"On what grounds?"

"That you attempted to coerce him into firing his lawyer."

"That's bullshit."

I wonder what the archbishop would say about that. "It's a sin to swear, Francis."

"I'll take it up at my next confession."

"We aren't going to resign."

"You made the same mistake twenty years ago. You still think you're bigger than the Church. Ramon suffers from the same malady."

And you suffer from being a self-righteous ass. "It wasn't true then," I say, "and it isn't true now." I look directly into his condescending eyes and force myself to keep my tone professional. "We aren't going to resign," I repeat.

"We'll wear you down."

"Are you threatening us?"

"I'm making a promise. Nobody is bigger than the Church."

Except for you. "And nobody is bigger than the State Bar."

It's a standoff.

He lowers his voice. "We'll destroy you," he growls.

God may have the power to smite me, but F. X. Quinn doesn't. "If you try to take us down, we'll bring you with us."

He sits there, fuming. "Well, then, you should know something else. Our insurance carrier informed me that your firm is not on their list of approved attorneys. Moreover, your firm is not on *our* list of approved lawyers, either. As a result, *we* are not in a position to pay your legal fees."

A huge surprise.

"You may wish to reconsider your decision in light of these new developments," he adds.

Asshole. "We've already told you that we're prepared to handle this matter pro bono."

He gives up. There's nothing else he can threaten us

with. "Suit yourself," he says, "but we're staying on as co-counsel."

Which will give him an opportunity to monitor our every move. I try to pursue our advantage by putting him back on his heels. "Did you hire somebody to follow us?"

There's a slight hesitation before he says, "Of course not."

"Did John?"

"No."

"Somebody was tailing us on our way over here."

"We don't hire investigators to follow co-counsel."

We'll see if the Impala reappears. I ask him if he hired a PI to tail Concepcion.

There's a longer pause before he says, "Obtaining information about opposing counsel is part of our due diligence. It isn't illegal and everybody does it."

He still hasn't answered my question. "Did you hire a PI to get a scouting report?"

"That's confidential."

"We're on the same side."

He fingers his reading glasses and says, "We have a PI on retainer."

At least he admitted it. "We'd like to talk to him."

"I can't allow you to do that."

"Sure you can."

"The information is privileged and confidential."

"Information gathered by a PI is not privileged."

"It's still confidential."

"You can get a protective order."

"It's a political issue. We can't admit that we hired a PI to spy on an attorney. It will look terrible."

You should have thought of that beforehand. "It will look worse if I have to send you a subpoena."

"No judge will enforce it."

"They might after your refusal to cooperate appears on the front page of tomorrow morning's *Chronicle*." Time to see if he'll blink. "What's the name of the PI?"

He sighs. Time to throw in the towel. "Nick Hanson. We've used him for years."

Well, that's a bonus. Nick "the Dick" Hanson is a local legend and one of the few living contacts to San Francisco's tawdry past. Still in robust health in his late eighties, the diminutive man-about-town has been a gumshoe for six decades. His agency in North Beach employs a dozen PIs, all of whom are related to him, and he writes mysteries in his spare time. I love Nick.

"We're going to talk to him," I say, "and we'll need you to tell him to cooperate."

His tone is grudging when he says, "I'll need to talk to John about it."

Fine. "Was Hanson watching Ms. Concepcion on the night she died?"

"I don't know."

"Who *does* know?"

"John."

CHAPTER 13

"This Is a Crime Scene"

Frequently, the most important single element in solving a murder involves the careful preservation of the crime scene.

—Inspector Roosevelt Johnson, *San Francisco Chronicle*

I IMMEDIATELY PLACE a call to Shanahan, who politely, but firmly, refuses to discuss any substantive issues by phone, then reluctantly agrees to meet me later tonight. Rosie goes back to the office while I make a beeline to the Mission, where Roosevelt Johnson is waiting for me in the dark hallway on the third floor of a nondescript, six-unit stucco building on Capp Street, between Twenty-fourth and Twenty-fifth. The carpet in Maria Concepcion's apartment building is worn and the walls are in need of paint. The postearthquake structure is in a corner of the Mission that's treacherous at night, and one of her neighbors gained some notoriety a few years ago when he started tossing bricks at the cars of the pimps who plied their trade on the street. It didn't stop their activities entirely, but it caused some of the hookers to move to another block.

"Technically," Roosevelt reminds me, "I'm under no legal obligation to do this. I invited you here because we're friends and out of respect for your father."

He's doing me a favor and I express my gratitude, but we both know that the California discovery rules will require him to show me the crime scene sooner or later. The fact that he didn't foist this exercise off on a uniform suggests he wants to ply me for information.

His partner is conspicuously absent. "Where's Marcus?" I ask.

"He's preparing for the prelim that you got pushed up on short notice."

And he doesn't want to talk to me. "I want to resolve this case by Christmas," I say.

"You can resolve it today by having your client plead guilty."

I tell him that I had a slightly different resolution in mind.

He lifts the obligatory yellow tape and opens the door, then he turns around and says, "This is a crime scene. If you touch anything, I will kill you instantly."

He isn't kidding.

I can feel the blood rushing to my feet as he escorts me inside Concepcion's apartment, which is even smaller than mine. You never get used to the feeling when you enter a murder scene, and my stomach starts churning. The tiny living room has been converted into a makeshift law office, and the kitchen is big enough for one. The dull beige carpet is tattered, and the paint is chipped. A narrow hallway leads to a cramped bedroom and a bath. The windows are closed, and the heavy air smells of industrial-strength cleaning solvent.

I ask him why a successful lawyer lived in such a modest place.

"She wasn't that successful," he says. "In fact, she was almost broke. She had about a thousand dollars in her bank account when she died, and she was behind on her rent."

I point out that she must have made some good money from her cases against the archdiocese.

"She considered it blood money and donated most of it to the battered-women's shelter."

I admire her principles, but it doesn't tell the entire story. "She had other clients," I say.

"It was small-time stuff, and she did a lot of work pro bono. Her ex-husband took everything in their divorce. She still had student loans and other debts."

I look around and observe that she wasn't much of a housekeeper. Her secondhand desk is covered with file folders, and DataSafe boxes are piled haphazardly on the tired olive sofa. A laptop computer, fax machine and photocopier are sitting on a table that came from IKEA. The only family mementos are photos of her parents and a younger brother who died in an auto accident about ten years ago.

I ask Roosevelt if anything was missing.

"Not as far as we can tell. There was no sign of forced entry, and there was some money and jewelry in her dresser. We're reasonably sure Ms. Concepcion knew her assailant and let him in. The back door was unlocked, and your client's fingerprints were on the handle."

"When did Ms. Concepcion's mother last speak to her daughter?"

"Seven-thirty that night." He gives me a stern look and says, "She told us there was nothing unusual about the conversation."

Duly noted. "Do you think she might be willing to talk to us?"

"I can't prevent you from approaching her, but I would ask you to be sensitive."

"Understood."

He leads me down the hallway to the bathroom where the sink, toilet and tub are original issue. The white floor tile has been scrubbed clean, but I can still make out traces of blood in the grout. "There was a lot of blood," he says. He promises to send over the photos, but I'm not looking forward to seeing them. He tells me that Concepcion's clothes were found in a pile on her bedroom floor.

"So," I say, "you think somebody knocked her unconscious, stripped off her clothes, put her into the tub, slashed her wrists and tried to make it look like a suicide?"

"No, I think *your client* knocked her unconscious, stripped off her clothes, put her into the tub, slashed her wrists and tried to make it look like a suicide."

"And the motive?"

"They had a fight. A woman who lives across the hall heard shouting at a quarter to ten."

Hmm, another witness. "What were they fighting about?"

"You'll have to ask your client."

"How did the witness know it was Father Aguirre?"

"She heard the voices of a man and a woman, and we know Father Aguirre was still here."

Unfortunately, we do. We'll need to talk to the neighbor. I point to the medicine chest and ask, "What did you find in there?"

"Nothing unusual." He rattles off a typical list of toothpaste, cosmetics and deodorant.

"Anything else?"

"Birth-control pills."

It shouldn't surprise me—even for a good Catholic.

His mustache twitches when he adds, "We also found an unused home pregnancy test."

Seems odd. "Why would she have a pregnancy test if she was taking birth-control pills?"

"Maybe she'd stopped taking them. We also found a number of prescription and over-the-counter medications." His mouth turns down slightly before he says, "Including Prozac."

Bingo. She was being treated for depression.

"I know what you're thinking," he says, "but just because she was taking an antidepressant doesn't mean she was suicidal."

"Says who?"

"Her mother and her shrink."

And Ramon. "It doesn't prove that she wasn't."

"Save it for your closing argument," he says.

I will.

His tone turns defensive when I ask him if he found any blood on Ramon's hands or clothing. "We didn't question him until several days later. He would have washed his hands and laundered his clothing."

"You can't prove it."

He doesn't respond.

I scan the bathroom again and ask, "Did you find his fingerprints in here?"

He studies the evidence markers and says they found

his prints on the flusher, the sink, the toilet-paper dispenser and the medicine chest.

"That suggests he used the bathroom for conventional purposes," I say.

"Maybe. But—" He lowers his voice and gestures toward the empty tub. "It was full of water when the body was found," he says.

"So what?"

"If it was a suicide, Ms. Concepcion would have drawn her own bath."

I don't like where this is going. "Are you saying that someone other than Ms. Concepcion started the bath?"

"Yes."

I know what he's going to tell me, but heart sinking, I ask, "How could you possibly have made that determination?"

He points to a yellow marker on the lip of the tub, just below the hot-water handle. "Because we found Father Aguirre's fingerprints on the handles to the bathtub faucet, too."

CHAPTER 14

"Everybody Knows Eduardo"

*With the downturn in the economy and the competition
from the big chains, it's become increasingly difficult for
independent markets to survive.*

— Tony Fernandez, *Mission District Weekly*

TONY'S PRODUCE HAS been a fixture around the
corner from St. Peter's for twenty years. It's an unusual
meeting place for a couple of lawyers, but it's convenient
and Rosie's older brother is an excellent source of gossip.

Rosie and I are sitting on crates in the back of the market, and the sweet aroma of fresh fruit surrounds us as she
takes in the details of my meeting with Johnson without
reaction. She tosses the core of her Fuji apple into the
trash and asks, "Have you talked to Ramon about it?"

"I didn't want to do it by phone. I'm going to see him
later tonight."

"My gut is telling me that he may not have been entirely forthcoming with us."

Her gut is usually very reliable.

Tony is about my age and height, but he spends his free
time at the gym and carries two hundred and twenty pounds
of pure muscle on his six-foot frame. Widowed almost
twenty years ago, he recently began dating an attractive di-
vorcée who works at the LaVictoria Pastry Shop across the

street. An upbeat guy with more street smarts than formal education, he never loses his cool and he's managed to run a clean operation in a business that's rife with payoffs and graft. His smile is wide when he asks me, "How did you like that smoothie?"

"Not bad," I say.

He put in a juice bar a couple of years ago in an attempt to siphon off business from a Jamba Juice that opened on Mission Street. He discovered that most of the locals can't afford four-dollar fruit shakes, and he freely admits it hasn't been a financial bonanza. Then again, success is often measured in relative terms. He's still in business, but Jamba Juice isn't.

I finish the blended orange/strawberry/kiwi concoction and say, "Do you have a Diet Dr Pepper in the cooler?" He stocks them just for me. "Old habits."

"Let me see what I can do." He returns a moment later with a can of my favorite soda, and his tone turns serious. "Do the cops really think Ramon killed Maria Concepcion?"

I assure him that they do.

He takes in the details with a pronounced scowl, then offers a concise analysis. "I don't believe it," he says.

I ask him what he knows about Concepcion.

"Off the record?"

"Any way you'd like it."

"She used to come in from time to time and was a Type Triple-A. I don't think she had a lot of friends. She helped us with the fund-raising auction at St. Peter's last year and was very good at it, but she wanted to run it like a Fortune 500 company. She treated anybody who disagreed with her as if they were stupid or nuts."

Sounds like her instincts for church politics were on a par with mine.

"A lot of people resented it when she filed those lawsuits against the archdiocese," he says. "I know that she was just doing her job, but you have to understand this community. A hundred people are holding a vigil for Ramon over at St. Peter's tonight. The church is the center of this neighborhood, and he's still a hero. Some people think she did it just to get back at her ex-husband after he took her to the cleaners in their divorce."

You can always count on Tony for the skinny. "We understand that she was recently seeing a man named Eduardo Lopez."

"She was."

"Do you know him?"

"Everybody knows Eduardo. I supply his produce."

"Is he a nice guy?"

"He's successful."

"Is he trustworthy?"

"He's always paid my bills, and he's donated a lot of money to St. Peter's."

I'm still looking for a straight answer. "Is he honest?"

"He's never been arrested."

Enough. "Is he the kind of guy you'd want as your business partner?"

The sage of Twenty-fourth Street pulls at his skin-tight sleeveless shirt and says, "Eduardo always has an agenda for which he's the primary beneficiary."

Progress. "What about his personal life?"

"What about it?"

I look at Rosie and say, "Is he the kind of guy you'd want your sister to date?"

"His idea of fidelity is a little different than mine. I know his wife. Everybody in the neighborhood knew he was cheating on her. She finally hired a PI who caught him red-handed with Maria. Vicky filed for divorce and blamed Maria for breaking up their marriage."

"Who ended the relationship between Maria and Eduardo?"

"Vicky told me Maria pulled the plug. Evidently, Eduardo was pretty upset."

This contradicts the story Maria told Ramon. She said Lopez broke up with her because he wasn't willing to leave his wife and start a family with her.

"I've never asked Eduardo about it," he says. "It isn't the sort of thing you talk about with one of your customers."

It's also a prototypical lose-lose-lose situation. Eduardo cheated on Vicky to sleep with Maria. Vicky got wind of it and it destroyed any chance of reconciliation with her husband. Then Eduardo and Maria split up. At the end of the day, everybody lived sadly ever after, except Maria, who didn't live at all. It will be interesting to get their respective sides of the story if they're willing to talk.

I ask, "Do you know the name of the PI that Vicky Lopez hired to watch her husband?"

"Nick Hanson."

That name keeps popping up.

"There's something else," he says. "Maria and Ramon had some history."

"He told us they grew up in the neighborhood, they were friends."

"There's more." He shrugs and says, "I assumed you already knew."

"Knew what?"

"They almost got married before he decided to go to the seminary."

CHAPTER 15

Pete

You just keep digging until you find something.

—Pete Daley, *Private Investigator Monthly*

SAN FRANCISCO'S LONGEST-RUNNING party has been in full swing for the last quarter of a century at Eduardo's Latin Palace at Twenty-third and Mission, a block and a half from Concepcion's apartment. Lopez's raucous eatery was serving fresh Mexican food long before various chains sanitized the concept and took it to malls across the country. The evening's festivities are already under way at six o'clock inside the cavernous space that smells of mesquite-grilled pork. The bar is packed with blue-collar workers, attractive singles and button-down yuppies. The margaritas are cheap and the crowd is electric.

My brother is sitting across from me in a corner booth, just beneath a neon Corona logo. We look almost identical, except he's five years younger than I am and has darker hair and a graying mustache. Pete was up all night, and he's unshaven and his hair is disheveled. It comes with the territory when you pay the bills chasing unfaithful husbands. He nibbles at a tortilla chip, takes a long draw on his Pacifico and says, "I heard you got bail."

He's never been much for small talk. "We did."

"Neat trick." He takes off his brown bomber jacket and says, "How'd you pull it off?"

"We got the archbishop to testify."

He winks and says, "I heard. Your little coup is making the rounds. By the end of the day, it will be part of local legend."

It's vintage Pete. He likes to ask questions for which he already knows the answers. It comes from his training as a cop, and it's bugged me for years. He would have made a great lawyer if he had the patience to sit behind a desk. He scratches the stubble that covers his pock-marked face. Pete spent a decade with the SFPD before he and a couple of buddies were unceremoniously shown the door after they broke up a gang fight with a little too much enthusiasm. He's still pissed off about it. He's worked as a PI for ten years. He doesn't have the bubbliest personality, but he's perceptive and an excellent judge of character.

He takes another sip of his beer and rasps, "Which judge?"

"Vanden Heuvel."

"I'm surprised. She used to be a prosecutor."

"She's fair," I say.

"And Catholic. Savor the victory. It won't happen again."

True enough.

He orders a second beer and asks, "Has my nephew started sleeping through the night?"

"Almost."

He gives me a half smile that represents a show of

great enthusiasm for him. "You don't make the concept of having children especially attractive," he says.

"Since when did you start thinking about having kids?"

"Donna and I talk about it."

Donna Andrews has been Pete's on-again, off-again girlfriend for the last two years. She works in the accounting department of one of the big law firms and provides a modicum of order in Pete's unpredictable schedule. They've talked about getting married, but they've both been divorced and they're cautious. She's turning forty this year, and Pete better get busy pretty soon.

"Conceptually," he says, "I like the idea."

"What about down here in the real world where you have to change diapers?"

"That's where I have a few minor problems."

I try to avoid giving him advice on his love life. My track record is terrible, and he's never forgiven me for introducing him to his ex-wife. Nevertheless, I decide to violate my policy and offer some low-key brotherly counseling. "The benefits outweigh the sleepless nights," I say. "Don't wait too long."

"I won't." That's as much as he cares to hear, and he returns to the matters at hand. "So," he says, "I take it you called me down here to ask if I'd help you with Ramon's case?"

"I did. Do you have time?"

"I can make time. Am I going to get paid?"

He's as practical as Rosie, and I play it straight. "Probably not. Our client is a priest."

"I'd be retired if I hadn't given away so much free time to your clients over the years."

"I'll put in a good word with the archbishop on your behalf."

"Cold, hard cash would be preferable."

"If it makes you feel better, we aren't getting paid, either."

"Maybe we could pass the hat around over at St. Peter's. There was quite a crowd over there when I walked by earlier tonight."

"They're trying to show support for Ramon, but they don't have a lot of money, either."

"If I'm not going to get paid, what's in it for me?"

"You'd be helping Ramon."

He acknowledges that this has some merit. "What else?"

"You can dig up as much dirt as you can on the archdiocese. Think of it as your chance for payback for all of those long, miserable hours you spent in Catholic school."

My brother never had the same affection for the Church that I did, and his eyes light up. "Are you serious?" he asks.

"Yes."

"What's the point?"

"Concepcion was about to start a huge case against the archdiocese. I want to know who was pissed off at her."

"You can start with the archbishop and F. X. Quinn, but I don't think you're going to be able to nail either of them with murder."

"I need to cover all the bases." And I have few other viable options at the moment.

My perceptive younger sibling offers me some solid advice. "You shouldn't turn this into a vendetta against the Church."

"I won't." I realize my tone is too emphatic when I say it.

"Come on, Mick. It's a bad idea to let a case get personal. Are you really going after Archbishop Keane?"

"Only if it helps Ramon."

"Okay," he says, "I'm in. What do you know?"

He keeps a close ear on the police scanner, and I throw it back. "What have you heard?"

"Concepcion was a small-time attorney who worked out of an apartment in the Mission and made a living suing the archdiocese. Her body was found in her bathtub last Tuesday morning. Her wrists had been slashed, and it looked like a suicide—or a fake. They found Ramon's fingerprints on the knife. She used to be married to the guy who is representing the archdiocese in the O'Connell case. That's all I know."

His information is always solid. He maintains a detached professionalism as I fill in the details, and his expression turns troubled when I tell him the police found Ramon's fingerprints on the back of Concepcion's neck and on the handles to her bathtub faucet. The mustache starts to twitch furiously when I tell him about their relationship twenty years ago.

He takes the items in order. "How did Ramon's prints get onto her neck?"

"He gave her a back rub."

"Bad idea. How did his prints get onto the bathtub faucets?"

"I don't know."

"They don't belong there. Was there any hanky-panky?"

"No."

"Says who?"

"Says Ramon."

"What about their history? Some guys never give up."

"He did."

He isn't convinced. "What does Rosie think?"

"What difference does it make?"

"She has better instincts than you do."

Thanks. "She didn't know. She's the lawyer in the family. Her brother is the gossip."

"We need to nail that one down. It will look terrible if they were getting it on."

Yes, it will. I ask him to canvas the area around Concepcion's apartment for witnesses. "I want to know if anybody went to her apartment on the night she died. And I want you to check out her ex-husband." He smiles when I mention Nick Hanson's name, and I tell him that I've already left him a message. I finish my beer and say, "I think somebody may have been following me earlier today." I tell him about the phantom green Impala.

He frowns and says, "You want me to have somebody watch your backside?"

"That might be a good idea."

He nods. "You may see a black Ford Explorer in your rearview mirror starting tomorrow morning. The driver's name is Vince, and it's the sort of thing that generally works better if you pretend he isn't there."

"Got it." My brother has access to a small army of operatives who seem to materialize on short notice. I explain that Concepcion recently broke up with Eduardo Lopez. "It so happens that he's the owner of this fine establishment."

"Maybe we should have a little talk with him." He summons our waitress with a big smile and asks, "Is Mr. Lopez in the building? We're old friends."

I love to watch my brother work. She returns the smile and says, "I'm afraid he's at a planning commission meeting."

Pete is undeterred. "Do you expect him back later?"

"He said he'd be in around eleven-thirty. Did you want to leave a message for him?"

"That's okay." Pete winks at her and says, "We may drop in to see him."

CHAPTER 16

"It Became Increasingly Difficult to Deal with Her on a Rational Basis"

The archdiocese is our largest client, but we are a full-service firm that provides the highest-quality legal services to a sophisticated and diversified client base.

—John Shanahan, *San Francisco Chronicle*

JOHN SHANAHAN IS eyeing me with a mixture of suspicion and contempt, but his voice is pure velvet. "We appreciate everything you're doing for Father Aguirre," he says. "It must be very difficult for you to represent a friend and classmate."

"It is." And you're completely full of shit.

Everything about the founding partner of Shanahan, Gallagher and O'Rourke is in muted tones of gray: the hair, the eyebrows, the suit and even the carpet. He's addressing me from behind a hand-carved rosewood desk in a museum-quality corner office on the twentieth floor of the historic Russ Building, a thirty-story neo-Gothic classic at 235 Montgomery Street that was the tallest building west of the Mississippi when it was completed in 1927, but is now dwarfed by its unsightly modern neighbors. He hasn't slept in a day and a half as we're meeting at seven-thirty on Wednesday night, but his appearance is still immaculate.

I try to keep my voice deferential when I say, "We'd like your help."

He leans back in his deep leather chair and says, "We'll make all of our resources available to you, Michael."

Sure you will. "I understand Ms. Concepcion used to work here."

"She did."

"Was she a good lawyer?"

He gets a faraway look in his eyes and says, "As I recall, her reviews were quite good, but she had difficulties managing the stresses of a full workload, and she elected to be taken off the partnership track."

And she was a woman who didn't have a big book of business who was working in a male-dominated, old-line firm. I ask him why she left.

"She was married to another attorney in the firm, and things became uncomfortable after they separated." He assures me that her departure was voluntary. "She developed an unhealthy anger toward the archdiocese that manifested itself in several unsuccessful lawsuits."

Nice try. I point out that the papers said she'd negotiated settlements that ran well into eight figures.

"They exaggerate. None of the cases went to trial. A few were settled for modest sums."

"How modest?"

"That's confidential."

We'll see. "Father Quinn told me that you hired a private investigator named Nick Hanson to watch her."

"He's on retainer, and it's part of our standard procedure."

He isn't hiding the ball. "Did he provide any useful information about Ms. Concepcion?"

"Nothing that we didn't already know."

Now he's hiding the ball.

"We wanted to see who she was talking to in preparation for the O'Connell case," he explains. "Quite honestly, there weren't any surprises."

I never trust people who toss around phrases like "quite honestly" in casual conversation. I ask him if Nick the Dick prepared a dossier about her.

He hesitates for just a beat before he decides, "Yes, he did."

"We'd like to see it."

Another pause. "Of course." He buzzes his night secretary and asks her to bring a photocopy of the materials that Nick prepared. His apparent willingness to provide the information probably means there is nothing in the report that may help us. "It will serve no useful purpose to withhold information in a murder investigation," he says.

"I appreciate your cooperation." And I'd feel better if I actually thought you meant it. I ask him if he provided a copy to the police.

"We will if they ask us for it," he says. "Quite honestly, we have researched the issue and we believe a private investigator's report will be discoverable."

I didn't think he'd give it to them out of the pure goodness of his heart. "I trust you have no problem if we want to talk to Mr. Hanson?"

"Of course not." He arches a gray eyebrow and adds, "After all, we're on the same side."

At least for the time being. "Do you happen to know what kind of car Mr. Hanson drives?"

"I'm afraid not. Why do you ask?"

"We have reason to believe that somebody may be watching us."

The corner of his mouth turns up slightly when he says, "I can assure you that we didn't hire a private investigator to conduct surveillance on our co-counsel."

I'm not entirely sure that I believe him. "I wasn't suggesting that you did. Do you have any idea who might have an interest in watching us?"

"Quite honestly," he says, "I can't imagine why anybody would be interested in following you. Perhaps you should ask the police."

"I will." We'll see if Pete's guy finds anybody on my tail.

When I ask him about the status of the civil case against Father O'Connell and the archdiocese, he says it's on hold until the plaintiff can hire a new lawyer. "I'm hopeful that we may be able to settle it in the interim. I'm an optimist by nature."

I disagree. I think you're an asshole by nature.

"With Ms. Concepcion's untimely death," he says, "it may be easier to persuade the plaintiff to listen to reason. We usually take a hard line to discourage people from bringing frivolous lawsuits, but we made an exception in the O'Connell case because of the seriousness of the charges and the notoriety of the defendant. The judge ordered us into mediation, but Ms. Concepcion was unwilling to compromise. Regrettably, it became increasingly difficult to deal with her on a rational basis as we got closer to the trial date. It was a disturbing case, and she was an unhappy person with an ax to grind. For better or worse, civil litigation is generally driven by pure economics. If somebody thinks they've been wronged, they go to court and ask for money. A jury can't fix your broken leg, but they can compensate you for it. Litigation is very risky, however, because juries are notoriously unpredictable. Most cases settle out of court because the parties know they can't control what happens inside the jury room."

He isn't telling me anything I don't already know, but it's interesting to hear his take on the process. The cold, calculating tenor of his lecture is disturbing and dead-on accurate.

"The system collapses when one of the parties tries to use civil litigation for a purpose other than a redistribution of wealth," he says. "Juries aren't equipped to fix social problems."

"And you think Ms. Concepcion was using the system for her own reasons?"

"Precisely. She refused to recognize the system's limitations or engage in meaningful settlement discussions. She wanted juries to hand out damage awards based on raw emotion."

And it appears she was effective. "Put yourself in her shoes," I say. "If you were representing somebody who had been sexually assaulted by a priest, wouldn't you use everything at your disposal?"

"Of course, but I wouldn't allow my ego or my emotions to cloud my judgment. The archdiocese cannot possibly restore the dignity of the people who have been wronged by their priests, but they can compensate them for their pain. In my view, she was attempting to generate publicity to serve her own ends."

I point out that she donated her legal fees to charity.

"That's all very well and good, but it wasn't in her client's best interests to dismiss our generous settlement offer out of hand."

"How much?" I ask.

"That's confidential."

"Ballpark?"

He thinks about it for a moment before he says, "Mid–six figures."

In the context of big-time civil litigation, half a million bucks is chump change. "She thought she could do better in court?"

"She *wanted* to go to court." His tone fills with self-righteousness. "I know it's fashionable to bash the Church," he says, "but the fact remains that our religious institutions hold together the moral fabric of our society. The overwhelming majority of priests do excellent work and are untainted by scandal. People like Ms. Concepcion want to bring down the institution because of the bad acts by a handful of priests."

I ask him when he last saw her.

"We had a settlement conference last Monday afternoon. The judge tried to persuade us to increase our offer, but Father Quinn was unwilling to do so. Her opening bid was fifty million dollars, which was out of the question. It wasn't the first time she had put forth an absurd settlement offer and we told her that we'd see her in court."

"Did you speak to her again?"

"I talked to her around seven o'clock that evening."

Interesting. "Where were you?"

"Here."

"Why did she call you?"

"Actually," he says, "I called her. I had persuaded Father Quinn to raise our settlement offer by a modest sum, but she turned us down. That was the last time I spoke to her."

I ask if she seemed agitated or distraught.

"Both. It was a big case, and she had difficult cards. We believe the plaintiff was getting cold feet."

"What's the plaintiff's name?"

"Jane Doe."

I sigh. It isn't uncommon for victims of sexual abuse to avoid using their names in court documents, but I obviously need to know more than that. "What's her *real* name?"

"That's confidential."

I give him a look. He knows that I can get it from the cops or from the prosecutors or even from the media, all of whom know her true identity. They can get into trouble only if they make the information available to the public. He takes a deep breath and says, "Her real name is Kelly O'Shea."

A nice Irish-Catholic girl. I ask him why she was reluctant to testify.

"Because she made the whole thing up. Do you know what she does for a living?"

"The papers said she's a waitress."

"Technically, that's true, but there's more to it than that."

"What does she really do?"

"She's a lap dancer at a girlie theater. And a hooker."

CHAPTER 17

"It Was a Wrongful Act"

The concept of abstinence is a fundamental principle that is deeply rooted in our theology. There are no exceptions.

—Father Ramon Aguirre, *San Francisco Chronicle*

AH. MAYBE NOT such a nice Irish-Catholic girl. "And the allegations?"

"They're claiming he was providing counseling to her and used his position and influence to procure sexual favors."

"Is it true?"

Shanahan taps his Montblanc pen on his desk and says, "Of course not. The DA agreed to give her immunity if she fingered her pimp and Father O'Connell. The criminal charges against the pimp were pleaded out, and Father O'Connell's case was dropped after he died."

Leaving only the civil case against the archdiocese.

"Things got more complicated a few weeks ago," he says. "The police caught Ms. Doe soliciting in the Tenderloin. Her immunity agreement didn't cover the new charge, and the episode wouldn't have enhanced her credibility in court. Ms. Concepcion was about to start jury selection in a high-profile case in which her star witness was a prostitute. Quite honestly, we were very confident we would prevail."

There's that phrase again. "Then why did you offer to settle?"

"Pure economics. Protracted litigation is prohibitively expensive."

The fact that the archdiocese would have been dragged through the mud never entered his mind. I ask him if he still intends to pursue a settlement.

"We are reevaluating our position."

"Was Mr. Hanson keeping Ms. Concepcion under surveillance on the night she died?"

"Yes."

Bingo. "Did he happen to see anyone other than Father Aguirre enter her apartment?"

"No."

Dammit. "Was someone watching Ms. Doe, too?"

"Yes." He tells me that Doe lives in a residential hotel in the Tenderloin and assures me that she was nowhere near Concepcion's apartment on the night she died.

"Is she going to testify?" I ask.

"The case against Father O'Connell will collapse if she doesn't."

And the archdiocese will be off the hook. I ask him why she isn't in jail on the solicitation charge.

"Ms. Concepcion posted bail for her."

She certainly was a full-service lawyer—especially if she didn't have a lot of money. "Where did she get the funds?"

"She had sources in the neighborhood." He places his bone-china coffee cup in its saucer to signify that our conversation is coming to an end.

I lean forward and tell him that I'd like to meet Dennis Peterson.

"He isn't available, Michael."

Don't knock yourself out trying to help. "Perhaps we can set up a time to get together tomorrow."

He stands and says, "I'll see what I can do."

RAMON'S HANDS ARE clasped on the table in front of him at eight-thirty on Wednesday night, and his eyes are locked onto mine. "What are you asking?" he says.

We're sitting in his makeshift room at Church headquarters that looks as if it was furnished by "Rectories R Us." There are a single bed, a small desk, a three-drawer dresser and a lamp. A cross hangs on the back of the door. It's been an eventful twenty-four hours since he heard my confession. We have a lot of territory to cover, and I wanted to have this discussion outside the presence of Quinn, Shanahan and, most important, the archbishop.

"I need you to tell me the precise nature of your relationship with Ms. Concepcion."

"I was her priest," he says.

"What else?"

"We were friends."

"Close friends?"

"Yes."

"Come on, Ramon."

There is exasperation in his tone when he says, "Just because you're a priest doesn't mean you can't have social friendships with your female parishioners."

"I was never the priest for one of my old girlfriends."

"What's that supposed to mean?"

"It has come to our attention that you and Ms. Concepcion dated for a period of time."

"We went out for six months, and we broke up twenty years ago. She went to law school and I went to the seminary."

"How would you describe your relationship?"

He doesn't try to spin it. "Boyfriend-girlfriend."

"So you were romantically involved?"

"Yes."

"How involved?"

"Are you asking me if I slept with her?"

I nod.

"The answer is yes."

Dammit.

"It was a wrongful act," he says. "I went to church and confessed."

"Did you enjoy it?"

"Confessing?"

"Sex."

"It was nice, but it isn't all that it's cracked up to be."

He's never done it with Rosie. "I need to know if there was anything in your relationship that may leap out and bite us."

"Except for the sex, nothing."

"I'm serious."

"Are you asking me if I still had feelings for her?"

"Yes."

He takes a deep breath and says, "I loved her as dearly as one can love a friend and I worried about her constantly, but I had no romantic feelings for her."

"Have you been romantically involved with anybody since you've been a priest?"

"Absolutely not."

Good enough. "You told me she was unhappy because Lopez had dumped her."

"That's true."

"Tony heard it the other way around."

"What difference does it make?"

"Maybe none, but if we're going to argue it was a suicide, it would help if he dumped her. In my vast experience, the dumpee is frequently in worse shape than the dumper."

"Thanks for your insight, Dr. Phil, but she told me that he broke up with her. If you don't want to take my word for it, you can ask Eduardo."

We will. "How well do you know him?"

"Pretty well. He's a big benefactor of St. Peter's."

"Did he have a habit of cheating on his wife?"

He doesn't answer.

"Is there reason to suspect he may have been involved in Maria's murder?"

"Get real, Mike."

"Work with me, Ramon."

His tone drips with sarcasm when he says, "While you're at it, you shouldn't rule out his wife. She was angry at him, too."

St. Peter's should be renamed St. Peyton Place. "Why didn't you mention it earlier?"

"Because neither of them is capable of murder and I was still operating under the misguided assumption that I was supposed to keep my parishioners' secrets confidential."

"From now on," I say, "you need to tell me everything."

"Even if it involves something told to me in confidence?"

"It beats spending the rest of your life in jail."

He responds with a stern scowl. We spend the next hour going through his visit with Concepcion again in painstaking detail. Thankfully, his story doesn't change. I try to sound casual when I ask him, "Did you use the bathroom while you were there?"

"Yes." He acknowledges that they may have found his prints on the toilet seat and the sink. "I had a headache and I took some aspirin from her medicine chest."

That accounts for most—but not all—of the fingerprints. Now comes a big one. "They found your prints on the handles to the bathtub faucet," I say.

He makes a face. "We got into an argument before I left. She didn't like it when I told her I thought it was time for her to move on with her life. Her trial was about to start, and I suggested that she take a bath to relax. I even started the water for her. That's all."

I breathe a little easier. It isn't an airtight alibi, but it's a plausible explanation—I can work with it. I ask if she called anyone while he was there.

"No."

"Did anyone call her?"

He frowns. "Yes. Her ex-husband called her around nine-fifteen, and they talked for a couple of minutes. She got very upset." He shakes his head. "She ended the conversation by telling him to go to hell."

CHAPTER 18

"What's the Worst-Case Scenario?"

Criminal-defense work is like putting together a puzzle. You study each piece of evidence and try to find ways to cast doubt on the prosecution's case. If you overlook something important, your client is in serious trouble.

—Rosita Fernandez, *Boalt Hall Monthly*

I GIVE MY daughter a parental nod and ask, "Is your homework done?"

"Yes, Dad."

I'm reminded that bedtime schedules frequently take a backseat to more pressing business as Grace's smile lights up her grandmother's living room at ten o'clock on Wednesday night. Rosie's parents bought the post–earthquake era bungalow in the shadows of St. Peter's almost fifty years ago for fifteen grand. Though it needs a fresh coat of paint and new appliances, it would fetch close to a half million bucks if Rosie's mom ever chose to sell it. There isn't a chance that she will.

Sylvia Fernandez's tidy living room looks much the same as it did when I first met Rosie, and the oatmeal-colored sofa and teak end tables have a comfortable familiarity. The faded black-and-white wedding photos of Rosie's

parents still adorn the mantel, and framed graduation por-
traits of Rosie and her siblings hang above the fireplace.
The only significant addition in the last decade is the photos of Sylvia's grandchildren.

Grace's inflection is a dead-on imitation of her
mother's when she says, "I saw you on the news tonight."

"How did I look?"

"Same as always."

Thanks. Her answers have gotten shorter as she's gotten older. She's also developed a fairly advanced sense of
irony for a twelve-year-old.

Her tone takes on a serious cast. "You said Father
Aguirre was innocent."

"Yes, I did."

"Is he?"

"Of course."

"That isn't what they're saying on TV."

"They're wrong."

No reaction. "I was reading about the case on the
Chronicle's website," she says. We keep a pretty tight lid
on her instant messaging contacts and we draw the line at
porn sites and chat rooms, but the speed of the technology is outpacing our ability to police it. "They found
Father Aguirre's fingerprints in Maria Concepcion's
bathroom."

"It's true," I tell her.

"Does that mean he's guilty?"

Nice try, Sherlock. "It means he went to the bathroom." And it may be time to revisit our Internet-access
policy.

She won't give up easily. "What was he doing in her apartment that night?"

"Visiting."

"That's all?"

It's like arguing with Rosie. "That's all."

"How much will you give me if I crack the case?"

Everybody's on the make. "Twenty bucks," I say, "but only if you prove he's innocent."

"What if I show that he's guilty?"

"I'll give you fifty bucks to keep your mouth shut."

She responds with an all-knowing smile.

My ex-mother-in-law walks in a moment later with Tommy on her shoulder. She and Rosie have matching features and identical constitutions. Sylvia was born seventy-five years ago in a village near Monterrey, Mexico, and moved to San Francisco when she was in her teens. A highly intelligent soul with little formal education and an uncompromisingly level head, she assumed the role of family matriarch when her husband died shortly after Rosie and I met. She remains a pillar of strength for her children, and we couldn't practice law without her.

She pats Tommy on the back and whispers, "He just fell asleep." She brushes the hair out of her grandson's eyes and says, "Maybe he'll make it through the night."

"Hope springs eternal."

She turns to Grace and says, "Get your things ready, sweetie. Mommy is going to drive us back to your house in a few minutes."

"Do I have time to do a couple more computer searches?"

"Five minutes, honey."

I hope she isn't instant-messaging any of the boys at school.

Sylvia rocks Tommy and lowers her voice in a manner that suggests she doesn't want him to hear her. "Father Aguirre isn't a murderer," she says. She's from a generation where it was considered taboo to refer to a priest by his first name.

"Let's hope the police agree with you."

Tommy stretches, and Sylvia kisses him lightly on the forehead. "I'll get him ready to go," she says to me.

"Thanks, Sylvia." She's about to go back to her room when I ask, "How well do you know Maria's mother?"

Her shrug causes Tommy's eyes to open wide. "Pretty well."

"Well enough to ask her if she'll talk to us?"

"Her daughter just died, Michael."

"And her priest has been accused of her murder."

"I'll call her in the morning."

I walk into the tiny kitchen where Rosie is studying copies of the police reports. She has an uncanny ability to concentrate on legal issues when Grace and Tommy are nearby. Her tone is deadly serious when she says, "I think I saw the Impala sitting on the corner by our office earlier this evening. I called the cops, but it disappeared before they got there."

Hell. "Did you get a license number?"

"There was no plate." She says she filed a report with the police, who searched the immediate vicinity and told her to keep her eyes open. She's pleased when I tell her that Pete is going to have somebody watch my backside.

I point to the stack of papers on the table and say, "Anything new?"

"Not much," she reports. She glances around to make sure that Grace is out of the room before she hands me the gruesome crime-scene photos.

I study the pictures for a moment and notice that Concepcion's face is covered with white cream. "What's that stuff?" I ask.

"It's a moisturizer called Essential Elements. They found it all over her body."

This is odd. "Including her hands?"

"Yes. For our purposes, the best-case scenario is that she decided to make herself comfortable before she committed suicide. The fact that they found her fingerprints on an empty plastic container that was sitting on the ledge of the tub would seem to support that conclusion."

So far, so good. "What's the worst-case scenario?"

"Ramon spread the skin cream on her body to cover the injuries that she sustained when he knocked her unconscious and to make the fake suicide look more convincing."

"Is there anything that suggests he was so meticulous?"

"They found his fingerprints on the empty bottle, too."

Dammit. His fingerprints are turning up in a lot of places where they shouldn't. I ask if she's heard anything from the chief medical examiner's office.

"I spoke with Dr. Beckert briefly," she says, "and he's willing to talk to us."

"Any hints?"

"He said it was definitely not a suicide, and the time of death was between nine-thirty P.M. and one A.M."

"That means she could have been alive after Ramon left," I say.

"If you believe Ramon's story."

I do. "It also opens up the possibility that somebody came in later and killed her."

"Or that she committed suicide," she says.

"Not if Beckert is right."

She hands me a stack of computer printouts and says, "These are the phone records from last Monday—both cell and landlines." There were no incoming or outgoing cell-phone calls. She confirms that Concepcion received calls at her apartment from Shanahan at seven, her mother at seven-thirty, Ramon at seven forty-five and Peterson at nine-fifteen. "The last incoming call was at nine forty-seven and lasted less than a minute."

"From whom?"

"It was placed from the general number at the headquarters of the archdiocese."

I can't wait to hear Quinn's explanation. "Were there any outgoing calls?"

"Just one. It was at nine-fifty, and it lasted for a minute."

"To whom?"

"Eduardo's Latin Palace."

"Maybe she ordered dinner."

"Or maybe she talked to her ex-boyfriend. Did you happen to notice any food in her kitchen when Roosevelt showed you her apartment?"

"Not that I recall."

She studies the police reports for a moment and says, "They found a partially eaten chicken burrito on her kitchen table. It was in a wrapper from Eduardo's."

CHAPTER 19

"Things Just Didn't Work Out"

I have tried to give something back to our community.
—Eduardo Lopez, *San Francisco Chronicle*

IT'S COOL OUTSIDE, but the heat is on at Eduardo's. The packed restaurant is pulsating with athletic bodies at eleven-thirty on Wednesday night. Pete and I have worked our way to a booth in the corner of the bar, where we're sweating profusely, nursing our beers and admiring the lead stallions on the dance floor. He leans across the table and shouts, "Oh, to be young and single."

I nod, but make no effort to respond above the roar.

Pete spent the last few hours talking to people in the alley behind Concepcion's apartment with little to show for it. He gestures to a shapely waitress with seductive eyes and long black hair and says, "Two more beers, please." He winks and asks, "Is Mr. Lopez in?"

She responds with an indifferent shrug.

He places a twenty on the table, and her reticence magically transforms into a warm smile. She sweeps up the bill with a graceful motion and says, "He just arrived."

"Would you ask him to come see us?"

"Of course, sir. What's your name?"

"Tell him we're friends of Tony Fernandez."

I love to watch my brother work.

She returns a moment later with our beers and her boss, a dapper man in his late fifties who looks as if he was transported intact from a *GQ* ad and bears a striking resemblance to Raul Julia. His tailor-made navy suit and crisp rep tie complement a perfect tan, slicked-back hair and neatly trimmed silver goatee. He flashes a practiced smile, extends an inviting hand and manages to sound charming, even above the din. "I'm Eduardo Lopez," he says in a lightly accented voice. The consummate host presents the beers to us himself. The warmth in his tone seems genuine enough when he says, "I understand you know Tony Fernandez."

Pete smiles back and says, "We do."

He winks at the waitress and says, "These are on the house."

She responds with a demure smile and walks away.

We thank Lopez profusely, and the crinkles at the corners of his eyes become more pronounced as his plastic smile broadens. We partake in small talk for a few minutes before he tries to disengage. "It's nice to meet you," he says. "Please give my best to Tony."

Pete stops him with an upraised hand and says, "We really need to talk to you."

"About what?"

"Business." The band launches into a raucous number that causes the dance floor to erupt. Pete gestures toward the back of the restaurant and shouts into Lopez's ear, "Can we go someplace quiet?"

Our genial host forces a smile as he tries to figure out

who we are and what we want. He motions us to follow him, and we weave our way through the crowd, where he has a handshake for every man and a peck on the cheek for each woman. It takes him ten minutes to lead us less than fifty feet to a soundproofed office above the kitchen, where I can still feel the reverberations from the drums downstairs. The windowless space is almost as large as Shanahan's office and has a comfortable, albeit kitschy, feeling. It houses an antique rolltop desk, two brown leather armchairs, a credenza and a conference table that holds a scale model of a low-income housing project to be built near the Sixteenth Street BART station. His cluttered desk is covered with photos of his numerous grandchildren, and the paneled walls are filled with citations, awards, testimonials and photos of Lopez with politicians, entertainers, sports figures and other celebrities. The most prominent is a signed picture of a young Lopez standing next to Orlando Cepeda at Candlestick Park. Next to it is a more recent photo of a graying Lopez with a retired Cepeda in front of Lopez's burrito stand behind the scoreboard at SBC Park.

He eyes us warily and says, "What can I do for you gentlemen?"

Pete is chomping to leap into interrogation mode, but I want to ease Lopez into this discussion more slowly. I look at his family photos and say, "How old are your grandchildren?"

His chest puffs out when he says, "They range from six months to seventeen years."

I was hoping this would get him talking, but he's a

man of relatively few words. I find another prop on the table and ask him about the development plans.

"It's called Riordan Square," he says. "We're going to provide housing for over five hundred low-income families."

"How did you happen to get involved in the development business?"

His eyes light up. "Our community has supported my business for a long time, and I wanted to give something back. Conventional developers can't make money on low- and moderate-income projects, so I created a template for establishing partnerships between private builders and nonprofit agencies. The developers handle the construction at a reduced cost and the nonprofits provide subsidies to make the units affordable." He says that the archdiocese is the lead investor on Riordan Square. "Construction will begin in the spring."

This calls for a platitude. "That's tremendous," I say. "Do you get any compensation for your efforts?"

"A lot of satisfaction." He hesitates before he adds, "And a modest fee."

I'm tempted to ask him how modest, but that would be pushing it. "Is there anything that could derail the process?"

"I certainly hope not. I've always been an optimist."

And I've always been a cynic. "There has been speculation that the archdiocese may face serious financial problems if it suffers an adverse result in its pending litigation."

He assures me that the archdiocese has more than adequate resources to fulfill its financial obligations. He sounds like a new father as he expounds about his plans, although the level of self-aggrandizement is a bit much for my taste. Finally, he decides it's time to see why we're really here. "Did you want to talk about the real-estate business?" he asks.

I come clean. "Tony's sister is my partner, and we're representing Father Aguirre. We're looking for information about Maria Concepcion."

The affable smile is still plastered on his face, but his eyes show the first hint of concern. I can hear tension in his voice when he says, "I am certain Father Aguirre is not a murderer."

It's reassuring to hear him say it. "We were hoping you would help us demonstrate the correctness of your view to the district attorney. We understand that you knew Ms. Concepcion."

"I did. She patronized this establishment, and I considered her a friend."

He strikes me as the sort of guy who considers everybody on his dance floor a friend.

He adds, "I am very saddened by her sudden and untimely loss."

Of course. "Do you know anything about her death?"

"I'm afraid not."

"Would you mind telling us where you were a week ago Monday night?"

"Are you suggesting I had something to do with it?"

"I'm not suggesting anything."

His inflection remains upbeat when he says, "I was in the restaurant from six o'clock Monday evening until twelve-thirty Tuesday morning." There's an almost-imperceptible hint of defensiveness in his tone when he adds, "You don't have to take my word for it. Feel free to ask any of our employees."

We will, and if they value their jobs, they'll give us the answer he wants us to hear. "We understand you knew Ms. Concepcion pretty well."

"In my line of work, you get to know a lot of people."

Too glib. "We're told you were involved with her."

"Involved?"

"Yes." He might be able to buffalo his employees, but he won't be able to do it to me.

"Where I come from," he says, "personal relationships are nobody else's business."

"I grew up in this neighborhood and I agree with you, but things tend to get complicated after somebody has been murdered."

"If you want to ask any additional questions, you'll have to talk to my lawyers."

That experience is likely to be considerably less than satisfying. "We aren't after you," I say. This isn't entirely true. If I could prove that he was at her apartment on the night she died, I would scream until somebody down at the Hall of Justice decided to question him. "We can talk about this politely and we'll get out of your hair, or I can bring over a subpoena and we can do this in a more unpleasant way."

His eyes narrow. "My lawyers will tie you up for years."

This is undoubtedly true. "You'll look like you're trying to hide something."

No reply.

Egomaniacs generally like to have their psyches massaged, and I try to butter him up. "You know everybody in the neighborhood," I say, "and we were hoping you might be willing to help us."

He thinks about it for an instant and decides to show a degree of cooperation. "This situation is difficult," he says in a subdued tone. "My wife and I are getting divorced. Obviously, my relationship with Ms. Concepcion has been a complicating factor."

I try to empathize. "I can understand why you don't want to do your laundry in public, and I can assure you we'll do everything to minimize your part in this matter." It's more than a little white lie, but still well south of a big whopper. I would broadcast everything I know about his divorce on KGO if it would help Ramon's case.

He isn't buying it. "I am most impressed by your sensitivity," he says.

I offer a realistic assessment. "The police will find out about your relationship with Ms. Concepcion. If you don't tell them about it, your wife will."

He decides to play it straight. "They've already asked me about it," he says.

It's the opening I wanted. It also indicates that Roosevelt knows more than he's told me. "What did you tell them?"

"That's none of your business."

It is now. I feed him the party line that the law requires the police to provide copies of their reports to us. "I'm going to find out," I say, "and I'd rather hear it from you." More important, I want to watch your expression as you tell me about it.

"I don't want to hear my name on the news tomorrow," he says.

I assure him that he won't hear anything about it from me.

"Ms. Concepcion and I were involved for a short time."

Was that so hard? "Was your wife aware of it?"

"Yes. I told her about it."

"Before or after she hired the private investigator?"

He stares daggers at me and whispers, "After. It made reconciliation less likely."

I'll bet. This isn't an opportune time to ask him to admit to serial adultery. "When did you start seeing Ms. Concepcion?"

"In March." He confirms that they split up in early September.

"What caused the breakup?"

"Things just didn't work out."

I'm hoping for a little more. "Can you be a bit more specific?"

His tone turns more emphatic when he repeats, "Things just didn't work out."

Dammit. "Did you break up with her?"

"It was a mutual decision."

That's never the case. "And did she give you any indications she was unhappy?"

"Things deteriorated over time. She was fifteen years younger than I am and wanted to start a family. We were at different points in our lives."

Not to mention the fact that you were still married.

"Obviously," he says, "the end result was not the one either of us had hoped for."

His tone suggests he's told us everything he plans to about that subject. Pete reads the cue and interjects a fresh voice. "How was Ms. Concepcion's mood the last time you talked?"

"Same as always."

It's a perfectly good answer that says nothing, and Pete keeps pushing. "Was she unhappy about the termination of your relationship?"

"She was getting counseling from Father Aguirre and seeing a therapist."

"Did you notice any unusual behavior?"

"None."

"Sadness or even depression?"

"No. Would you mind getting to the point?"

I tell him that the cops found Prozac in her medicine chest.

"I run a restaurant. I'm not a therapist."

His tone is more callous than I might have expected. "There is some evidence that she may have committed suicide," I say. "Do you think it's possible?"

"It would trouble me to think she took her own life."

"But you wouldn't rule it out?"

"No, I wouldn't."

It isn't as good as getting a diagnosis from her shrink, but it may help. "Mr. Lopez," I say, "when was the last time you saw her?"

He says she came into the restaurant for dinner a couple of weeks ago by herself, and they had a polite, albeit strained, conversation. She appeared nervous about the

O'Connell case and expressed problems with a key witness. He says they didn't speak again.

I tell him that there was a call from Concepcion's apartment to this restaurant at approximately nine-fifty on the night she died.

"We receive hundreds of calls a day," he says. "I have no idea who she talked to or what she was calling about. She may have ordered a take-out dinner."

"Is there any way you can tell if she did?"

"Only if she paid with a credit card."

I ask him to check it out, and he agrees to do so. I tell him the police found a partially eaten burrito in a wrapper from his restaurant in her apartment.

"Are you suggesting I had something to do with it?"

"I'm trying to find out whether you or anybody else from your restaurant delivered a burrito to her apartment last Monday night."

The last remnants of cooperation disappear. "I did not talk to her last Monday night," he says, "and we don't deliver."

MY BROTHER IS less than convinced of the veracity of our host's story. "He was lying, Mick," he says.

"About what?"

"I'm not sure."

"How could you tell?"

"His lips were moving."

Pete's instincts are significantly better developed than his communication skills. I press him, but he sets his jaw and refuses to elaborate.

It's after midnight, and the raucous crowd is pouring out onto Mission Street. Traffic is still heavy as we watch a homeless man pushing his shopping cart down the street in search of a place to sleep. Just another night on the strip in my old neighborhood.

We shuffle down Mission and turn left at Twenty-fourth, where my car is parked at the corner. I look at my beat-up Corolla and immediately see that the driver-side window has been smashed in. Tiny shards of glass cover the driver's seat. "Dammit," I say.

"It happens," Pete says. "You've been living out in the suburbs too long."

"There was nothing in the car worth stealing," I say.

He shrugs. "You couldn't tell that from the outside."

I glance at a pristine Mercedes that's parked behind my Corolla and say, "If I were a garden-variety car thief, I would have taken my chances with the Mercedes."

"That car has an alarm," Pete observes. "Yours doesn't."

I'm not convinced. "There is a bunch of people who aren't excited by the fact that we're involved in this case. Maybe somebody is trying to send me a message."

"It may be nothing, Mick. If you're really worried, my guy will be on your tail starting at six o'clock tomorrow morning."

"Thanks." I wish he were there already.

Pete reads the troubled look in my eyes and says, "You aren't going to back down, are you?"

"Of course not."

"Good." He takes inventory of my car and says, "I think

it's still driveable, but it may be a little cold going over the bridge."

"I'll take care of it tomorrow," I say.

He takes a deep breath of the damp night air and says, "Are you in any hurry to get home?"

The thought of crossing the Golden Gate Bridge in a cold drizzle with a broken window isn't especially appealing. "Not really," I say. I haven't slept in two days, but I'm game.

"I'm going to see if anybody is hanging out behind Concepcion's apartment."

"Want some company?"

"Absolutely."

CHAPTER 20

"Looking for a Good Time?"

I have instructed the chief of police to give high priority to prostitution and other "victimless" crimes in the Mission District, where law-abiding citizens should not have to suffer the indignity of being accosted by prostitutes and drug dealers.

—The Mayor of San Francisco

MY BROTHER'S CATLIKE eyes are darting as we're standing in the alley behind Concepcion's apartment building at twelve-twenty A.M. The rain has given way to a dank fog, and I can see my breath. The tightly packed low-rise buildings are covered with graffiti, and the only source of illumination is a single light that's mounted on a power pole. Cars are parked haphazardly, and threatening signs warn interlopers not to block the garages. An emaciated cat is pawing for food in an overflowing Dumpster, and the pungent odor envelops us.

We're only a block and a half from Lopez's sleek restaurant, but it's a different world. The alley rivals Mission Street as the neighborhood's hub of nighttime commerce, and traffic is continuous. The selection of goods is limited and the quality is spotty, but all the products are illegal. We've been here for fifteen minutes and we've been offered coke, crack, heroin, meth and women. I can hear a wailing siren from Mission Street, but there is no discernible police presence. An imposing entrepreneur is peddling pharmaceutical products with impunity from the back of his van. He was more interested in selling heroin than providing information, and he assured us he hadn't been in the vicinity last Monday night.

We're leaning against a decaying garage door and trying to engage the sliver of humanity that inhabits this flea market for vice. In other words, we're looking for trouble. We've chatted up drug dealers, hookers, gang members and petty thieves, with nothing to show for it so far. One dealer pulled a knife and tried to extort a little extra cash, but quickly reconsidered when Pete flashed a small, but intimidating, twenty-two-caliber pistol. My anxiety is somewhat tempered by the fact that there is an armed ex-cop standing next to me. He's licensed to carry the gun, but legal niceties lose much of their meaning in a dark alley in the Mission.

I ask Pete, "What are the odds we'll get some useful information?"

"Better than fifty-fifty."

"And the chances we'll get ourselves killed?"

He pats the handgun under his jacket and says, "Worse than fifty-fifty."

Twelve-thirty turns into one o'clock as we continue talking to the addicts and low riders who parade by us. The vignettes in our immediate proximity are typical for this hour: a man selling drugs to a young woman; a hooker arguing with a john; a group of boisterous teens wearing matching gang jackets. In the distance, we can hear gunfire and the sound of cars doing donuts in a parking lot behind a long-closed movie theater. Police have been trying to crack down on these so-called sideshows for years, with limited success.

By one forty-five, the Mission is settling in for the night. Traffic has slowed to a trickle, and the hookers and johns have retired. The next shift is the homeless, who materialize from the crevices and cautiously push their shopping carts into doorways in their nightly attempt to find sheltered places to sleep. The mist is getting thicker, and my hands are getting colder. Pete's leather jacket and mustache are covered with moisture. His eyes keep moving as the alley becomes ominously still. A dirt-encrusted man toasts us with a kind word and a bottle of gin. He lavishes us with slurred thanks after we oblige his request for change, but he provides no helpful information.

At two o'clock, Pete motions down the alley toward a tall Latina who is walking in the shadows with a halting gait. I can't tell if she's injured, intoxicated or trying to navigate high heels. I ask, "What's she doing here?"

"Working," Pete says.

"Excuse me?"

"Shut up, Mick."

I always feel like Barney Fife when I'm on a stakeout with Pete.

Despite the fog, the woman is clad only in a miniskirt and a loose-fitting, white cotton blouse. Her heavy makeup is smeared, and her long hair is disheveled as she limps toward us. Her exact age is difficult to discern in the dim light, but she can't be much older than twenty.

We've made no attempt to remain inconspicuous, and

Pete invokes a nonthreatening tone when he approaches her cautiously and says, "Do you need some help, Miss?"

The worldly hooker reaches into her blouse, and the dim light reflects off the blade of a small knife. "Is your name Gary?" she asks.

I'm guessing Gary isn't her boyfriend. "I'm afraid not," Pete says. He's just far enough away from her so that she can't reach him. I can feel my heart pounding as Pete holds up his palms. "My name is Pete," he says, "and this is Mike." I step forward to show her that I'm unarmed. Pete tries to keep his tone reassuring, "Are you in some kind of trouble?"

"Are you vice?"

"Nope."

"Undercover?"

"Nope."

"Mayor's Task Force?"

"Nope."

I admire her directness.

Her eyes turn hopeful. "Looking for a good time?"

"We're here on business."

"So am I."

"I'm a private investigator," Pete says. He gestures to-ward Concepcion's building and adds, "A woman died in there last Monday night. Were you here?"

"Maybe." She hesitates and says, "Maybe not." There is recognition in her eyes when he tells her that we're working for Ramon. "I've met him," she says. "I get dinner at the church a couple of nights a week."

"Then help us."

Reality intrudes. "My pimp is going to beat the crap

out of me because I can't find a guy named Gary and now you want me to help you solve a murder?"

"Tell us who else works on this street. Maybe somebody can help us."

"What's in it for me?"

"The knowledge that you helped keep Father Aguirre out of jail."

She's unmoved. "You're going to have to do better."

"What was Gary supposed to pay you?"

"Fifty . . . a hundred bucks."

"We'll give it to you."

I'm not sure about the precise legalities of this transaction, but her dull eyes light up, and she tries to raise the ante. "A hundred and fifty."

"A hundred—that's going to be my best offer."

"All right, but I want you to find me a new apartment," she says.

Give her credit for trying, but there are limits on what we can offer. "I'm a PI, not a social worker," Pete tells her.

This is a spot where I might be able to add something useful. "I'm a lawyer," I say, "and I know some people who can help you."

"Lawyers are assholes."

At least we're starting on a positive note. "Not all of them," I say. "I represent people who get accused of crimes that aren't their fault."

"Like what?"

"People who sell their bodies to make money for asshole pimps. I'd like to buy you a cup of coffee and talk about it."

"Forget it." She fingers her knife and says, "Coffee doesn't pay the bills."

"Money does." I pull out my wallet and hand her five twenties. "Here's the hundred that Gary owed you. Now you're in good with your pimp. Let's start with your name."

She tucks the money inside her blouse and says, "Anna."

"That's a pretty name. Is it real?"

"Yes."

"What's your last name?"

"That's going to cost you another fifty."

"That's a little steep." I hand her a twenty.

"Moreno," she says.

Progress. Our window of opportunity may be very small. "How old are you?" I ask.

"Twenty-five."

She's lying. "How long have you been doing this?"

"A couple of years." She says she grew up just south of here on Garfield Square. Her father left home when she was a baby, and her mother died when she was thirteen. She did foster care for a few years and then went into business for herself. Now she lives in a women's shelter.

"Hypothetically," I say, "would you be interested in meeting some people who might be able to help you go back to school?"

"What's it going to cost me?"

"Nothing."

"There's no free lunch."

"There is with me."

"You're an unusual lawyer."

So I've been told. There are limits to what one can accomplish in an alley in the middle of the night, but she seems genuinely interested. I give her my business card and ask her to call me at the office. She gives me a phone number that I hope is real. I try to ease her into a discussion of the matters at hand. "How often do you work here?"

"Six nights a week."

Jesus.

"I can make five hundred a night," she says, "but most of it goes to my pimp. Every once in a while, the vice cops clear everybody out for a few weeks."

"Have you ever been arrested?"

"Of course." Her tone suggests this is an accepted cost of doing business. She says she's done a little jail time. "It sucked."

I'll bet. "Is there anybody who might have seen something last week?"

"Maybe."

"What's it going to cost us?"

"Another hundred."

This is getting pricy. "Tell me who it is." I flash another five twenties, which she tries to grab, but I snatch them away.

Her voice goes down a half octave. "I thought we had a deal."

"We did."

"Then give me my money."

"Not until you give me a name and tell us where to find him."

She hesitates for an interminable moment, then she

leads us down the alley and to a building a half block from where we started. She points to a closed garage door and says, "His name is Preston Fuentes."

"Is he your pimp?"

"Do you think I'd give you the name of my pimp?"

Probably not. "Who is he?"

"My cousin."

"What does he do?"

"He's a mechanic."

Seems innocuous enough. I'm about to pursue it when the quiet calm is broken by the sound of violent barking.

"That's Fluffy," she explains. "She's Preston's Doberman."

Everybody should have a pet.

"He's restoring a Corvette in this garage," she explains. "He works on the car at night, and Fluffy keeps an eye on it when he isn't around."

Two thoughts flash through my mind. First, I wonder where a mechanic got the money to purchase a Corvette. Second, I decide to stay on Fluffy's good side.

CHAPTER 21

"I Figured You Might Be Up"

It takes some babies longer to calibrate their sleeping patterns, but they should make it through the night by their first birthday.

—*Parenting for Dummies*

MY BROTHER'S VOICE is raspier than usual when he says, "You sound terrible, Mick."

It may have something to do with the fact that I just spent the last three hours interviewing prostitutes and drug dealers next to a Dumpster in an alley off Capp Street, and my left arm is numb from the freezing rain that's whipping through the broken window in my car as I'm driving past the north tower of the Golden Gate Bridge at three-ten A.M. My tone is less than convincing when I say, "I'm fine, Pete."

He's still looking for witnesses behind Concepcion's apartment. I offered to stick around, but there are times when he prefers to work alone. This doesn't mean he's planning to do something sordid, but it doesn't rule out the possibility.

I glance to my right, where the clouds are obstructing my view of the Alcatraz beacon and the Berkeley Hills, then I ask him if he found anything after I left.

"I can score you some of the finest-quality crack this side of the Mississippi."

It's too late for jokes. "What about Preston Fuentes?"

"He works at a body shop on Valencia Street when the sun is up. He runs a different kind of body shop after the sun goes down."

"Excuse me?"

"Seems he supplements his income by selling drugs and pimping out of his garage."

"Is Anna Moreno one of his girls?"

"No, she's really his cousin. And the stuff about restoring cars in his spare time is true. Evidently, he's quite good at it."

Maybe he can fix the window on my Corolla. I ask him how he managed to uncover the treasure trove of information at this hour.

"The Mission is always open for business, and I talked to a couple of his neighbors. Then I disconnected his alarm and broke into his garage. I didn't stay long."

I'm not hearing this. "You realize that breaking and entering is still a crime."

"Yes, I do. I didn't find anything illegal, but I met Fluffy. You know I've always had a way with animals."

Pete once ran over our dog with his bike and he felt terrible about it for years. He and the bike recovered, but the dog was never the same. "What's Fluffy doing now?"

"I persuaded her to take a nap."

Most Dobermans aren't terribly receptive to friendly suggestions. "Did your persuasive skills include the use of a tranquilizer gun?"

"Perhaps."

"Do me a favor," I say. "Don't do anything illegal for the rest of the day."

"Deal. Do you want to know what else I found out about Fuentes?"

"You realize we won't be able to use anything you tell me in court."

"I'm not a cop anymore, Mick. I'll let you lawyers worry about it."

I'll take what I can get. "Okay, give."

"Fuentes lives by himself in the building behind the garage and spends his nights restoring a beautiful sixty-six 'Vette and collecting dough from his girls. He likes to play loud music out in the garage. This doesn't make him especially popular with his neighbors, but there isn't much they can do. Nobody wants to get on Fluffy's bad side."

Quite understandable. "They could get the landlord to evict him."

"He owns the building."

Sounds like he's successful at all of his various professions.

Pete asks, "Do you want me to talk to him?"

"Absolutely."

"Now?"

The fading digital clock on my dash says it's three-fourteen A.M. "He'll be more cooperative in the morning," I say. "Besides, you don't want to wake up Fluffy."

"She won't be up anytime soon."

"WHAT ARE YOU doing here at this hour?" Rosie asks me.

"I saw the lights, and I figured you might be up."

"You figured right."

She's sitting on her sofa at three-forty on Thursday morning. The furniture is pushed against the walls, and the room is dominated by a hand-me-down playpen. The rain has stopped, and the crickets are chirping in her small front yard. Grace is asleep in her room, which she graciously shares with her grandmother when Sylvia is staying on this side of the bay. Tommy's eyes are wide open as he clings tightly to his mother's shoulders.

I hold up my hands and say, "Hand him over."

Rosie kisses his forehead and sends him down to my end of the couch. Tommy cries when he's hungry or wet, but that's reasonably infrequent. He's more of a worrier than a screamer. He gets it from me. If you walk by his crib in the middle of the night, you're likely to find him staring up at the ceiling with a troubled expression on his face.

"Come on, partner," I say to him. "Daddy had a busy day. I'll tell you all about it." I go to my confessional voice and give him a full report. He dozes off as I'm describing my meeting with Shanahan, and he's sleeping soundly by the time I get to my visit with Lopez. "I'll fill you in on the details tomorrow," I whisper to our sleeping son.

Rosie is still wide awake. "Are you going to get your car fixed tomorrow?" she asks.

"I hope so."

"Do you think your smashed window was something other than a random act?"

"I don't know." There was no sign of the phantom Impala. "I stopped at Mission Station and filed a report with the police, but there isn't a chance they'll find the perp."

She sighs. "We had a little excitement over here, too," she says.

Uh-oh.

"My kitchen window was broken when I got home."

Hell. "Do you think it was something other than a random act?"

"Hard to tell. Nothing was stolen, and nobody came inside the house. The cops said they've been having some problems with vandalism by some high-school kids."

I look directly into her eyes and say, "Are you going to be all right with this?"

"It may be completely unrelated to Ramon's case."

"Or it may not."

"There's something else," she says. Her neighbors reported seeing a man sitting in a black Chrysler parked across the street. "He was there until about eleven o'clock. He was gone by the time I got home."

"Did they call the cops?" I ask.

"No. He wasn't doing anything illegal."

"Maybe he smashed your window," I say.

"Maybe, but Jack and Melanie didn't hear anything."

"Did they get a license number?"

"There was no plate." She says the police did a thorough search of the neighborhood, but the car was long gone. She takes a deep breath and says, "I don't know if any of this has anything to do with Ramon's case, but we need to be careful."

"We don't have to look for trouble," I tell her. "I don't like the idea of somebody watching the house."

"I don't like it either, but I'm not going to be intimidated. The cops promised to drive by every half hour tonight. My mother is going to stay here with Grace and Tommy tomorrow, and I'm going to talk to the principal at school. It seems pretty unlikely that the broken windows in your car and my kitchen could somehow be related, but I'm not inclined to take any chances."

We sit in silence for a long moment. It's something of a relief to turn back to the more mundane matter of representing an accused murderer. "Did Lopez break up with Concepcion?" she asks.

"He wouldn't say either way, and he claimed he didn't talk to her on the night she died."

"Do you believe him?"

"I don't know. A lot of people call the restaurant, and I'd love to know how the burrito got to her apartment that night."

She reacts with exasperation when I tell her about my reconnaissance mission with Pete. "I thought we agreed you were going to leave the cops-and-robbers stuff to the professionals."

"Pete wanted some company."

"I need you to stay alive until Tommy finishes college. If Pete needs some muscle, Terrence should help him." I get another suitably incredulous look when I tell her about our conversation with Anna Moreno. "You're planning to use the testimony of a hooker?" she says.

"It's all that we have so far."

The corner of her mouth turns up slightly at my description of Fuentes and his pet Doberman. "So," she says, "if somebody attacks Fuentes, he gives the command 'Kill, Fluffy. Kill!'"

"Something like that." I leave out any mention of Pete's decision to raid Fuentes's garage and sedate his dog.

"Do you plan to call him as a witness?"

"If he provides any useful information."

"So, our only witnesses are a hooker and a pimp?"

"More or less."

"I trust Pete is going to keep looking."

"Yes, he is."

We listen to Tommy's rhythmic breathing and she says, "There is a little good news. My mother spoke to Concepcion's mother. She's willing to talk to us."

Sylvia does it again. "Your mother is a gem."

"So is Maria's."

She looks at Tommy and says, "I'm going to try to get some sleep. Can you keep an eye on him if he wakes up? My mother will be up soon to relieve you."

"Of course." Sylvia is usually watching CNN by four-thirty every morning.

I put a hand on Rosie's cheek and say, "I'll try to persuade her to sleep in until five."

"She won't."

"I know." I lower my voice and ask her if she wants me to stay.

"It's okay, Mike." She glances at the baseball bat that's strategically positioned by the front door and says, "The Fernandez women can take care of themselves."

Yes, they can.

Rosie gives me a thoughtful look through tired eyes.

"Did I ever tell you that except for all of your well-documented flaws, you're fundamentally a good man, Michael Daley?"

"You've mentioned it from time to time."

She winks and adds, "You shouldn't put too much credibility in anything I say in my sleep-deprived stupor. I'll make it up to you after Tommy starts sleeping through the night."

"Will that include sexual favors?"

She reaches over and kisses Tommy's forehead, then she takes my hand and squeezes it. "Possibly," she says.

SYLVIA WAKES UP for the third and final time at five-fifteen and refuses to go back to sleep, so I make the three-block journey to the fifties-era apartment building just behind the Larkspur fire station where I've lived since Rosie and I got divorced. My place would be serviceable for a starving college student or a young couple, but it's tight for a grown-up. My sofa is from IKEA, and my bookcases are made of bricks and boards. The Sony TV was a wedding present, and the appliances date back to the Eisenhower administration.

I flip on the lights and look around the cramped surroundings. I'm not a great housekeeper, and my home will never be featured in a Martha Stewart magazine. I'm relieved to find no broken windows or other damage. My head is throbbing, and my throat is scratchy. I pull out the last Diet Dr Pepper in the venerable fridge and punch the flashing button on my answering machine, where the cheerful computer-generated voice informs me that I have one message. There is a pronounced smoker's hack before I recognize the unmistakable voice of Jerry Edwards, the *Chronicle*'s ace investigative reporter and a regular contributor to the morning news on Channel 2. He's an unbearably antagonistic man, but he's also a superb muckraker when he's sober. "Mr. Daley," he rasps, "I'm sorry to bother you at home."

Right.

"We've discovered some very disturbing information about your client," he says, "and I need to speak with you about it right away."

As if I don't have enough on my mind. I glance out the window, and my heart starts to beat faster when I see the taillights of a Chevy Impala speeding around the corner and into the night.

CHAPTER 22

"Father Aguirre Provided More Than Counseling"

Father Aguirre has an outstanding record of community service.

—John Shanahan, *San Francisco Chronicle*,
Thursday, December 11

I'M JOLTED AWAKE from a brief and uneasy sleep by my ringing phone, and there is tension in Rosie's voice when she says, "Put on *Mornings on Two*."

I fumble the remote and click to Channel 2, where the graphic in the lower right corner indicates it's seven-twenty A.M. and the temperature is forty-four degrees. I recognize the gravelly voice from the answering machine and look straight into the bloodshot eyes and pit bull face of Jerry Edwards. It takes just an instant to figure out why he wanted to talk to me. "In a late-breaking development," he croaks, "our sources have informed us that Father Ramon Aguirre was involved in a sexual relationship with Maria Concepcion."

Rosie is unimpressed. "It was twenty years ago," she says.

Edwards is still going. "It has been reported that Father Aguirre had a romantic relationship with the victim twenty years ago. Sources tell us that he was also providing counseling to Ms. Concepcion after she recently terminated a relationship with noted restaurateur Eduardo Lopez, who declined to comment." Edwards leers into the camera and adds, "It also seems Father Aguirre provided more than counseling to Ms. Concepcion. In fact, they were romantically involved immediately prior to her death."

"That's bullshit!" Rosie snaps.

I turn up the volume. "Father Aguirre hasn't returned our calls," Edwards says, "and neither have his attorneys at the firm of Fernandez and Daley. We believe this represents a tacit admission of the veracity of our reports."

"The hell it does," I say. "He left a message on my machine at eleven-thirty last night."

"He's trying to bait us," Rosie says.

He's succeeding.

MY PHONE RINGS AGAIN, and Ramon's voice is shaking when he says, "Did you see Jerry Edwards?"

"Yes." I tell him that we're going to set the record straight at a press conference later this morning.

"I want to be there," he says.

"That's a very bad idea." The chance he'll say something that could come back to bite us is too great. "As your lawyer, I'm recommending against it."

"As your client, I'm telling you it's my reputation at stake."

"Let us handle the legal strategy."

"What does that leave for me?"

Prayer. "You have to stay calm and trust us."

THE PARADE CONTINUES when Pete calls a few minutes later. "Where are you?" I ask.

"Outside the body shop where Fuentes works."

"Car repair or other activities?"

He isn't amused. "Car repair, Mick. I tried to talk to Fuentes, but he's no dummy and he referred me to his lawyer."

Dammit.

"Do you want me to rough him up a bit?" he asks.

Not a good idea. "No. We'll pay him a visit at home tonight. He may be more receptive away from his job—especially if we bring along a subpoena."

"What about Fluffy?"

"We won't need a subpoena for her."

I don't get the chuckle I was hoping for. "What do you want me to do in the meantime?" he asks.

"I need you to find Jane Doe."

I GLANCE AT my rearview mirror, and I'm relieved to see a black Explorer two cars behind me. My brother has kept his word, but I'm still uneasy—even with his friend Vince riding shotgun. I called the Larkspur police to report the Impala outside my apartment early this morning, but they weren't able to locate it. I live a block from the police station, and they've promised to keep a close eye on my place.

I answer my cell phone as I'm driving down Van Ness Avenue toward the office. "Mr. Daley," the scratchy voice says, "Jerry Edwards, *Mornings on Two*."

Asshole. "Nice to hear from you, Jerry."

"Thank you. What can I do for you?"

Like every good reporter, he's being engaging to see if I'll let my guard down, but I know better. He's taken his share of potshots at Rosie and me over the years, and we have long memories. I keep my tone professional when I tell him that I was returning his call.

"Did you see today's paper?" he asks.

"Yes, I did. I also saw you on TV this morning."

"I was trying to reach you last night to see if your client might be available for an interview."

"He isn't."

"Give me a break, Mr. Daley. When I couldn't get you by phone last night, I drove all the way to your partner's house to see if I could find you, but nobody was home."

What? "How late did you stay?"

"Until eleven."

"You just missed her."

"I couldn't stay there all night. I have deadlines, Mr. Daley."

I ask him what kind of car he drives.

"What difference does it make?"

"There was a suspicious black Chrysler parked in front of my partner's house last night."

"It wasn't suspicious. It was me."

My relief is tempered by the fact that it still doesn't account for the Impala. "I trust you're aware that stalking is illegal."

"I wasn't stalking anybody. In my line of work, we call it investigative reporting."

Right. "Do you always drive a car with no license plates?"

"I took it out of the *Chronicle* motor pool last night," he says. "I didn't check it carefully."

"Do you know anybody who drives a green Impala?"

"No. Is somebody following you?"

"I don't know."

"It wasn't me. Now that I've confessed that I was parked in front of your ex-wife's house, I think you should reconsider your decision not to let me interview your client."

"Forget it." I tell him that we're going to hold a press conference later this morning. "You're welcome to join us."

"I will. How about a consolation prize? If your client won't appear, how about you?"

This may give me a chance to spin the story our way. "Deal."

"Mr. Daley," he says, "my sources have reported that Father Aguirre was romantically involved with Ms. Concepcion immediately prior to her death. Would you be kind enough to confirm it for me?"

"Absolutely not."

"Are you denying it?"

"I will confirm that Father Aguirre and Ms. Concepcion dated for a short time twenty years ago."

"My sources tell me they were engaged in a romantic relationship more recently."

"Who are your sources?"

"You know I can't reveal that information."

Sure you can. I hold out a carrot. "I'll give you an exclusive interview with my client if you do."

He's tempted. "I'm afraid not, Mr. Daley."

It was a bluff. "Sorry to hear that, Jerry."

He tries again. "So," he says, "do you wish to comment about Father Aguirre's recent relationship with Ms. Concepcion?"

"*Alleged* relationship."

"Whatever. Do you wish to comment?"

"Yes. The accusation that Father Aguirre was romantically involved with Ms. Concepcion before her death is completely false."

"Are you calling me a liar?"

Yes. "I'm saying that your source is either mistaken or lying and that a good journalist like yourself would have double-checked a story that is so obviously false."

CHAPTER 23

"God Never Gives Us More Than We Can Handle"

There is nothing more painful than burying a child.

—Father Ramon Aguirre

ROSIE'S VOICE IS barely a whisper as she addresses Concepcion's mother. "Thank you so much for seeing us," she says.

"You're welcome, Ms. Fernandez."

"It's Rosie."

She clutches her tissue tighter and says, "I'm Lita."

It's only ten-thirty, but it's been a busy morning. We held an impromptu press conference in front of the El Faro to rebut Jerry Edwards's claim that Ramon was sleeping with Lita's daughter and to ask for help finding witnesses who were on Capp Street last Monday night. Things got heated when Edwards showed up and accused us of lying. We didn't back down, and the situation quickly degenerated into the legal profession's version of mud wrestling. It was great theater and will be the lead story on the news tonight. We spent a few minutes with Ramon, then we made a beeline over here. My head is throbbing from sleep deprivation. A triple dose of Extra-

Strength Advil will be a part of my daily routine until this case is over.

We're meeting in Lita's tidy apartment in a nondescript two-story building on Valencia, not far from Mission Dolores. She's at least ten years younger than Sylvia, but considerably more frail, and there's a slight quiver in her high-pitched voice. She's wearing a polka-dot housedress and a pair of Reeboks as she's sitting in an embroidered armchair in a living room that makes Sylvia's look spacious. The two-bedroom apartment could use a coat of paint, but our fastidious hostess shares Sylvia's view about upgrades. Her daughter's high-school graduation photo is prominently displayed on the mantel, and a single candle is burning on the kitchen table.

"I know this must be very difficult for you," Rosie says.

"It is." There is a sense of grave purpose in her eyes when she tells us she wants to find out what happened to her daughter. "She was everything to me."

The pained expression on Rosie's face indicates to me that she's thinking about Grace. She bites her lip and says, "How long have you lived here?"

"We moved here shortly after Maria was born." Her husband was a maintenance worker for MUNI who died almost twenty years ago. She glances at the same photo of her son that I saw in Maria's apartment. "It was difficult enough to bury our son. I never imagined that I would have to bury both of our children."

In the course of defending accused murderers, we sometimes forget that the lives of the families of the victims are changed forever. All the lines I practiced at the seminary for occasions such as this seem to ring hollow, but I go with an old standby. "I'm so sorry, Lita. This apartment must have a lot of memories for you."

"It does." She bravely tries to sound philosophical. "My husband used to say that God never gives us more than we can handle."

It's a kind sentiment, but it garnered mixed results when I used it in my priest days.

She adds, "I suspect he may have reconsidered his view if he had lived a few more years."

No doubt. We sit in silence for a long moment before Rosie says, "Tell us about Maria."

Lita dabs at her eyes and says, "She was beautiful, sensitive and intelligent." She fills in the details of her daughter's tenure at the Shanahan firm and her relationship with her ex-husband. "Dennis likes to collect things: antiques, money, guns and women. I think he viewed Maria as another trophy." She swallows hard and says, "He cheated on her from the beginning of their marriage, and she filed for divorce only two years later. She'd signed a one-sided prenuptial agreement and learned some hard lessons. That's when she decided to move back to the neighborhood and to help the community."

She says things became more strained when Maria and her ex ended up on opposite sides of several legal battles. "Their personal animosity added to the tension, and her faith helped her through the most difficult times. St. Peter's was her anchor, and she attended mass regularly. She was terribly uncomfortable about suing the Church, but she believed that somebody had to represent the people who had been abused by the priests."

Rosie eases her into another sensitive topic. "We understand your daughter was seeing a man named Eduardo Lopez."

The mention of his name brings a noticeable cringe and a terse response. "It didn't work out."

Rosie has to push forward. "Can you tell us what happened?"

Lita chooses her words carefully. "I've known Eduardo since he was an altar boy at St. Peter's. I was troubled that Maria was seeing a married man—especially one who was so much older than she was. It was even more difficult because I've known Eduardo's wife for years."

This created a rather delicate situation. "How did she feel about it?"

"I haven't spoken to her since Maria started seeing her husband. In addition to everything else, I lost a friend."

Rosie asks her if she talked to her daughter about her relationship with Lopez.

"A little. I told her I didn't think it was a good idea, but young people don't always listen to reason. Maria was certain he was going to leave Vicky to marry her. She wanted things to work out so badly she didn't see the warning signs."

"So she ignored your advice?"

Lita sighs. "You want the best for your children, but she was capable of making decisions for herself. She was desperate to have a child, and she thought Eduardo wanted to start a family with her. She was wrong." The sadness in her tone turns to barely containable anger when she says, "People like Eduardo think they can make up for their behavior by donating money to the Church and building housing for the poor. I think it's admirable that he's given back to the community, but I still believe Jesus looks at your character after you die and adds up the debits and the credits. If you're evil, you can't make up for it by donating money to charity."

That's the way they taught it at the seminary.

Rosie asks if Maria broke up with him.

"Just as soon as she was convinced that he wasn't going to leave his wife. She was devastated. It became even more difficult when she found out Eduardo had been seeing another woman while he was going out with Maria."

This is news. Any lingering doubts that I have about Lopez's character have now been erased. I ask, "Do you know the other woman's name?"

"Mercedes Trujillo. She's a hostess at the restaurant."

It's an example of the classic adage—if they cheat with you, they'll cheat on you.

"Evidently," she says, "Maria made quite a scene at the restaurant after she found out."

"Is Ms. Trujillo still seeing Mr. Lopez?"

"No."

"Is she still working at the restaurant?"

"As far as I know."

You have to pay the bills.

Rosie touches Lita's hand and says, "When was the last time you talked to Maria?"

"I left her apartment at six o'clock, and I spoke to her by phone around seven-thirty." She says her daughter was in good spirits. "She was going to have a session with Father Aguirre. She was very fond of him, and the counseling seemed to be helping."

It seems like an inappropriate time to ask if they were sleeping together.

"How well do you know him?" Rosie asks.

"He's been our priest for a long time."

"Do you trust him?"

There is no quiver in her voice when she says, "Absolutely."

"We understand that he and Maria once dated for a while."

"They did. It was a long time ago and I was hoping they would stay together, but it didn't work out. She wanted to go to law school and start a career."

"Do you think she ever regretted her decision?"

"From time to time."

"Do you think Father Aguirre has regrets?"

"We've never talked about it."

Rosie gently explains that there have been suggestions that Ramon and Maria still had feelings for each other.

"I read about it in this morning's paper," Lita says. "Father Aguirre is a principled man. If I thought he had been engaging in immoral behavior, I wouldn't have asked him to officiate at Maria's funeral. I don't believe he and Maria were romantically involved, and I think it's disrespectful to her memory and his reputation to suggest it."

This helps. Rosie asks her if she would be willing to testify to that effect.

"I'll have to think about it."

Rosie measures her words carefully as she turns to a

final sensitive issue. "We understand that your daughter was taking antidepressants."

"They seemed to be helping."

"There is some evidence that Maria may have taken her own life."

Lita Concepcion gives Rosie a hard look and doesn't parse. "Maria was a fighter," she says. "She did not commit suicide."

CHAPTER 24

"Eduardo Is a Cheating Asshole"

It is with great pleasure that I present this community-service award to Eduardo Lopez for his fine efforts on behalf of Mission District residents. He sets an excellent example for his neighbors and is to be highly commended.

—The Mayor of San Francisco

LOPEZ'S SOON-TO-BE EX-WIFE is considerably less diplomatic than Concepcion's mother when the subject turns to her husband's shortcomings. "Eduardo is a cheating asshole," she says.

I'm glad she doesn't feel compelled to sugarcoat her feelings.

We're sitting at a table near the window of the trendy Ti Couz creperie on Sixteenth, between Guerrero and Valencia, down the street from Mission Dolores in the gentrified corner of the Mission. The early lunch crowd of yuppies and Gen-Xers mingle comfortably at the cheerful wooden tables, and the sweet smell of fresh crepes wafts through the inviting room that looks as if it were transported directly from a village in Brittany. If you walk two blocks down to the BART station, you'll find junkies shooting up and hookers plying their trade in broad daylight. The Mission caters to many constituencies.

Victoria Clemente Lopez isn't a waif-thin beauty, but the successful designer of upscale clothing carries herself with style and a feisty self-confidence that has its own charged appeal. Eduardo may be debonair, but Vicky has charisma. She runs a fashionable boutique at Twenty-fourth and Noe, about a mile from here. Her broad shoulders and toned muscles indicate some serious gym time, and you'd have to look closely at the corners of her Botoxed eyes to notice the remnants of the crow's-feet. I'd guess she's in her mid-fifties from the dyed black hair and the hints of a second chin that's been surgically modified, but it's hard to tell. She appears comfortable in tight leather pants and a modest cotton blouse that is fighting a reasonably successful battle to control her ample bosom.

Rosie tries for an offhand tone when she asks how long she's been married.

"Twenty-seven years. I was working as a hostess at the restaurant when we met."

So is Mercedes Trujillo.

Vicky gives us a quick rundown on their four children and nine grandchildren. "Our youngest daughter is expecting twins in March. Eduardo and I need to work out some arrangements to see our grandchildren."

Rosie lowers her voice and says, "Forgive me for asking some personal questions—"

"You're just doing your job. After everything Eduardo has put me through, I don't have any secrets."

"How long were you married before your husband started . . . straying?"

"I'd guess about two weeks. Eduardo has always tried to portray himself as a family man who doted on his children, but it was all a lie. I knew that running a restaurant required him to keep late hours, but I ignored the signs for years." Her inflection turns decidedly bitter when she says, "Maybe I was naive or stupid, but I feel like I did this to myself."

"You shouldn't blame yourself," Rosie says. She casts a scornful look in my direction and says, "A lot of men are pigs."

It distresses me to be lumped in with the Neanderthals, but I take one for the team and keep my mouth shut.

Vicky appreciates the sentiment and says, "I've accepted the fact that it would be best for our children and grandchildren if Eduardo and I remain on reasonably civil terms. I have a business to run, and I'd like to get on with my life." She gives us a wicked smile and adds, "I wouldn't mind taking him to the cleaners for every penny I can get."

Go for it.

She says their divorce settlement is almost final. "My barracuda is in negotiations with his shark. With a little luck, we should have everything divided up by the end of the year. He'll get the restaurant, and I'll keep my business. I'll get the house, and we'll each get a car. Everything else will be split fifty-fifty."

Rosie treads into choppier water. "How did you find out that your husband was seeing Ms. Concepcion?"

"A couple of my friends told me about it. I was skeptical, but Eduardo didn't come home for four nights running. That's when I hired a private investigator." She says it took Nick the Dick only one day to catch her husband in bed with Concepcion at a Union Square Hotel. "That's when I hired a lawyer."

Rosie turns to another subject. "We understand some questions have been raised about your husband's business dealings."

"I'd say he's as honest in business as he is in his personal relationships. He has friends down at City Hall who help him get approvals for his projects."

"Has he ever done anything illegal?"

"He's never been caught."

Hardly a ringing endorsement. Rosie asks, "How does he react when he's angry?"

"Are you asking if he ever hit me?"

"Yes."

Vicky pauses to consider the ramifications of her answer. She can do irreparable damage to his reputation by accusing him of anything from wife beating to child molestation, whether or not the allegations are true. She opts for a frank tone, and provides what I surmise is an honest response. "My husband is a manipulator and a cheat," she says, "but he also has shown many moments of great kindness and generosity, and he never laid a hand on me."

This is good for her health, but it doesn't enhance his status as a suspect.

Rosie lays it on the line. "Do you think there is any possibility he may have been involved with Ms. Concepcion's death?"

There is no hesitation this time. "No, but he was upset that they split up. To Eduardo, a good lay is still a good lay."

How delicate. We can add another notch to his belt,

but we still have no evidence that he was violent or that he was anywhere near Concepcion's apartment on the night she died.

"I have to ask you where you were last Monday night," Rosie says.

"At my store."

"Until what time?"

"Around twelve-thirty. I was working on some designs for next year's line."

It's the same time her husband left work. I'm not big on conspiracy theories, but it can't hurt to probe. Rosie asks, "Was anybody else there with you?"

In other words, can anybody corroborate your alibi?

"I was by myself. I spoke to my husband briefly around eight. We were trying to set up a time to get together with our lawyers to finalize our settlement. There were no other calls."

Which means nobody can confirm her whereabouts that night.

She sees where we're going and takes the offensive. "I don't appreciate what you're implying," she says. "You're trying to portray me as the angry ex-wife."

"We're trying to rule you out as a suspect," Rosie says.

Which means we're also trying to rule her *in* as a suspect.

Rosie asks, "Were you anywhere in the vicinity of Ms. Concepcion's apartment that night?"

"I drove down Twenty-fifth Street on my way home."

Which means she was within a block of Concepcion's apartment.

CHAPTER 25

"My Ex-Wife Had Serious Emotional Problems"

Ms. Concepcion was a worthy adversary. It would be inappropriate to comment upon the pending case against the San Francisco Archdiocese.

—Dennis Peterson, *San Francisco Daily Legal Journal*

"**WHAT DID YOU** think?" I ask Rosie. We're waiting for the downtown train on the platform of the Sixteenth Street BART station.

"Eduardo Lopez is a jerk."

No argument from me. "I was referring to his wife."

She looks at the TV monitor, which notes that our train will arrive in two minutes, then she turns to me and says, "We gave her a chance to accuse her husband of everything from spousal abuse to murder, but she didn't. It suggests to me that he may be a pathological liar who cheated on his wife, but murder seems out of character."

"Maybe she was protecting him."

"Why?"

"To avoid the humiliation to her family—and herself."

"I don't think so," she decides. "We can't afford to rule anybody out, but we can't place him closer than a block away from Concepcion's apartment."

I ask her about the burrito.

"She could have picked it up two days earlier. We have no evidence he or anybody else from his restaurant delivered it."

Still too many holes to make a meaningful accusation. "What about Vicky?" I ask. "She can't provide an alibi for the night Concepcion died."

I hear the distinctive beep of the BART train horn, and the musty air starts to swirl. "The jealous wife is such a cliché," she says. "Besides, we can't place her in Concepcion's apartment that night, either."

DENNIS PETERSON greets me with a firm handshake, a gracious smile and a polite "How can I help you, Mr. Daley?"

The hallowed and virtually silent halls of Shanahan, Gallagher and O'Rourke look as if they were designed by the same guy who picked the furniture for the staid—and all male—Pacific Union Club in the old Flood mansion on Nob Hill. The dark paneling and subdued artwork suggest you need to pass an initiation ritual before they'll let you in. Virtually every other law firm in San Francisco has gone to business casual, but not SG and O. The lawyers who speak in hushed tones are dressed in the same uniform: European-cut charcoal business suits, starched white shirts and subdued rep ties. It gives me the creeps.

Concepcion's ex-husband fits squarely in the mold. He's in his mid-forties and could pass for Shanahan's long-lost illegitimate son. He has the same blue eyes, perfect tan, rugged features and erect bearing, along with the modulated tone, impeccable wardrobe and understated mannerisms. The only significant difference is that Peterson's hair is a chemically enhanced jet black, whereas Shanahan's has faded to a dignified gray.

I lean back in an armchair that's opposite his mahogany desk. The people who work here place a premium on good manners—even when they're sticking it to you—so I summon a respectful tone when I say, "Thank you for seeing me."

"You're welcome."

"I need to ask you some questions about your ex-wife."

The Young Turk adjusts the maroon kerchief in his breast pocket and looks admiringly at his "ego wall," where diplomas from Dartmouth, Harvard Business School and Yale Law School hang among various certificates from the state and federal courts to which he's been admitted to practice. Most of us keep these trophies in boxes, but guys like Peterson seem to require constant reassurance that they are, in fact, licensed to practice law. "Mr. Daley," he says, "I need you to bear with me for a moment. John wants to join us."

This is unplanned, but hardly surprising. Shanahan's name is on the door, and he has home-field advantage. I have no choice. "Fine with me," I say.

He buzzes his secretary and asks her to summon the head honcho. Big John saunters in a moment later with a subdued smile and an outstretched hand. He's had a shower and a shave since I last saw him, and I'm pretty sure he's wearing a fresh suit, but it's hard to discern any difference from the one he was sporting yesterday. I wonder if there is a closet next to the mail room where the lawyers get their costumes every morning.

Shanahan feigns interest in my well-being. "Good to see you again, Michael," he lies. "Did you get some sleep?"

"A few hours."

So ends the chitchat. Shanahan nods to Peterson and then turns his back to me. It's his firm, and he's going to call the shots. He tries to sound forthcoming. "Michael," he says, "I was just talking to the archbishop."

I can guess what's coming.

"He asked me once more to try to impress upon you his great desire to have a member of our firm take the lead in Father Aguirre's case."

"That isn't going to be possible as long as Father Aguirre wants me to be his lawyer."

"We were hoping you might be able to convince him otherwise."

"I can't do that."

"I'm asking you as a professional colleague and a friend—is there anything that I can say to change your mind?"

"I'm afraid not."

He sighs melodramatically and throws in the towel. He looks at his partner and says, "I've asked Dennis to be as open and candid as he possibly can."

Which means he isn't going to tell me anything.

Shanahan segues into the inevitable backpedaling. "You'll have to bear in mind, however, that Dennis is representing the archdiocese. Obviously, if there is any information that may be confidential or sensitive, he will have to make a decision as to whether it is appropriate to reveal it to you."

Obviously. "The O'Connell case has no bearing on the charges against Father Aguirre," I say.

"The victim was the plaintiff's attorney."

"That has nothing to do with the matters at hand."

"We'll see." Shanahan turns to his partner and says, "Do what you can to help him, Dennis. We're all on the same side."

Peterson takes his cue. His inflection is almost a perfect imitation of Shanahan's when he says, "The O'Connell case is on hold until the plaintiff finds another attorney. It will probably take a couple of weeks." I pepper him with questions about the procedural status of the case and he gives me polite, but guarded, answers. He isn't going to tell me anything more than he absolutely must, and Shanahan is here to make sure he doesn't overstep his bounds.

I move in another direction. "How long have you been working here?"

"Since I got out of Yale."

Why do people who attend Ivy League schools always manage to work their alma mater's name into every conversation?

His chest juts out two inches when he says, "I made partner after only six years. I was the youngest person ever elected, and I sit on our firm's Executive Committee."

This is far more important to him than it is to me, but I want to make him feel good about himself. "That's very impressive," I say. "You must be on the fast track in firm management."

His false modesty is transparent when he says, "I suppose."

If this place is anything like the law firm where I used to work, Shanahan presides over a puppet regime where he makes the calls on everything from partner compensation to the coffee in the lunchroom.

Shanahan interjects, "Dennis is too modest to admit it, but he's the chairman of our Litigation Department and he has a seat on our Compensation Committee. We think he has a very bright future in operations, but we don't want to take him away from trying cases." He nods to his disciple and adds, "He's a superb trial lawyer."

I'm sure he is. Now that I've buttered him up a bit, it's time to make him squirm. "I understand your ex-wife used to work here."

"She did. She left the firm shortly after our divorce. It was her decision."

Sure, it was. "Was it for professional or personal reasons?"

"Both. The specific circumstances surrounding her departure are confidential."

That's all I'm going to get on this subject. I ask, "How long were you married?"

"Two years."

"What happened?"

"Excuse me?"

You heard me. "Why did you split up?"

"It didn't work out."

The fact that you were cheating on her didn't help. "Why not?"

Shanahan intercedes. "This has nothing to do with Father Aguirre's case," he says.

Not true. "We're trying to determine Ms. Concepcion's state of mind immediately prior to her death, and we have reason to believe she never fully recovered from her divorce. If we can prove she committed suicide, Father Aguirre will be released and I'll get out of your hair."

Shanahan nods to Peterson. "Go ahead," he says.

His tone becomes more emphatic. "It just didn't work out," he says.

I'll have to do this in baby steps. "Let's start with the basics. Who filed?"

"She did."

"Why?"

"She was under the mistaken impression that I had been unfaithful."

"Were you?"

"Of course not."

He's lying. "Did things get acrimonious?"

"Not really."

"I understand you had a dispute over the division of property."

"Not true."

"That's not the way I heard it."

"Where are you getting your information?"

"I talked to your ex-mother-in-law this morning."

This elicits another awkward glance toward Shanahan. Peterson measures his words carefully when he says, "We signed a valid, binding and enforceable prenuptial agreement."

For a guy who is supposed to be cooperating, he's sounding a lot like a lawyer.

He adds, "She wasn't happy about it, but she did it."

"I assume she liked it even less after she got nothing in the divorce."

"It was an enforceable agreement."

I can see why Concepcion's mother didn't feel especially warm and fuzzy about this guy. I ask him if his ex-wife was a good lawyer.

"Yes, she was."

"And you were opposing counsel on several cases, weren't you?"

"Yes, we were."

"And she won some of those cases, didn't she?"

He shakes his head. "Absolutely false," he says. "She never beat me in court."

It's good lawyerly parsing, but it doesn't tell the whole story. I sense defensiveness in his tone, and I want to try to use it to my advantage. "You settled several of the cases, didn't you?"

A grudging nod. "Yes."

"How many?"

His irritation is turning into modulated anger. "A few."

"How many is a few?"

"That's none of your business."

"It is now."

"Bullshit."

Temper, temper. "How much money are we talking about?"

"That's none of your business, either."

"The *Chronicle* said you were well into eight figures."

"The *Chronicle* exaggerates."

"I'll subpoena the settlement documents."

"They're confidential and covered by a protective order."

"I'll go to a judge."

"You won't get very far."

We'll see.

"Look," he says, "a lot of people sue the archdiocese, and we have a compelling legal interest in keeping our settlement discussions confidential. We need to make it clear that our client isn't going to be a sitting duck for shakedowns by every small-time plaintiff's lawyer."

"Like your ex-wife?"

"That's right."

Now we know where we stand. "I understand you were engaged in settlement discussions right before she died."

He hesitates for just an instant before he says, "That's true."

"Were you close?"

"Our settlement discussions are subject to the attorney-client privilege. It's none of your business."

I fire back. "This isn't a civil case where we have time to shower each other with paper and play games for ten years. Father Aguirre's life and career are at stake. If we don't resolve this in the next couple of weeks, he'll never be able to work again. It isn't in your best interests or his to be uncooperative."

Shanahan has heard enough and answers for him. "The judge ordered us into mediation and we made a bona fide, good-faith effort to settle. We were unsuccessful."

Was that so hard? I turn back to Peterson and ask, "Do you think there was any chance the case was going to settle?"

"No. My ex-wife had serious emotional problems that began during our marriage, were compounded by our divorce and were exacerbated by this case. She was on medication, and her judgment was impaired. We put forth a generous offer prior to her death, and she dismissed it. The plaintiff is a lap dancer and a hooker who has drug problems. Maria was out of touch with reality if she thought she was going to do better in court."

I ask him when he last spoke to his ex-wife.

"Nine-fifteen last Monday night. I'd gotten authority from Father Quinn to increase our settlement offer. Maria rejected it out of hand."

I ask him why he upped his offer if he was so sure he was going to win.

"You can run the numbers. It costs our client about a thousand dollars an hour for John and me to sit in the same room. It costs more than ten grand a day for us to sit in court. A couple of weeks of trial can result in legal bills that run well into six figures. Maria knew how to work the system, and we made a strategic decision to try to settle for purely economic reasons. Bottom line: we thought it would cost more to try the case than to settle it."

Bottom line: they didn't want to risk putting their case in the hands of a group of retirees, courthouse groupies, students, goof-offs, misfits and other hangers-on. In legal terms, we call these people a jury.

CHAPTER 26

"It Wasn't a Suicide"

Dr. Roderick Beckert is the dean of big-city medical examiners and a distinguished author and scholar. His textbook on forensic science is the seminal work in this field.

—Course Catalogue, *UCSF Medical Center*

DR. RODERICK BECKERT strokes his gray beard and strikes a chatty tone. "It's a pleasure to see you again, Mr. Daley," he lies. "It's been awhile since we've had a chance to work together."

Are you ever going to retire? "It's nice to see you, too," I say.

The chief medical examiner of the city and county of San Francisco is sitting in an ancient swivel chair in his cluttered office in the basement of the Hall at three o'clock on Thursday afternoon. With his bald dome, aviator-style glasses and cheap paisley tie, his appearance may be unimposing, but you can't let your guard down. He knows more about forensic science than anybody in the Bay Area—and he's more than happy to let you know it. The heavy bureaucratic furnishings and mundane assortment of medical texts, charts and scientific instruments are overlaid with nearly forty years of personal memorabilia that ranges from the ego-driven (honorary degrees and photos with local politicians) to the whimsical (a life-size skeleton sporting a Giants' cap). A compulsive perfectionist with a photographic memory, his only hobby is teaching pathology at UCSF. An inveterate publicity hound, the forensic guru handles the autopsies and courtroom theatrics for every high-profile case in San Francisco, and he's frequently called upon to lend his expertise to other jurisdictions. He detests defense attorneys on general principles.

His tone is always authoritative. "It wasn't a suicide," he tells me before I have a chance to ask. "Ms. Concepcion was murdered. She bled to death."

He may be hardheaded, but he usually gets it right. It's also frustrating to argue with him because he's unfailingly polite. I summon my most respectful tone and ask, "Would you mind explaining how you came to that conclusion?" I lean forward and prepare to receive his wisdom.

He slides a photocopy of a meticulously typed document across his immaculate steel desk. You'd think he'd just handed me the stone tablets when he says, "It's in my report."

If past history is any indication, this will be his response to every question I ask. "This is the first time I've seen it," I say.

He tries to cut off the discussion before it starts. "This copy is for you," he says. "Call me if you have any questions."

This will be my only chance to talk to him before the prelim, and I have to press. A flip remark will get me a quick exit, and I have no choice but to genuflect. "Dr. Beckert," I say, "I would be extraordinarily grateful if you would answer a few questions."

One corner of his mouth turns up slightly, and he makes a big show of pulling up the left sleeve on his camel-hair sport jacket to look at his Rolex. "I have another meeting," he says, "but I can spend a few minutes with you."

It takes every ounce of my self-control to avoid making a sarcastic remark. "Thank you, Dr. Beckert."

"You're very welcome."

I start with an easy one. "When did you conduct the autopsy?"

They say that great baseball hitters can remember the exact count and location of every pitch they ever hit for a home run. Great coroners are the same way. He pretends to study the report through the bottom half of his bifocals, but I'm convinced he can remember the details of every autopsy he's performed since he got out of medical school. He flips through the pages and finds what he's looking for. "Tuesday, December second," he tells me. "Three-thirty P.M."

"That's about seven hours after they found the body," I say.

"Correct."

He isn't going to offer anything voluntarily, so I'll have to lead him along. "Were you called to the scene?"

"Yes." He says he arrived at Concepcion's apartment at ten-thirty that morning.

"That was about an hour after the initial police call?"

"Correct."

It isn't a big point, but it gives me room to argue about the level of decomposition of the body when he first saw it and, by extension, the time of death. "I understand you've placed time of death between nine-thirty on Monday night and one o'clock on Tuesday morning."

"Correct."

"Which means at least ten hours had elapsed from the time of death until the time you first saw the body, and seventeen hours had elapsed until you began the autopsy."

"You can do the math as well as I can, Mr. Daley."

Yes, I can. I ask him if the body was still in the bathtub when he arrived.

"No, it wasn't." He explains that the paramedics removed the body from the tub in their attempts to revive her. "Except for the fact that the body was taken out of the tub and moved to the floor, the area was preserved intact." He confirms that she was pronounced dead at the scene.

"Was the body still submerged when it was found?"

"Yes, it was, except for her head and shoulders, which were above the water level, and her left arm, which was dangling outside the tub."

"The fact that the body was underwater for up to twelve hours would have made it more complicated to determine the time of death, right?"

"I gave myself a three-hour window because the body was found in standing water," he says. "The rate of decomposition would have changed depending upon the initial temperature of the water when the body was placed in the tub."

"*If* it was placed in the tub," I argue.

He doesn't budge. He explains that the presence of the water made the usual measurements of body temperature, lividity and rigor mortis somewhat less precise. "I was also able to do some calculations based upon the rate of digestion of food in her stomach," he says.

"What food was that?" I ask.

"A chicken burrito."

At least we know she ate some of the burrito that was found in her kitchen. Whether she purchased it that night still remains to be determined.

Beckert adds, "If she had bled to death on the floor, I may have been able to call time of death within a narrower window." He adds that Concepcion drank a small amount of alcohol on the night she died, and no drugs were found in her system.

His analysis gives us wiggle room to argue that she could have died after Ramon left the scene. It would help even more if we could prove that somebody else entered her apartment after he left. I pretend to thumb through the report for another moment and ask, "How were you able to rule out a self-inflicted wound?"

He knows I'm looking for a preview of his testimony. "It's in my report, Mr. Daley."

I tap his report and say, "I'm sure it's all here, but I would be very grateful if you would explain your conclusion to me."

"We can do that in court next week, Mr. Daley."

"If we do it now, we may not have to do it again next week."

He glances at his watch again and says, "If you turn to page seven, you'll see that there were three deep cuts on each of the victim's wrists that resulted in massive blood loss."

I'm prepared to accept the conclusion that she bled to

death. "It still doesn't explain how you determined the wounds weren't self-inflicted," I say.

He places a photograph of the back of Concepcion's head and shoulders on the desk in front of me and uses his gold Cross pen to point at several areas circled with a black felt-tip marker. "Do you see any unusual marks in these areas?"

I study the photo for a long minute and then answer honestly. "No."

"Look more closely. We found the defendant's thumbprints on the back of the victim's neck in these locations using the glue fuming process."

"He may have given her a back rub," I say, "but it doesn't prove he killed her."

He points toward a spot where her right shoulder meets her neck and asks, "Do you notice anything here?"

I'm not going to give him the satisfaction of acknowledging anything short of a fully disembodied head.

"If you look at this spot right here," he says, "you'll see a bruise on Ms. Concepcion's right shoulder, just below the nape of her neck."

I never graduated from medical school, and I can't see any blood or other evidence of a significant wound. In a rare instance of the truth lining up with an appropriate legal response, I tell him, "I'm afraid I don't see it, Dr. Beckert."

He hands me a copy of the photo and says, "Your medical expert will confirm that Ms. Concepcion experienced a blow that rendered her unconscious and caused a hematoma."

I know just enough medical lingo to understand that

he's referring to a bruise resulting from a direct hit, but I'm not buying it. "Broken bones?" I ask.

"None."

"Blood?"

"No."

"Swelling?"

"Not discernible to the naked eye."

I argue that the wound could have been self-inflicted.

"It would have been impossible for her to have hit herself in that location," he says.

"She could have fallen or bumped into something."

"You have no evidence she did."

"You have no evidence she didn't. It's your job to prove the cause of death was a homicide. It isn't our job to prove it wasn't."

He strokes his beard and lowers his voice. "I'll win that argument in court," he says.

I'm not going to win it here. I'll feed the information to a hired medical expert who will massage it to fit our needs. "So," I say, "you believe Ms. Concepcion was knocked unconscious and then placed in her bathtub, where her wrists were slashed and she bled to death."

"Correct." His expression turns smug. "There's more, Mr. Daley." He pulls out another photograph and lays it out in front of me. "They took this picture just before they moved the body from the scene." Unlike the first photo, which was taken in his lab, this one was taken in Concepcion's bathroom, and it shows her body on the floor in a pool of bloody water. Her head is propped up against the wall and her eyes and mouth are open. "Did you notice that Ms. Concepcion's body was covered with white skin cream?"

"Yes. It suggests to me that she wanted to relax before she committed suicide."

"It suggests to me that somebody made a clumsy attempt to fake a suicide. We found your client's fingerprints on the empty skin cream container. More important, we discovered that the amount of cream in the area around the wound on her shoulder was greater than on other parts of her body. This indicates somebody was trying to cover the hematoma."

"If her shoulder was covered with cream, how were you able to find the fingerprints on her neck?"

"Her neck wasn't covered."

It doesn't add up. "If Father Aguirre was smart enough to try to cover the bruise, he would have covered the prints."

"He was in a hurry and got careless."

"Or somebody else hit her and didn't know enough to cover the prints."

"You can argue that theory to the judge, Mr. Daley. We also found skin cream on and around her genital area and rectum. Women know that it is inadvisable to use such compounds in sensitive areas."

"I suspect she wasn't worried about reading warning labels that night."

"She had a rash around her labia majora and her anus. If she was trying to make herself comfortable, she wouldn't have put that type of compound on those areas."

I point out that he found the cream on her hands. "That suggests she put it on herself."

He fires right back. "That suggests your client put it on her hands."

I can't refute any of this on the fly.

Beckert isn't finished. He points toward the photo and asks, "Do you notice anything unusual about the position of her body?"

He would have been a great law professor. Like his medical students, I have no choice but to play along. "Nothing leaps out at me."

"Look at her head."

I don't see any bruises. "Give me a hint."

"When the paramedics pulled her out of the tub, they placed her body on the floor facing the same direction as it was when she was in the water. Her head is at the end of the tub where the faucet and handles protrude from the wall."

"So?"

"Nobody sits in a bathtub that way because you'd bang your head on the faucet or the handles."

He's right.

He closes his report and hands it to me. "I really need to get to this other meeting," he says, "and you really ought to give some serious thought to a plea bargain."

"That isn't going to happen, Dr. Beckert."

"You're a good lawyer, but you're making a big mistake."

Duly noted. "Thank you for your time."

"You're welcome." He taps his fingers on his desk, and his professorial tone changes to one that is almost fatherly. "Michael," he says, "we go back a long way, don't we?"

It's the first time he's ever called me by my first name, and my guard goes up. "Yes."

"And we've always played it straight with each other, haven't we?"

More or less. "Yes."

He takes off his glasses and wipes them with a small cloth, then he puts them back on and says, "There's something else in my report that's very troubling and you aren't going to be able to refute."

Uh-oh. "What is it?"

"Ms. Concepcion was pregnant."

CHAPTER 27

"God Hasn't Been Charged with Murder"

A priest cannot accept confessions if his morals are in question. It's a credibility issue.

—Father Ramon Aguirre

"THIS IS NOW a first-class nightmare," Rosie says.

Her succinct analysis is dead accurate. My mind is racing as I'm standing in the pay lot next to the McDonald's down the block from the Hall in a howling wind at four o'clock on Thursday afternoon. I slipped out the back door and took a circuitous loop to avoid the press and three dozen of Ramon's parishioners, who are holding a vigil on Bryant Street. It's difficult to hear her over the roar of the freeway, and I press my cell phone tightly against my right ear. The rain has subsided, but black storm clouds are gathering to the west. I can see a black Explorer parked across the street.

First things first. "Have you talked to Pete?" I ask.

"Yeah. He says Vince has been following you all day."

Good. "Has he seen Mr. Impala?" I ask.

"Not yet."

Dammit. At times like this, you start to question your sanity. I know I saw the Impala outside my apartment earlier this morning, but I start to wonder if it's all just a figment of my overactive imagination.

She asks me if I've talked to Ramon

"Not yet." I tell her that I didn't want to call him because I'm paranoid enough to suspect that somebody may be listening in on the phones at the archdiocese—or even on my cell. "I'm heading over there now."

"Do you want me to come with you?" she asks.

Yes. "No. I'll handle it."

"Have they identified the father?"

"No, but they're going to do DNA testing." She doesn't need to remind me that such tests are virtually infallible. In normal circumstances, it takes several weeks to get the results, but Beckert has asked for expedited handling. We leave the obvious unspoken—if Ramon is the father, our problems may be insurmountable. "We should have the answer by Sunday," I say.

"The media is going to be all over this," she says.

It's true. The DA's office, the cops and the press must know about it already, and Jerry Edwards will undoubtedly appear any minute now. We consider the possibility of trying to persuade a judge to seal the autopsy report, but we'll lose the argument and give the impression we have something to hide.

She gives me a realistic assessment. "The public will turn on Ramon in a nanosecond if there is any reason to think he's the father," she says.

They'll turn on him even if he isn't if they think he killed a pregnant woman and an unborn child.

$$* \qquad * \qquad *$$

I LOOK INTO the tired eyes of my client and lower my voice to confession level. "We need to talk," I say.

Ramon's body tenses. He's sitting in a wooden chair in his makeshift lodgings at archdiocese headquarters. The pressure is starting to take its toll and his complexion is gaunt. "What is it?" he asks.

I don't have time to be subtle. "She was pregnant."

There is no discernible reaction before he whispers, "She told me it was possible."

What the hell?

He closes his eyes for an interminable moment, then he opens them and understates, "It's so terribly sad."

"We need to discuss this, Ramon."

"Maria and her baby are in heaven. Maybe it was God's will."

We aren't going to be able to foist this one off so easily. "God hasn't been charged with murder," I say. My voice starts to rise when I add, "The autopsy report is now a matter of public record. I need to know the truth."

"I've found the truth is often very elusive."

His cryptic answer is troubling. I give him another moment to think about it, but he doesn't engage. Finally, I say, "Did you have anything to do with her death?"

"Absolutely not."

I'll never speak to you again if you're lying. "How did you know she may have been pregnant?"

"She told me she was trying."

"When did she tell you about it?"

"About a month ago."

"Why didn't you say something to me?"

"Life is complicated."

"It's going to get even more complicated if you don't start telling me the truth."

He takes a deep breath and says, "Maria asked me to keep her situation confidential until she could sort out some issues."

"Such as?"

"She was concerned that she would lose the moral high ground in her cases against the Church if it was discovered she was having a child."

"Her personal circumstances had nothing to do with the validity of the legal claims."

"That's a nice lawyerly argument, but she didn't buy it."

"She was wrong."

"She disagreed. She was also going to have to explain the situation to her mother."

"Who strikes me as a very understanding person."

"She is until you get into discussions about theology. Like many good Catholics, she views most moral issues in black and white."

"In my experience, people become more flexible when they're presented with the prospect of having their first grandchild. She would have come around."

"I'd like to think so, but she wasn't making things any easier for Maria."

I ask if Lita knows about her unborn grandchild.

"She knew Maria was trying to get pregnant."

"She didn't mention it to us."

"It isn't the sort of news you talk about with strangers."

"How did she find out?"

"When the police indicated it may have been a homicide, I knew there would be an autopsy. I told her that Maria had confided to me that she was trying to get pregnant. I thought it was better for her to have heard it from me."

"Did you tell the police?"

"No. I didn't know if she was pregnant, and I was hoping the issue would go away."

"You must have known that everybody would have found out about it sooner or later."

"Not if she wasn't pregnant."

Now everybody is going to know about it. I think back upon Lita's pain at having buried two of her children, and I realize she's added an unborn grandchild to the list. "You should have told me about it right away," I say.

He swallows hard and says, "I'm sorry, Mike. I was trying to protect Lita's feelings."

And I'm trying to save your life. "Is there any possibility Maria committed suicide?"

"She wouldn't have taken the life of her unborn child."

"She was in a lot of pain."

"She wanted that baby more desperately than you can imagine." He gets a faraway look in his eyes. "Remember our first week at the seminary when Father John told us about the great wonders of going to heaven?"

I'm not sure where he's heading. "I'll never forget it."

"I've tried to persuade Lita that her daughter is there, but I can't imagine anything I've said has provided any solace."

I know the feeling. There were times when I was called upon to provide comfort when I was certain I was only making things worse. The possibility that Maria may have committed suicide is difficult enough for her mother. The chance she may have also killed her unborn child is unbearable.

"Lita has endured so much sadness," he says. "I wish there was something I could do to stop the pain."

"We can find out what really happened to her daughter."

"I'm a priest, Mike, not a cop, and I can't leave this building without a police escort. Besides, it will never bring back Maria or the baby."

No, it won't, but finding the killer may provide some closure. "We need to focus on your case," I say. "The revelation of an unborn child has serious ramifications. You'll lose the goodwill of the public and the potential juror pool if they think you were involved in the death of a pregnant woman."

"I wasn't."

"Then we need to prove it—preferably before your preliminary hearing begins."

"It's impossible to prove a negative," he observes.

"We'll have to try. If all else fails, we'll need to provide the cops with one or more viable suspects who may have been at her apartment that night. Did you see anybody as you were leaving?"

"No."

"They found a partially eaten burrito from Lopez's restaurant on her kitchen counter. Do you have any idea how it might have gotten there?"

"No."

Dammit. "Do you recall her making a phone call to Lopez's restaurant before you left?"

"No."

"You were the only people there. How could you *not* have noticed?"

He thinks about it and he says, "I used the bathroom right before I left, and I started her bath. Maybe she was on the phone."

"That doesn't help."

"It's the truth."

I take a deep breath and say, "There's another complicating factor." I tell him that the state of California views an unborn fetus as a living person in the context of a murder trial. "The DA is likely to amend the charges to include double murder." I add, "It also raises the specter of a more serious charge."

"What can be more serious?"

"The death penalty."

The color leaves his face, but he doesn't say anything.

"It's another lever they'll pull to pressure you to confess," I say.

The air leaves the room, and Ramon's eyes are on fire. "I didn't kill her," he says.

I believe him, but it's time to turn all the cards faceup. I ask, "Are you the father?"

He swallows hard and whispers, "It's possible."

CHAPTER 28

"The Technology Outpaced the Theology"

Thou shalt not commit adultery.

—Exodus 20:14

RAMON'S TONE IS maddeningly even when he says, "It isn't what you think."

"It's precisely what I think." I may have found a way to forgive him for not revealing Maria was pregnant right away, but this is far more damaging. "The last immaculate conception happened two thousand years ago."

"Hear me out."

"I know where babies come from."

"This is different."

"No, it isn't. You lied to me."

"No, I didn't."

"What would you call it? I asked you flat-out if you were sleeping with her, and you looked me right in the eye and said you weren't."

"I wasn't."

"When I turned fifty last year, Rosie bought me an X-rated videotape that promised to improve our sex lives. It showed one hundred and fifty-three different positions. I think it covered every possible permutation as to how one can get pregnant."

His jaws tighten. "You aren't listening. I wasn't sleeping with Maria. I agreed to be a sperm donor."

It stops me dead in my tracks. "Are you serious?"

"Yes."

"When?"

"About three months ago." He says he took care of business at a clinic in Berkeley. "She was desperate to have a child, and I had a chance to help."

I'm reeling. "Priests aren't allowed to do that," I stammer.

"I'm familiar with the theological rules on the subject." He assures me he hasn't performed a similar service for any of his other parishioners.

Here we go. "Are you the father?"

"I don't know."

"How can you *not* know?"

"She decided to be inseminated after she broke up with Lopez, but I didn't know the process had been successful, and she said there were other donors. I don't know who they were and some were anonymous."

Swell. "Were you planning to find out if you were the father?"

"Yes, but for obvious reasons, we had agreed to keep my part in this process a secret."

Everybody is going to find out now, and I struggle to sort out the scenarios. If he's the father, the complexion of the case changes significantly for the worse. If he isn't, we may be able to deflect some attention to the person who is—if we can identify him. The most obvious candidate is Lopez, but I learned long ago that there are no sure bets in murder cases, and we'll still have to deal with the fact that Ramon is accused of murdering a pregnant woman. We also have an immediate issue as to what, if anything, we should tell the press and our esteemed co-counsels, Quinn and Shanahan, who are certain to find out that Concepcion was pregnant within minutes, if they haven't already.

I ask him if Maria told anyone about their arrangement.

"No."

"What about her mother?"

"Maria swore to me that she didn't say anything to her. As far as I know, Lita doesn't know the identity of the donors, including me."

"What did you say when you told her Maria was trying to get pregnant?"

"That there was an anonymous donor."

I don't relish withholding material information from Maria's mother. Ideally, we should also try to find somebody at the clinic who can corroborate the fact that Ramon went there, but it will only draw attention to him if we show up on their doorstep and start asking questions. I ask him if he used his real name at the clinic.

"No. Everything was done anonymously."

"How did they identify your . . . uh . . . donation?"

"They asked me to give them an alias."

"What pseudonym did you use?"

"Michael Daley."

Perfect.

I watch the second hand on the clock go around twice before he speaks again. "What do we do now?"

Our alternatives aren't attractive. "We have three-options," I say. "We can issue a vehement denial and hope the DNA tests prove negative, in which case this problem goes away." Leaving us only with the small task of defending Ramon against a double murder charge.

"And if the results are positive?"

"We'll look like lying idiots, and our credibility will be completely shot."

He asks what's behind door number two.

"We'll come clean and explain that you attempted to assist a woman who was desperate to have a child. We'll tell the truth—that you didn't engage in sex with Maria."

"It will rank right up there with President Clinton's denials about Monica Lewinsky."

"You were helping a person in need. In a way, you were doing God's work."

"The perception is always more important than the truth."

"There are mitigating circumstances. You'll apologize for the lapse in judgment and make a confession seeking the forgiveness of the Church and the public."

"The Church isn't going to give me a pass."

That's no longer my department. "It's a risk," I say, "and you'll be criticized for not coming forward in the first place."

He drums his fingers on the table, but doesn't say anything.

I lay it on the line. "I know your intentions were good, but you crossed the line. I can make good legal arguments, but you're going to have to make your own peace with the Church."

"I'm out of a job."

I feel bad about that, but it's the least of my concerns. "We'll make your case to the archbishop after we get the murder charges dropped. You didn't do anything illegal, and you shouldn't be penalized just because the technology outpaced the theology."

"The archbishop isn't going to buy it."

"Then we'll go to Rome and talk to the head guy as soon as the charges are dropped."

"This is serious," he says. "I made a commitment to this vocation. Being a good priest is important to me."

"I understand that, too, and I believe you did something to sanctify the beauty of human life and you brought hope and comfort to someone in need. If that's a sin, so be it. Surely, there must be somebody in the Church who is willing to lend a sympathetic ear."

"You were always the guy who argued with the priests about being flexible."

"Maybe I was preparing to become a lawyer even then."

He asks about the third option.

"We say nothing for the time being, and then we reevaluate our alternatives after the DNA tests come back."

"That will only delay the inevitable."

"At least we'll know what the inevitable is. It's better to know for sure before we say anything that could embarrass us later. If you aren't the father, the problem goes away and we may have another viable suspect."

"Lopez?"

"Precisely."

"So, if the tests show that I'm not the father, you're saying we'll invoke the time-honored theological doctrine of 'No harm, no sin.' "

"That's one way of looking at it."

His lips form a tight line across his face. "I don't like it," he says. "It's lying."

"No, it isn't. You're simply electing not to reveal certain facts that could be used to incriminate you. It's your legal right."

"It isn't my moral right."

"That's out of my jurisdiction."

"You can dress it up however you'd like," he says, "but lying was still on the hot list of sins last time I looked."

It may be a cop-out, but I'm no longer charged with interpreting laws that aren't written in the Penal Code. "You're under no legal obligation to talk about your case," I say.

"That may be true insofar as the state of California is concerned," he replies, "but I still have to answer to a higher authority."

"I'm no longer licensed to practice in that courtroom."

"What do we tell Quinn and Shanahan?"

"The truth."

"Are you out of your mind?"

"As long as they're your legal counsel, anything you tell them is privileged. If they reveal this information to anybody—including the archbishop—I'll haul their asses before the State Bar. It's a clumsy metaphor, but the sooner you tell them, the sooner they're pregnant."

CHAPTER 29

"You've Put Me into an Impossible Position"

Our faith is predicated on the principle that God loves us and is understanding of our human frailties.

—Father F. X. Quinn, *San Francisco Catholic Magazine*

IT TAKES A supreme effort by Quinn to keep his deep voice modulated after he learns of Concepcion's pregnancy. "This is now a complete disaster," he says.

We're meeting in his office at archdiocese headquarters. A grim Shanahan is standing in the corner. Every major TV channel is broadcasting from the steps of the Hall, and a fleet of news vans is undoubtedly barreling down Van Ness Avenue toward us. We'll need to begin defensive maneuvers right away.

Quinn is just warming up. He points a threatening finger in my direction and says, "Jerry Edwards called for you."

"I'll deal with him."

"*We'll* deal with him," he says. "What were you planning to tell him?"

"That we have no comment."

"That's the best you can do?"

"Until we know more facts, it's the correct answer."

"We'll get crucified for looking evasive."

Interesting metaphor. "We'll look careful," I reply.

Quinn turns to Ramon and asks him straight up. "Are you the father of Ms. Concepcion's unborn child?"

Ramon glances my way and I say to Quinn, "Are you still representing Father Aguirre?"

"Of course."

I ask the same question of Shanahan, who nods. I turn back to Quinn and say, "And you would therefore agree this conversation is covered by the attorney-client privilege, right?"

His bushy right eyebrow goes up slightly before he responds with a tentative "Yes." Shanahan agrees with him again.

That's all I need. I nod to Ramon, who swallows hard and whispers, "It's possible."

The explanation takes just a moment and Quinn's eruption comes fast and hard, followed by a diatribe that lasts a full five minutes. He punctuates his fury with hand gestures, table thumping and an occasional expletive. His tirade is directed in equal parts toward Ramon, who created this mess, and me, who put him in a position where he can no longer rat out our client to the press, the DA or the archbishop without violating the attorney-client privilege. Every once in a while, the California Rules of Professional Conduct work to your advantage, but this doesn't seem like an opportune time to gloat about my satisfying legal conquest.

Quinn finally regains a small portion of his composure and turns the full impact of his venom in my direction. "What do you plan to do?" he asks.

"Keep our mouths shut until the DNA results come back."

"That isn't a legal strategy."

"It is until we know more facts."

"What if he isn't the father?"

"It may help us deflect the blame toward another suspect," I say.

"And if he is?"

"It won't."

He's unmoved by my glib response. "I don't like it," he says. "We're withholding material evidence."

He's never tried a criminal case, and I remind him we aren't obligated to reveal anything that may tend to incriminate our client.

"We're lying," he says.

"No, we aren't. Besides, that's a moral issue, not a legal one."

"Some of us think they're the same."

"I don't." Not anymore.

"You sucker-punched me," he says.

"We told you the truth. The only people who know about Ramon's visit to the sperm bank are the employees there and everyone in this room. I can assure you that Ramon and I aren't about to say anything. If this information leaks out, I'll take you before the State Bar for revealing privileged information." I look at Shanahan and say, "The same applies to you."

"Are you threatening us?" Shanahan asks.

Yes. "I'm reminding you of your legal obligations under the California Rules of Professional Conduct." I turn back to Quinn and say, "The same goes for you."

He's in no mood for a lecture from me, but he knows his cards aren't good. He opens and closes his right fist and pushes himself up from his chair. "You've left us no choice," he says. "For the moment, our official line is that we have no comment with respect to the autopsy report, except to say that we are deeply saddened by the news that Ms. Concepcion may have been pregnant." He points a finger at Ramon and says, "You will have no contact with the outside world until your preliminary hearing begins on Monday."

It's heavy-handed, but it's also the right legal call. Good lawyers don't let their clients talk to anybody before trial.

Ramon's voice regains its edge. "I didn't kill her, Francis," he says.

"I didn't say you did."

"I don't like your tone."

"I don't like yours, either."

Quinn turns to me and says, "You haven't heard the last of this."

I'm sure this is true. "It's the correct decision, Francis."

"It's morally reprehensible, and you've put me into an impossible position."

This is one of the few times when I'm actually inclined to agree with him. "This isn't about you, Francis," I say.

It isn't the sentiment he wanted to hear. "I hope to God you know what you're doing," he says. "I've worked long and hard to protect the interests of the archdiocese. If this case comes back to bite the archbishop—or me—I promise I will bring both of you down with me."

I try to parry by diverting his attention to another subject. "Francis," I say, "we got a copy of the phone records from Ms. Concepcion's apartment from the night she died. It seems a call was placed from the archdiocese to her apartment."

"So?"

"Do you have any idea who called her?"

"I did."

Really? "What were you talking about?"

His eyes dart toward Shanahan before they return to me. "I made a slightly increased settlement offer, which she rejected. That was the last time I talked to her."

TERRENCE THE TERMINATOR'S high-pitched voice has an unusual sense of urgency. "Where are you?" he asks me.

My left hand is on the steering wheel and my right is clutching my cell phone as I'm driving down Gough Street toward Market. I was a starting running back and all-conference pitcher at St. Ignatius, but I don't seem to have the coordination to drive and talk at the same time. "I'm on my way back to the office."

"Rosie needs you to make a slight detour to the Tenderloin."

"Why?"

"Pete found Jane Doe."

CHAPTER 30

"Meet Jane Doe"

All tenants must check in at the front desk. Absolutely no visitors allowed.

—Alcatraz Hotel

BEFORE THE 1906 earthquake, the area immediately to the east of City Hall was a fashionable neighborhood with graceful apartment buildings and elegant shops, but those days are long gone. The Tenderloin, as it is now called, is a forgotten cesspool of decaying tenements and residential hotels whose teeming streets are populated by poor immigrants, welfare recipients, drug addicts, prostitutes and the homeless.

The Alcatraz Hotel is typical of the accommodations in this heavily populated and largely ignored corner of downtown. The decrepit three-story building on Eddy Street is down the street from the Federal Building and next door to the YMCA. The first thing that strikes you is the indelible stench of urine that permeates the area in front of its grated iron door. The ground-floor windows have been boarded up, and a muscular young man with tattoos covering his arms is selling crack in plain view.

I hand a homeless man a dollar and push my way inside the heavy door. The check-in desk is behind bullet-proof Plexiglas. It's only five o'clock, but several hookers are already getting instructions on their cell phones. Their workday is just beginning, and I realize I'm standing in their reception area.

Pete is talking to Terrence the Terminator just inside the lobby. They make an oddly intimidating pair, and the residents give them a wide berth. My brother is wearing his beat-up bomber jacket with a pair of black jeans and a flannel work shirt. Terrence towers over him by almost a foot, and his shaved head, massive shoulders and sleeveless Gold's Gym T-shirt suggest he could still stand toe-to-toe with Mike Tyson. Ironically, Pete is far more likely to inflict serious damage. Terrence's rap sheet may be a mile long, but he isn't as tough as he looks.

I nod to Terrence and address my brother. "Where's Rosie?" I ask.

"Upstairs."

"By herself?"

"She's fine, Mick. She wanted to talk to her alone."

I'm less than reassured. "How did you find Doe?"

"I did some poking around."

I never ask him for specifics. Working with Pete is always a need-to-know deal. I look around at the decaying lobby and observe no discernible police presence anywhere in the vicinity. "Why aren't the cops watching her?" I ask.

"She's a plaintiff in a civil case. It's out of their jurisdiction."

I remind him of the prostitution charge.

"She's out on bail."

"She may be a witness in a murder investigation."

"I'm sure they know where to find her. I saw a couple of undercover cops out on the street. As far as I can tell, they aren't involved in the Concepcion case."

I ask Pete if anybody followed him here.

"No."

I turn to a more immediate question. "Did anybody follow *me* here?"

He gives me a sheepish grin and says, "Just Vince, but he's on our side."

"When was the last time you talked to him?"

"About two minutes ago. He's been watching you all day."

"And?"

"Nobody's following you, Mick. Either somebody got word to the guy in the Impala to stay clear, or he's taking the day off."

I look my brother straight in the eye and say, "Is Vince reliable?"

"Only the best for my brother."

"I'll have to meet him someday."

"Not until the case is over."

Pete leads me past the nonworking elevator and up a rickety stairway with a missing banister. You see some marginal accommodations when you represent criminals for a living, but the squalor upstairs is more disturbing than I had anticipated. The heat is on, and the stairwell reeks of feces. We stop at the first landing, and he opens the door to a stifling hallway that's piled with discarded mattresses and bed frames. The tile floor is sticky, and the only illumination comes from a bare lightbulb. The odor of frying Spam fills the corridor. We pass the open door to the bathroom, where a young woman in scanty clothes is smoking crack.

Pete bangs on the steel-reinforced door of room six, and Rosie answers immediately. I follow her inside, and Pete takes up a post in the hall. The drab room measures no more than ten by ten and is dominated by a sagging double bed. There is a cracked white pedestal sink with a dripping faucet. Jane Doe's panties and bras are hanging on a line strung across the room.

Rosie nods toward a petite Caucasian woman who is sitting with her arms crossed in the middle of an olive green bedspread. "Meet Jane Doe," she says.

Her razor-thin body appears to have about thirty years of mileage and her facial features are strikingly similar to those of Julia Roberts, but her dull eyes look considerably older. Her frizzed hair and eyebrows are an enhanced jet-black with red highlights, and her full lips are covered with purple lipstick. She's wearing a black leather miniskirt and a skimpy halter top. Her deep voice is a tired mixture of worldliness and sarcasm when she says, "Welcome to my office. I was explaining to your partner that I can't help you. My attorney advised me not to speak to anybody except her."

And now she's dead.

"I'm not going to talk about my case until I find another lawyer," she says.

I need to put something on the table in a hurry. "We can help you," I say.

The streetwise operator immediately senses an opportunity to barter. "I might be willing to talk to you if you're willing to take my case against the archdiocese—for free."

The possibility of a contingency fee is enticing, but it would create a conflict of interest if she's asked to testify at Ramon's trial, not to mention the fact that we've never handled a civil case. "I'll give you the names of a couple of attorneys who might be willing to help you," I say.

"That's the best you can do?"

It's all I have to offer. "For the time being." And if you don't cooperate, we'll come back with a subpoena and make your life a lot more unpleasant.

She's savvy enough to realize that she may be able to get more if she plays along. "Are you willing to keep my identity a secret?"

"Of course." That's the truth.

"Are you willing to keep my answers confidential?"

"Yes." That's a bald-faced lie. If she tells us anything that might exonerate Ramon, we'll sprint to the Hall to tell Roosevelt about it.

She remains legitimately skeptical. "I have to leave in ten minutes," she says.

I'll have to work quickly. "Where are you from?"

"The lower Sunset."

My old stomping grounds. She isn't exactly the type that my mother always wanted me to marry. She says she went to St. Anne's and Mercy High School. I leave out any mention that I may have heard her confessions twenty years ago. I ask if her parents still live in the neighborhood.

"Yes." There's an awkward silence before she adds, "I haven't spoken to them in years."

"Why not?"

"Among other things, they don't approve of what I do for a living."

"Which is?"

"I'm a dancer."

I'm guessing she isn't a lead ballerina at the San Francisco Ballet. "Where?"

"The Mitchell Brothers."

The pieces are starting to fit together. In its unique way, the Mitchell Brothers O'Farrell Theater is as much a Bay Area institution as Coit Tower. Jim and Artie Mitchell were fun-loving brothers from the East Bay who opened a girlie theater on Independence Day of 1969 in a converted vaudeville house a few blocks from here. Roosevelt Johnson and my father had the privilege of participating in the first raid a few weeks later, which foreshadowed decades of turmoil. The brothers got lucky in 1971 when Marilyn Chambers, the star of their X-rated feature film *Behind the Green Door,* also appeared as a model on boxes of Ivory Snow soap. The attendant publicity made the film a huge hit and landed the plucky Mitchells right up there with Hugh Hefner and Larry Flynt in the higher echelons of adult-entertainment purveyors. The savvy brothers were among the first to bring high-class porn to a mass audience, and their empire soon expanded to a dozen locations. The lawsuits brought by local communities trying to keep them out generated substantial press coverage and free publicity. It was front-page news when Chambers was arrested for solicitation at the theater in 1985, and she spent most of her brief jail time posing for photos with the cops. In response to

changing times and the AIDS epidemic, the astute busi-
nessmen produced a sequel to *Green Door* starring porn
diva Missy Manners, which was widely recognized at the
time as the first safe-sex adult film.

The train started to derail in the late eighties as Artie's
drug and alcohol problems worsened, and things came to
a tragic head when Jim shot his brother to death in Feb-
ruary of 1991. At Jim's murder trial, his lawyers argued
that Artie's death was an accident arising out of a drug
and alcohol intervention that had gone awry. The prosecutors pointed out that Jim had parked his car a few
blocks from Artie's house, kicked the door down and shot
him three times, including one to the brain. He was convicted of manslaughter, and he served three years at San
Quentin before his release in 1997. He's been back at
work at the theater ever since.

I have to ask. "How did a nice girl from St. Anne's
Parish end up working for Jim and Artie Mitchell?"

"Things don't always work out the way you'd hope
after your father touches you in inappropriate places and
beats your alcoholic mother. I left home as soon as I got
out of high school and enrolled at State. I got my degree,
but I need to support a pretty spectacular drug habit, and
dancing pays more than flipping burgers. I'm not especially proud when I take off my clothes in front of
strangers, but I'm making a living and I'm not hurting
anybody."

You always get a dose of reality in the Tenderloin.
Rosie asks her if she ever considered the possibility of
bringing legal action against her father.

"I talked to Maria about it, and she said it would be

difficult to win a swearing contest against my father. He can afford good lawyers."

It's a realistic analysis.

I take her in another direction. "We understand you were arrested a few weeks ago."

"It was a setup. An undercover cop asked me for a date, and they were all over me. I should have seen it coming. The archdiocese wanted to smear me before the start of the O'Connell trial."

"Who fingered you?" I ask.

"The PI who's been following me for the last two months—Nick Hanson."

Nick the Dick strikes again. "Was he arrested, too?"

"Of course not. He didn't do anything illegal."

"It's entrapment."

"If I ever find a new lawyer, he'll argue it at the trial."

The fact that she may end up in jail doesn't seem to faze her. I ask if anybody is representing her on the solicitation charge.

"At the moment, no."

Rosie darts a glance in my direction and then turns back to her and says, "We might be able to do it."

The conflict isn't as blatant as if we agreed to represent her in her case against the archdiocese, but it's a liberal interpretation of the rules that prohibit offering legal services in exchange for favorable testimony. We aren't going to quibble about it for now.

"I don't have any money to pay you," she says.

Rosie tells her that we'll handle it pro bono.

"Why?"

"You have information about Ms. Concepcion. You

can play ball with us or we can come back with a subpoena, in which case you'll have to tell us everything *and*
you'll have to find somebody else to represent you."

The pragmatic hooker makes the call. "Maria was my
lawyer," she says. "I guess you could say she was my
friend. I got her name from the Tenderloin Legal Clinic
after I was picked up for solicitation last year. She got the
charges dropped, and I asked her to help me sue Father
O'Connell."

Rosie bores in. "How well did you know her?"

"Pretty well. She wasn't holding up very well. She
was nervous about my case, and she had stomach problems."

"Did you know she was expecting a baby?"

Her eyes open wide. "No, I didn't," she says. "She
really wanted to have children."

Our attempts to elicit additional information about
Maria's personal life are met with silence. It's hard to decide if she's withholding information or she simply
doesn't know.

Rosie asks her where she met Father O'Connell.

"At mass at St. Boniface." It's the magnificent church
in the heart of the Tenderloin. She reads the look of surprise on Rosie's face and says, "Just because you take
your clothes off to pay your bills doesn't mean you aren't
a good Catholic."

Quinn might have a different view. We're getting to
the good stuff, and Rosie nods to me. It's time for the
priest voice. I ask, "When did Father O'Connell start
making advances?"

"Shortly after we met. He asked me if I would come to

him for private counseling about my drug problems. At the end of one of my sessions, he hugged me and told me he was proud of me. That was the first time he touched me. He did it again the next time I saw him, then he tried to kiss me. I told him it wasn't appropriate. He pretended to agree with me, but he did the same thing the following week."

"Why did you keep going to see him?"

Her eyes turn down and she says, "Because he was my priest. I know it sounds strange, but I didn't want to let him down. Then he started showing up at the theater and following me home."

Dear God. A priest who was also a stalker. "Why didn't you report him?"

"He said he would tell the cops that I had solicited him. He was a well-known priest, and I work at the Mitchell Brothers—who do you think they would have believed?"

Easy answer. "How long did this go on?" I ask.

"Almost a year. Then he started hitting on one of the younger girls at the club, and I decided I needed to do something."

If she's telling the truth, Ramon's mentor was even more evil than his portrayal in the press indicated. "We'd like to talk to the other woman."

"You can't. She disappeared about six months ago."

Uh-oh. "Is she still alive?"

"We think somebody paid her to leave town, but nobody knows for sure. A lot of people in this neighborhood disappear, and there isn't much the cops can do about it. Nobody takes attendance around here."

I'll ask Roosevelt about it. "So you went to Ms. Concepcion for help?"

"Yes. She was willing to handle my case for a contingency fee, and she was realistic about the fact that it was going to boil down to my word against Father O'Connell's. He was popular and had friends in high places. He also had the full backing of the archdiocese. Their lawyers are going to portray me as a drug addict and prostitute who is making wild accusations."

I ask her about the possibility of a settlement.

"Maria and I talked it over, but we decided not to accept anything out of court. You may find it hard to believe, but I didn't file the lawsuit for the money. I did it to expose Father O'Connell for what he did, and I'm prepared to donate any judgment to the battered-women's shelter. This is about doing what's right." Her eyes fill with tears when she says, "My father was abusive, and there was nothing I could do about it. I wasn't going to let the archdiocese get away with covering up this monster's acts."

"We understand they upped their settlement offer on the night Ms. Concepcion died."

"They did."

"To what?"

"A million dollars, but I turned it down. I told you this case isn't about money." She looks at her watch and stands. "I really have to get to work," she says.

I throw up a Hail Mary pass. "When did Ms. Concepcion tell you about the final settlement offer?"

"On the night she died."

"What time was that?"

"Around ten-thirty."

I can hear the audible gasp from Rosie's lips. If Doe is telling the truth, she spoke to Concepcion a half hour *after* Ramon left her apartment.

CHAPTER 31

"I Think We Can Do Business"

Our case against Father Ramon Aguirre is airtight.

—Inspector Marcus Banks, *KGO Radio,*
Thursday, December 11

MY EYES ARE now boring straight into Doe's when I ask, "Are you absolutely sure about that time?"

There is no equivocation in her voice when she says, "Yes."

Yes! I try to temper my excitement when I quickly recognize a practical evidentiary problem. "We have the records from Ms. Concepcion's cell and home phones for that evening," I say, "and there was no record of an outgoing call to you."

"She called me from a pay phone."

Huh? "Why?"

"She was afraid her phone was bugged."

It's a legitimate concern. "Where did you take the call?"

"At a pay phone at the club."

I can't think of any reason why she would be making this up, but her background puts her credibility into question. Pete's moles at SBC will be able to identify any pay-phone-to-pay-phone calls to the Mitchell Brothers' last

Monday night, but it will be impossible to prove Concepcion was on the line without an eyewitness. Then again, if we can demonstrate she was still alive after Ramon left, we may have hit the defense attorney's mother lode.

I ask her if she answered the phone at the club.

"Yes."

"Was anybody else around?"

"No."

So much for a corroborating witness there. "What exactly did she say?"

"That the archdiocese had upped its offer to a million dollars. I told her I wasn't interested, and I went back to work."

Ever the consummate professional. Maybe we can find a witness at the other end. "Where was she?"

"I don't know, but it was difficult to hear her because it was noisy."

She may have been in a bar or restaurant near her apartment. The obvious choice is Eduardo's. "How long did you talk to her?"

"Less than a minute. That was the last time we spoke."

"Have you talked to the police about this?"

"Yes. I spoke to Inspector Johnson and Inspector Banks earlier today."

Roosevelt didn't mention it. It's unrealistic to expect him to call every time he receives information that may be helpful to us, but this could create a substantial hole in his case. I ask, "Are you willing to testify about this?" I'm just being polite. If she refuses, we'll send her a subpoena.

"What's the big deal?"

I explain that Ramon left Concepcion's apartment at ten o'clock. "If you talked to her at ten-thirty, it means she was alive after he left."

"She was definitely alive at ten-thirty."

Excellent answer.

She arches an eyebrow and says, "I guess my testimony is pretty important to your case."

"Yes, it is."

"Then we have some interesting issues to discuss, don't we?"

"Yes, we do."

"Are you willing to make it worth my while?"

We could serve her with a subpoena and end this discussion right now, but it may impact her willingness to testify. "We'll represent you on the solicitation charge," Rosie says.

"Are you willing to represent me if I want to bring legal action against my father?"

"Yes."

"And are you willing to help me find a new job and another place to live?"

"Yes."

The worldly prostitute is now a key witness in a murder case. She extends a hand and says, "I think we can do business."

CHAPTER 32

"You Can Look, but You Can't Touch"

Highest-quality adult entertainment in a safe and clean environment. Continuous show times.

—Mitchell Brothers' O'Farrell Theater

MY BROTHER IS chewing on a toothpick as we're standing beneath the marquee in front of the Alcatraz Hotel. "This case is over, Mick," he says. "You just won."

"If Jane Doe is telling the truth," Rosie adds, "Concepcion was still alive after Ramon left her apartment. That's more than enough for reasonable doubt."

Not so fast. "*If* she's telling the truth," I say, "and *if* the jury believes her."

"Why would she lie?"

"I don't know, but I'm going to hold off on buying the champagne for now."

Pete asks, "Why are you always so pessimistic?"

It's my proper Catholic upbringing. "I've seen a lot of cases go sideways long before the charges are dismissed. They may know something that we don't. It isn't over until Ward and McNulty say it is."

"We need to talk to them," Rosie says.

"We will as soon as we can corroborate Doe's story," I say.

"At the very least," she says, "we ought to get her to sign a declaration that she received a phone call from Concepcion at ten-thirty that night."

The unbending voice of caution. We've assigned Terrence to keep an eye on Doe, but if something happens to her or she changes her mind, we'll want some record of what she told us tonight. We'll write something up as soon as we get back to the office, then we'll see if we can get her to sign it. We still have to deal with the small matter of Concepcion's unborn baby.

I turn to Pete and say, "I need you to do a little research over at the Mitchell Brothers'."

His eyes light up. "Hands-on research?"

He's a few credits short of a master's in political correctness. "You can look, but you can't touch."

"You're no fun."

"I'll tell Donna."

"Exactly what do you want me to do?"

"I need you to get the numbers of every pay phone in the building, then I want your mole down at SBC to identify any calls around ten-thirty last Monday night."

"Can I use a little muscle to get backstage if I have to?"

"Finesse and bribery are always preferable, but do what you have to do."

I'M IN MY CAR heading toward archdiocese headquarters to give Ramon the good news when my cell phone rings. "Mr. Daley," Jerry Edwards rasps, "you've been withholding information. You didn't tell me that Ms. Concepcion was pregnant."

I need to get off the phone as fast as I can. "I just found out."

He sigh is punctuated by violent coughing. He catches his breath and says, "It would be in your client's best interest to come clean about this."

"We are still gathering facts and we have nothing to say at this time."

"Is your client the father of Ms. Concepcion's unborn child?"

"We have no comment."

"You'll dig yourself an even bigger hole if you're evasive."

"I'm prepared to give you a quote right now."

"I'm listening."

"Father Aguirre did not murder Ms. Concepcion, and he will be fully exonerated. We will provide the testimony of a witness that will conclusively prove Ms. Concepcion was still alive after Father Aguirre left her apartment last Monday night."

"Who's the witness?"

There is no reason to hide it. "Jane Doe."

PETE CALLS ME at the office at seven-thirty. "You got a minute, Mick?"

"Yeah. How are things down at the Mitchell Brothers'?"

"The early show was more tasteful than I had anticipated."

"I'll have to check it out one of these days. Did you call just to give me a review?"

"No, I called to tell you that there are two pay phones in the theater. One is in the lobby, and the other is backstage. My guy at SBC checked on calls to both. We owe him a couple of six-packs."

I'll take care of it. "And?"

"Doe's story is checking out. There was an incoming call to the backstage phone at ten thirty-one last Monday night that lasted forty-seven seconds." He says there were no other incoming calls until after midnight.

"Was he able to tell where the call originated?"

"A pay phone by the front door at Eduardo's Latin Palace."

Bingo. "I'll meet you there in twenty minutes."

CHAPTER 33

"Nobody Saw Her"

Eduardo's makes every effort to ensure your dining experience is a pleasant one. If you are dissatisfied with your food or service for any reason, please see our hostess.

—Eduardo's Latin Palace

PETE POINTS TO a battered pay phone in the entry vestibule next to the pickup window in Lopez's restaurant and says, "That's it."

With the proliferation of cell phones, it's hard to find functioning pay phones nowadays, and many that remain intact are in need of repairs. The beat-up wall model that may hold the key to our case fits squarely into this category. The phone-book holders are empty, the steel-encased cord is dangling by a thread and the emergency numbers and dialing instructions have been obliterated by black Magic Marker. Nowadays, if you want to reach out and touch someone, you really have to work at it.

The young woman at the podium has the requisite model-perfect qualities that fall somewhere between Jennifer Lopez and Salma Hayek. She flashes a radiant smile and tosses her silky black hair. "Party of two?" she asks.

"Yes, please."

"Right this way."

Pete and I follow her to a booth in the rear of the

raucous eatery. It's eight o'clock, and the evening shift is filing in. I say, "We're looking for Mercedes Trujillo."

She's still smiling when she says, "I'm Mercedes. Who's asking?"

"Mike Daley."

She's flirting out of habit—it's in her job description. "And who is Mike Daley?"

"Tony Fernandez's brother-in-law." And Ramon Aguirre's lawyer.

I get the response I'm hoping for. "It's nice to meet you, Mr. Daley."

"It's Mike."

"Mike," she repeats. She looks at Pete and says, "And who might you be?"

He gives her a big smile and says, "I might be Pete."

"Nice to meet you, too." As if she would have any interest in two middle-aged guys with graying hair and expanding midsections.

I order a couple of beers and say, "We were hoping you could help us. We were trying to figure out if somebody we know came in to pick up an order last Monday night."

The phony smile transforms into a pout. "We get a lot of customers, Mike."

"She was a regular," I say, "and we think you may have known her."

"What's her name?"

Here goes. "Maria Concepcion."

The flirting stops. "You'll need to speak to Mr. Lopez," she says.

*   *   *

LOPEZ IS EYEING us from the leather chair behind his desk. Trujillo is conspicuously absent, and his pronounced scowl indicates that he's going to be the sole spokesman on matters relating to the Concepcion case. He strokes an unlit Cuban cigar and says, "I assume you're looking for additional information concerning the matters we discussed last night?"

"We are." And if you don't cooperate, we'll come back with a subpoena for a far less engaging visit. "Last time we talked, I mentioned that a call was placed to this establishment from Ms. Concepcion's home phone at approximately nine fifty-one last Monday night."

He tries to sound cooperative. "I recall discussing it with you."

"We were hoping you were able to determine who she talked to."

"Mercedes."

His forthrightness catches me off guard. "You could have called us," I say.

"And you could have called us. I gave the information to the police. I assume they're required to share it with you."

They are, and I'm not going to argue about who has better manners. "Why did she call?"

"To place a takeout order. She talked to Mercedes for just a moment. We were busy."

On to the main event. "Did she come to the restaurant to pick it up?"

"We don't know. It was picked up at the delivery window by the door, but Mercedes didn't see her."

I ask him if he has a receipt.

"Yes, we do." He reaches into his desk and hands me a photocopy of a computer-generated receipt indicating that a phone order for a chicken burrito was placed by someone identified only as Maria at nine fifty-one P.M. "Payment was made in cash, but we don't record pick-up times." He says they checked their security videos, but they didn't see her there, either.

It proves that she called in, but it doesn't place her in the restaurant or confirm that she called Doe. I ask who was working at the takeout window.

"A new employee. You can talk to him if you'd like." He tries to sound magnanimous when he adds, "In fact, you can talk to everybody who was working that night."

"We'll need a list."

"Fine. You can use my office." He calls Trujillo and tells her to start rounding up the troops. His apparent co-operation is admirable, but it means his employees aren't going to impart any information that may help our case.

I try another direction. "Did you happen to see the news tonight?"

The genial smile returns when he says, "I'm afraid not."

"It seems Ms. Concepcion was pregnant."

He pauses for a beat before he says, "I hadn't heard."

"Do you know anything about it?"

"No."

"You realize they're going to do DNA testing."

"Of course."

There's no reason to be subtle. "If it turns out you're the father of the unborn baby, it will cast suspicion in your direction."

"I'm not."

"How can you be so sure?"

His smile turns patronizing as he pantomimes the motion of cutting with scissors. "Because I had a vasectomy over twenty years ago," he says.

CHAPTER 34

"You Don't Want to Base Your Defense on the Testimony of a Hooker"

Fame and fortune are great, but a man's most valued possession is his reputation.

—Pete Daley, *Private Investigator Monthly*

PETE TAKES A sip of bitter coffee and says, "It isn't enough, Mick."

And he thinks *I'm* the pessimist. "It's close," I say.

"Not close enough." My brother is stewing over a Styrofoam cup of scalding java at the McDonald's at Twenty-fourth and Mission, around the corner from Concepcion's apartment. She may have passed this spot last Monday night on her way to Lopez's restaurant, where we just finished interviewing the employees. Nobody remembered seeing her that night. The scared kid who was working at the pick-up window recognized her photo, but he couldn't confirm that she had come to the restaurant. "The cops already know about the call to Doe," he says. "Roosevelt would have contacted us if we'd solved the case. Besides, you don't want to base your defense on the testimony of a hooker."

It's sound advice, but I take glimmers of hope wherever I can. "It's more than we had."

"It's not enough to get the charges dropped."

He still thinks like a cop. "It may be enough to get them to reopen the investigation."

"I'd feel better if we had somebody who actually laid two nonbloodshot eyes on Concepcion at Lopez's restaurant after ten o'clock last Monday night."

So would I. "At least we know Lopez isn't the father of the baby."

"That doesn't help, either," he says. "If he was the daddy, he would have moved up several notches on our list of potential suspects."

I gnaw on a french fry and try to find something positive. "Trujillo will testify that she talked to Concepcion."

"That's irrelevant. It proves Concepcion made a phone call ten minutes before Ramon left her apartment."

"It isn't inconsistent with Doe's testimony."

"It doesn't corroborate it, either."

"Doe has no reason to lie."

"Unless she was trying to get something in return."

"Like what?"

"Free legal services."

"You think she's using us?"

"Maybe. She's been around the block."

"I don't think so. She couldn't have faked the phone call to the Mitchell Brothers'."

"She's bright enough to know that she needed to offer you something. Maybe it was a setup. Maybe her pimp called her at that hour every night."

"The jury will be able to connect the dots."

"I wouldn't want to be in your shoes if you're wrong."

Neither would I. I look for a reality check. "Do you think Concepcion called Doe?"

He takes another long drink of scalding coffee and decides, "Probably."

"But?"

"I can't prove it yet, and I wouldn't want to go to court until we can."

"How *can* we prove it?"

"First, you need to get your ass on TV to tell everyone that we have a witness who spoke to Concepcion at ten-thirty last Monday night without looking like one of those hack defense lawyers who get on the tube and blame everything on aliens from outer space or a cult."

"I like to think I have a little more finesse."

"Don't kid yourself, Mick. Second, we need to find a credible witness who saw Concepcion after ten o'clock last Monday night—preferably at Lopez's restaurant or in the immediate vicinity."

PRESTON FUENTES IS less than thrilled to see us as he buffs the grill of his treasured red Corvette. He's a wisp of a young man with a dark buzz cut, narrow shoulders and arms covered with tattoos. He weighs no more than a hundred and forty pounds dripping wet, but I'd take him even up in a twelve-rounder with Terrence the Terminator. There is a small-caliber handgun in his belt. He doesn't look up at us when he says, "I told you I can't help."

His garage door is open, and the cool night air smells of a mixture of chrome polish and paint fumes. In addition to the fire hazard, we're probably standing in a toxic swamp.

Pete uses his cop voice when he says, "We aren't trying to start trouble. We're looking for information about what was going on last Monday night."

"Talk to the cops."

"They won't tell us anything."

"Neither will I."

"A woman was murdered across the alley."

"It happens. I didn't know her, and I don't know who killed her."

Nice guy. "You may be able to help us find out who did."

"Getting involved in a police investigation will make my life more complicated. I like to keep things simple."

"It doesn't bother you that a murderer is walking the streets of your neighborhood?"

He glances at Fluffy, who is sitting at high alert in the corner. The only thing keeping the Doberman from dismantling us is a heavy choke collar that's been securely tethered to a thick block of cement that looks like it could be used to weigh down a body in the bay. "That's why I have her," he says.

Pete tries his persuasive powers for a few more minutes with no success, then he decides to up the ante. "Look," he says, "we have reason to believe you may be engaging in some questionable activities in your spare time."

"Says who?"

"Your cousin."

"It isn't true, and she has a big mouth."

Sounds like the Fuentes and Moreno families have some issues.

Pete is still talking. "I have some friends in the SFPD. I could make a couple of calls."

Guys like Fuentes don't respond well to threats. "I could make a couple of calls, too."

Or he could simply turn Fluffy loose.

Pete isn't backing down. "I know a lieutenant at Mission Station who could shut your operation down tomorrow."

"Your friend isn't going to bother me. I fix the cars of all of the top brass." He takes a deep breath of the pungent air and says, "I think this would be a good time for you to leave."

They stare at each other in an icy silence for a long moment. Fuentes returns to his work, and Pete heaves a frustrated sigh.

My father used to say that you get more with honey than with vinegar. "What would it take to get you to help us?" I ask.

Fuentes doesn't fudge. "Money."

"What else?"

"More money."

"We can't do it."

"Then I can't help you."

I lateral the ball back to Pete, who looks at the Corvette and says, "Are you almost done?"

"Yeah. I have a buyer who wants to take delivery next week, but I've been having trouble getting some parts."

This gets Pete's attention. Among macho hard-ass types, auto parts are the universal currency. "What do you need?"

"A carburetor. They're hard to find for a sixty-six."

"Have you tried the Internet?"

"Of course."

The animosity between them disappears for a moment as they bemoan the dearth of auto-parts suppliers in the Bay Area. To the untrained eye, it appears to be an academic exercise between two car junkies, but Pete never engages in small talk just for fun. "If I can find you a carburetor," he says, "would you be willing to help us?"

"Depends on the quality of the equipment."

"It will be top of the line—I guarantee it."

"Who's your supplier?"

"Pick."

Fuentes's eyes light up. "You can still get parts from Pick?"

"Yeah."

I have no idea what they're talking about.

"He went out of business," Fuentes says.

"He's reopened, but he only services his best customers, and everything is cash up front."

Fuentes's slim shoulders sag. "He won't talk to me," he says. "We got into a fight about the cost of some equipment."

"Pick doesn't negotiate price."

"So I learned. How can I get in touch with him?"

"You can't, but I can."

"What's it going to cost me?"

"The price of a carburetor and information about last Monday night. We might be willing to pay for the carburetor if you can provide us with some good dish."

Fuentes weighs the potential upside against the risk of abandoning his long-standing policy against talking about police matters. The buyer of this Corvette is probably going to pay well into six figures, and the economic analysis tilts in our favor. "What do you want to know?" he asks.

"Were you here last Monday night?"

"Yes." He says he was in the garage until one o'clock.

Pete holds up a photo of Concepcion and asks, "Did you see this woman?"

"No."

"Did you see anything unusual?"

He ponders for a moment before he says, "A black SUV was parked in the alley a few minutes before one."

"What model?"

"I don't recall."

He's playing hard to get. A car fanatic like Fuentes knows every make and model. "Was it somebody from the neighborhood?"

"People around here don't drive SUVs, and they know it's a bad idea to block this alley."

"I don't suppose you caught a license number."

"No." He says the car was parked for about ten minutes.

"Was anybody else in the alley that night?"

"I can ask around."

"How soon?"

"How soon can you get me my new carburetor?"

"I'll call Pick right away."

"Meet me back here at ten o'clock on Sunday night with a carburetor, and maybe I'll have something for you."

CHAPTER 35

"Who's Pick?"

Our workouts and camps stress baseball fundamentals for elite players. Our coaches are experienced and knowledgeable in all aspects of the game.

—Brochure for Jeff Pick's Baseball Academy

"**FUENTES KNOWS SOMETHING,**" Pete says. He's simmering as we're sitting on crates in the back of Tony's market at eleven o'clock on Thursday night. Tony is sweeping up, and I can hear the bells of St. Peter's chime as the aroma of fresh fruit wafts through the closed business.

Rosie's always-levelheaded brother offers a succinct explanation. "Preston is an asshole," he says, "but he's a great mechanic."

I take a bite out of an apple and turn to Pete. "Who's Pick?" I ask.

"Jeff Pick." His matter-of-fact tone suggests that I should recognize the name.

Tony stops sweeping and says, "You know Pick?"

"Yeah."

Tony's tone fills with reverence when he says, "I need some stuff for my truck. Can you talk to him for me?"

"I'll see what I can do."

I'm still clueless. "Who's Jeff Pick?" I ask.

"The best baseball player ever to come out of Serra High School," Pete says.

The powerhouse Catholic School in San Mateo has produced as many great athletes as St. Ignatius. "Barry Bonds went to Serra," I remind him.

"Pick was better. He was unhittable. He got a full ride to Santa Clara and was an all-American his senior year. He signed with the Giants and had a couple of seasons in the minors before he hurt his arm. He still throws in the mid-eighties, but he was never the same."

I was an all-conference pitcher at St. Ignatius, but my fastball topped out at eighty-two miles per hour and I had to rely on finesse and guile and there were no scholarship offers. Pete says Pick now pitches for a couple of semi-pro teams and coaches high-school and college kids.

"What does this have to do with getting a carburetor for a sixty-six Corvette?" I ask.

"There isn't a lot of money in pitching lessons," Pete says.

There's even less in semipro baseball. "So?"

"He has a side business dealing in auto parts that's quite lucrative. Most pitching coaches don't live in Hillsborough."

I'm beginning to get the picture. "How did you meet him?"

"I played against him in high school. More precisely, I heard three fastballs go by before I took a seat on the bench. Our paths crossed again when I was working at Mission Station."

"He became a cop?"

"No, he became a criminal. He was dealing in stolen auto parts, but we never pressed charges."

"Why not?"

"He's a good guy, Mick. He got me some parts for my old Mustang. He supplies half of the SFPD, including a couple of the assistant chiefs, and he pitches on the department's semipro team. They came in second in the nationals last year. Everybody wins."

I'm not hearing this. I ask if he now acquires the parts by legitimate means.

The corner of his mouth turns up slightly. "Depends on your definition of 'legitimate.'"

"Are they stolen?"

"Sometimes they're borrowed."

Got it. "What are the chances he can find a carburetor for Fuentes?"

"Excellent."

"How soon?"

"I'll call him right now. We should have something to offer Fuentes in the next day or two."

"Don't forget to ask him about the struts for my truck," Tony says.

I glance at my watch. It's eleven-eighteen. I turn to my brother and say, "Pick operates at this hour of the night?"

"Most of his inventory becomes available after the sun goes down."

JEFF PICK ISN'T the only guy who works late. I strain to hear Roosevelt Johnson's voice as the wind is whipping through the broken window in my car while

I'm crossing the Golden Gate Bridge at midnight. "You're up late," he says.

"So are you."

"You really need to get more rest, Mike. You'll live longer."

I'll live even longer if I get my window fixed. "I'd sleep a lot more if you'd drop the charges against Father Aguirre."

"Only if you find me another murderer. Otherwise, it will screw up our conviction statistics."

"Maybe I can help you. I've solved the case."

"Really? Nobody said anything to me about a plea-bargain deal, so I assume this means you think your client is innocent."

"Correct."

"You'll forgive me if I don't break down the door to Nicole Ward's office to demand that she drop the charges immediately."

"I understand your reluctance, but we have some information that blows your case out of the water."

"I'm listening."

"We've found a witness who is prepared to testify that she had a telephone conversation with Ms. Concepcion at ten-thirty on the night she died. That's a half hour *after* our client left her apartment."

His tone doesn't show the tiniest hint of concern. "What else did Jane Doe tell you?"

I push the phone more tightly against my ear and say, "You knew?"

"Of course."

"Since when?"

"This afternoon."

"Why didn't you say something?"

"I've been busy investigating a murder."

"Alleged murder," I correct him.

"I was going to call you in the morning."

"How did you find out?"

"I'm a good cop. Doe told us she received a call from Concepcion at ten-thirty last Monday night. We confirmed that a call was placed from a pay phone at Lopez's restaurant to one at the Mitchell Brothers' at that time, but we couldn't identify the parties. We also got some help from Jerry Edwards. It's always nice to hear from the Dark Lord of the Sith. Evidently, he spoke to Doe, too."

"The fact that Ms. Concepcion was making calls from Lopez's restaurant a half hour after Ramon left her apartment doesn't trouble you?"

"First, you can't prove she was at Lopez's restaurant."

"We have Doe's testimony."

"She's a hooker."

"She's credible."

"Second, you can't prove Doe ever talked to her."

"We have Doe's testimony about that, too."

"She's still a hooker."

"She's still credible."

He exhales heavily and says, "You'd better keep looking, Mike."

He usually plays it straight with me. "Is there something else you haven't told me?"

"We're still checking a couple of things."

I remind him that he has a legal obligation to share any evidence that might tend to exonerate Ramon.

"I'm well aware of that, and I can assure you this evidence does not."

"Mind if I ask you something off the record?"

"I can't promise that I'll answer, but go ahead."

"Are you having me tailed?"

"What makes you think so?"

"A guy in a green Impala seems to have taken an unusual interest in my whereabouts."

The line goes silent for a long moment. "Off the record?" he says.

"Yes."

"It isn't us."

"ROOSEVELT KNOWS SOMETHING," I say to Rosie.

"He always knows more than he lets on," she says. She yawns and adds, "There's nothing we can do about it tonight."

It's one A.M., and I'm lying down on Rosie's sofa with my head resting in her lap. We've scheduled a meeting with Ward and McNulty to go over evidentiary issues in a mere twelve hours. I'd like to have something significant to show them.

She senses my frustration and tries to find something positive. "Doe's testimony proves that Concepcion was still alive a half hour after Ramon left," she says.

"We can't corroborate her story."

"We still have three days until the prelim starts."

"Got any good news?"

One corner of her mouth turns up slightly when she

says, "Pete talked to Vince. Nobody was following you today."

Mr. Impala seems to be lying low or has other things to do. "Where's Vince?" I ask.

"Sitting in his car across the street. Pete said we shouldn't talk to him—he doesn't want us to blow his cover."

I glance out the window and see the outline of an Explorer, then I look up at Tommy, who is sitting on top of me with his eyes wide open. I've always believed that babies know more than they let on, and he cocks his head slightly. Rosie thinks that Tommy's dreamy personality means he's going to be an artist, but I think he's going to be a lawyer. I look into his perplexed eyes and we share a big yawn. He stretches himself out to his full length and gives me a half smile. Tommy always looks as if he can't quite make up his mind if he's happy. He seems to have inherited my view that if something good happens, the roof is likely to cave in a moment later. I sit up and raise him to my shoulder. "I think it's time for you to call it a night," I whisper to him.

He responds with another yawn. I take him into Rosie's bedroom and gently place him down in his crib, where he gives me another Mona Lisa smile. He's going to be a terrific poker player.

I'm sitting in the dark on the chair next to the crib and listening to Tommy's rhythmic breathing when I hear Rosie's voice by the door. "Is he asleep?" she whispers.

"Barely."

She motions me into the living room, and we take our places back on the sofa. She runs her fingers through my hair and says, "I think you're getting grayer."

Thanks. "It's just the light."

"You're a lousy liar."

"I could start dying it."

"What color?"

"How about pink?"

"Maybe not. It wouldn't play well in court. Besides, I think you look distinguished."

"I'd rather look studly."

"Better stick with distinguished." I give her a playful pat on the cheek, and her tone turns serious. "How are you holding up?" she asks.

"Not bad," I say, "all things considered." This case arrived on our doorstep a little more than forty-eight hours ago, and my head is throbbing. "I wasn't getting any sleep before the case started. This gives me something to do late at night that's more productive than surfing the Net."

"Do you ever stop making wisecracks?"

"It's the only thing that keeps me going in my sleep-deprived state." I touch her cheek and lower my voice. "Do you have the juice to take this to the finish line?"

"It's Ramon."

"It could get ugly."

"I know." She leaves it there. It's unwise to get introspective in the middle of a murder investigation, and she turns back to business. "I got Doe to sign an affidavit about her phone call. I'm worried she might make a run for it."

"She'll stay put," I say. "We're her best hope."

"Terrence is watching her," she says. "He knows his way around, and he isn't going to let her out of his sight."

Not to mention the fact that he'll get to watch the

shows at the Mitchell Brothers' for the next couple of nights. "Is anybody else keeping her under surveillance?"

"Not as far as we can tell."

I ask her if she's ever heard of Jeff Pick.

"He's a pitching coach who makes ends meet by selling stolen auto parts," she says. "I was thinking of signing up Grace for one of his camps this summer."

"It's nice to know that someone who engages in illegal activities can still serve as a role model for our daughter."

Her eyes twinkle. "So," she says, "in addition to cutting deals to represent hookers, we're now trading stolen auto parts for information?"

"It's basic economics. Supply and demand. It doesn't mean that I like it."

The crow's-feet at the corners of her eyes crinkle as she smiles. She leans forward and kisses me. "Don't be such a prude, Mike. We're going to get through this, and Ramon will be found innocent."

"I know." I wish I had her confidence.

"And then Tommy is going to sleep through the night."

"I'm not so sure about that."

She lowers her voice and says, "We have to get the charges dismissed at the prelim. If this goes forward, Ramon's reputation will be annihilated, even if we win at trial."

"That's a tall order," I say.

"We're good lawyers, and we have some evidence to work with. Besides, we have to make some time to deal with our other cases."

Huh? "What other cases?"

"We've promised half the hookers in San Francisco that we're going to represent them after this case is finished."

"It's a living." I take her hand and give it a gentle squeeze. "If all else fails, we can go into the auto-parts business with Jeff Pick."

Her smile transforms into a pronounced frown as she hears the sound of the phone, and she leaps up and grabs it just before the second ring. Criminal-defense lawyers have to deal with calls in the wee hours, but this is definitely beyond the bounds. Her eyes turn to cold steel and she nods intently as she listens. Finally, she hangs up and starts to put on her jacket.

"We have to get downtown right away," she says. She glances at Grace's room and says, "I'll let my mother know."

What the hell? "It's one o'clock in the morning."

"I know, but there was a fire at the El Faro and our office is going up in smoke."

CHAPTER 36

"You're Making a Huge Mistake"

The most important element in developing a case is devoting enough resources to get the facts right.

—Nicole Ward, *San Francisco Chronicle*

THERE ARE FEW things more disheartening than the sight of plumes of smoke billowing out of the windows of a burning building. First Street is deserted except for the emergency vehicles whose flashing lights are creating a strobe-light effect, and a couple of news vans that stopped to shoot some easy footage for the morning shows. I feel utterly helpless standing on the sidewalk next to Rosie as the firefighters assault our office with jets of water. We're accompanied by Carlos Cerventes, the customarily gregarious man who has owned the El Faro for twenty years and is stoically watching the destruction of his restaurant.

Our building is within a mile of the Sansome Street fire station, and the blaze was reported almost immediately by a Muni bus driver who was pulling into the Transbay terminal. I suspect the fire and the water have destroyed our files and furniture, but things could have been worse. Nobody was hurt, and it appears that structural damage will be minimal. The fire started in the kitchen of the El Faro and destroyed most of the cooking equipment, then spread to the seating area, where the tables and chairs were consumed. It's going to be a while before we'll be able to get a burrito downstairs.

Carlos turns to us and says, "Are you insured?"

"Yeah. Are you?"

"Yeah. We'll put it back together. I'm too old to start over somewhere else."

I ask him if he was here when the fire started.

He shakes his head. "We were closed. They think it was an electrical short that ignited some grease on the grill."

"What do you think?"

"There may have been an electrical problem, but I can assure you that there was no grease. I closed down tonight, and I cleaned everything myself."

We stand in silence for a long moment as we watch the smoke begin to dissipate. I look at my neighbor and say, "Does that mean you think somebody started this fire on purpose?"

"I don't know." His voice fills with frustration when he says the police have promised to look into it. "I've been here for a long time, and I can't imagine why anybody would want to do this to us. We've been good neighbors."

"Maybe it was an accident," I say.

"Maybe," he replies without conviction. He gives us each a perfunctory handshake and heads across the street to try to salvage what he can of his business.

Rosie flips open her cell phone and dials her home number. She gives her mother an update and explains that we're going to be working out of the house for a while. She snaps the phone shut, and we exchange a somber glance. "I'll call the insurance company first thing," she says.

"We'll be back up and running in no time," I say.

"Right." She exhales heavily and says, "Do you think somebody was trying to send a message to the El Faro?"

"I can't imagine why."

Her next question is predictable. "Do you think somebody was trying to send a message to *us*?"

I take a deep breath of the acrid air. I don't want to unduly alarm her, but she isn't naive. "There are people who aren't ecstatic about the fact that we're representing Ramon," I say, "but they don't strike me as the type who would burn down our building to prove a point. Frankly, there are simpler ways to threaten somebody."

"Like following you around and smashing windows?"

"Yeah."

"Maybe they figured we weren't getting the message."

"We're getting it now."

It's almost five A.M. when a tired fire captain whose gear is drenched approaches us and says, "The fire is under control, but we need to watch a few hot spots." He tells us that it probably started by accident in the kitchen of the El Faro and that it is unlikely that we'll be able to salvage much. He's about to head back to his crew when he says, "Do either of you happen to drive a green Impala?"

Rosie and I exchange a quick glance. "No," she says. "Why do you ask?"

"It's probably nothing," he says, "but the bus driver

who called nine-one-one said he saw an Impala pulling out of the alley behind your building right before he saw the flames."

I TRY NOT to dwell on the fire as I'm pulling my second consecutive all-nighter. At six-thirty A.M., I'm crossing the Richmond Bridge on my way to the Channel 2 studios in Oakland for my interview with Jerry Edwards. My cell phone rings, and F. X. Quinn invokes a priestly tone and feigns interest in my well-being. "I saw the fire on the news this morning," he says. "Are you all right?"

"Yes, Francis. Nobody was hurt."

"Thank God." There is a hesitation before he lowers his voice. "Listen, Michael," he says, "we will understand completely if you need a few days to regroup."

"We're fine."

"We can always ask for a continuance."

"That won't be necessary."

"And if you and Rosie need to reconsider your generous offer to handle Ramon's case, we'll understand that, too."

No doubt. "We'll manage."

He keeps pushing. "We can always bring in some people from John's firm to help you."

"That won't be necessary, either."

"Are you sure, Michael?"

"I'm sure, Francis." I'm tempted to ask him if he knows anybody who drives a green Impala, but I'm sure he'll deny it.

The phony concern leaves his voice when he says,

"Are you going to be able to salvage anything from your office?"

"Not much, but we have what we need for Ramon's case." Fortunately, our laptops and the police files for Ramon's case were at Rosie's house.

"John said that you can use a conference room at his firm for a few weeks."

How magnanimous. He'll probably charge us rent. The last thing we need is to be camped out at Shanahan's office, where he'll have a chance to monitor every move we make. When you earn your stripes as a public defender, you have to get used to working out of cramped space. "That's very generous of him," I say, "but we'll manage."

NICOLE WARD'S TONE is irritatingly deferential. "I'm so sorry to hear about the fire," she says. "I hope everything is going to be all right."

I assure her, too, that we're fine.

Not a strand of hair is out of place as she leans on the delicate elbows that she's placed on her broad desk at one o'clock on Friday afternoon. She's just returned from a fund-raising luncheon at the Fairmont for the governor, and she looks relaxed in a chic cream-colored silk blouse with a dark blue scarf. The fact that we're starting a preliminary hearing in a high-profile murder case three days from now appears to have no substantial bearing on her demeanor. Then again, her office didn't go up like a bedsheet last night. Her patronizing tone becomes even more grating when she says, "Have they been able to determine the cause of the fire?"

"The fire inspectors are looking into it."

"We'll understand if you need to delay Monday's prelim."

"We'll be ready to go."

So much for the feigned compassion. "I saw you on *Mornings on Two*," she says. "Have you found anybody who saw Ms. Concepcion at Mr. Lopez's restaurant last Monday night?"

"Not yet."

"You'll keep us informed?"

"We will."

Her stylish clothing and confident air are a stark contrast to those of her subordinate, Bill McNulty, who is wearing a rumpled Men's Wearhouse suit and is sitting in one of the chairs adjacent to her desk. Johnson and Banks are standing behind him. Rosie and I are on the sofa, and Quinn and Shanahan have assumed defensive postures directly across from us. You can tell the pecking order from the seating arrangements: the lawyers get to sit, but the cops have to stand.

"You called this meeting," Ward says. "What did you want to talk about?"

This is not a time for subtlety. "We think you should seriously consider dropping the charges and reopening the investigation."

Banks and Johnson exchange a quick glance, but they remain silent. McNulty's eye roll is more pronounced, but he stays quiet, too. This is Ward's office and it's her show. One corner of her mouth turns up slightly and she responds with a sugary, "We think you should seriously consider taking more realistic positions."

"Hear me out. We've found a witness who is prepared to testify that she spoke to Ms. Concepcion at ten-thirty last Monday night. We've obtained a written statement from her that proves Ms. Concepcion was still alive after Father Aguirre left her apartment." Thankfully, the statement was in Rosie's briefcase and didn't burn up in the fire.

No reaction. "We've talked to Ms. Doe," she says calmly. "You're welcome to put her on the stand, but she's a convicted hooker and druggie who is selling her testimony to the highest bidder. She would have told us anything we wanted to hear if we'd agreed to drop the solicitation charge. We aren't in the business of trading information for testimony—especially from an unreliable witness."

They do it all the time.

"Moreover," she adds, "we'll crucify her on cross-exam."

Either she is truly unconcerned about Doe's testimony or she's bluffing. You never want to use a heavy hand with a witness who is also a victim. "If I were in your shoes," I say, "it would bother me that a witness is prepared to testify that the victim was very much alive a half hour after our client was supposed to have murdered her."

"You aren't in my shoes, and you can't corroborate her story. We confirmed that a call was placed from Lopez's restaurant at ten-thirty last Monday night to a pay phone at the Mitchell Brothers', but we have no way of proving that Ms. Concepcion initiated it or that Ms. Doe answered. And besides—"

And here she smiles. She only does that when she's about to pounce. I *hate* it when she smiles.

"—it doesn't matter anyway."

Huh? "What are you talking about?"

"I'm talking about the fact that we have a witness who can place your client *back* at the scene, later that night."

What? "Who?"

"Nick Hanson. He saw your client walking back to Ms. Concepcion's apartment . . . at a quarter to twelve."

CHAPTER 37

"Indeed I Am"

*The longer I do this job, the more I realize there's no sub-
stitute for hard work.*

—Nick Hanson, *San Francisco Chronicle*

FIOR D'ITALIA IS a crowd-pleasing North Beach
classic that opened its doors in 1886 and now caters
mostly to tourists. Despite the occasionally snippy wait-
ers and the brusque service, the food is bountiful and, at
times, excellent. The aroma of tomato sauce and moz-
zarella fills the elegant dining room as Nick the Dick
Hanson shoots to his feet and greets me with a broad
smile and a warm handshake at nine o'clock on Friday
night. Ever the man-about-town, the diminutive octoge-
narian has a fresh rose on his lapel that's a perfect match
for his red face, and his new charcoal toupee comple-
ments his double-breasted Armani.

"How the hell have you been, Mike?" he croaks. It's
his standard greeting, but you manage to suspend disbelief long enough to think he actually means it.

"Just fine, Nick," I say.

"Sorry to hear about the fire."

"Thanks." We took a quick and depressing tour of
what's left of our office earlier this evening. The smoke

and water did more damage than the flames, and little is salvageable. We'll be working out of Rosie's living room for the foreseeable future.

"You aren't pulling out of the Aguirre case, are you?"

He's never backed away from a fight, and neither will I. "Of course not."

"Good man."

"So," I say, "I understand you've been keeping pretty busy."

He arches a bushy gray eyebrow and says, "Indeed, I have."

So have I. Our less-than-satisfactory visit with Nicole Ward was followed by a heated conversation with our client in which he admitted he went for a walk in the vicinity of Concepcion's building late last Monday night, but he vehemently denied that he reentered her apartment. He said he had forgotten to drop off some flyers for a church function earlier that evening and he left a stack by her back door. There was no record of any such materials in the police inventory, and his story sounded a bit forced. Then we got another earful from Quinn and Shanahan, who reiterated their displeasure that they're duty-bound not to reveal the possibility that Ramon may be the father of Concepcion's unborn child, and who made it abundantly clear that there would be serious repercussions if it turns out that he is. You can't please everybody. Next, Pete, Rosie and I spent six fruitless hours pounding on doors in the vicinity of Concepcion's apartment, but not a soul saw her out for a stroll last Monday night. We'd just finished another friendly chat with Preston Fuentes, who'd told us in no uncertain terms that he wouldn't talk to us again until we show up with a carburetor.

As always, tonight's festivities begin with appetizers and the ceremonial recitation of the accomplishments of Nick's children, grandchildren and great-grandchildren. Nick does all the reciting, and the bullshit flows as freely as the Chianti. He reports that the four generations of Hansons who work at his agency are doing well, and that he's especially proud of his great-granddaughter Dena, who will start law school at USF next fall if she can pry herself away from answering the phones at her great-grandpa's business.

Our salads arrive next, and Nick shoves a plate of tomatoes in front of me. "You need vegetables," he insists, "and more protein. I've been on the Atkins Diet for sixty years. I could have made a mint if I'd started writing diet books instead of mysteries." He's still going strong at eighty-eight, and he must be doing something right. He says his latest novel has been optioned to Hollywood, although he expresses disappointment that Danny DeVito will not reprise his role in the lead. "Bruce Willis is interested," he says. "He wants to give it more of an action-adventure feel."

I can see it now: *Nick the Dick Dies Hard.*

Our entrees arrive at ten o'clock, but he's still warming up. Dinner with Nick is like getting married—it requires a commitment. I nibble at my petrale as he cuts his veal scallopini in half and passes his plate over to me. "Try it," he says. "You need to keep your strength up." He orders a second helping for himself. "I've always had fast metabolism," he explains.

The former welterweight boxer played baseball on the North Beach Playground with his boyhood pal Joe DiMaggio, and ran the grueling seven-and-a-half-mile Bay to Breakers race in May for a record sixty-ninth straight year. He tells me he's training for the Dipsea Race that starts in Mill Valley and goes over Mount Tam to Stinson Beach. "A ninety-four-year-old guy ran it last year," he says. "I'm going to beat him."

I don't doubt it.

The restaurant is packed and I can hear the clock in the bell tower at St. Peter and Paul's around the corner chiming eleven times when Nick finally finishes his second helping of veal, drains what's left of his third glass of wine and orders dessert. He sounds like Edward G. Robinson when he says, "So, did your guy do it?"

It's taken two hours and a couple of pounds of veal, but we're finally getting to the good stuff. "No, he didn't," I tell him. "I know this guy. He's clean."

"Whatever you say." He motions to the waiter, who brings him a double espresso. Nick doesn't drink decaf.

"I understand you're involved in the O'Connell matter."

"Indeed I am."

"Was he clean?"

"Indeed he was not."

It takes all of my self-control not to start mimicking him. "Can they prove it?"

"No way. It's going to be Doe's word against his. Doe's a whore, and he's dead."

Ever the consummate professional. "He can't defend himself," I say.

"He's better off. When he was still alive, the trial was going to be about *him*. Now the trial is going to be about *her*. The archdiocese paid me a bundle to dig up some dirt about her, and it wasn't hard. I was able to persuade a couple of vice cops to pick her up a few weeks ago on a solicitation rap. Her credibility is shot."

Doe was right: her arrest was a setup.

Nick is still talking. "Father O'Connell had a propensity for offering counseling services to attractive young women who came to mass at St. Boniface. It so happens that a lot of those sessions took place at the Mitchell Brothers'."

"I take it this included illicit sex with his parishioners?"

"Indeed it did." He washes down his cheesecake with a healthy shot of espresso, then he absentmindedly adjusts his toupee. "They'll never be able to prove it. Doe is the only witness, and she's a druggie."

Nick Hanson has many virtues, but diplomacy isn't one of them.

"She's a Catholic girl from the Sunset whose father molested her and beat the crap out of her alcoholic mother," I say. "It won't play well if Ward and McNulty try to nail her."

"She's a lap dancer. That doesn't make her a very credible witness in my book."

Mine either. "Give her a break, Nick. She's been through a lot."

"This is just business," he says. "I've been on retainer for the archdiocese for four decades. Shanahan asked me to get some dirt on her and I did. Do you think I got any pleasure spending day after day at the Mitchell Brothers'?"

I don't think he's really expecting me to answer.

"I feel sorry for her," he says, "but I'm not a social worker. I hope she gets herself straightened out and finds something more productive to do with her life."

I ask him if he had anybody watching her last Monday night.

"My son, Rick, was keeping an eye on her at the theater."

"Did she receive a phone call?"

"I don't know. He didn't go backstage."

I ask if he bugged Doe's room or her phone.

"No. It's against archdiocese policy. Jerry Edwards would nail them if they tried it."

Yes, he would. "Where were you last Monday night?"

"On the roof of the garage across the alley from the back door of Concepcion's apartment." Another one of his sons, Nick Jr., was watching the front door. "For the record," he adds, "we didn't bug her apartment or her phone, either."

I'm inclined to take his word for it. I ask him how long he'd been watching her.

"For about six months. Lopez's wife hired me to watch her husband, who was seeing Concepcion at the time. She got really pissed off when I told her that her husband was cheating."

Always a pillar of decorum. "Enough to murder his mistress?"

"No. Just enough to take him to the cleaners in their divorce."

"Are you still working for her?"

"Yeah. She wants me to keep an eye on him until the

divorce is final. He isn't seeing anybody now, but just wait a few days. You can't paint new spots on an old dog."

I ask him about Concepcion's breakup with Lopez.

"It was one for the ages. She read him the riot act when she found out he was boinking the hostess from the restaurant."

That would be Mercedes Trujillo. "She broke up with him?"

"Definitely."

"How do you know?"

"I heard everything."

"You just said you didn't bug her apartment."

"I didn't. I bugged Lopez's office."

I'm confused. "You said that violates archdiocese policy."

"It does. I was acting on behalf of Mrs. Lopez."

You can't tell the players without a scorecard.

"Among other things," he continues, "she took a swing at him with his Orlando Cepeda autographed bat, and he's lucky she didn't connect. She took a chunk out of one of the towers of the Riordan Square model. They didn't see each other again."

I tell him that the phone records indicated that Concepcion placed a call to Lopez's restaurant at nine fifty-one on the night she died. "Did she talk to him?"

"She didn't."

"How do you know?"

"We bugged his phone, too."

I love it. "Did you bug anybody else's phone?"

"No."

"Do you think he was pissed off enough about their breakup to have killed her?"

"He's a dick, but he's not a murderer."

Nick's a good judge of character. On to a more important question. "Did you see her leave her apartment that night?"

"Yes."

Yes! "What time was that?"

"About twenty minutes after ten."

Perfect. "You realize Father Aguirre left her apartment at ten o'clock."

"I saw him leave."

Excellent. "Do you know where she went?"

"No, but she returned about twenty minutes later."

It's plenty of time for her to have walked over to Lopez's restaurant and made a phone call to Doe. I ask him why he didn't follow her.

"I couldn't get down from the roof without being seen."

Good enough. "I can understand why you were watching Doe, but why did the archdiocese ask you to keep an eye on her attorney?"

"Belt-and-suspenders lawyering. They wanted to discredit the messenger—especially if she was a depressed, quasi-suicidal loon who had a grudge against the archdiocese."

"Was she?"

"Not really, but that's the portrait we're going to present to the press. We were able to take a look at her file in her shrink's office. She was unhappy and on medication, but she wasn't any loopier than the two of us."

The fact that Nick was able to study Concepcion's file at her therapist's office with complete impunity is more than a little disturbing.

He adds, "I'm not prepared to testify about the contents of that file."

"Understood." We'll ask the shrink about it.

"She was also becoming a monumental pain in the ass who was hell-bent on tweaking her ex-husband and her old law firm. She filed dozens of suits against the archdiocese. She never beat them in court, but Quinn and Shanahan were getting tired of explaining it to the archbishop. They settled a few cases for a couple of million bucks. In the grand scheme of things, that isn't a helluva lot of dough when you're talking about priests who did creepy things."

I suppose.

"It started to get more personal in the last couple of months," he says. "Shanahan didn't like her, and her ex-husband hated her. Oddly enough, Quinn was the voice of reason. He agreed to settle a couple of the more serious cases to avoid the bad publicity."

"He couldn't settle the O'Connell case," I say.

"He tried. She wanted too much money."

I ask him if he saw anybody come or go from her apartment last Monday night.

"Just your client. He arrived around eight and left a few minutes after ten."

So far, so good.

He adds, "Then I saw him again around eleven forty-five that night."

Not so good, but it jibes with Ward's account earlier today. "Where?"

"Walking down the alley behind Concepcion's apartment."

"Did you see where he went?"

"Inside the gate to Concepcion's building."

"How long was he there?"

"A few minutes."

This is consistent with Ramon's story that he dropped off some flyers at Concepcion's back door. "Did you see him enter her apartment?"

"I couldn't see the back entrance to Concepcion's apartment from my vantage point, but he was clearly heading for the door."

I ask if he could see inside the apartment.

"No. The curtains were pulled and the lights were off."

"Were the lights off the entire time he was there?"

"Yes."

Ward will argue that Ramon killed Concepcion in the dark. I try not to show my concern when I ask, "How was his demeanor?"

"He was in a hurry."

He would have been running if he'd just committed a murder. "Not to belabor this, but did you happen to see him kill her?"

"No."

Good. "Can I ask you a question off the record?"

"You can ask me anything you want."

"Do you or any of your people drive a green Impala?"

He gives me a knowing look and says, "Somebody's watching you, eh?"

"We think so."

"Off the record," he says, "we aren't watching you, and nobody in my operation drives an Impala."

I believe him.

"On the other hand," he says, "just because we aren't watching you doesn't mean that you aren't being watched. There are a lot of people in town who have a vested interest in the O'Connell case, including the cops and the archdiocese. If I were in your shoes, I'd keep my backside covered."

It's good advice. "How late were you at your post behind Concepcion's apartment?"

"Until about twelve-thirty."

I ask him why he didn't stay all night.

"My son called me from the Mitchell Brothers'. Somebody was hassling Doe, and he needed some help. It turned out to be a false alarm."

"Have you spoken to the police about all of this?"

"I talked to Roosevelt this morning. He looks great."

Yes, he does. "Can you rule out the possibility that somebody entered her apartment after you left?"

"No."

It helps a little. "Are you prepared to testify to that effect?"

"Indeed I am."

FRIDAY NIGHT TURNS into Saturday, and Saturday turns into Sunday. We spend the weekend pounding on doors in the vicinity of Concepcion's apartment, but we find no witnesses. We regroup in Rosie's apartment at six o'clock on Sunday night, and the mood is already somber when the call comes in. Roosevelt's voice has an ominous cast when he says, "Did you get a fax from Ward?"

"Not yet." I can feel my heart starting to pound. "Is it the results of the DNA tests?"

"Yes."

I take a deep breath and say, "And?"

"I thought you'd appreciate hearing it from me. Your client is the father of Ms. Concepcion's unborn baby."

CHAPTER 38

"A Sin Is Still a Sin"

DNA testing has confirmed that Father Ramon Aguirre is the father of Maria Concepcion's unborn child.

—Nicole Ward, *KGO Radio*,
Sunday, December 14, 6:20 P.M.

RAMON REACTS WITH a combination of sadness and despair. His face is ashen and his voice is a whisper when he understates, "That isn't good news."

I can't disagree with him.

Quinn is sitting behind his desk with his arms folded. His view is decidedly more direct. "This is a disaster," he says.

A stoic Shanahan nods in agreement.

Rosie and I are sitting in the stiff chairs adjacent to Quinn's conference table at seven o'clock on Sunday night. Ramon's subdued reaction suggests the information didn't come as a great surprise to him. Quinn's lack of histrionics indicates that he had braced himself for the possibility as well.

I try to focus on the bigger picture. "It doesn't change the fundamental nature of the case or provide a shred of additional evidence," I say.

Quinn's scowl becomes more pronounced and his response is more lawyerly than I might have anticipated. "It provides a motive," he says. "The DA will argue that it was a clumsy attempt to cover up a sexual indiscretion. If word got out he'd fathered a baby, his career would have ended right there."

In all likelihood, it's probably going to end right here.

Ramon's eyes are on fire. "You think I murdered my own unborn child?" he asks.

Quinn's tone turns patronizing. "It happens, Ramon."

"It didn't happen here, Francis."

Shanahan raises a calming hand and invokes a practical tone. "It's time to take a hard look at the facts," he says. "They've placed you at the scene, and you're the father of the baby. The prosecution will argue you killed her to cover it up. Maybe she was trying to blackmail you, or maybe it was in a fit of rage. In the final analysis, it doesn't matter."

"That isn't what happened, John."

"Do you think anybody is going to believe you?"

"It's the truth."

I'm tempted to defend him, but it won't help. I try to shift from recriminations and finger-pointing to problem solving. "We'll need to talk to the people at the fertility clinic," I say.

"We already know that Ramon is the father," Quinn says.

"But it will demonstrate that he fathered the baby through artificial insemination."

"A sin is still a sin."

"Come on, it isn't as sinful as having sex out of wedlock. You know that. We need to show it wasn't some cheap one-night stand. It won't look quite so bad."

The room fills with an uneasy silence. Quinn looks at the etching of Jesus above his desk in an effort to seek divine inspiration. Shanahan takes off his reading glasses and holds them tightly in his right hand. Ramon is sitting ramrod straight. Guilty people tend to panic at times like this, but Ramon doesn't.

Rosie breaks the silence. "We still have tonight and tomorrow morning to gather as much evidence as we can," she says.

"It isn't enough time," Shanahan says. "We should ask for a continuance."

"I don't want to postpone the hearing," Ramon says. "This will drag on for months."

"We're going to talk to a man who lives down the alley from Concepcion's apartment," I say. "He was working on his car last Monday and might have something for us."

Quinn is unimpressed. "How did you find him?"

He was recommended by his cousin—a hooker—and we agreed to trade stolen auto parts for information. "We spent the last couple of days asking around."

"What does he do?"

He's a pimp. "He's a mechanic."

"What are the chances he might be able to help us?"

"Hard to tell. He told us there was a black SUV parked in the alley behind Ms. Concepcion's apartment around twelve forty-five A.M."

Shanahan's interest is piqued. "Did he see anybody get out?"

"No."

"And this is supposed to give us some level of comfort?"

"It's all we have so far, John. We're checking SUV registrations."

Quinn says, "There must be thousands registered in the Bay Area."

There are.

There is a long silence before Quinn turns to Shanahan and adds, "You tell them."

"Tell us what?" I ask.

Shanahan's silver hair gleams against the artificial light coming from the fluorescent tubes above us. "I received a call from Ms. Concepcion's mother," he says. He turns to Ramon and adds, "She wanted me to convey her extreme disappointment at your behavior."

"I'll talk to her," Ramon says.

"She has no interest in talking to you. She informed me that she has retained separate legal counsel to initiate a civil action against you and the archdiocese."

"On what grounds?" I ask.

"Wrongful death."

"That's absurd."

"That's for a jury to decide. "

It's true, and the threshold for finding liability will be lower. In a criminal case, the prosecution needs to prove guilt beyond a reasonable doubt, but in a civil case, the plaintiff must prove its case only by a preponderance of the evidence. They couldn't nail O.J. on murder, but they got him on the civil charges. Moreover, the civil discovery rules are more liberal. Ramon will be able to invoke his fifth amendment rights, but he can't refuse to testify altogether.

And now I know what's coming next.

Shanahan's voice is its customary modulated tone when he says to Ramon, "Your behavior has put us into a decidedly difficult position that creates inherent conflicts of interest."

It's what I'd been warning people about all along.

"We may have to make a decision in the civil case that will be adverse to your client's interests."

I don't like the fact that he's referring to Ramon as *my* client.

"More precisely," he continues, "it may be in the best interests of the archdiocese to settle all or some portion of the civil suit before the criminal case is resolved."

"Meaning you're prepared to sell out Ramon if it's better economically for you."

"It's my job to protect the interests of the archdiocese."

"You're willing to admit liability even if it means your client's life and career will be put into jeopardy?"

Shanahan clears his throat and says, "Obviously, that would not be an optimal result."

I turn to Quinn and say, "Do you agree with John's analysis?"

"It's also my job to look out for the best interests of the archdiocese, even if it might result in a less-than-ideal situation for your client."

Ramon points a finger at his colleague and says, "*I'm* your client."

"Not anymore. You brought this upon yourself, Ramon."

"I'm willing to admit I made a mistake by helping Maria, but I didn't kill her."

"You lied about your relationship, and you may be lying now."

"Go to hell, Francis."

"Your ticket there is already punched."

Shanahan steps back like a hockey referee and lets them go at it as the vitriol escalates. Rosie looks to me for guidance, but I let them blow off steam. Murder cases are stressful, and it's helpful to let everybody cut loose every once in a while. I'd rather let Ramon take out his frustrations on Quinn.

The sniping subsides after a couple of minutes, and I reassert myself. I turn to Shanahan and say, "Where does this leave us?"

"We cannot represent Father Aguirre as long as the civil case is pending."

I turn to Quinn and say, "Is that your position, too?"

His face is still red from his tirade, but his tone is even when he says, "We have no choice but to withdraw as counsel."

"You realize you're still bound by the attorney-client privilege."

"Only with respect to issues that we've discussed prior to our resignation."

Not true. "If you reveal any confidences, I'll take you before the State Bar." I point to Shanahan and say, "The same goes for you."

"Calm down, Michael."

No, I won't. "You should expect to receive a subpoena later tonight. We're going to call you as a witness in Father Aguirre's case." I shift my gaze slowly over to Quinn and say, "You'll be getting one, too."

"Judge Tsang will never let you do it," he says.

"He may be inclined to rule our way after I explain to him that both of you spoke to Ms. Concepcion on the night she died." I turn back to Shanahan and say, "We're going to send a subpoena to Dennis Peterson."

"He's skiing."

"We'll find him." I don't say it out loud, but we will also subpoena Archbishop Keane. That should liven things up around archdiocese headquarters.

Shanahan hands me a letter noticing the resignation of his firm and Quinn as counsel of record in Ramon's case. "I was hoping we might have been able to do this in a civilized and orderly manner," he says. "Even in difficult circumstances, it's important to maintain your professionalism."

Rosie has heard all that she can stomach. "Professionals don't quit on their clients the night before their prelims," she snaps.

"We have no choice."

"Yes, you do."

"It's out of my hands. My partners won't let us continue."

"Your name is at the top of the letterhead. You can do anything you want."

"I can't put my firm's reputation at risk."

"But you're prepared to ruin your client's."

Genteel John tries to strike an imposing posture as he folds his arms and lowers his voice. "Let me give you some free legal advice," he says.

There's no way I can possibly stop him.

"I've been doing this for more than forty years," he

says. "I know you're angry, but I think you should sleep on this before you start shooting out subpoenas to people who have the wherewithal to make your lives miserable."

Rosie responds before I can. "We don't intimidate that easily," she says.

"I'm not trying to intimidate you," he lies. "I'm looking out for your best interests."

Her tone oozes contempt when she says, "Thank you for your wisdom, John."

Their minds are made up, and I need to address some practical considerations. I turn to Quinn and say, "I trust your decision to withdraw from this representation will have no bearing on your decision to post bail for Father Aguirre?"

"We will honor that obligation."

"And you will continue to provide a place for Father Aguirre to stay?"

"We intend to fulfill that commitment, too." He isn't happy about it, but it would be a public-relations disaster if they went back on their word.

"I don't want you to discuss any matters with Father Aguirre unless I am present."

"Understood. I hope you will have no objection if we're polite when we have contact from time to time. After all, he's our guest."

"You can talk about the weather. I will make your lives a living hell if anybody in this building is talking to Father Aguirre without my permission, and I will bring the mother of all legal actions if Father Aguirre's room or phone is bugged."

"You've made your position crystal clear."

"We'd like to talk to our client for a few minutes," I say. "In private."

In addition to everything else, we are now officially at war with the San Francisco Archdiocese.

CHAPTER 39

"It's Better to Come Clean"

We must always bear in mind that the actions of one priest can cast a long shadow upon the archdiocese as a whole.

—Father Ramon Aguirre, *San Francisco Chronicle*

RAMON'S VOICE IS a whisper. "I'm sorry, Mike," he says. "I was trying to help Maria."

We're meeting in his room at archdiocese headquarters at eight o'clock on Sunday night. His surge of energy has dissipated, and the harsh realities are sinking in. His freedom is at stake, the cards are stacking against him and nobody in this building is his friend.

I put on my game face and try to sound reassuring. "We'll deal with it," I say. "You're family."

"They say it isn't a good idea to represent relatives."

"Sometimes you have to break the rules."

"Seems I've done enough of that in the last few months to last a lifetime."

He certainly has.

Rosie starts with pragmatics. "You have to be careful about whom you talk to," she says. "Everybody here is a potential witness. We're the only people you can trust."

"I understand."

"We need to deal with Maria's unborn child," I say. "It's better to come clean and move forward."

"It will cost me my job."

"We can address that issue after the charges are dropped."

The reality check is now complete. He lowers his voice and asks what he can do to help.

"We need a description of everybody you met at the fertility clinic. With a little luck, we'll find a witness who can corroborate that you made a . . . donation. We need to show that it wasn't a one-night stand. We also need a detailed chronology of precisely what you did and where you walked after you left Ms. Concepcion's building last week. Maybe we can find somebody who will testify that you never reentered her apartment."

"I told you I left some flyers by her back door."

Which doesn't help much without corroboration. I decide to shift gears. "Both Quinn and Shanahan spoke to Ms. Concepcion last Monday."

"So?"

"I think they know more than they've told us."

"They might. What do you want me to say?"

"That they had a grudge against her and would sell their souls to protect the reputation of the archdiocese."

"They did and they would, but I don't think they'd get involved in murder."

"I'm not as forgiving as you are."

"I've been in the forgiveness business longer than you have."

And I got out before I got good at it.

He acknowledges that he has no great love for either of

them, but he's adamant in his belief that neither man would engage in criminal activity. "They wouldn't cross the line," he says. "There's too much at stake."

We push him, but he doesn't change his view. We explain that McNulty will present his case at the prelim as expeditiously as possible and we'll put on a full-court defense. "The prosecution will probably finish by the middle of the day," I say. "We'll have to be ready to go."

"When do I testify?"

Rosie and I respond in unison with an emphatic "You don't."

He gives up quickly after he hears the adamance in our respective tones. There is a slight chance that Rosie and I will put him on the stand if this case goes to trial, but it's far too risky to let him testify at a prelim, where Bill McNulty will tie him in knots.

"We'll pick you up first thing tomorrow morning," I tell him. "Wear your collar."

"I will." He takes a deep breath and says, "Where are you off to now?"

"I have to deliver a carburetor."

CHAPTER 40

"It Can't Possibly Get Any Worse"

The preliminary hearing for Father Ramon Aguirre will begin at nine o'clock tomorrow morning. Pull up a comfortable chair, get a big bowl of popcorn and prepare to enjoy the show.

—Legal Commentator Mort Goldberg, *Channel 4 News,*
Sunday, December 14, 10:00 P.M.

PRESTON FUENTES STUDIES every inch of the carburetor that Jeff Pick located for him with the same precision that a jeweler would use in examining a fine diamond. "This looks good," he finally decides. "Where did Pick find it?"

"I didn't ask," Pete says.

We're standing inside Fuentes's garage at ten o'clock Sunday night. The door is closed, and Fluffy is sitting quietly in the corner. The cramped area smells of car wax.

"What do I owe you?" Fuentes asks.

"Nothing."

"What's it really going to cost me?"

"Information about the woman who died in the building across the alley."

"I didn't know her, and I don't know what happened to her."

"You said you'd try to find somebody who did."

"I can ask around."

"We were under the impression you were *already* doing that."

"I told you'd I'd see what I can do *after* you delivered the carburetor."

Pete's voice gets louder. "So, you haven't done a damn thing."

"Correct."

"We had a deal."

"Yes, we did. Now that you've fulfilled your part, I'll fulfill mine."

Pete can't mask his irritation. "How soon?"

"Come back tomorrow night. Same time, same place." He looks down at the carburetor and says, "Give my best to Pick."

PETE IS SEETHING. "That was a fucking waste of time," he says.

What my brother lacks in eloquence he makes up for with directness. We're sitting in my car behind Tony's market at ten-thirty on Sunday night. I need to get back to Rosie's to continue preparations for the prelim. Pete is going to relieve Terrence the Terminator, who is spending some quality time at the Mitchell Brothers' watching Jane Doe.

He adds, "He should have had his ass in gear. He knew I would get him the carburetor."

As if Fuentes would have any reason to think Pete has a reputation for procuring auto parts.

"We don't have time to screw around," he continues. "I'll go around and knock on a few doors tonight."

I admire his tenacity. "I want you to relieve Terrence."

He nods. His dark brown eyes reflect the glow of the streetlight above us as he gives me his honest assessment of our situation. "We're fucked, Mick," he says.

"We've been in tougher spots. Besides, what else can they do to us? They've followed us around, smashed my car window, broken into Rosie's house and tried to burn down our office. It can't possibly get any worse."

My ever-resourceful younger brother admits that I may have a point.

I'm about to start the ignition when my cell phone rings. I can tell from the Terminator's shaky voice that something is very wrong. "She's dead, Mike," he whispers.

Uh-oh. "Who?"

"Jane Doe."

No! "What the hell happened?"

"Somebody shot her as she was leaving the theater."

Hell. "Did they catch him?"

"No."

"Do you have any idea who did it?"

"No."

"Did you call the cops?"

"They're here." He's choking back tears. "I'm sorry, Mike. I did the best that I could."

"I know. We'll be right there." I snap the phone shut, and Pete gives me an inquisitive look. "Things just got worse," I tell him.

CHAPTER 41

"Follow the Money"

There's been a shooting in the alley behind the Mitchell Brothers' Theater. The victim has not been identified.

—*KGO Radio,* Monday, December 15, 12:30 A.M.

THE TERMINATOR IS inconsolable as he's sitting on a milk crate just outside the yellow crime-scene tape in the alley behind the Mitchell Brothers' at twelve forty-five A.M. He won't look up at me, and his voice is child-like when he says, "I let you down."

The flashing lights and haphazardly parked news vans create a surreal carnival-like atmosphere in a neighborhood where many crimes go unreported and most go unsolved. Reporters from the major TV stations jockey for position to get the best angle of the backdrop of a girlie theater offset against the foggy night sky.

I put a hand on his muscle-bound shoulder and say, "You couldn't have prevented it."

"She was out of my sight for less than two minutes. It's my fault."

"No, it isn't. Somebody was waiting for her." He says he saw a green Impala pull out of the alley, when he came around to find her. He didn't see the driver or a license plate.

I look down the alley, where I see Marcus Banks escorting Rod Beckert toward the body. I try to get their attention, but they ignore me. I stay with Terrence as Pete walks along the perimeter of the restricted area. He returns a moment later with Roosevelt, whose tired voice has a cast of respect and sorrow when he says, "I can't let you inside." I pepper him with questions for which he provides precious few answers. Yes, Doe was shot and killed. No, the murder weapon hasn't been found. Yes, it appears that it was a single bullet. No, they haven't been able to identify the caliber of the weapon. Yes, a green Impala was seen in the alley immediately after the shooting. No, they don't have anybody in custody.

He tries to pull away, and I stop him. "Do you have any idea who did this?" I ask.

"Too soon to tell. Her purse was missing, and it could have been a robbery—or somebody trying to make it look like one." He responds to my skeptical expression. "The fact that it was a clean kill hasn't gone unnoticed, but she wasn't on the best of terms with her drug suppliers."

"What about the Impala?"

"We're looking for it."

I remind him that somebody has been following us in a similar car.

"I'm well aware of that."

I was hoping for a little more. "You're saying this has nothing to do with Doe's case against Father O'Connell?"

"I didn't say that."

"You seem to be ruling out a professional job." Or trying to.

"I didn't say that, either."

"What *are* you saying?"

"Anything's possible. She was going to be the star witness in a civil case against the archdiocese and a criminal case against your client. You can do the math."

ROSIE'S LIVING ROOM has a morguelike cast as we regroup at three A.M. I just arrived from archdiocese headquarters, where Ramon took the news of our star witness's untimely demise with deep resignation. Pete is sitting on the windowsill. He spent the last two hours hounding his former colleagues for additional information about Doe's death with no luck.

The Terminator walks in with a tray of sodas and leftover tortilla chips. I didn't want to leave him by himself tonight, so I told him that he could bunk with me. He's barely spoken since we got here. He says to Pete, "Donna's on her way."

"What does she need?" My brother has an unwritten rule that his girlfriend isn't supposed to get involved with his job.

"She's bringing you dinner."

"I'm not hungry."

As far as I know, Terrence has never had a long-term or even a short-term relationship, but his instincts on domestic matters are usually dead accurate. "When somebody does you a favor," he says, "you're supposed to say thank you."

My brother is smart enough to back off, and Donna arrives a few minutes later with a bag of turkey sandwiches. Her straight blond hair cascades down her back, and her melancholy eyes evoke a sense of sadness. She's a lapsed Catholic who grew up in the Sunset and attended Mercy High. Her no-nonsense demeanor and crackling sarcasm keep the partners in line at the law firm where she works. More important, she provides adult supervision to my brother.

The sandwiches are homemade and hearty, and I thank her profusely while devouring mine. "What's the word on the street?" I ask. We lawyers tend to get so caught up in our own little worlds that we frequently ignore what's going on outside.

"The bad news is that everybody is going crazy about the fact that your client is the father of the baby. The good news is that Doe's death is taking everybody's mind off the bad news."

Not for long.

"They interviewed Marcus Banks on TV," she says, "but he didn't say much. Jerry Edwards is going nuts. He thinks somebody involved in the O'Connell case murdered Doe."

It's a great angle for a reporter, and we may be able to channel his energy to our benefit. I ask, "Did he happen to mention whom?"

"He was speculating it was somebody connected with the archdiocese."

That doesn't narrow the field by much. "Did he offer any proof?"

"Of course not. That's not his job."

It's ours.

She adds, "John Shanahan said such claims are totally preposterous."

That's his job. "Did you believe him?"

"I believe everything he says. He looks like Paul Newman." She takes a deep breath and says, "How badly does Doe's death hurt your case?"

It's a key question, and I answer her honestly. "We can still introduce her statement at the prelim," I say. It was still in Rosie's briefcase. "It sounds harsh, but her death may not be such a bad thing for us. Given her background, she may not have been a very credible witness."

"You think she'll come off any better now that she's dead?"

"At least they won't have a chance to cross-examine her."

I turn to Rosie and ask if all of our subpoenas have been served.

"Yes. They found Dennis Peterson on the slopes at North Star."

It isn't easy to find process servers who ski. I arch an eyebrow and ask, "Was our process server able to serve the archbishop?"

"Yes."

"Where?"

"In church."

Perfect. Quinn is going to get an earful. "Does that mean our server is going to hell?"

"I don't think so. He's Jewish."

I'm not sure that entitles him to a free pass.

Rosie turns serious. "It's fun to tweak them," she says,

"but we have to connect Concepcion's death to Doe's murder."

"We have no evidence that they're related."

"We have no evidence that they aren't."

I ask her how she plans to prove it.

"I can't."

We sit in silence for a moment before Pete speaks up. "I checked the auto registrations for some of the players," he says. "Lopez and his wife drive matching Lexus SUVs, and Shanahan and Peterson drive the same model. The archdiocese owns a couple of Jeep Cherokees to chauffeur the archbishop and the power priests."

It raises some intriguing possibilities, but we can't prove that any of the cars were parked behind Concepcion's apartment last Monday night.

He adds, "I'm trying to find out if anyone has reported a stolen green Impala."

Donna has been listening to our conversation intently when she says, "If you want to get some dirt on Shanahan, you might check on the trust accounts maintained by his firm."

Law firms are required to maintain separate bank accounts to hold funds on behalf of their clients. They're used to advance costs and to pay settlements.

She adds, "I've seen some hanky-panky in our firm's trust accounts. A couple of the power partners exert more control over them than they should."

Too vague. "Meaning?"

"They take care of certain matters on behalf of our clients without going through the usual channels. They have the discretion to make some problems go away."

"Payoffs?" I say.

"We refer to them as settlements. They probably won't release the information voluntarily, but they're no different than any standard corporate bank account." She turns to Pete and says, "Surely you must have experience in this area."

He nods.

"Follow the money," she says, "and maybe you can find a connection to Jane Doe."

It's a long shot. "We can subpoena the financial records for the archdiocese and Shanahan's law firm," I say, "but that will just invite a discussion with their lawyers." I look at my brother and ask, "Can you get their bank account information another way?"

"Probably."

"Can you do it legally?"

"Depends on your definition of the term *legally*."

CHAPTER 42

"I Won't Let You Turn My Courtroom into a Circus"

*I expect every lawyer who appears before me to be pre-
pared and to treat everyone in my courtroom with respect
and dignity.*

—Judge Ignatius Tsang, *California State Bar Journal*

THE HONORABLE IGNATIUS Tsang is stroking
his chin as he studies the legal papers before him. A slight
man in his late fifties with a quiet, but authoritative,
voice, a receding hairline and a scholarly demeanor, the
judge could pass for a college physics professor. His tone
is measured when he says, "We need to discuss some issues before we can begin the preliminary hearing."

The dignified jurist is sitting in an old leather chair behind a standard-issue metal desk in his cramped chambers at nine-ten on Monday morning. The native of Hong
Kong moved to San Francisco when he was in his teens
and he grew up in Chinatown, where his parents held
down multiple low-paying jobs to allow young Ignatius
to focus on his studies. A brilliant student with a photographic memory and a knack for language, he absorbed
English quickly and graduated at the top of his class at
San Francisco's supercompetitive Lowell High. He raced

through UC-Berkeley in three years and was first in his class at Boalt Law School. He clerked for Justice Byron White before he took an entry-level position at the San Francisco DA's office, where he labored tirelessly for two decades while pursuing his academic interests by writing law-review articles and teaching criminal procedure at Boalt. He has brought the same tenacity and intellectual strength to the bench for the last eight years.

The room is packed with dusty legal tomes reflecting his cerebral approach to the law, as well as several photos of his son, Nathan, a professor at Northwestern Law School. A bronze rendering of the scales of justice sits on his desk, and a tasteful lithograph of the U.S. Supreme Court hangs next to his law school diploma. The only nod to the twenty-first century is the state-of-the-art notebook computer on a credenza that is piled high with papers.

We had barely completed the attorney introductions when Judge Tsang summoned us into his chambers. Quinn and Shanahan presented their papers to withdraw as Ramon's counsel of record first thing this morning, and the cautious judge called a time-out to talk things over. It's helpful to know who is representing whom, and good judges abhor disarray.

Rosie and I have taken positions in armchairs to the left of the judge's desk, and McNulty and Ward are sitting on an old green couch to his immediate right. Quinn and Shanahan are forced to stand against the bookcase. If this were a baseball game, Rosie and I would be in the luxury boxes and they'd be in the bleachers.

Judge Tsang looks up and tells us we're off the record,

then he turns to me and says, "I understand one of your witnesses is no longer available."

"That's true. Ms. Kelly O'Shea—also known as Jane Doe—was killed outside her place of employment late last night." I leave out any mention of the Mitchell Brothers.

"Does this mean you'll need a continuance?"

"No, Your Honor. We've discussed this matter with our client, and we wish to proceed."

"Are you sure? I understand you had an emergency at your office over the weekend, too."

"We're sure, Your Honor."

He nods politely, but his expression indicates that he was hoping we'd bump the prelim until we have more information about Doe's death. "Does this suggest that the testimony of this witness is not essential to your client's defense?"

"We intend to introduce a sworn statement that we obtained from her before she died."

This gets McNulty's attention. "That's unacceptable to us," he says. "We didn't have an opportunity to interview the witness to make a judgment as to her credibility."

And now you never will.

"Moreover," he continues, "we haven't reviewed the document and confirmed its authenticity. For all we know, Mr. Daley could have generated it on his word processor."

The bombast is typical McNulty, yet I'm surprised he's making a big deal about it. Nick Hanson is going to testify that he saw Concepcion leave her apartment at ten-twenty and return at ten-forty. The fact that Concepcion spoke to Doe at ten-thirty now has little relevance to their case. Unless they want to undermine his testimony, they'll have to show that Ramon killed her when he came back to her building later than night.

"Your Honor," I say, "the police interviewed Ms. Doe before she died. If Mr. McNulty is concerned about her credibility, he should consult with Inspector Roosevelt Johnson. If he wishes to challenge the authenticity of her statement, he's free to do so at trial."

"May I see the document, Mr. Daley?"

"Yes, Your Honor." I hand it over to him.   •

He studies it for a moment, then he turns to McNulty and says, "I'm inclined to admit it."

"But, Your Honor—"

"I've ruled."

"Yes, Your Honor."

It's a small victory. We still have to deal with the fact that Ramon was spotted in the vicinity of Concepcion's apartment later that night.

Judge Tsang is just warming up. "I called you in here because I want to sort out who is representing the defendant," he says.

"Your Honor," Shanahan begins, "let me try to shed some light on the situation—"

The judge cuts him off. "With all due respect," he says, "these are my chambers and I get to ask the questions. I'll let you know if I need you to provide illumination."

It isn't a good sign when a judge addresses you with the words "With all due respect."

Shanahan sucks it up. "Yes, Your Honor."

Judge Tsang turns to McNulty and Ward and says, "I

assume the lineup on your side of the aisle hasn't changed?"

Ward answers for them. "That's correct, Your Honor. Mr. McNulty and I will be representing the people."

The judge is pleased. "Have you made any progress in negotiating a resolution of this case?" Plea bargains are a judge's best friend.

"No, Your Honor. Mr. Daley and Ms. Fernandez have been unwilling to seriously consider our generous proposal."

The judge's eyes shift in our direction and I try to sound as respectful as I can when I say, "Our client did not kill Ms. Concepcion, and he is unwilling to say that he did."

"Does the revelation that he is the father of the victim's unborn child cause him to reconsider?" Judges watch the news just like the rest of us.

"That fact has nothing to do with the identification of Ms. Concepcion's killer," I say.

Ignatius Tsang is one of the most intelligent judges on the San Francisco bench—smart enough to know that presiding over the murder trial of an accused priest is likely to turn into a quagmire that will do little to enhance his reputation. His stoic expression transforms into a pronounced scowl when he says, "It's been suggested it provides your client with a motive."

"That suggestion is mistaken," I say.

He shoots a glance toward Ward, which indicates he's thinking "I tried," then he turns back to me and says, "I take it you and Ms. Fernandez are still representing Father Aguirre?" He's still a prosecutor at heart—he's going to ask leading questions in a manner that elicits the answers he wants to hear.

"Yes, Your Honor," I say.

He addresses Quinn and Shanahan. "I have reviewed your papers, and I understand you wish to withdraw as counsel of record."

Shanahan elects himself as spokesman. "That's correct, Your Honor. We have a conflict of interest."

"Didn't you have the same conflict on Friday?"

"No, Your Honor." He says the situation changed when Lita Concepcion advised him that she was going to file a civil lawsuit naming Ramon and the archdiocese as co-defendants.

"I would think your interests line up with Father Aguirre's."

"In this case," Shanahan says, "circumstances may require us to take positions that are adverse to Father Aguirre's interests."

"In other words," the judge says, "you may want to cut a deal in the civil case that would implicate Father Aguirre."

Shanahan starts to tap-dance. "We hope that situation will not arise."

"But it might."

"If it does, it would place us in the untenable position of having to represent clients with adverse interests."

"And the DNA test indicating the defendant was the father of Ms. Concepcion's baby and the attendant publicity had nothing to do with your decision?"

He isn't making this easy for them.

"No, Your Honor," Shanahan says.

"And you believe the situation has changed so precipitously since Friday that you are no longer in a position to provide adequate representation to Father Aguirre?"

"The Rules of Professional Conduct don't allow it, Your Honor."

Judge Tsang exhales heavily and says, "I find it very troubling that you would withdraw on the day of a preliminary hearing."

"We have no choice, Your Honor."

"Yes, you do. You can refer the civil matter to another firm and continue as counsel for Father Aguirre."

This would require Shanahan to do the unthinkable—to let another firm handle a major matter for the archdiocese. He'd rather remove his internal organs with his bare hands. He starts dancing faster. "Your Honor," he insists, "the archdiocese is already a client of our firm."

"So is Father Aguirre."

"Nevertheless, we may obtain confidential information that could require us to take positions that are adverse to the interests of the archdiocese."

"That problem will go away if you refer the case to somebody else."

Quinn interjects, "The archbishop would like Mr. Shanahan's firm to act on behalf of the archdiocese."

"I'm sympathetic, but I'm troubled that Mr. Shanahan is prepared to do so at Father Aguirre's expense."

"We have no choice, Your Honor."

Shanahan adds, "I agree with Father Quinn."

He always does.

I keep my mouth shut as the stately judge lambasts them, but when it becomes apparent that Quinn and Shanahan aren't going to cave, he turns to Ward and says, "Do you have any objection to this change in Father Aguirre's representation?"

She's thrilled. Shanahan and Quinn have enough resources to turn this case into a circus. Ward summons her best solemn tone when she says, "No, Your Honor."

The judge turns to me and says, "Do you or your client have any objections, Mr. Daley?"

It would be bad form to appear ecstatic. "No, Your Honor."

He turns back to Shanahan and Quinn and says, "You're off the case, gentlemen."

Shanahan can't contain a smirk. "Thank you, Your Honor."

Judge Tsang takes off his glasses and places them on the desk in front of him. He points a finger at Shanahan and says, "Let me give you some free legal advice."

The smile disappears. "Yes, Your Honor?"

"I'm going to contact the judge who is assigned to the civil case. I intend to inform him or her that you have obtained privileged and confidential information with respect to Father Aguirre and you should therefore be disqualified from representing the archdiocese."

The color leaves Shanahan's face. "But Your Honor—"

"You can't have it both ways, Mr. Shanahan. This court does not approve of lawyers who abandon criminal defendants in order to handle more lucrative civil work."

Shanahan is watching a potential seven-figure fee go out the window. "We've researched this question," he says, "and we believe no such conflict exists."

"I believe it does, and I'm the one wearing the robes.

I think you should consider your next step carefully before you embarrass your firm and yourself."

Looks as though the all-nighter pulled by one of Shanahan's associates to research this issue is going to waste. "Yes, Your Honor," Shanahan says. He holds up a thin hand and says, "There is another issue we'd like to discuss. Father Quinn and I were served with subpoenas to be called as witnesses in Father Aguirre's case. So was my partner Dennis Peterson, as well as Archbishop Albert Keane."

"So?"

"We believe the aforementioned individuals should not be compelled to testify."

It isn't a good idea to use legalistic words like *aforementioned* when addressing a smart judge like Ignatius Tsang, who isn't going to be impressed by Shanahan's vocabulary.

The judge's annoyance is starting to grow. "On what grounds?" he asks.

"We may be asked to reveal privileged and confidential information about his case."

Judge Tsang listens to Shanahan drone on for a moment before he stops him. "We just decided you're no longer representing Father Aguirre," he says. "There is no reason to prevent you from testifying."

"You're putting us into the untenable position of compelling us to reveal privileged information."

"You can ask for a protective order."

"It isn't good enough."

The judge gives us equal time. "How do you feel about this, Mr. Daley?"

"We have no intention of asking Father Quinn or Mr. Shanahan about any matters that may be subject to the attorney-client privilege," I say. "We plan to ask them about their contact with the victim on the night she died. That information has nothing to do with Father Aguirre, but it has everything to do with them. They can't withdraw from representation and then expect to be immune from questioning."

Shanahan's face is red. "This is highly irregular," he says.

The judge snaps right back. "It's even more irregular for counsel to withdraw on the day of a preliminary hearing."

"Surely you can't expect Mr. Peterson to testify. He was the victim's opposing counsel in the O'Connell case."

I interject, "We aren't planning to ask any questions about that case."

"Why do you need to call him as a witness?" the judge asks.

"He was one of the last people who spoke to Ms. Concepcion on the night she died. He was married to her, and he may be able to provide information concerning her state of mind."

"How would that be relevant?"

"He may be able to help us prove Ms. Concepcion committed suicide."

Shanahan is becoming more animated. "Mr. Peterson isn't a therapist."

"No," I say, "but he knew his ex-wife better than anybody else did."

"There are no legal grounds to compel him to testify."

"There are none for him to avoid it, either."

The judge makes the call. "I don't see any legal justification for concluding that Father Quinn, Mr. Shanahan and Mr. Peterson should not testify," he says. "I am therefore ruling that they will do so, subject to the caveat that they may seek appropriate relief if they believe they are being asked to reveal confidential and/or privileged information."

Shanahan is livid. "But, Your Honor—" he says.

"I've ruled, Mr. Shanahan. In addition, I see no legal justification for concluding that Archbishop Keane should not be required to testify, either."

It's a slap in the face to Quinn, who has let Shanahan do the talking until now. "Your Honor," Quinn says, "it is unfair to call upon the archbishop to testify as to legal matters involving the archdiocese. The information is privileged."

Not to mention the fact that it could turn into a public-relations nightmare and cost Quinn his job. "Your Honor," I say, "we are cognizant of the sensitivity of the issues that could arise by calling Archbishop Keane to testify, but no legal basis exists to conclude that he should be exempt." Now I'm really trying to tweak Quinn.

Quinn's voice starts to rise. "Your Honor," he says, "Archbishop Keane has no information that is relevant to Father Aguirre's case."

How the hell do you know? "Not true," I say. "He's been involved in preparations for the O'Connell case and he was present during settlement discussions with Ms. Concepcion."

"Those discussions were confidential and off-the-record," Quinn says.

"Not in the context of a murder trial," I say. This may not be entirely true, but I'm on a roll. "Archbishop Keane spoke with Ms. Concepcion in the days leading up to her death. The status of the O'Connell case and her demeanor during that time are relevant to Father Aguirre's case. The only items that aren't fair game are those covered by attorney-client privilege and those that may tend to incriminate the witness."

Quinn points a finger at me and bellows, "Are you suggesting that Archbishop Keane is a suspect?"

"I'm simply noting that he doesn't get a free pass just because of his position."

"That's preposterous," he says.

"That's the law."

Judge Tsang says, "I'm going to allow Mr. Daley to call Archbishop Keane."

Excellent.

"But, Your Honor—" Shanahan says.

"I've ruled, Mr. Shanahan."

It's a win for us, and I keep my mouth shut.

The judge isn't done. "There are several other issues that I want to address," he says. "First, I'm going to ban television cameras from this proceeding. As much as I like being on TV, I want to try to keep the media hype for this case to a minimum."

The only mild protest comes from Ward, who will lose face time on the news tonight.

"Second," the judge says, "I'm imposing a strict gag order on everybody involved in this case." He jabs a finger in my direction and says, "I don't want to see you on *Mornings on Two* spreading wild rumors and spewing propaganda."

Ignatius Tsang isn't going to let us play this one out in the media.

"Third," he continues, "I expect all of you to behave in a dignified and professional manner. I will not hesitate to hold you in contempt if you start grandstanding, and I won't let you turn my courtroom into a circus. Understood?"

We reply in unison with an unenthusiastic, "Yes, Your Honor."

He reminds Quinn and Shanahan that they are on the witness list and are therefore not allowed to be present in the courtroom during the testimony of the other witnesses. Then he stands and heads for the door and says, "Let's get to work."

CHAPTER 43

"All Rise"

Mr. Daley and Ms. Fernandez should ask for a continuance.

—Legal Commentator Mort Goldberg, *Channel 4 News*, Monday, December 15, 8:30 A.M.

A FAULTY HEATING duct has left Judge Tsang's packed courtroom unbearably hot, and the air reeks of mildew from the torrential rains as the bailiff calls for order at nine-thirty. Umbrellas and raincoats are strewn haphazardly, and the jury box is filled with reporters. The sketch artists are sitting in the rear, their pencils poised, and Jerry Edwards is perched in his usual spot in the second row, just behind Lita Concepcion. Quinn and Shanahan have to wait in the corridor, but a couple of dutiful associates from Shanahan's firm are taking copious notes. We can keep witnesses out of court before they testify, but we can't prevent their colleagues from spying.

McNulty and Ward look like twins who were separated at birth in their matching gray suits. Ramon's hands are folded as he sits at the defense table between Rosie and me. He's wearing the traditional collar and black slacks. I've instructed him to be attentive and respectful, but to avoid drawing undue attention to himself. In other words, I need him to look like a priest.

"All rise."

Judge Tsang hustles to the bench and motions us to sit down. He buys a moment to gather his thoughts by turning on his computer, adjusting his microphone and pouring himself a glass of water. He wants to give the impression that this is just another day in the office, but his act is unconvincing. He dons his reading glasses, looks down at his docket and says, "Are counsel prepared to proceed?"

The attorneys inch forward. "Yes, Your Honor," we recite in unison.

He asks the bailiff to state the case.

"The People versus Father Ramon Aguirre."

The murmuring stops, the house lights go down and the curtain goes up.

The judge patiently reminds the few people in the gallery who don't tune in to *Law and Order* that the purpose of this prelim is to determine whether there is sufficient evidence to suggest that Ramon committed murder. "The threshold for holding a defendant over for trial is significantly lower than to convict," he notes, "and just because a defendant is bound over does not in any way suggest he is guilty. It is a fundamental principle of our legal system that the accused is presumed innocent until proven guilty beyond a reasonable doubt in a court of law."

The younger reporters may be impressed by his solemn recitation of the customary legal catechism, but the rest of us are unmoved, and other practical ramifications are left unsaid. Our system is as good as any, but once you've been accused of a serious crime, your life is never the same.

Ramon's career probably ended when Judge Tsang banged his gavel.

The seating arrangements in courtrooms are similar to weddings, and Ward and McNulty are akin to the bride's side of the family. Their guest list is longer than ours, and their invitees are jockeying for the seats on their side of the aisle. Our only invited guest is Terrence the Terminator, who is surrounded by a half dozen of Ramon's parishioners who waited in line overnight to get the few seats that are available to the public. Their support is appreciated, but when you cut your teeth in the PD's office, you get used to being outnumbered.

Judge Tsang asks Ward if she's ready to proceed, and she responds with a radiant smile. "Yes, Your Honor," she says.

"Will we be hearing from you or Mr. McNulty today?"

"Both of us." Her smile gets broader. "Initially, you'll be hearing from me."

It isn't uncommon for the DA to appear in court to provide moral and political support to her subordinates, but it is unusual for her to conduct any real business. The media-savvy Ward recognizes this is a high-profile matter that requires serious attention. She's also interested in generating face time. District attorneys are first and foremost politicians.

Judge Tsang looks over his reading glasses and says, "We're pleased to have you back in our courtroom, Ms. Ward."

"Thank you, Your Honor."

Oh, please.

The judge turns my way. "Will you be addressing us on behalf of the defense, Mr. Daley?"

"Yes, Your Honor." I glance over at Ward and take a gratuitous swipe. "We are also pleased that the district attorney has decided to take an active role in this case. It's encouraging to see our tax dollars at work." I give Ward a nod that says "If you want action, you've got it." She responds to my trash talk with a magnanimous plastic smile.

The judge decides not to dip his toe into our petty pissing contest. He says to Ward, "Did you wish to make an opening statement?"

Are you kidding? She's going to play this for all it's worth.

"Yes, Your Honor." She nods toward Edwards as she saunters to the lectern, where she stands erect and adjusts the microphone. She tosses her hair back and locks eyes with Judge Tsang. She may be self-serving and compulsively ambitious, but she has charisma. She also has a feel for staging as she works without notes. "May it please the court," she begins in a crisp voice, "we are here to discuss a serious matter." She points a finger at Ramon and then looks at the poster-size photo of a smiling Concepcion that she's placed at the front of the jury box. "We face a difficult situation in which a respected member of our community stands accused of murdering the beautiful woman whose picture appears before you. Maria Concepcion was a successful attorney who was only forty-two years old when her life was tragically snuffed out."

I want to break up the rhythm of her memorized speech,

and I take a calculated risk by objecting. "Excuse me, Your Honor," I say in my most respectful tone. "These proceedings will move along more quickly if Ms. Ward would go a little lighter on the hyperbole."

The judge looks at our DA, who is rolling her eyes. "Ms. Ward," he says, "I'm going to overrule Mr. Daley's objection, but I would encourage you to get to the point."

She casts a sarcastic glance in my direction. "Your Honor," she says, "if Mr. Daley is planning to interrupt me at every turn, these proceedings will move at a snail's pace."

That's the whole idea.

Judge Tsang's tone remains diplomatic. "I would ask each of you to be respectful of opposing counsel," he says. Good judges are masters of understatement.

Ward goes back to work. "Your Honor," she says, "we will present sufficient evidence to hold the defendant over for trial for the murder of Ms. Concepcion."

One more time. "Object to use of the term *murder*," I say. "I would ask you to instruct Ms. Ward to use the term *alleged murder*." Now I'm being petty.

I get another nasty look from Ward. "In the interest of having an opportunity to conclude my *very* brief opening statement," she says, "let the record show that I am hereby adding the term *alleged* to the term *murder* in my earlier remarks."

The judge says to me, "Are you happy, Mr. Daley?"

"Yes, Your Honor." I've done what I needed to do. It's time to sit down and shut up.

"Your Honor," Ward continues, "we will demonstrate that the defendant was present at Ms. Concepcion's apartment on the night she died, that the defendant had physical contact with the victim and the murder weapon, and that the defendant attempted to cover up his crime with a clumsy attempt to fake a suicide."

Somebody coached her to say the words *the defendant* as many times as she can.

She's still going. "The defendant has also admitted that he was the father of Ms. Concepcion's unborn child. This suggests the defendant murdered her to protect his position as a priest. The defendant had motive, means and opportunity, and there is sufficient evidence to bind the defendant over for trial for the murder—I mean alleged murder—of Maria Concepcion."

She sits down. Her workmanlike opening was more than adequate despite my attempts to throw off her pacing, but somewhat south of sensational. Most important, it was brief.

The judge turns to me and says, "Do you wish to offer a statement?"

"Yes, Your Honor." We have the option of opening now or after the prosecution has finished its case. I want to take a few potshots right away.

Rosie leans over and whispers, "Stay on point and keep it short."

I stand as erect as my six-foot frame allows, and I walk to the lectern. I place three handwritten note cards in front of me and look up at Judge Tsang, who eyes me with a somber expression. The courtroom is still as I button my charcoal jacket and address the judge as if he's the only other person in the room. "Your Honor," I say, "Father Ramon Aguirre is a respected priest, scholar and community leader, who has been accused of a terrible crime that he did not commit. We will demonstrate that the police and the district attorney have made a colossal error by rushing to judgment without carefully examining the evidence. We intend to conduct a full defense to clear his name so that he may return to his duties at St. Peter's."

I pause to see if I can sense any reaction from the judge, but I'm out of luck. He has a better poker face than Tommy.

"Your Honor," I continue, "our only objective is to find the truth." This is complete bullshit, but I want to try to win a few credibility points by acknowledging certain indisputable facts. "Father Aguirre visited Ms. Concepcion's apartment to provide counseling on the night she died. He used a kitchen knife to cut an apple. Coincidentally, it appears the very same knife was used to slash Ms. Concepcion's wrists. Ms. Ward will introduce evidence suggesting Father Aguirre inflicted those wounds, but we will show that he didn't." I don't want to telegraph the portion of our defense where our medical expert will testify that she committed suicide—it's too early in the game. "I would ask you to keep an open mind and weigh the evidence carefully."

I have a tendency to try to provide for all the holes in our case before the prosecution points them out, and Rosie gives me a signal to speed it up. We agreed that I would also address the most damaging issue. "Your Honor," I say, "it has been reported that Father Aguirre is the father of Ms. Concepcion's unborn child."

The courtroom is hushed, and Judge Tsang leans forward.

"In the spirit of finding the truth, I can confirm that he is, in fact, the father of the unborn fetus. He has admitted it, and he has no reason to lie—about anything."

I get a muted reaction from the back of the courtroom.

"Your Honor," I say, "Father Aguirre is deeply saddened by the death of Ms. Concepcion and his unborn child. He attempted to help a parishioner who was desperate to have a baby by acting as a donor so she could be artificially inseminated. The procedure was successful, and Ms. Concepcion became pregnant. Father Aguirre acted out of compassion, and any suggestion that this matter was the result of a sordid affair is absurd. The accusation that he murdered Ms. Concepcion is an unsubstantiated claim of the worst kind. Those are the facts, Your Honor. Two lives have been lost. Let us not compound this tragedy by sending a moral man to prison for a crime he did not commit."

JOHNNY NEVINS IS a good cop and a great character. The outgoing younger brother of one of my classmates at St. Ignatius has a quick smile and a glib manner. At five-five and a wiry hundred and thirty pounds, Johnny was a lightning-fast running back who still holds several school records. He was also the guy who organized the illicit beer parties with the girls from St. Mary's. His dad and four older siblings are all cops, and it was preordained that he would end up with the SFPD. Johnny developed a deft touch for undercover work that has taken him to some of the seamiest corners of San Francisco. Now in his mid-forties, he gave up Vice a couple of years ago after he took a bullet in a drug bust. He trains new recruits at his old stomping grounds at Mission Station, where the kids can't keep up with him.

Ward approaches the witness box, and Johnny greets her with an affable smile. His crow's-feet and graying hair reveal his age, but the boyish eyes haven't changed. He tells her he's been a cop for twenty-two years. "I enrolled at the academy on my twenty-first birthday," he says, "just like my dad and my brothers."

It's Ward's turn to beam. You can't find a more engaging witness. She furrows her brow in a manner that suggests she's attempting to elicit great wisdom when she asks, "Were you the first officer called to the victim's apartment on Monday, December first?"

"Yes, ma'am."

He uses the term *ma'am* only when he's in court.

"What time was that?"

"Nine thirty-six A.M." He says he responded to a nine-one-one call placed by Concepcion's mother. "I was driving by myself toward Mission Station when the call came in. I was returning from an errand."

"Where?"

"The donut store."

A smattering of laughter. Johnny can charm the chrome off a tailpipe.

In response to Ward's question about what he did when he arrived, Johnny leans back and says, "I followed standard police procedures for securing a crime scene."

I didn't expect him to say he stole all of Concepcion's valuables.

He adds, "I provided comfort to Ms. Concepcion's mother and I called for help."

"I trust you didn't disturb any evidence?"

I need to put an end to this lovefest. "Objection, Your Honor," I say. "Leading. We'll stipulate that Officer Nevins complied with all applicable rules in securing the scene." I'm not going to win any claims that Johnny mishandled the evidence.

"Sustained."

Ward remains unfazed and asks him if he checked the body for a pulse.

"I did." He glances at Lita, and his tone turns solemn when he says, "Unfortunately, I was unable to find one."

Ward lets the answer hang. The fact that he found the body is no bombshell, but from a prosecutorial perspective, she's ticked off the first item on her checklist: there is a victim. Johnny confirms that the paramedics took the body out of the bathtub in an unsuccessful effort to revive her. "Inspector Banks and Inspector Johnson of the Homicide Division arrived a short time later and took over responsibility for the scene," he says. "We assembled a team, and we began to canvass the area for witnesses."

"Did you find any?"

"A neighbor heard the defendant and Ms. Concepcion arguing at approximately nine forty-five the previous night. Another witness saw the defendant leave Ms. Concepcion's apartment at ten-oh-two. A third witness, Mr. Nicholas Hanson, saw the defendant return to Ms. Concepcion's building at approximately eleven forty-five P.M., and leave a short time later."

She's ticked off another item on her list: she's placed Ramon at the scene—not just once, but twice. She keeps Johnny up on the stand to talk about crime-scene procedures and evidence collection, and she introduces a poster-size diagram of Concepcion's apartment. I make a few gratuitous objections, but his testimony is factual and I have no grounds to complain. Good lawyers know you have to pick your spots. She has all that she needs less than ten minutes later when she turns to me and says, "Your witness."

I button my jacket and head to the lectern. Johnny has established a rapport with everybody in the courtroom, and I don't want to crowd him. It's unwise to mount a full frontal attack on a likable witness, but I can't afford to roll over. "Officer Nevins," I say, "you mentioned that you spoke to a witness who heard Father Aguirre's voice inside Ms. Concepcion's apartment at approximately nine forty-five that night."

"That's correct."

"Did she see him enter Ms. Concepcion's apartment?"

"No."

Good. "How did she know it was Father Aguirre?"

"She had met him on a couple of occasions."

"Did she know him well?"

"No, she didn't."

"Yet she was able to positively identify his voice?"

"Yes, she was."

"Do you know the approximate age of the witness?"

"Sixty-four."

I ask if she was in good health.

Ward decides to try to slow me down. "Objection. Officer Nevins isn't a doctor."

"Sustained."

"I'll rephrase." I turn back to Johnny and say, "Without making any medical determinations, did it appear to you that the witness was in good health?"

Ward starts to stand, but reconsiders.

Nevins says, "As far as I could tell."

"Did she have any trouble hearing you when you questioned her?"

"No."

"Did you ask her what she was doing that night?"

"Watching television."

"Was her door open?"

"No."

"So a woman in her mid-sixties who was watching TV was able to positively identify the voice of a man whom she'd met on only a couple of occasions?"

"That's correct."

"And she was absolutely sure it was Father Aguirre?"

"Yes."

In other circumstances, I might be able to win this case by claiming she was mistaken or that her hearing was bad, but we already know that Ramon was there and I'll lose credibility if I suggest he wasn't. I move on to a more important legal point when I ask, "Did she see Father Aguirre stab Ms. Concepcion?"

"No."

"Did any witnesses see him stab Ms. Concepcion?"

"No."

"So, as far as you know, it is possible that someone other than Father Aguirre may have stabbed her, right?"

I get the expected objection from Ward. "Speculative," she says.

Time for semantic games. "Your Honor," I say, "I'm not asking Officer Nevins to speculate. I'm asking for his personal knowledge based upon his expertise as to whether it's possible that someone other than Father Aguirre may have stabbed Ms. Concepcion."

Judge Tsang sees it my way. "Overruled."

Nevins rolls his eyes and says, "I have no personal knowledge that the defendant stabbed the victim, nor did I interview anyone who had personal knowledge that he had done so."

We're on the board. I've established that this is a purely circumstantial case. "Officer Nevins," I say, "you don't know how Ms. Concepcion died, do you?"

"It isn't my job to make that determination."

"But as far as you know, she may have taken her own life, right?"

Ward is up again. "Objection. The question is speculative and calls for the witness to come to a conclusion based on expertise for which no foundation has been established."

"I'm not calling upon Officer Nevins to make a medical determination," I say.

Judge Tsang doesn't buy it. "It sounds to me that it is exactly what you're asking."

True. "Not true. I'm simply trying to demonstrate that Officer Nevins has no personal knowledge as to the cause of Ms. Concepcion's death, and, thus, he cannot rule out a suicide."

Judge Tsang exchanges a glance with Nevins, then he turns back to me and says, "I'm going to sustain the objection, Mr. Daley. If you want to ask someone to provide a medical opinion as to the cause of death, I would suggest you talk to the chief medical examiner."

That's precisely what I intend to do.

CHAPTER 44

"It's in My Report"

Dr. Roderick Beckert has handled the autopsy in every major murder investigation since Richard Nixon was in the White House.

—Profile of Dr. Roderick Beckert,
San Francisco Chronicle

THERE'S BEEN A change in the lineup when we resume, and Bill McNulty has taken Nicole Ward's place at the podium. Ward had her moment of glory when she opened in front of a packed house, but she's astutely handed the ball over to her best nuts-and-bolts interrogator. McNasty's face is contorted into the familiar grimace. What he lacks in charm, he makes up for in preparation and tenacity. His voice fills with reverence when he says to the next witness, "Please state your name and occupation for the record."

"Dr. Roderick Beckert." His tone exudes the confidence of Barry Bonds when he's swinging at a belt-high fastball over the middle of the plate. "I've been the chief medical examiner of the city and county of San Francisco for thirty-seven years." He settles into the uncomfortable wooden chair and pours himself a glass of water. The camel-hair jacket and the cheap paisley tie have been replaced by a charcoal Wilkes Bashford double-breasted

suit and a subdued rep tie. He may be a character in the
bowels of the Hall, but he's all business in court.

McNulty is clutching a copy of the autopsy report with
the same respect that one would use when holding a Bible.
He approaches Beckert cautiously and lobs the first soft-
ball. "Would you be kind enough to summarize your academic and professional qualifications?"

Some of the younger reporters might be interested in
hearing about Beckert's advanced degrees from Johns
Hopkins and his teaching career at UCSF, but I've heard
it before and I'm inclined to skip the recitation. "Your
Honor," I say, "we're prepared to stipulate to Dr. Beckert's expertise in the field of pathology."

Judge Tsang is pleased. "The record will reflect the
fact that the defense has stipulated to Dr. Beckert's qualifications," he says.

McNulty takes a moment to find his place in his carefully scripted notes. He was planning to walk Beckert
through his credentials, and now he has to fast-forward
his presentation. He holds up a copy of the report and
asks, "Do you recognize this document?"

Beckert identifies his report, and McNulty introduces
it into evidence. I don't challenge its existence, but I'll
take a few potshots at what's inside.

McNulty approaches the witness box, hands Beckert
his report and begins slowly. "When did you first see Ms.
Concepcion's body?"

"It's in my report." He leafs through the document and
says, "I arrived at her apartment at ten-thirty A.M. on
Tuesday, December second."

McNulty lowers his voice and asks if Concepcion was still alive at the time.

"No, she was not."

The courtroom is silent.

"Dr. Beckert," McNulty continues, "where was the body when you first saw it?"

"On the floor of her bathroom." He glances at Lita and explains that she found her daughter's body in the bathtub at nine-thirty that morning. "She called the police and the paramedics immediately, but it was too late. The paramedics moved the body from the tub to the floor in their attempts to revive her, but their efforts were unsuccessful."

"At what time was Ms. Concepcion pronounced dead?"

"Ten thirty-four A.M." Beckert correctly notes that an official pronouncement doesn't necessarily coincide with the time of death. "The victim is pronounced when medical personnel arrive. Ms. Concepcion had passed away quite some time before her body was discovered."

Medical examiners never use euphemisms such as *passed away* unless a member of the victim's immediate family is present.

"Dr. Beckert," McNulty continues, "were you able to make a determination as to the time of death?"

"It was between ten forty-five on Monday night and one o'clock on Tuesday morning. He goes through a clinical analysis of blood loss, body temperature, lividity and extent of digestion of the food in Concepcion's stomach in support of his conclusion.

McNulty gives him an inquisitive look and says, "As I

recall, the initial version of your report set forth a different time frame."

"It did." Beckert acknowledges that he first concluded Concepcion could have died as early as nine-thirty. "Based upon credible evidence provided by a witness who was present at the scene, I revised my original analysis."

"Would you describe that evidence?"

"The witness saw the victim walking to her apartment at approximately ten-forty P.M."

"Which means she was still alive at that time."

Nothing escapes McNulty's keen eye.

"That's correct," Beckert says. "The name of the witness is Nicholas Hanson."

We'll be hearing from him shortly.

McNulty is still doing damage control. "It isn't uncommon for you to change your conclusions from time to time, is it?"

"No. When new and better facts become available, we add them to the analysis."

"Can you be more precise about the time of death?"

"I'm afraid not. The fact that the body was submerged in water prior to its discovery made an exact determination impossible."

"Dr. Beckert," McNulty says, "you concluded the cause of Ms. Concepcion's death was blood loss, correct?"

I can't make it that easy for him. "Objection," I say. "Leading."

"Sustained."

McNulty gives me an impatient sigh and says, "I'll rephrase the question, Your Honor."

I knew he would.

"Were you able to make a determination of the cause of Ms. Concepcion's death?"

"Yes. She experienced significant injuries that led to acute hypotension, which ultimately resulted in a cessation of vital bodily functions. In layman's terms, she bled to death."

"And you have no reason to doubt your conclusion?"

"Objection," I say. "Asked and answered."

"Sustained."

McNulty darts an apologetic look toward Concepcion's mother and then launches a preemptive strike in anticipation of our next argument. "Did you consider the possibility that Ms. Concepcion may have committed suicide?"

"I did, and I concluded she did not." He parrots the analysis he gave me at his office. He emphasizes Ramon's thumbprints on the back of Concepcion's neck and swears that he found evidence of a trauma on her right shoulder. I object sporadically and for all practical purposes, inconsequentially.

McNulty returns to the podium. "Dr. Beckert," he says, "did you find any alcohol in the victim's bloodstream?"

"A slight amount. She was well below the threshold for driving under the influence."

"What about prescription medications or other substances, illegal or otherwise?"

It's a standard ploy: he's ruling out an accidental overdose.

"None," Beckert says. He confirms that Concepcion's medical records indicated she had been given a prescription for Prozac.

McNulty picks up his notes and rolls them into a tube that he uses to gesture. "Was there anything else of note about Ms. Concepcion's physical condition prior to the time she died?"

"She was pregnant."

McNulty reacts as if he's just revealed a deep, dark secret. "Did you conduct any tests on the baby?"

He could just as easily have chosen the term *fetus* or *unborn child,* but *baby* has greater emotional impact and I'll sound like a jackass if I object.

"Yes, we did," Beckert says. "The baby was approximately eight weeks in gestation and was approaching a point where viability was possible."

McNulty is standing at the podium with his chin resting in his right palm. "Were you able to make any determination as to the health of the baby?" he asks.

"The baby had no identifiable medical complications."

"In other words, Ms. Concepcion was carrying a healthy baby?"

How many times are they going to use the word *baby*? "Objection," I say. "Asked and answered."

"Sustained."

"Dr. Beckert," McNulty says, "did you conduct DNA tests to determine the identity of the baby's father?"

"Objection," I say. "We've stipulated that Father Aguirre is the father."

"Sustained."

The fact that we've admitted it doesn't diminish its impact.

McNulty folds his notes and tucks them into his breast pocket. "No further questions."

I DON'T WANT Judge Tsang to call a recess, and I walk to the lectern before McNulty sits down. I'm not going to win this case during cross-exam, but I have to set a tone that casts doubt on some of Beckert's conclusions. If I can't prove it to the judge, maybe I can get Jerry Edwards to pick up the scent.

"Dr. Beckert," I say, "you concluded Ms. Concepcion died between ten forty-five P.M. on Monday, December first, and one A.M. on Tuesday, December second."

"Correct."

"You had to change your original opinion as to the time of death after you received information from a witness who said Ms. Concepcion was still alive at ten-forty that night, didn't you?"

"I received evidence of the later sighting after I had released my original report. As a matter of good practice, I was compelled to amend it."

"Is it possible your conclusion as to time of death could change even more as additional information is compiled?"

"I look at the totality of the evidence, and I draw my conclusions based on the best information and science available at the time. If you present credible evidence that

I have made a mistake, I will reevaluate my conclusions and reissue my report."

"How often does this happen?"

"Occasionally."

"When was the last time you reissued a report?"

"Objection. Relevance."

"Overruled."

Beckert looks up at the ceiling to suggest he's trying to remember something that happened a long time ago, in a galaxy far away. "I believe it was about five years ago."

"What did you get wrong?"

"I concluded that a homicide was a suicide."

"What made you change your mind?"

"The perpetrator confessed."

We are unlikely to have a similar result in this case. "Dr. Beckert," I say, "there is evidence that Ms. Concepcion committed suicide." I state it as a fact and I'm surprised McNulty doesn't object, but Beckert doesn't need a lot of help.

"Intelligent people can disagree about many things," Beckert says.

"Your report indicates Ms. Concepcion bled to death after her wrists were slashed by a kitchen knife that was found adjacent to the bathtub, yet you didn't take into account the fact that Ms. Concepcion's fingerprints were on that knife."

"So were your client's."

"My client has admitted he handled the knife to cut an apple."

"So?"

You don't get to ask the questions. "Ms. Concepcion

was distraught and taking antidepressants. Based upon your earlier testimony, it appears that she hadn't taken her Prozac that night. Reasonable people might put these facts together to conclude she used the knife to slash her own wrists."

"That isn't what happened."

I didn't expect him to agree with me, but I want to cast a little doubt. "You also concluded that Ms. Concepcion was knocked unconscious before she was stripped, placed in the tub and had her wrists slashed."

"Correct."

"Yet your report contains no specific explanation as to how you concluded Father Aguirre did any of these things."

"We found an injury to her right shoulder. I therefore concluded that he inflicted a blow that rendered her unconscious. He then removed her clothing, placed her in the tub and inflicted the fatal wounds. We found his fingerprints on the back of her neck."

"Is it possible that Father Aguirre's fingerprints could be explained in another manner? Perhaps he gave her a back rub."

McNulty pops up. "Objection. Speculative."

"Overruled."

Beckert's tone turns condescending when he says, "Anything's possible, Mr. Daley."

Yes, it is. "How do you account for the fact that there were no substantial bumps or bruises to Ms. Concepcion's head or neck?"

"There was a bruise on the back of her right shoulder

that was not easily discernible to the naked eye. This suggests he hit her just hard enough to knock her out."

"He didn't hit her at all!" I snap.

"Yes, he did."

"Did you find any broken bones or bruises from weapons—perhaps a stun gun?"

"I would have mentioned it in my report if I had."

"It sounds like you made the same mistake about five years ago."

McNulty gets up and says, "Objection, Your Honor. Argumentative."

"Sustained."

I'm just warming up. "Your report also indicates that much of Ms. Concepcion's body was covered with a skin cream called Essential Elements."

He nods.

"Did it occur to you that she may have been trying to make herself comfortable as she was taking her own life?"

"I thought it might be possible, but I found the cream in certain sensitive areas where it would have caused her great pain. She simply wouldn't have done it."

"Maybe she was careless."

"Maybe she was murdered."

"Did you find skin cream on her neck?"

"No."

"If Father Aguirre was trying to cover his tracks by faking a suicide and he knew his fingerprints were on her neck, wouldn't he have tried to cover them with skin cream?"

"Perhaps the defendant wasn't that careful or sophisticated."

"Yet you think he was sophisticated enough to try to fake a suicide?"

"Yes, I do."

I return to the lectern, pick up my notes and say, "It's your belief that Father Aguirre killed Ms. Concepcion when he returned to her apartment building at approximately eleven forty-five on the night of Monday, December first, isn't it?"

"Yes."

"And it's your theory that he entered her apartment, knocked her unconscious, removed her clothing, took her into her bathroom, covered her body with skin cream, placed her in her bathtub, slit her wrists and drew her bath water?"

"We've covered this issue, Mr. Daley."

Okay. "How long do you think it took him to do it?"

"I have no idea."

"Ballpark guess."

McNulty is up. "Objection. Speculative."

"Your Honor," I say, "I have stipulated to the fact that Dr. Beckert is an expert in his field. In determining the time of death, he must have factored in the length of time it would have taken a perpetrator to do all of the things I just mentioned."

"I'll allow it."

I wasn't sure he'd give me that one.

Beckert tries evasion. "It would be difficult for me to hazard a guess," he says.

Not good enough. I ask the judge to instruct Beckert to answer, and he obliges.

Beckert gives McNulty a helpless look and says, "He could have performed all of those tasks in just a few minutes."

I bore in. "How many minutes?"

"It's difficult to say."

"Two minutes? Five minutes? Ten minutes?"

"Less than five minutes, but I don't know for sure."

Good enough. "And you would acknowledge that if Father Aguirre never entered Ms. Concepcion's apartment for the second time, or was there for a very short time, it is unlikely he could have done all of the things I just mentioned, right?"

"Objection," McNulty says. "Speculative."

I'm also trying to put words into the witness's mouth.

Judge Tsang gives me a look that says "Nice try." "The objection is sustained."

I've made my point. "No further questions, Your Honor."

CHAPTER 45

"Nice to See You Again, Your Honor"

It isn't just the story—it's how you tell it.

—Nick Hanson, *San Francisco Chronicle*

"THAT DIDN'T GO very well," Ramon observes.

We're sitting in the consultation room behind Judge Tsang's courtroom during the morning break. His glass of water is untouched, and his face is flushed.

I give him a reasonably honest appraisal. "We scored some points," I say, "but the prosecutors always have the upper hand at the beginning."

In reality, things went downhill after my cross of Beckert. McNulty called a veteran crime-scene expert named Kathleen Jacobsen, who deftly placed Ramon's prints on the knife, Concepcion's neck and the bathtub faucets, and handled my challenging questions about glue fuming with great dexterity. Concepcion's neighbor then gave a compelling account of the tension between the two former lovers when she testified that she heard them arguing. McNulty continued with a brief, but powerful, presentation by Concepcion's therapist, an articulate New Age guru named Pamela Swartz, who told us in no uncertain terms that

pregnant women don't commit suicide. This led to an out-
burst by Maria's mother, who was gently escorted from the
courtroom by a burly bailiff. That's when Judge Tsang decided it was time for a break.

Ramon pushes his glass of water aside and says, "I
was hoping you would have persuaded Dr. Beckert to
change his mind about suicide."

"He won't."

"He reconsidered his conclusion on the time of death."

"Only after he was presented with Nick Hanson's
testimony."

"I trust you've saved some good stuff for our defense."

It's still a work in progress. "We have."

"Have you reconsidered your decision not to let me
testify?"

"We haven't."

FOR COURTROOM AFICIONADOS, an appearance
by Nick the Dick is as rare and as widely anticipated as a
Bruce Springsteen concert. The jaunty PI looks like a
politician as he makes his way down the center aisle and
pumps the hand of everybody within reach. An inveterate
and equal-opportunity schmoozer, he greets Ward, Mc-
Nulty, Rosie and then me.

When the bailiff asks Nick if he swears to tell the
truth the whole truth and nothing but the truth, he responds with a wide smile and says, "Indeed I do." He
extends a hand to Judge Tsang and chirps, "Nice to see
you again, Your Honor."

The judge ignores the outstretched palm and motions

him toward the stand. "Please take your seat, Mr. Hanson."

The chuckles in the gallery are cut off by Judge Tsang's gavel. Nick climbs up into the witness box, adjusts his boutonniere, runs a hand through his toupee and pours himself a glass of water. He flashes another grin at Judge Tsang, then nods toward McNulty, who is standing at the podium with an uncharacteristic expression that almost resembles a smile.

McNulty asks, "Would you please state your name and occupation for the record?"

"Nick Hanson. In the daytime I'm a PI, and at night I write mysteries. My next book is coming out after the first of the year."

He always manages to work in a plug for his favorite author.

McNulty asks him how long he's been a PI.

"Sixty-eight years." Nick takes his own sweet time telling us his life story—and it's a good one. He was born in North Beach and educated on the tough streets of the Barbary Coast. He became a PI out of necessity after his father was jailed for bootlegging. It would be suicidal for me to interrupt him. Our only saving grace is that McNulty is questioning him in the monotone that he uses for cops and forensic experts.

McNulty turns to the business at hand. "Mr. Hanson," he says, "you were conducting surveillance on the evening of Monday, December first, at the apartment building where the victim lived, weren't you?"

"Indeed I was." He says the archdiocese hired him to

obtain background information on Concepcion and to identify any potential witnesses.

"How long were you employed by the archdiocese?"

"For about six months. We were hired to keep Ms. Concepcion's apartment under surveillance twenty-four hours a day." He explains that he and his sons worked in ten-hour shifts. "I was situated on the roof of a garage across the alley that runs behind Ms. Concepcion's building."

"How did you happen to choose that vantage point?"

"It gave us an unobstructed view of the back of Ms. Concepcion's apartment, and it allowed us to remain inconspicuous."

"Could you also see the back door to Ms. Concepcion's apartment?"

"No. Our view was obstructed by her garage. However, we could see the gate that led to the passageway, as well as the windows to her bedroom and kitchen."

"Was anyone assisting you in these surveillance activities that night?"

"My son Rick was watching the front of the building from a parked car on Capp Street."

"Could anyone have gone in or out without having been seen by you or your son?"

"We're professionals, Mr. McNulty." His story doesn't change. He confirms that Ramon entered through the front door at eight o'clock and left via the rear door at ten. He saw Concepcion depart at ten-twenty and return at ten-forty. Ramon returned on foot at eleven forty-five, went in the back gate and left a few minutes later. There is nothing new, except the story is being told by a master.

Most important for McNulty, it places Ramon at the scene a second time that night.

"Mr. Hanson," McNulty says, "do you have any idea why the defendant returned to Ms. Concepcion's apartment?"

"Objection," I say. "Speculative, and Mr. McNulty is mischaracterizing this witness's earlier testimony. Mr. Hanson said he saw Father Aguirre enter the backyard to Ms. Concepcion's building, but he did not—and could not—see him enter her apartment. In fact he testified that he could not see the back door from his vantage point."

"Sustained."

McNulty tries it another way. "Could you see into her apartment last Monday night?"

"No."

McNulty freezes. "Why not?"

"The blinds were closed."

McNulty acts as if this isn't a significant issue, but it will give me a little ammunition, and he changes course. "Why did the defendant return to Ms. Concepcion's building?" he asks.

I'm up. "Objection. Speculative."

"Sustained."

McNulty presses forward. "Is it likely he may have gone inside?"

"Objection. Still speculative."

"Sustained."

"Is it possible he may have gone inside?"

"Objection. More speculation."

"Sustained."

"Mr. Hanson," McNulty says. "Did you or your son

see anybody else enter Ms. Concepcion's apartment that night?" He can't prove that Ramon went inside, but he can try to confirm that nobody else did, either.

"No."

"How was the defendant's demeanor when he left the second time?"

"Objection," I say. "Speculation as to the defendant's state of mind."

"Your Honor," McNulty says, "I'm asking him to describe the defendant's appearance."

I'm going to lose this one.

"Overruled."

Nick says, "He was in a hurry."

"Do you know why?"

"Objection. Speculative."

"Sustained."

"Mr. Hanson," McNulty says, "is it possible the defendant was in a hurry because he had just murdered Ms. Concepcion and was trying to leave the scene as quickly as possible?"

"Objection. Speculative."

"Sustained."

He's placed Ramon at Concepcion's building at eleven forty-five and demonstrated a likelihood that he went inside, but he can't go any farther. "No further questions, Your Honor."

Rosie leans over and whispers, "You have to go after him."

I button my jacket and remind myself to keep my tone unfailingly professional. I'll lose points if I question his credentials or stamina, and I'll go down hard if I start trading wisecracks with him. I nod respectfully from the lectern and look into the congenial eyes of the legendary PI. "Mr. Hanson," I say, "you testified that you were keeping Ms. Concepcion's apartment under surveillance last Monday night, right?" I'm trying to elicit yes-or-no answers.

"Correct."

"Were you there all night?"

"No." McNulty and Ward exchange a glance, but they don't say anything. Nick gives me a fatherly nod and says, "I had to leave for a short time around twelve-thirty."

"I thought you were hired to provide round-the-clock surveillance."

"I was, but I received a phone call from my other son, Nick Jr., who was keeping Ms. Concepcion's client under surveillance. He was concerned somebody was following her, but it turned out to be a false alarm."

"Did you leave your post at Ms. Concepcion's apartment to assist him?"

"Yes. I went to her client's place of employment."

"That would have been the Mitchell Brothers' Theater?"

"Correct."

A few murmurs in the back of the courtroom.

"That would be an adult theater, wouldn't it?"

"Objection," McNulty says. "Relevance."

"Sustained."

No problem. I ask Nick if he returned to his post later that morning.

"Around two A.M."

"By which time Ms. Concepcion was already dead."

"I don't know."

Here goes. "Did you enter Ms. Concepcion's apartment that night?"

"No."

"Did you enter it on any occasion?"

"No."

"Did you use electronic eavesdropping equipment or bug her phone?"

"The archdiocese has a policy against such tactics."

Quinn will be pleased that he recited the party line. "Mr. Hanson," I continue, "you testified earlier that you couldn't see the rear door to her apartment."

"That's correct."

"So," I say, "you couldn't see if anybody entered her building that night, could you?"

He responds with a grudging "True."

"And although you saw Father Aguirre enter her backyard at eleven forty-five, you have no direct personal knowledge as to whether he actually went inside her apartment, do you?"

"The only logical reason was to go back to her apartment."

I can't let him fudge. "Yes or no, Mr. Hanson—did you see Father Aguirre enter Ms. Concepcion's apartment at eleven forty-five that night?"

"No."

Good. "And it is therefore possible that he never did. In fact, he may have stayed in the gangway or left something outside her door without ever entering the building, right?"

"Objection. Speculative."

"Overruled."

Nick shakes his head and says, "I couldn't say, Mr. Daley."

I switch gears. "Mr. Hanson," I say, "you told the police that you saw Ms. Concepcion return to her apartment at approximately ten-forty that night."

"Correct."

"I trust she was very much alive at the time?"

"Of course."

Just checking. "What did Ms. Concepcion do when she got home?"

"I don't know. I just explained that I couldn't see inside."

"You couldn't see inside," I repeat. "She turned on the lights, didn't she?"

"Of course."

"When did she turn them off?"

Nick darts a glance toward McNulty, then he turns back to me and says, "Eleven-thirty."

"Were they still off when Father Aguirre returned?"

"Yes."

"Did Ms. Concepcion turn them on again when Father Aguirre entered her yard?"

"Not that I recall."

Good answer. "Were the lights on in her apartment at any time between the moment you saw Father Aguirre enter her yard and the time that he left?"

"Not that I recall."

"So, if she let Father Aguirre inside, they were conducting their business in the dark?"

"So it would seem."

"Didn't that strike you as a bit odd?"

"It didn't occur to me until you just raised it."

"According to Dr. Beckert, Father Aguirre entered Ms. Concepcion's apartment, knocked her unconscious, stripped off her clothing, started her bath, slashed her wrists, placed her in the bathtub and spread facial cream over her body in a clumsy attempt to fake a suicide."

McNulty is up. "Is there a question there somewhere?"

Not really. "How long was it from the time Father Aguirre entered Ms. Concepcion's gate until the time he left?"

"A few minutes."

"How many minutes is a few?"

"More than two, but less than ten."

"Less than five?"

"Maybe."

Close enough. "But it could have been even shorter, right? Maybe one or two minutes?"

"Maybe"

"So," I say, "based upon your sixty-eight years of experience, do you think it is plausible that Father Aguirre was able to do everything Dr. Beckert said in two or three minutes?"

McNulty is up again. "Objection, Your Honor. Speculative."

"Overruled."

Nick shrugs and gives me an honest answer. "I don't know."

I add, "Not to mention the fact that he did all of it in the dark?"

"Anything is possible, Mr. Daley."

Just the answer I wanted. "And it is also possible somebody other than Father Aguirre could have entered Ms. Concepcion's apartment while you weren't there and killed her, right?"

"Anything is possible," he repeats.

In the world of criminal defense attorneys, possibilities frequently lead to acquittals. "No further questions," I say.

CHAPTER 46

"A Classic Case of Motive, Means and Opportunity"

You continue to ask yourself if you have enough credible evidence to prove the defendant's guilt beyond a reasonable doubt. If you settle for anything less, you're wasting everybody's time.

—Marcus Banks, *San Francisco Chronicle*

"PLEASE STATE YOUR name for the record."

"Inspector Marcus Banks." He always includes his title when he introduces himself. He turns to the court reporter and adds, "B-A-N-K-S."

As if she didn't know.

Eleven-thirty. Nick the Dick's testimony was entertaining and may have piqued the interest of some of the reporters in the gallery, but it's time to get back to business. McNulty is bringing his presentation to a close by calling a battle-tested warrior to have the last word. Banks is ideally suited for the role—he looks and sounds like James Earl Jones.

McNulty remains at the podium as Banks recites his stellar credentials: forty-two years with the SFPD, with thirty-four in homicide; an array of commendations, decorations and medals. I let Marcus brag for a moment before I stipulate to his expertise. I want to get him off the stand as soon as possible.

"Inspector Banks," McNulty says, "you and your partner are the lead homicide investigators in the death of Ms. Concepcion." He's making statements instead of asking questions, but I'm not inclined to interrupt just yet.

"Correct."

"Could you please describe your investigative procedures?"

McNulty got caught up in the moment with Nick Hanson and got a little sloppy, but he's reverting to form. He's going to walk Banks through each and every piece of evidence in his customary methodical manner. It isn't scintillating theater, but it's effective. McNulty leads him through thirty minutes of textbook direct exam. I object inconsequentially as Banks starts with the securing of the scene, continues with a description of every shred of evidence found in Concepcion's apartment and concludes with a concise analysis of how the pieces fit together. It's also a blatant attempt to run out the clock on this morning's court session, thereby giving Judge Tsang a long lunch hour to digest a turkey sandwich and the prosecution's case without significant interference from me. McNulty finishes by asking Banks to summarize his reasons for concluding that Ramon murdered Concepcion.

The warhorse clears his throat and says, "The defendant was present at Ms. Concepcion's apartment on two occasions that night. She left her apartment for about twenty minutes, but she came back a short time later, and there is uncontroverted evidence she was present when he returned. We originally thought the defendant may have killed her during his first visit, but the eyewitness accounts thereafter led us to conclude he killed her on his return."

He's tailored his story to account for Nick the Dick's testimony.

Banks is still talking. "The defendant and Ms. Concepcion had a volatile history and exchanged heated words earlier that evening. His fingerprints were on the murder weapon, the victim's body and in the room in which the victim was found. He has offered no explanation for his actions, and our chief medical examiner has ruled out a possible suicide." Banks turns and addresses Judge Tsang directly. "Your Honor," he says, "this is a classic case of motive, means and opportunity. There is sufficient evidence to bind the defendant over for trial."

That's that.

The judge glances at his watch, and then he turns to me and asks, "Do you plan to conduct a lengthy cross-exam?"

"Just a few questions, Your Honor." It's the sort of blatant lie you use when you're trying to recruit somebody to serve on the PTA or coach Little League. You suck them in by telling them the time commitment will be minimal.

The judge gives me a legitimately skeptical look and says, "Proceed."

The gloves are off, and it's time for hand-to-hand combat. The reporters in the gallery will be heading outside to do live updates as soon as we're done, and I want to give them something to talk about. I walk up to Banks and get in his face. "Inspector," I say, "when we first met, you believed that Ms. Concepcion was killed prior to ten o'clock last Monday night, didn't you?"

"It was one of the scenarios we had considered."

"But your analysis changed when you discovered she was very much alive after ten o'clock, didn't it?"

"We obtained new evidence from a reliable source, and we adjusted our analysis to account for it. The fact remains that your client was seen entering her building at eleven forty-five P.M. last Monday night, and Ms. Concepcion wasn't seen alive after that."

I correct him. "Mr. Hanson testified that he saw Father Aguirre enter the gate leading to Ms. Concepcion's backyard. He didn't actually see anyone enter her apartment."

"You can put two and two together."

So can everybody in this courtroom. "For the record," I say, "did Mr. Hanson or anyone else see Father Aguirre reenter Ms. Concepcion's apartment that night?"

"No."

Good enough. I suggest that Ramon couldn't have knocked Concepcion unconscious, undressed her, slit her wrists, covered her body with skin cream and drawn her bath in the short time he was seen in the vicinity by Nick the Dick.

"It doesn't take long to commit murder," he says.

"And you think he could have done all of this in a matter of a couple of minutes?"

"Desperate people do desperate things."

So do desperate lawyers. I steal a glance at Rosie, who touches her index finger to her nose—the signal to move on. "Inspector," I say, "did you ever consider any other suspects?"

"The evidence didn't lead in any other direction."

Time for some smoke. "Ms. Concepcion phoned a restaurant called Eduardo's Latin Palace earlier that evening, didn't she? And you found a partially eaten burrito from that establishment in her kitchen, didn't you?"

"Yes."

"You are aware that Ms. Concepcion and the proprietor of that restaurant had terminated an extramarital affair a few months earlier, aren't you?"

"Yes."

"The fact that she called his restaurant on the night she died didn't cause you to consider him as a suspect?"

"We questioned him, and we concluded that she did not have any direct contact with him that night."

"You took his word for it?"

"We were able to corroborate his story by talking to his staff."

"You didn't consider the possibility that his employees lied on his behalf?"

"We never take anybody's statement at face value."

I ask, "Did you also question Mr. Lopez's estranged wife?"

"Yes. We ruled her out, too."

And I can't place either of them in her apartment that night. "Ms. Concepcion also spoke to her ex-husband by phone that night, didn't she?"

"Yes, she did, but we have no evidence he was anywhere near her apartment that night."

Neither do we. "But you would acknowledge that their relationship was contentious?"

"So is my relationship with my ex-wife."

A smattering of laughter in the back of the courtroom.

I keep pushing. "Ms. Concepcion also had contact with the general counsel of the San Francisco Archdiocese that night, didn't she?"

"They spoke by phone."

"And their relationship was also contentious, wasn't it?"

"They were on opposite sides of litigation."

"Did you ever consider anybody associated with the archdiocese as a suspect?"

"We consider every possibility, but it's our job to look at the evidence to see what we can prove in court."

"Does that mean you've ruled out somebody connected to the archdiocese?"

"It means the evidence points toward your client."

I press him, but he doesn't budge, and I sense Judge Tsang is getting hungry. I return to the lectern and lower my voice. "Inspector," I say, "did you interview a woman known as Jane Doe?"

"Yes."

"Could you please explain to everybody in this courtroom who she was?"

McNulty interrupts us. "Objection," he says. "Relevance."

"Your Honor," I say, "Ms. Doe was going to be a key witness in this case. She was one of the last people who spoke to Ms. Concepcion before her death."

"I'll allow it," Judge Tsang says.

"Ms. Doe was Ms. Concepcion's client," Banks says. "She had brought a civil case against the archdiocese."

Not good enough. "For what?"

"Sexual harassment."

McNulty tries again. "Your Honor," he says, "I still fail to see the relevance of this line of questioning."

It's my turn to testify. "Ms. Doe spoke to Ms. Concepcion at approximately ten-thirty last Monday night, which means she may have been the last person to have talked to her before she died."

The judge goes my way. "The objection is overruled."

I turn back to Banks. "Inspector," I say, "can you please tell everybody in this courtroom why Ms. Doe is not available to testify today?"

"She was shot to death outside her place of employment last night."

"So now both the attorney and the plaintiff in that case are dead."

"Yes, they are."

I glance at Edwards and say, "It has been reported that Ms. Doe had a strong case against the archdiocese."

"That's for a court to decide."

"Does it strike you that it may be more than coincidental that Ms. Doe and her attorney are now both dead?"

McNulty is up. "Objection. Speculative."

"Sustained."

"Is it disturbing to you that the plaintiff in a high-profile civil case and a key witness in a murder trial was gunned down just as both cases were about to start?"

"Yes, it is."

"Do you have any idea who may have killed her?"

"The investigation is ongoing, and we are looking into all of the possibilities."

"Have you ruled out the possibility that Ms. Doe's death may be related in some manner to the death of Ms. Concepcion?"

"We haven't ruled out anything, Mr. Daley."

"Have you considered the possibility that somebody associated with the archdiocese may have decided to silence both of these women?"

McNulty leaps up and says, "Objection, Your Honor. Relevance. Speculative. Argumentative."

All of the above. The judge gave me more leeway than I had anticipated, and I need to tone down the rhetoric. "Withdrawn," I say. "No further questions."

Judge Tsang turns to McNulty and says, "Do you have any other witnesses?"

"No, Your Honor. The prosecution rests."

The judge looks to me and says, "I take it you'd like to make a motion?"

"Yes, Your Honor." I make the standard request that the charges be dropped as a matter of law on the theory that the prosecution hasn't met its threshold of proof.

"Denied. I'll expect you to be ready to call your first witness at two o'clock sharp."

CHAPTER 47

"How Long Can You Blow Smoke?"

The older I get, the less interested I am in money and fame. I'm far more interested in finding the truth.

—Dr. Robert Goldstein, *San Francisco Chronicle*

"WHAT THE HELL are you doing?" Rosie asks.

We're standing outside the courtroom during the lunch break. Ramon is in the consultation room down the corridor, where a uniform is standing guard.

"Trying to give the judge some other options," I say.

"Are you planning to accuse everybody who ever talked to Concepcion of murder?"

More or less. It's a variation on the time-tested defense strategy known as S-O-D-D-I—some other dude did it. "I'm trying to make something happen."

"That isn't the game plan."

"The game changed when they conceded that Concepcion was still alive after Ramon left at ten o'clock. It makes Doe's statement irrelevant, and we have to give the judge some alternatives."

"Then we should wait until trial."

"Ramon can't wait that long. His career is over if we can't show somebody else did it."

"His life may be over if we keep telegraphing our defense."

"Do you have any better ideas?"

She takes a deep breath and says, "At the moment, no."

I promise to lighten up on the hyperbole a bit, then my cell phone rings and I flip it open. "How far did the prosecution get?" Pete asks.

"They wrapped up. No bombshells."

"I take it that means you weren't able to persuade the judge to drop the charges?"

"Not yet. When will you be here?"

"As soon as I can. I went to see Fuentes again. He said he may have something for us. How long can you blow smoke?"

"How long do you need?"

"At least until tonight."

OUR FIRST WITNESS goes on at the stroke of two. "My name is Dr. Robert Goldstein," he says with genial authority. His jowls wiggle when he adds, "I'm an emeritus professor in the departments of pathology and trauma surgery at UCSF."

He's also one of the most accomplished bullshit artists in the San Francisco medical community. Now in his late sixties and semiretired, the once-impressive scholar works the lecture circuit and acts as a hired gun. Thankfully, Quinn's last official act before he withdrew as Ramon's attorney was to authorize payment of ten grand to Dr.

Goldstein, who spent a good two hours browsing through Beckert's report. Nice work if you can get it.

"Dr. Goldstein," I begin, "would you describe your expertise in the field of pathology?"

His impeccably coiffed gray hair matches his subdued Wilkes Bashford suit. His résumé can stand toe-to-toe with Beckert's, and his blue eyes gleam as he tells us he graduated from Stanford and went to medical school at Johns Hopkins. McNulty grudgingly stipulates to his qualifications.

I walk up to the witness box and offer him a copy of Beckert's report. "Are you familiar with this document?" I ask.

"I've studied it in great detail."

Or in as much detail as he could muster in a couple of hours of preparation time after he got home from the Warriors game on Saturday night.

He straightens his tie and his tone is deferential when he adds, "I've worked with Dr. Beckert for many years, and I have great respect for him."

Just the way we rehearsed it.

"That's why I was very surprised when I read this report," he says.

It's my cue. "Why is that, Dr. Goldstein?"

He shakes his head in feigned disbelief when he says, "I believe Dr. Beckert made an error in his analysis of the cause of death."

Gee, big surprise. I dart an incredulous glance at Edwards, then I turn back to Goldstein and ask, "Could you explain why?"

"Dr. Beckert concluded that Ms. Concepcion had been

knocked unconscious, but I could find no evidence of any such injury."

"Are you sure about that?"

McNulty makes his presence felt. "Objection," he says. "Asked and answered."

"Sustained."

No problem. I continue playing the straight man. "Would you please explain your conclusion?"

He responds with a transparent smile. "Of course, Mr. Daley." He addresses the judge directly when he says, "Would you mind if I took a moment outside the witness box to point out a couple of items from the autopsy photos?"

McNulty offers no objection.

Goldstein walks over to an easel that I've set up adjacent to the witness box where the judge and the gallery can watch him. He buttons his double-breasted suit and takes a gold Cross pen out of his pocket to gesture. He works without notes as he points to an enlarged photo of the area where Concepcion's neck meets her right shoulder. He makes a circling motion and says, "This is the area where Dr. Beckert claims that Ms. Concepcion was struck." He moves in closer and puts on his reading glasses—just the way I told him to. "Your Honor," he says, "I have studied this photograph along with various enhancements thereof with great care."

Grace spends more time on her math homework every night.

He straightens up and prepares to recite his carefully scripted lines. "Your Honor," he continues, "I cannot find any evidence of a significant trauma that would have caused Ms. Concepcion to have lost consciousness." He shakes his head vigorously and adds, "I did not have the benefit of examining the body, but our current photographic technology is excellent and it is very difficult for me to disagree with one of my most respected colleagues."

Unless somebody is willing to pay him ten grand to do it.

"As a result," he continues, "I believe Dr. Beckert's conclusion that Ms. Concepcion was knocked unconscious was incorrect. I'm sure Dr. Beckert would be willing to reconsider his determination if given the opportunity."

He's starting to ad lib, and I need to get to the punch line. "Dr. Goldstein," I say, "would you please state your conclusion as to Dr. Beckert's determination concerning the cause of Ms. Concepcion's death?"

He puts the pen into his pocket and returns to the stand. He clears his throat and summons his most authoritative tone. "I have concluded that it is highly unlikely that Ms. Concepcion committed suicide."

Air raid! Emergency! It's a trial lawyer's worst nightmare—a perfectly coached witness with an impeccable setup who fumbles the delivery. I struggle to keep my composure. "Dr. Goldstein," I say, "didn't you mean to say exactly the opposite?"

His confident demeanor gives way to a deer-in-the-headlights look. "What did I say?"

"You said it is *unlikely* that Ms. Concepcion committed suicide."

"I did?"

"Yes." You idiot.

"That's not what I meant," he stammers. "I meant to say that it is very *likely* that Ms. Concepcion *did* commit suicide."

"You're sure about that?"

"Absolutely."

I have him reiterate the correct conclusion once again, but the damage is done. As Nick Hanson likes to say, it isn't just the story—it's how you tell it. The judge's expression indicates that whatever points we made at the beginning of Goldstein's testimony were lost at the end. He turns to me and asks, "Do you have any more questions for this witness?"

"No, Your Honor."

The judge turns to McNulty and says, "Cross-exam?"

"No, Your Honor." He may as well have added, "I don't need it."

You can write the perfect script and have the perfect cast, but the show can go down the tubes if somebody flubs his lines.

The judge turns to me and says, "I need to take a short recess."

As we're leaving the courtroom, Edwards buttonholes me and says, "How much did you pay Goldstein?"

"Ten grand."

"Next time you ought to pay him a little extra to get it right."

CHAPTER 48

"Things Didn't Work Out"

Whereas, Eduardo Lopez is one of the moral pillars of St. Peter's Parish and the Mission District Community.

—Commendation issued by the San Francisco
Board of Supervisors

MERCEDES TRUJILLO ISN'T flirting today. She looks as if she'd rather be anywhere else in the world than the witness box when I ask her, "How long have you been a hostess at Eduardo's Latin Palace?"

Her long hair is pulled back into a tight ball, the big earrings are gone and her makeup is subdued. "For about two years," she whispers.

By the time we're finished, she may be unemployed. "Do you know a man named Eduardo Lopez?"

"He's my boss."

"Do you know him well?"

"Pretty well."

I'm tempted to ask her if she knows him in the biblical sense, but I'd be getting ahead of myself. "Did you know a woman named Maria Concepcion?"

"Yes, I did. She used to come to the restaurant. You could say she was a regular."

I could. "Ms. Concepcion knew Mr. Lopez pretty well, didn't she?"

"They were friends."

"In fact, they were more than friends, weren't they?"

She takes a deep breath, and her pouty lips form a tight ball. She looks around for help, but none is forthcoming. "Yes," she finally decides, "they were more than friends."

"In fact, they were lovers, weren't they?"

"I'm really uncomfortable talking about this."

I turn to the judge for help. "Ms. Trujillo," he says, "you'll have to answer the question."

"Mr. Lopez and Ms. Concepcion were involved in a romantic relationship," she says.

"Ms. Trujillo," I continue, "are you aware that Mr. Lopez and his wife have filed for a divorce?"

"I've never talked to them about it."

I'm sure this is true. "One might conclude that one of the reasons for their separation involved Mr. Lopez's extramarital affair with Ms. Concepcion."

"Objection, Your Honor. Assumes facts that have not been introduced into evidence."

"Sustained."

"Ms. Trujillo," I say, "you also had a relationship with Mr. Lopez, didn't you?"

She freezes for an instant before she says, "He was my boss."

"He was more than your boss, wasn't he?"

She doesn't respond immediately, and the judge instructs her to answer. "Mr. Lopez and I were romantically involved for a short time," she says. "Things didn't work out."

For anybody. "When were you seeing Mr. Lopez?"

"Last August and September."

"Was Mr. Lopez also seeing Ms. Concepcion during that time?"

"Yes, he was."

"So, Mr. Lopez was seeing both you and Ms. Concepcion earlier this year?"

McNulty tries to slow me down. "Objection," he says, "asked and answered."

Judge Tsang goes my way. "Overruled," he says.

Trujillo takes a deep breath and says, "Mr. Lopez was dating both of us for a short time."

Good. "And just so we're clear, he was still married at that time, wasn't he?"

Everybody in the courtroom knows the answer. "Yes, he was."

"Did Ms. Concepcion find out that Mr. Lopez was also seeing you?"

"Yes, she did."

"And how did she react?"

"Badly. She came to the restaurant and made a scene, then she went upstairs to Mr. Lopez's office and ended their relationship."

And she took a swing at him with his Louisville Slugger. "I take it she was upset?"

"That would be an understatement."

"Was Mr. Lopez also upset?"

"Very."

"Ms. Trujillo," I say, "did you and Mr. Lopez continue to see each other after that?"

"No. I told Mr. Lopez that I thought it would be better if we parted company."

"Yet you still work for him?"

"You have to pay the bills, Mr. Daley."

And she has a gold-plated sexual-harassment claim if she's fired. On to the pyrotechnics. "You mentioned that Mr. Lopez was upset that Ms. Concepcion broke up with him."

"Yes, he was."

Here goes. "Upset enough to kill her?"

This gets McNulty out of his chair. "Objection, Your Honor," he says. "Speculative."

"Sustained."

I'm just starting to speculate. "Ms. Trujillo," I say, "did Mrs. Lopez know that her husband was seeing you and Ms. Concepcion?"

"Yes. She called me and told me she'd hired a private investigator who had seen us."

"Did Mr. Lopez know about this?"

"Yes. I confronted him about it, and he told me that she already knew."

"Did he seem to care?"

"Not as far as I could tell."

Here we go again. "Was Mrs. Lopez upset about it?"

"Very."

"Upset enough to murder Ms. Concepcion?"

McNulty shoots up again. "Objection!" he shouts. "There isn't the slightest bit of foundation for this speculative line of questioning. Mr. Daley is desperately grasping at straws in order to suggest there may be other possible suspects in this case."

Yes, I am.

Judge Tsang knows exactly what I'm doing. "Sustained."

I glance at Edwards, then I turn back to Trujillo and ask, "When was the last time you spoke to Ms. Concepcion?"

"She called the restaurant to place an order last Monday night."

"Did she pick up the order?"

"I don't know."

"Did she have any contact with Mr. Lopez that night?"

"I don't know that, either."

"Did he leave the building at any time during your shift?"

"Not as far as I know."

"And what time did your shift conclude?"

"Twelve-thirty A.M."

"Ms. Trujillo," I say, "did you happen to leave the restaurant through the rear door?"

"Yes."

"And did you walk down the alley?"

"For about a block."

"Are you aware that Ms. Concepcion lived in a building that backs onto the same alley?"

"Yes, I am."

"Did you happen to see Ms. Concepcion or anyone else in the alley that night?"

"No."

"Was Mr. Lopez still at the restaurant when you left?"

"Yes. We walked out the back door at the same time."

It's around the same time Nick the Dick left his post—that would explain why he didn't see Trujillo or Lopez. "Is it possible that he paid a visit to Ms. Concepcion at some point after you left the restaurant that night?"

McNulty stops me. "Objection, Your Honor. Speculative."

"Sustained."

"It's possible that Mr. Lopez could have gone to Ms. Concepcion's apartment and killed her that night, isn't it?"

"Objection. The question is speculative and there is no foundation."

Yes, it is, and no, there isn't.

"Sustained."

"No further questions."

MERCEDES TRUJILLO may have been a reluctant witness, but Vicky Lopez most certainly is not. She's dressed in her own creations as she adjusts the microphone. Her olive skin is gleaming against an understated beige blouse. She tells an impressed gallery that she runs one of the most successful independent fashion-design firms in the country, and she appears quite ready to inflict a full-blown frontal assault on her husband's character. Never underestimate the pent-up anger in a jilted spouse.

"How long have you been married?" I ask.

"Twenty-seven years." I notice an approving nod from Judge Tsang as I take her through a brief recitation of a listing of her children and grandchildren.

"Mrs. Lopez," I say, "is it true that you and your husband have filed for divorce?"

"Yes, it is."

"Would you mind telling us why?"

Her voice doesn't go up a single decibel when she says, "My husband is a cheating pig."

Just the dignified tone I was hoping for. Judge Tsang silences the gallery with a single bang of his gavel.

The marriage counseling is over and the gloves are off as Vicky Lopez catalogues her husband's infidelities. She acknowledges that she hired Nick the Dick, who reported on her husband's relationships with Concepcion, Trujillo and several others. "Eduardo was probably cheating from the day we got married," she concludes.

This confirms that he's a jerk, but it still doesn't place him at Concepcion's apartment last Monday night. "Mrs. Lopez," I say, "how did you feel when you first heard that your husband was cheating on you?"

"How do you think I felt?"

This works better when I ask the questions. "Angry?"

"Irate. It was humiliating."

Fair enough. "Did you confront him?"

"Yes. He denied everything. I told him that I would leave him if he cheated again. He didn't think I meant it, but believe me, I did."

I believe you. "You knew Ms. Concepcion, didn't you?"

"Yes, I did. I was furious when Mr. Hanson told me about it."

"At Ms. Concepcion?"

"At my husband."

Not the right answer for establishing the ever-popular Jealous-Wife-with-a-Motive theory, but it throws a little more mud on his reputation. "Did you confront her about it?"

"I confronted my husband."

Dammit. "And?"

"He denied it."

True to form. "Is that when you filed for divorce?"

"Yes." I let her vent. It's entertaining to wash the Lopez family's dirty laundry in public and I realize she's building an impressive case for her divorce proceedings, but the purpose of this exercise is to provide evidence that Eduardo may have been so angry at his ex-girlfriend that he killed her. Unfortunately, there is none. Our next option involves smoke and mirrors.

"Mrs. Lopez," I say, "where were you on the night of Monday, December first?"

"At my shop." She says she was there until about twelve-thirty A.M. "I like to work at night because it's quiet."

"Did you go straight home?"

"Yes." She says she lives within a mile of her store. "I'm still living at our house, which is at Twenty-fifth and Bryant. My husband has taken an apartment at Twenty-fifth and Folsom."

"Did you have any contact with Ms. Concepcion that night?"

"None."

I didn't expect her to say that she bumped into her in the alley behind her apartment just before she went upstairs and killed her. "Did you speak to your husband that evening?"

"We had a telephone conversation around eight o'clock. We were trying to work out a time to get together with our lawyers to iron out the final details of our divorce settlement."

McNulty stands and says, "I fail to see the relevance of this questioning."

Judge Tsang says, "I'm inclined to agree with Mr. McNulty."

So am I. "Just a couple more questions," I say.

He gives me the benefit of the doubt. "Proceed."

"You saw your husband later that night, didn't you?"

"Briefly," she says. "I almost drove into his car as I was heading east on Twenty-fifth at about twelve forty-five A.M. He was pulling out of the alley between Mission and Capp. It would have been pretty ironic if we'd wrecked our cars just before we were about to finalize our divorce settlement."

True enough. It also places both of them within a half block of Concepcion's apartment after Ramon left. "What kind of cars do you drive?"

"Matching Lexus SUVs."

It still doesn't place either of them in Concepcion's apartment. "Your husband was coming home from work, wasn't he?"

"Yes."

"And he drove right by the back of Ms. Concepcion's apartment building, didn't he?"

"Yes."

"Is it possible he may have gone into Ms. Concepcion's apartment?"

"Objection," McNulty says. "Speculative."

"Sustained."

I can place her husband within striking distance of

Concepcion's apartment after Ramon left, but that's as far as I can go. I probe for another minute, but she can't provide any additional details regarding his whereabouts that night. McNulty passes on cross-exam.

The judge looks at his watch and asks me to call my next witness.

It's time to rock and roll. "The defense calls Eduardo Lopez," I say.

CHAPTER 49

"Mutual Decisions Generally Don't Involve Baseball Bats"

Defense attorneys for Father Ramon Aguirre have placed Eduardo Lopez in the alley behind Maria Concepcion's apartment on the morning she died.

—*KGO Radio,* Monday, December 15, 3:00 P.M.

EDUARDO LOPEZ STROKES his neatly trimmed beard and nods politely to the judge after he's sworn in. He could pass for a lawyer at Shanahan's firm. The silk shirt and designer tie have been replaced by an executive ensemble from Brooks Brothers. He exudes a serene self-confidence as he sits in the witness box, and I approach him with caution. This may be akin to wrestling a rattlesnake. He's been lurking outside and I wanted to question him before he got debriefed by his attorney, an equally dapper man named Alex Schwartz, who is sitting in the back row of the gallery. Everybody involved in this case has a designated spy.

I try to get him to lower his guard by starting with an easy one. "You've operated Eduardo's Latin Palace on Mission Street for almost thirty years, haven't you?"

"Yes." No elaboration. He's been coached to keep his answers short.

"You've been quite successful, haven't you?"

I catch the hint of a proud smile behind the goatee. "My competitors seem to think so."

His attempt to sound disarming falls flat. "Mr. Lopez," I say, "we heard testimony earlier today from Ms. Mercedes Trujillo."

"She's an excellent employee," he says.

In many ways. "Is she also excellent in bed?"

"Objection," McNulty says. "Argumentative."

It's also insulting, but that isn't one of the prescribed legal grounds for an objection.

"Sustained."

"I'll rephrase." I approach Lopez and say, "You and Ms. Trujillo were involved in a romantic relationship earlier this year, weren't you?"

No response.

"Mr. Lopez," I say, "you'll have to answer my questions."

"Whatever you say, Mr. Daley."

"I'm saying Ms. Trujillo admitted that you were having an affair with her and with another woman—Maria Concepcion. Your wife testified that she hired a private investigator who discovered that you were cheating on her. The PI was gracious enough to confirm it."

Still no response.

"Mr. Lopez," I say, "this isn't your restaurant where you call the shots. In business, you may call it bluffing, but in court, we call it perjury—and you can go to jail for it."

His jaws clench when he says, "It is no secret my wife and I have had our differences and we are getting divorced.

The circumstances are highly regrettable, and I can assure you that's all I intend to say about it."

And I can assure you it's nowhere near what you're going to say about it. "Are you denying that you had an affair with Ms. Concepcion?"

"No."

"Are you denying that you also had an affair with Ms. Trujillo?"

"No." Lopez tries to take the offensive. "I fail to understand how this is remotely relevant to the issue of whether your client murdered Ms. Concepcion."

I turn to the judge and strike a patient tone. "Your Honor," I say, "would you please instruct the witness to answer my questions?"

"Your Honor," Lopez whines, "my personal relationships are nobody else's business."

"Answer the questions, Mr. Lopez."

"I had relations with Ms. Concepcion and Ms. Trujillo."

The negotiations in his divorce settlement just became stickier. "Mr. Lopez," I say, "Ms. Concepcion terminated your relationship when she found out you were also seeing Ms. Trujillo, didn't she?"

"It was a mutual decision."

Bullshit. "Mutual decisions generally don't involve baseball bats."

"I don't know what you're talking about."

"Your wife's private investigator was keeping your office under surveillance. He told us Ms. Concepcion broke up with you and she took a swing at you with your Orlando Cepeda autographed model."

"My office has no windows," he says. "There is no way he could have seen inside."

"Your office was bugged, Mr. Lopez."

He studies my face to see if I'm bluffing, but doesn't offer a response.

I add, "And so was your phone."

His Adam's apple bobs up and down, and he glares at me through slitted eyes. If he lies, I'll trot out Nick Hanson and make Lopez look like a buffoon.

Now that I have his undivided attention, it's time to rumble. "Just so we're clear," I say, "Ms. Concepcion broke up with you in early September after she found out you were also seeing Ms. Trujillo, didn't she?"

"The situation was complicated."

"Not to mention the fact that Ms. Trujillo dumped you a short time later."

McNulty stands up and says, "Objection. Relevance."

"Your Honor," I say, "we are trying to establish the circumstances surrounding a very traumatic event in Ms. Concepcion's recent past that will have direct bearing on this case." Especially if I want to try to pin the blame on Lopez. "I would be grateful for a little leeway."

The judge isn't entirely convinced, but he isn't prepared to pull the plug. "Proceed."

I turn back to Lopez. "You were very upset when Ms. Concepcion terminated your relationship, weren't you?"

"It wasn't the conclusion that I had hoped for. I was very fond of her."

"Did you love her?"

"I don't know."

"When was the last time you saw her?"

"She came into the restaurant a couple of weeks ago."

"Was she still angry?"

"She didn't want to talk to me."

I'll bet. "How did you feel when you saw her?"

"Sad."

"Angry?"

"A little."

"Jealous?"

"There was nothing to be jealous about, Mr. Daley."

"Did you know she was pregnant?"

"She didn't mention it."

"Were you concerned that you might be the father of her unborn child?"

"I just told you that I didn't know she was pregnant."

I've made him look like an ass, but I haven't gotten any closer to finding a motive for murder or placing him at her apartment. I say, "You're planning to run for office, aren't you?"

"I have made no secret of the fact that I intend to run for the Board of Supervisors."

"If word got out that you were having an affair or were the father of an illegitimate child, it would have been a huge setback for your political aspirations, not to mention your marriage."

"My personal life is not a public issue, and it has nothing to do with this case. A lot of people get divorced."

Tell me about it. "Did Ms. Concepcion know any deep, dark secrets that could have adversely impacted your political ambitions?"

"No."

"Was she trying to blackmail you?"

"Absolutely not."

It's as far as I can go. "What time did you leave work last Tuesday morning?"

"Approximately twelve-thirty A.M."

"Why didn't you stay until closing time?"

"I had an appointment at the Planning Commission early the next morning."

"Did you drive home?"

"Yes."

"You drive a Lexus SUV, don't you?"

"Yes, Mr. Daley. It was parked in the alley behind my restaurant."

"The same alley that runs behind the back of Ms. Concepcion's apartment building?"

"Yes."

"So you drove by her building after you left work, didn't you?"

"It's on my way home."

"Did you stop at her place?"

His tone is a bit too emphatic when he says, "Of course not."

"Did you see anybody in her apartment?"

"I wasn't looking."

"Were the lights on?"

"I didn't notice."

"Was anybody else in the alley?"

"Just the guy down the block who restores cars in his garage."

That would be Preston Fuentes. "Did you see anybody else that night?"

The corner of his mouth turns up slightly. "Ironically,"

he says, "as I was preparing to turn onto Twenty-fifth Street, I came within a foot of barreling into my wife's car."

Ordinarily, I would be skeptical when the testimony of a husband and wife matches up so perfectly—one might suspect they compared notes to provide alibis for each other. In this case, I find it unlikely that he and Vicky got together to swap stories. Moreover, the fact that they almost collided doesn't place either of them inside Concepcion's apartment. "Mr. Lopez," I say, "did you kill Maria Concepcion in the early morning hours of Tuesday, December second?"

"No, Mr. Daley."

There's nothing else that I can do. "No further questions, Your Honor."

"WHAT NOW?" Ramon asks. The air of resignation in his tone has been replaced by the sound of abject fear as we're meeting during the afternoon break.

"It's only a preliminary hearing," I say, "and we're still in the game."

"Barely," he replies.

"We have two options," I say. "Plan A is that we shut down now and put on a full defense at the trial." I explain to him that delay is frequently a defense attorney's best friend. "The upside is that this will allow us to interview witnesses and gather additional evidence in an orderly way. The downside is that nothing will be resolved for a year or two, perhaps longer."

"What's Plan B?"

"We'll put the San Francisco Archdiocese on trial right now."

CHAPTER 50

"You Thought You Were Going to Win"

Trials never go as planned. The best trial lawyers are masters of improvisational theater.

—Legal Analyst Mort Goldberg, *Channel 4 News,*
Monday, December 15, 4:05 P.M.

DENNIS PETERSON IS wearing his big-firm-hard-ass-trial-lawyer costume as he eyes me from the stand at four o'clock on Monday afternoon. The ace litigator from Shanahan's law firm isn't used to being on the receiving end of this drill, and his demeanor suggests that he isn't going to be especially pleasant about it.

I go right after him. "Your marriage broke up three years ago, didn't it?"

"Correct."

"Why?"

"My ex-wife and I found it was extremely difficult to live and work together."

There was a little more to it. "Was infidelity involved?"

McNulty pops up. "Objection, Your Honor. Relevance."

"Your Honor," I say, "the circumstances surrounding

Ms. Concepcion's divorce are essential to an analysis of her psyche at the time of her death."

"It was three years ago," McNulty whines.

"I was divorced eleven years ago, and I can assure you the psychological scars take a long time to heal." Just ask Rosie.

Judge Tsang agrees with me. "Overruled."

Peterson responds immediately. "My ex-wife erroneously believed that infidelity was involved," he says, "but I can assure you it was not."

Right. "Can anybody corroborate your claim?" It's an unfair question—he can't prove a negative.

"You know there is no way I can do that. You'll have to take my word for it."

It's the right answer. "Your ex-wife had psychological and emotional problems that included depression, didn't she?"

"Correct."

"And she sought the help of a therapist, who prescribed antidepressants, right?"

"Correct."

McNulty invokes a respectful tone. "Your Honor," he says, "we covered this territory with Ms. Concepcion's therapist. Unless Mr. Daley is prepared to offer some new information, I would suggest that he move on."

"Mr. Daley," the judge says to me, "you need to get to the point now."

"Yes, Your Honor." I turn back to Peterson and say, "You and your ex-wife were opposing counsel on a high-profile case that was about to go to trial, weren't you?"

"It would be a violation of the attorney-client privilege to discuss it."

"I'm not going to ask you about any substantive legal or evidentiary issues, but I would like to know about your ex-wife's mood. You were communicating with her frequently in the weeks leading up to her death, weren't you?"

"That's always true before a significant trial is about to start."

"And the days leading up a high-profile trial are very stressful, aren't they?"

"Yes."

I walk up to Peterson and say, "In general terms, how was the case going?"

"From our standpoint, very well."

"You were confident your client would prevail?" He can't very well say they were about to lose.

"Yes, Mr. Daley."

"That suggests Ms. Concepcion's case was weak, doesn't it?"

"That would be the flip side."

"You thought you were going to win, didn't you?"

"I still do." If he's smart, he'll shut his mouth, but his ego gets ahead of his judgment. "We were extremely confident a judgment in our favor would be the likely result."

Perfect. "Yet you attempted to settle the case, didn't you?"

"Yes, but we didn't think settlement was a likely outcome."

"But you did proffer one or more settlement proposals, didn't you?"

"Only in an attempt to terminate the case without incurring additional legal fees. We were confident we would prevail on the merits at trial."

"And how did Ms. Concepcion react to your proposals?"

"She rejected them."

"Because they were too low?"

"Because she had unrealistic beliefs about the strength of her case."

The same might be said of you. "Mr. Peterson," I say, "your ex-wife was suffering from severe emotional distress and she had a difficult, if not unwinnable, case against an excellent lawyer, right?"

He can't deny it. "Correct."

"Do you think the strain was so severe that her emotions got the better of her and she decided to take her own life?"

McNulty's up again. "Objection, Your Honor. Speculative."

"Sustained."

It isn't the last time I'm going to ask him to speculate. "Mr. Peterson," I say, "did your ex-wife appear distraught or unhappy to you?"

"Both."

"As unhappy as she did around the time of your divorce?"

"Yes."

"Unhappy enough that she may have considered desperate options?"

"Objection. Speculative."

"Sustained."

I'd be objecting like mad if I were in McNulty's shoes. "Mr. Peterson," I say, "you were at a settlement conference with Ms. Concepcion on Monday, December first, weren't you?"

"Yes."

"How was her demeanor?"

"Agitated. She was unwilling to discuss our final settlement offer in a rational way, and she had difficulties controlling her emotions. I think she had a panic attack, and she spent a long time in the bathroom. She said her stomach was bothering her."

It could have been the pregnancy, but I'm not going to suggest it. "Did you sense Ms. Concepcion was out of control?"

He measures his words carefully. "She was under a lot of pressure, but she conducted herself in a professional manner. Maria had her faults, but she was a fighter. She was also desperate to have a child and never would have hurt an unborn baby. It is inconceivable to me that she committed suicide."

It's the answer I expected. I ask, "When was the last time you spoke to her?"

"Nine-fifteen last Monday night. I had received authorization from my client to tender a final settlement offer. She rejected it."

"How was her mood?"

"She was tired."

I ask if he had any additional communication with the archdiocese that night.

"I reported on the results of my conversation to Father Quinn. He said he was disappointed, but not surprised."

"Did you speak to anybody else about it?"

"I briefed my partner John Shanahan. He wasn't surprised either."

"What time did you go home?"

"Around midnight."

"Why so late?"

"I was preparing for trial."

"Did you drive anywhere in the vicinity of Ms. Concepcion's apartment that night?"

"No, Mr. Daley."

I didn't expect him to admit that he went down to Twenty-fifth and Capp and committed murder. "Mr. Peterson," I say, "what kind of car do you drive?"

"A black Lexus SUV."

Of course. I give Edwards a knowing look and say, "No further questions."

CHAPTER 51

"I Am the Archbishop's Chief Advisor on All Major Legal Matters"

We have to avoid any appearance of impropriety.

—F. X. Quinn, *San Francisco Chronicle*

F. X. QUINN PLACES his hand on the Bible and swears he will tell us the truth, the whole truth and nothing but the truth, so help him God. If God's busy, I'm sure Quinn would be willing to provide the same assurances himself. In response to the bailiff's request that he state his full name and occupation, he says, "Father Francis Xavier Quinn." He struggles to maneuver his torso into the narrow wooden chair and adds, "I am the archbishop's chief advisor on all major legal matters."

And you wouldn't want to disappoint him.

The courtroom is hushed at four-fifteen, and all eyes are glued on the commanding figure of the archdiocese's chief legal eagle. Quinn is glaring at me with eyes that are filled with contempt, giving new meaning to the concept of a hostile witness.

"Father Quinn," I say, "did you know an attorney named Maria Concepcion?"

"We had a professional acquaintance. We were on opposite sides of several legal matters involving claims against the archdiocese."

"Was she a good lawyer?"

"She was a tenacious, if misguided, adversary."

"Yet she was successful, wasn't she?"

He invokes a fake apologetic tone. "The attorney-client privilege doesn't allow me to discuss the details of the matters she handled."

And if it didn't, you'd find another reason. "Ms. Concepcion did, in fact, obtain several meaningful victories on behalf of her clients, didn't she?"

He turns to the judge and says, "This information is privileged and confidential."

"I can't expect you to talk about any matter that is pending or the subject of an appeal," he says, "but the resolution of a particular case is a matter of public record, subject to any relevant protective orders or seals."

"But, Your Honor—"

"You'll have to answer Mr. Daley's question, Father Quinn."

It's the first time in years that somebody made Quinn do something he didn't want to do. He sucks it up and says, "We reluctantly agreed to settle several minor matters to avoid the costs of protracted litigation. The claims were wholly without merit, and the amounts are confidential."

I ask, "Then why did you settle them?"

"I just told you—we wanted to avoid the costs of litigation."

"And adverse publicity?"

"That's one of the factors we consider, but it isn't an important one."

The hell it isn't. "Who has the final authority to decide if a case should be settled?"

He pauses to consider his options. If he tries to kick it upstairs, I'll put the archbishop on the stand and ask him the same question. "I have the final say on all litigation matters," he says.

It's akin to suggesting that the chairman of the board of a public company would delegate the final decision on a bet-the-company lawsuit to his general counsel. It's indicative of how far he's willing to go to keep the archbishop out of the line of fire.

"Father Quinn," I say, "are you saying Archbishop Keane has no input on the resolution of major legal matters that could cost the archdiocese millions of dollars?"

"I consult with him, of course, but he's delegated the primary responsibility for concluding such matters to me."

"That makes you the most powerful person in the archdiocese."

"I am aware of the responsibility that goes along with this job, but I like to think moral and theological issues still take precedence over legal ones."

They do until the archdiocese is hit with a huge judgment. "Father Quinn," I say, "what was the magnitude of the settlements in the matters Ms. Concepcion had brought against the archdiocese?"

"That's confidential, Mr. Daley."

The judge doesn't help me this time, and I ask Quinn about the nature of the claims brought by Concepcion on behalf of her clients.

"She alleged unsubstantiated misdeeds by employees of the archdiocese."

Parsing works in politics, but it isn't terribly effective in court. "Would that include allegations of financial and sexual improprieties by certain priests and members of the archdiocese staff?"

"Ms. Concepcion was never able to prove any such claims."

"And now she'll never have the chance to try."

He doesn't respond.

On to the good stuff. "Father Quinn," I say, "Ms. Concepcion had brought a major case alleging illicit sexual acts by a priest named Father Patrick O'Connell, hadn't she?"

"There was no proof of any of the alleged acts."

"His accuser was murdered, wasn't she?"

"So it appears."

"As a result, she can't testify at Father O'Connell's trial, can she?"

"No, she can't."

"And she can't testify in this matter, either, can she?"

McNulty tries to slow me down. "Objection, Your Honor," he says. "These matters have already been addressed."

Judge Tsang says to me, "Please move along, Mr. Daley."

"Yes, Your Honor." I've been standing at the lectern at

a respectful distance, but now it's time to turn up the heat. I approach Quinn and say, "Do you have any information concerning the death of the plaintiff in the O'Connell case—a woman known as Jane Doe?"

"The police tell me the investigation is ongoing."

"You would acknowledge that her death will have a material bearing on the direction of the O'Connell case, right?"

"Of course. She was the plaintiff."

"And it is helpful to your client that she is no longer available to testify, right?"

McNulty's up again. "Objection, Your Honor. Relevance."

"Your Honor," I say, "any information about Ms. Doe may be relevant in determining who is responsible for the death of Ms. Concepcion."

"Answer the question, Father Quinn."

"Ms. Doe's unavailability is a factor that we will have to consider if her survivors elect to pursue her claims."

It's a perfect answer that says absolutely nothing. "When was the last time you saw Ms. Concepcion?"

He confirms that he was present at the settlement conference at Shanahan's office. "I can't discuss the details without violating the attorney-client privilege."

I give the judge a hopeful look, but his glare suggests this topic is not open for discussion. "You put a settlement offer on the table, didn't you?"

"Yes."

"May I ask how much?"

"No."

"What was Ms. Concepcion's response?"

"She rejected it." He pauses a beat and adds, "Emphatically."

"Why?"

"It wasn't enough money."

"Did she have a figure of her own in mind?"

"It was far beyond anything we would have considered."

"Millions?"

"I'm not at liberty to say."

"Tens of millions?"

McNulty interjects. "Objection, Your Honor. Asked and answered."

"He hasn't answered," I say.

"And he isn't going to!" the judge snaps. "The information is confidential, and the objection is sustained."

I didn't think he'd give me that one. "How was Ms. Concepcion's demeanor?"

"Agitated."

"Was she acting rationally?"

McNulty is up. "Objection, Your Honor. Calls for speculation as to state of mind."

"Sustained."

I try another adjective. "Was her behavior erratic?"

"She was always strident, but she seemed unusually distracted."

"Was that the last time you spoke to her?"

"No. I called her at a quarter to ten last Monday night."

This jibes with the phone records. "What did you discuss?"

"I wanted to see if we could bridge the gap in our settlement discussions."

"Does that mean you made another offer?"

"A generous one."

I ask him why he upped the ante.

"Litigation is expensive, Mr. Daley."

"Especially when you lose."

He clenches his jaws and says, "We weren't going to lose. We receive excellent advice from our regular outside counsel at the firm of Shanahan, Gallagher and O'Rourke."

I could ask him to speculate about whether she was suicidal, but that line of questioning hasn't been a winner. "How did Ms. Concepcion react to your offer?"

"Badly. I explained to her that it was our last and best offer, and she rejected it."

"How long did she consider it?"

"About two seconds. I didn't speak to her again."

"You didn't go over to her apartment to make one final plea to her better judgment?"

"No, Mr. Daley."

I ask him if he informed the archbishop of the break off in settlement negotiations.

"Yes. He expressed his disappointment and said he would pray for an equitable result."

MY BROTHER FINALLY makes his grand entrance at four-thirty. He's been going all night and lends just the right touch of dignity to the defense table when he saunters in wearing faded jeans and his bomber jacket.

"You're late," I whisper.

He pulls up the heavy chair next to mine. "I've been busy, Mick."

Just another day in the life of a PI. I turn to the judge and say, "If we might have just a moment to confer with our investigator, Your Honor."

"Make it quick, Mr. Daley."

We adjourn to the consultation room, where I ask Pete if he found anything.

"Maybe."

"We don't have time to play Twenty Questions," I say. "Spill it."

"One," he whispers, "the guy from the fertility clinic is willing to testify that Ramon donated sperm on two occasions."

The issue of whether Ramon is the father is no longer in question. It's helpful that we can show it wasn't a one-night stand, but it won't get the charges dropped.

"Two," he continues, "Vince said there was nobody on your tail this morning."

I'm glad to hear it, but I'm not prepared to let my guard down just yet.

"Three," he says, "the cops found an abandoned green Impala in an alley behind Moscone Center. It was stolen a week ago in South City and stripped completely clean."

This may explain why nobody has been following us. I hope Jeff Pick isn't involved. "Is it *the* Impala?"

"I don't know for sure, but the odds are pretty good."

The odds are also pretty good that the driver is long gone. "Were they able to lift any prints?"

"No way. It was cleaned by a pro."

"Can they connect the car to Doe's killing?"

"Not yet."

"What about the fire at our office?"

"I talked to one of my moles down at the fire department. There wasn't anything in the car that tied it to the fire, but he told me that there's a good chance it was arson."

"To get to us?"

"More than likely. To be on the safe side, I've asked Vince to stay on your tail."

This isn't making me feel any better. "What else is on your list?"

"Fuentes wants to meet us at ten o'clock tonight. He says he may have something."

My heart starts to beat faster, but I try to keep my hopes under control.

"I was able to obtain some information about the Shanahan, Gallagher and O'Rourke trust account," he says. He opens a battered manila envelope and removes a printout that has some computer-generated numbers on it.

I ask him how he got it.

"Legally. You'd be amazed what you can access if you know what you're doing. I can tell you how much Judge Tsang is worth if you're interested."

"That won't be necessary. Is there anything in this report that may help us?"

"Maybe." He points to a column of numbers toward the bottom of the first page and says, "A cashier's check was drawn on this account on Monday, December first."

"To whom?"

"Cash."

Which means it could have been converted into cold, hard currency at any bank. "How much?" I ask.

"Five million bucks."

What? "Why did they pull so much money out of the trust account?"

"My guess is that they were trying to settle the O'Connell case."

"Maybe. Who authorized the withdrawal?"

"Shanahan."

CHAPTER 52

Dirty Little Secrets

While we anticipate that Father Aguirre will be fully exonerated, our firm's primary loyalties lie with our good client, the San Francisco Archdiocese.

—John Shanahan, *San Francisco Chronicle*

AS ALWAYS, JOHN Shanahan's appearance is one of understated elegance as he sits in uncharted territory—the witness box—at five minutes to five. Judge Tsang has made it clear that we will adjourn as soon as I've completed my direct exam, and my hopes for a stunning grand finale have faded. Shanahan uses a grandfatherly tone as he says, "I am the senior partner of Shanahan, Gallagher and O'Rourke. We have over three hundred lawyers in nine offices in California and other major metropolitan areas. We have been the primary outside counsel for the San Francisco Archdiocese for over four decades."

I'm impressed. "Mr. Shanahan," I begin, "your firm is defending the archdiocese in a lawsuit alleging certain misdeeds by a priest named Father Patrick O'Connell, isn't it?"

"Correct."

"That lawsuit is currently on hold, isn't it?"

Shanahan turns to Judge Tsang. "Your Honor," he

says, "we cannot comment on legal matters relating to the archdiocese without violating the attorney-client privilege."

"You can address issues that are a matter of public record."

"But, Your Honor—"

"Answer the question, Mr. Shanahan."

I like the show of control.

Shanahan sighs melodramatically and says, "The O'Connell case is in abeyance because the plaintiff and her attorney are no longer available."

No kidding. "Why is that, Mr. Shanahan?"

"They've passed away."

"You mean they're dead."

"Yes, Mr. Daley. They're dead."

"The plaintiff was shot to death behind the Mitchell Brothers' Theater, wasn't she?"

"That's been reported in the papers."

"Do you know anything about it?"

"Just what I've read in the papers."

"And it's been alleged that Ms. Concepcion was murdered."

"That's why we're here, Mr. Daley."

Yes, it is. "It's certainly convenient for your client's case that neither the plaintiff nor her attorney is available to testify, isn't it?"

"It's highly unfortunate."

I can see that you're heartbroken. I approach the witness box. "Mr. Shanahan," I say, "Ms. Concepcion started her career at your law firm, didn't she?"

"Correct."

"Was she a good lawyer?"

"She was competent and very conscientious."

"Did your opinion of her legal skills change after she left the firm and began initiating lawsuits against the archdiocese?"

"She was still competent and very conscientious." He should stop right there, but he can't resist a swipe. "For some reason," he adds, "she decided to devote her time to bringing spurious lawsuits against the archdiocese. She was unsuccessful."

I wouldn't expect you to admit otherwise. "It's been reported that Ms. Concepcion had negotiated lucrative settlements in several of those lawsuits."

"The press exaggerates."

I point out that Peterson and Quinn confirmed that the archdiocese settled several suits.

Shanahan holds firm. "We never lost a case to Ms. Concepcion," he says. "It is inaccurate to state that the settlement of a couple of cases for modest sums was anything other than an attempt to avoid the costs of protracted litigation."

He certainly has his lines down. "How did you feel about the O'Connell case?"

"Our position was very strong."

"But the charges have not been dismissed, have they?"

"No."

"You were at a settlement conference with Ms. Concepcion on Monday, December first, weren't you?"

"Yes, I was."

"And you made a settlement offer there, didn't you?"

"It was rejected."

"And Mr. Peterson made another settlement offer later that evening, didn't he?"

"Also rejected."

"If you had such a strong case, why did you try so hard to settle it?"

"Trials are fraught with uncertainty, Mr. Daley. Settlements are not."

It isn't a bad answer. "A moment ago you said you were certain of the outcome. Now you seem to be saying you weren't."

"I said we made an economic determination that we would be willing to settle for a modest amount in order to avoid the costs of litigation—nothing more."

"And any settlement would have included an agreement in which neither the archdiocese nor Father O'Connell would have admitted any culpability, right?"

"Those are customary terms in settling civil cases."

It's an absolute deal-breaker in any settlement. "And the terms would have been strictly confidential, right?"

"Correct."

"Which would have also avoided adverse publicity."

"We take many factors into account."

"Did you have any other contact with Ms. Concepcion?"

"No. I provided a status report to Father Quinn later the same evening. He was disappointed, but not surprised."

"Did you speak to Archbishop Keane?"

"No. Father Quinn indicated to me that he would inform the archbishop."

I glance at Pete, who has taken a seat next to Ramon at

the defense table; then I turn back to Shanahan and say, "Your law firm maintains a client trust account, doesn't it?"

I catch a slight twitch in the corner of his mouth. "It's required by law, Mr. Daley."

"Can you explain its purpose?"

McNulty is up. "Objection, Your Honor. Relevance."

The judge gives me an inquisitive look and I say, "I'll tie this together in the next two minutes, and I promise this is the last subject on my list of questions for today."

"Overruled."

Shanahan folds his arms and lectures. "It's a bank account maintained by our firm to hold funds in trust on behalf of our clients. We are frequently asked to advance filing fees, court costs and other expenses. On rare occasions, we hold advances of our legal fees."

"Sometimes you hold larger amounts to expedite the payment of settlements, don't you?"

"From time to time, it's easier to facilitate the mechanics of a closing or a settlement if all funds are placed in our trust account."

"You have several subaccounts for the archdiocese, don't you?"

"It facilitates bookkeeping. Many of our clients ask us to provide detailed reports on advances and expense reimbursements."

McNulty finally runs out of patience. "Your Honor," he says, "this line of questioning is highly educational and very interesting, but I still fail to see the relevance."

Judge Tsang gives me a stern look and says, "I'm going to give you one more minute to show some relevance, Mr. Daley."

"Yes, Your Honor." I turn to Rosie, who hands me four copies of the account information Pete obtained, and I distribute them to the judge, McNulty and Shanahan. "Your Honor," I say, "the defense would like to introduce this bank account information into evidence." He studies the paperwork as I keep talking. "This document shows the transactions in a subaccount maintained by Mr. Shanahan's law firm on behalf of the archdiocese."

McNulty reacts immediately. "Where did you get this?"

"An information service that may be accessed over the Internet by payment of a fee. Our private investigator would be happy to provide details if necessary."

In reality, the only people who should have any objection are Shanahan and Quinn. McNulty sits down and mutters, "No objection, Your Honor."

All eyes turn to Shanahan, who recognizes that his firm's trust account records will be on the front page of the *Chronicle* in the morning. The experienced spin doctor makes the correct call. "Your Honor," he says, "our firm has nothing to hide and we have no objection if Mr. Daley wishes to have this document admitted into evidence. We're prepared to confirm that it shows transactions in a subaccount that we maintain on behalf of the archdiocese."

Either he truly has nothing to hide or he doesn't want to look evasive. I notice a wry grin on Edwards's face. The judge enters the document into evidence, and I turn back to Shanahan and ask him to describe the purpose of the subaccount.

"It was established to facilitate payment of miscellaneous expenses."

"Sort of a slush fund for contingencies?"

He repeats, "It was established to facilitate payment of miscellaneous expenses."

"Do you have any other secret accounts to settle matters for the archdiocese?"

"If it were a secret, Mr. Daley, I wouldn't be discussing it with you, and I can assure you that Father Quinn is well aware of its existence. In fact, he's the only person who can authorize deposits into the account."

Probably true. "And what is the current balance of that account?"

He puts on his reading glasses and studies the statement. "About twenty-five thousand dollars," he says.

"Is that generally the balance maintained in the account?"

"More or less."

"Mr. Shanahan," I say, "this document indicates that five million dollars was moved into this account on Friday, November twenty-eighth, doesn't it?"

"Yes."

"It appears the same amount was withdrawn from this account on the afternoon of Monday, December first, in the form of a cashier's check made payable to cash."

"Correct."

"The same amount was redeposited into the account the following day, and the funds were moved to another subaccount the same day."

"That's also correct."

It confirms that a big chunk of money was moved

around his firm's trust account for a couple of days, but tells us nothing else. I ask, "Who has signature authority over this account?"

"I do. So does my partner Dennis Peterson."

"Did you or Mr. Peterson authorize the five-million-dollar withdrawal?"

"I did."

"A cashier's check made payable to cash is essentially the same as cash, right?"

"It will be honored by any bank in readily available funds."

"Would you mind explaining why you decided it was necessary to have such a large amount of cash on hand?"

"We were in the process of trying to resolve several matters, and we wanted to be sure we had sufficient funds to cover all contingencies."

"Including a settlement with Ms. Concepcion on the O'Connell case?"

"I can't comment on any specific case."

"Does that mean you were prepared to offer up to five million dollars to settle the O'Connell case?"

"I told you I can't comment on any specific case. I am prepared to say we wanted to have enough cash on hand to handle any contingencies that arose at the time, which may have included the O'Connell case."

Sure. "You were sitting around in your conference room at the Russ Building with a readily negotiable document worth five million bucks?"

"It was in our safe-deposit box at the bank."

"And it's purely coincidental that the money was withdrawn from your account just before the start of the

O'Connell case and redeposited immediately after Ms. Concepcion's death?"

"Yes, Mr. Daley, and I resent any suggestion that the transfer of these funds was in any way related to Ms. Concepcion's death."

I push him, but I can't prove anything beyond the fact that there was a significant withdrawal and redeposit of cash around the time Concepcion died. I ask, "Did you have any further conversations with Ms. Concepcion that night?"

"No."

"Did you go to her apartment that night with the financial equivalent of a briefcase full of bills to try to persuade her to settle the O'Connell case?"

"Of course not."

"Did you use the money from your slush fund to try to fix a matter that still promises to be highly embarrassing and potentially very expensive for the archdiocese?"

"No, Mr. Daley."

I still can't place him in the vicinity of Concepcion's apartment. "Are there any other dirty little secrets relating to the O'Connell case that you'd like to share with us?"

"Objection, Your Honor. Argumentative."

"Sustained."

"No further questions."

Judge Tsang looks at the clock and says, "We're adjourned until nine A.M. How many witnesses do you plan to call, Mr. Daley?"

Time to up the ante again. "Just one, Your Honor. The archbishop of San Francisco."

*   *   *

ROSIE IS FURIOUS when we meet in the consultation room a short time later. "That was complete bullshit," she says. "Senior partners at big law firms don't have unfettered access to that kind of money."

"Evidently, this one did," I say.

"He's lying," Rosie says. "Anybody with half a brain would realize they were going to use the money to try to settle the O'Connell case or to buy off Concepcion."

"We have no proof," I say. "A cashier's check isn't a smoking gun."

"It's the equivalent of five million dollars in unmarked bills."

Pete's tone turns practical. "We still need to place somebody else at Concepcion's apartment that night."

"Then that's precisely what we'll have to do."

THE GREEN NUMERALS on the digital clock on my dashboard indicate that it's nine P.M. Rosie and I are driving toward the Mission when I punch the familiar number on my cell phone and Roosevelt picks up on the first ring. "What's up, Mike?" he asks.

"How did you know it was me?" I ask.

"Spy phone."

"I have an unlisted number."

"I have a really good spy phone."

Sometimes it's fun to be a cop.

His voice is tired, and he cuts to the chase. "What do you need?" he asks.

"To see if you're prepared to exercise some degree of

rationality and reopen the investigation in the Concepcion case."

"You need more rest, Mike."

"I won't get it until Tommy is in high school."

"The issues become more complicated when they become teenagers."

"Something to look forward to. Have you made any progress on Doe's murder?"

"We don't have anything solid yet."

"I'll take wild, unsubstantiated speculation."

"Off the record," he says, "it looks professional. It was a quick hit from a Saturday-night special. It was carefully executed, and the killer was gone in seconds."

"Did you find the murder weapon?"

"In a Dumpster. The serial number and all other identifying marks were removed."

"Prints?"

"Forget it."

"Witnesses?"

"None."

"Suspects?"

"The usual."

"Chances?"

"Slim."

I ask him if there might be a connection to the disappearance of Doe's former colleague.

"I don't know." He says he can't connect the Impala to Doe's killing, either. "The car was wiped completely clean. It doesn't mean that there isn't a connection. It just means that we haven't found it yet."

"Any chance I can persuade you to take a look at the

records for the trust account for Shanahan, Gallagher and O'Rourke?"

"I'll give it a look, but if Shanahan was really trying to hide something, he wouldn't have talked about it."

"He had no choice. He would have looked evasive. Maybe we caught him red-handed with his fingers in the cookie jar."

"A cashier's check doesn't add up to murder, Mike." He exhales heavily and says, "Let me give you some free advice."

His advice is usually very good.

"If you really want to crack this case," he says, "you're going to have to find an eyewitness who can place somebody other than your client in Concepcion's apartment after twelve-thirty last Tuesday morning."

Tell me something I don't know. "That's going to be tough."

"You're a good lawyer."

I ask him if he's going to be at work for a while.

"Yes. What do you need?"

"Protection. We're going to be talking to some people tonight. If we find a witness who knows something, I want to be sure he or she doesn't end up like Jane Doe."

"Do you want me to come with you?"

"No, but I may need you later."

"I'll keep my cell phone on."

CHAPTER 53

"Luis Does Not Exist"

The black market for illegal auto parts has skyrocketed thanks to a lack of resources and lax enforcement.

—*San Francisco Chronicle*

ROSIE, PETE AND I are standing a respectful distance from Preston Fuentes, who is sitting on a stool next to his workbench. The Corvette is conspicuously absent, but Fluffy is not. She's straining against the choke collar in the corner of the garage, and our escape options are nonexistent if she chooses to pounce. A clock that bears a Giants logo tells us it's ten minutes after ten. The door is closed, and an acrid combination of cigarette smoke and paint fumes fills the cluttered space. This garage could go up like a sheet at any moment.

Rosie insisted on accompanying us this time to be sure we didn't do anything stupid or reckless. She says to Fuentes, "Does this mean you sold the Corvette?"

He takes a long pull on a cigarette and says, "Yes."

"I'm sorry I didn't have a chance to see it."

"It turned out nice." He doesn't say anything else.

I try to engage him. "Did you do pretty well on the deal?"

"I did okay."

"Pick's carburetor worked?"

"Never underestimate the value of good auto parts."

Enough. "Preston," I say, "you said you had something for us."

"I found somebody who was in the alley last Tuesday morning."

Yes! "When can we meet him?"

"He's waiting for my call."

"Whatever it takes," I say.

Fuentes drops his cigarette on the floor and snuffs it out with his boot. He flips open a cell phone and conducts a brief and rather heated conversation in Spanish. I'm fluent enough to understand that the other party is expressing a degree of reluctance. He puts his hand over the mouthpiece and says, "I've persuaded him to talk to you."

"Great."

"There are some conditions."

Not so great. "What are they?"

"No cops."

"Agreed."

"No wires."

"Agreed."

"No photographs."

"Agreed."

"No names."

For the moment, I have no choice. "Agreed."

He holds up a finger and says, "This last one is a deal breaker."

"What?"

"No testimony."

No way. "He's useless to us."

"It's the best I can do."

"We got your carburetor on short notice."

"It isn't negotiable."

Dammit.

Rosie steps forward and says, "Tell him we'll talk to him."

"Does that mean you're accepting his conditions?"

"For now."

Fuentes scowls and puts the phone back up to his ear. He speaks in Spanish for another moment and flips the phone shut. "He's on his way," he says.

"Who is he?" I ask.

"He works for me."

"An employee?"

"An independent contractor."

"What does he do for you?"

"Whatever I ask."

"Does it involve procuring auto parts?"

"Whatever I ask."

"What's his name?"

"I told you no names."

"Give us just his first name."

"Luis."

"Why is he so paranoid?"

"Luis does not exist."

"Excuse me?"

"He's an illegal alien with a criminal record and several outstanding arrest warrants who has no interest in getting involved in a police matter."

CHAPTER 54

"I Was Going to Steal the Car"

Neighborhood patrols in the Mission District have done little to stem the tide of auto thefts.

—*San Francisco Chronicle*

THE WIRY YOUNG man with the shaved head, wisp of a mustache and tattoo of a serpent on his right arm looks at us through darting eyes. He's sporting a sleeveless black shirt with the logo of a hip-hop group whose name I don't recognize and faded Levi's that are shredded at the knees. A single stud punctures his left ear and his muscular hands are clenched. "Who are you?" he asks me in lightly accented English.

"We're representing Father Aguirre."

"Why?"

It's a fair question. "He's a friend and a classmate," I say, "and because he's innocent."

A nod of silent approval.

"Can you help us?" I ask.

"Maybe."

"Were you here late last Monday night and early Tuesday morning?"

"Maybe."

"Did you see anybody in this alley after twelve-thirty in the morning?"

"Maybe."

I get his drift. "What will it take to get the whole story?"

"I have some legal problems with the immigration authorities."

Rosie jumps in. "I've handled dozens of immigration cases," she says. "I'll take care of you."

"I have no money."

"Father Aguirre isn't paying us," she says. "We'll handle your case pro bono if you're willing to cooperate." It's all we have to offer.

"I need protection from the cops and the INS."

"I'll get a judge to sign a court order that will prohibit anybody from deporting you—I've done it in the past and I'll do it again."

The judge is our old law partner and my ex-girlfriend. It is doubtful that an order issued by a California Superior Court judge would be binding against a federal agency like the INS, but we've successfully stalled the bureaucracy from time to time.

The corner of his mouth turns up slightly, and Rosie responds with a warm smile. "What's your name?" she asks.

"Luis Alvarado."

It's a start. "I'll tell you what," she says. "Before we talk about what happened last week, why don't you tell us about your problems with the INS."

"It's a long story," he says.

"We have time."

ALVARADO'S STORY TAKES only a few minutes and is not atypical. He was born in Tijuana and slipped over the border five years ago. He did farm labor in the Central Valley and eventually worked his way up to San Francisco, where he tapped into the Mission District community and made enough money—legal or otherwise—to rent a ramshackle room above a garage near St. Peter's. Life became more complicated when he was diagnosed with high blood pressure and diabetes, and he had to turn to stealing to pay for his medication. His health has improved, but his medicine is expensive and he can't apply for standard welfare or other benefits because he'll be escorted out of the country. It's the ultimate catch-22— he can only avail himself of our safety net if he turns himself over to the authorities, who will send him packing.

"Nobody is going to send you anywhere," Rosie assures him.

His eyes turn hopeful. "Thank you, Ms. Fernandez."

"It's Rosie." They shake hands, and she gives him a business card. "You can reach me on my cell phone," she says. "Our office is being remodeled."

"Thank you, Rosie."

"You're welcome." Down to business. "Were you here last Tuesday morning?"

"Yes. I dropped off some parts at Preston's, and I was on my way home."

"What time was that?"

"A quarter to one."

Right after Nick the Dick left. Rosie asks him what he saw in the alley.

"A black Lexus RX 330."

This helps. "Was anybody inside?"

"No."

This doesn't. "Where was it parked?"

"Down the alley."

"Show us."

We take him outside, and he directs us to the area just outside the back gate of Concepcion's building. He gives us a sheepish look and says, "Is this conversation covered by the attorney-client privilege?"

"Of course," Rosie says.

"I had a standing order for a Lexus, and I was going to steal the car," he says. "It was just business." His tone fills with disappointment. "The driver came back just as I was about to hot-wire the ignition."

Bad timing. "Where did he come from?"

He gestures toward Concepcion's building. "I didn't want to be seen, so I ran. He got into the car and drove away."

"Why didn't you take him down and take the keys?"

"I just steal cars. I never hurt anyone."

It's a good policy. "Did you get a good look at him?"

"It was dark, but I might be able to identify him."

Might isn't good enough. "Did he say anything to you?" I ask.

"He told me to get away from his car. I was scared, and I got the hell out of there."

"Do you think you can identify his voice?"

"Maybe."

He's the only person on the face of the earth who might be able to identify Concepcion's killer. "Luis," I say, "we need you to testify. You can help us solve a murder."

"I'm not going to do anything unless I get some protection."

"We have friends in the SFPD who will take care of you."

"No cops."

"I have a friend who's a homicide inspector. He worked with my father for thirty years. You can trust him, Luis."

"I want to meet him first," he says.

"That's fair." I pull out my cell phone and punch in the familiar number.

"Johnson," the voice says.

"Daley."

"What?"

"I may have something for you, but I need you to be discreet. Can you meet me in twenty minutes?"

"Where?"

I need someplace safe, public and relatively inconspicuous. "St. Mary's," I say. "Come by yourself. We'll be on the far right side in the back."

"Can you tell me why?"

"You might say we're going to have a 'Come to Jesus Meeting.'"

CHAPTER 55

A Final Confession

Kindly respect the dignity of this institution by maintaining appropriate levels of decorum at all times.

—The Cathedral of St. Mary of the Assumption

IT TAKES A lot of arm-twisting, but I'm able to persuade the brain trust of the San Francisco Archdiocese to assemble in front of the modern altar in the Cathedral of St. Mary of the Assumption at eleven-thirty on Monday night. F. X. Quinn is standing between John Shanahan and Archbishop Keane, and Dennis Peterson has positioned himself a couple of paces to one side. The massive sculpture above them is supposed to symbolize the channel of love and grace from God, and its sheer size suggests that God has a lot of love and grace to give. It's made up of fifteen stories of triangular aluminum rods suspended by gold wires, and it weighs more than a ton. Nobody is admiring the architecture.

The contemporary white building is the third St. Mary's to serve the archdiocese. The first was erected in 1854 and still stands at the corner of California Street and Grant Avenue in what is now Chinatown. The second was built on Van Ness Avenue in 1891, but it burned down in 1962. The existing structure was completed in 1970 and was the subject of immediate controversy because of its dramatic, modern architecture, and was derisively referred to as "God's Maytag" when construction was finished. Its striking design flows from the geometric principle of the hyperbolic paraboloid, in which four corner pylons support a huge cupola, which rises nineteen stories above the floor. Expansive windows at each corner provide spectacular views of the city of Saint Francis.

I'm sitting by myself in the third row of the hushed cathedral that seats over two thousand people. I used to love to sit in church late at night when I was a priest. There was a serenity that is difficult to reproduce during the daylight hours. It was a spiritual time for me—perhaps the only time of the day when I felt truly connected to God. I look up at the magnificent vaulted ceiling, then I walk up to the altar and make the sign of the cross.

Quinn breaks the silence. "You said it was an emergency, Michael."

"It is." I address the archbishop. "We appreciate everything you've done for Father Aguirre."

"Our prayers are with him."

I'm sure they are.

Quinn hasn't taken his eyes off mine, and he tries to direct the discussion. "Why did you call us here?" he asks.

"I came to hear a final confession."

"I don't understand."

I look up at the cupola and then toward the back of the cathedral, where Rosie and Pete are standing. Luis Alvarado and Roosevelt Johnson are out of sight somewhere behind the mammoth northwest pylon. Rosie touches her right ear, and I address the archbishop. "Out of respect for you and for the Church," I say, "I wanted to give you a last chance to tell the truth tonight." And I want to conduct this exercise in a setting where the California Rules of Evidence don't apply. "If you and your attorneys aren't interested, we can discuss this in open court tomorrow."

The archbishop is undaunted. "I don't know what you're talking about, Michael."

"Your legal team let you down, Archbishop Keane."

The charismatic priest isn't going to take my word for it. "I have full faith and confidence in Father Quinn, Mr. Shanahan and Mr. Peterson," he says. "They've served the archdiocese well for many years."

"They've bent the rules to avoid embarrassment to the archdiocese and to yourself."

"That isn't true, Michael."

"Are you aware that Father Quinn testified that he has complete authority to settle major cases on behalf of the archdiocese without first getting your approval?"

"He was attempting to protect me. In fact, he does have the authority to settle major matters without my approval." He clears his throat and says, "And if you are serious about calling me as a witness tomorrow, I'm prepared to testify that the buck stops with me."

He's good. "I appreciate your willingness to discuss that subject, but there are some other issues that may not be quite so easy to dispose of."

"What issues?"

"Your general counsel and your chief outside counsel admitted in open court today that they maintain a slush fund to dispose of litigation matters involving the arch-diocese."

"I'm well aware of that subaccount, Michael, and it's hardly a slush fund. There is nothing illegal about it, and we have nothing to hide."

"Did you know Father Quinn moved five million dollars into the trust account at Mr. Shanahan's law firm?"

"I found out about it earlier today. I am disturbed by the magnitude of the amount, but I knew we were attempting to settle some difficult matters. There is nothing wrong with defending the Church against unfounded charges."

"And you had no problem spying on Father O'Connell and his attorney?"

"It isn't an ideal situation, but it's an accepted strategy in the litigation process. We trust Mr. Shanahan to solve our legal problems."

"You still believe Father O'Connell was innocent?"

"Yes."

"You realize the media will view this as the equivalent of having withdrawn five million dollars of unmarked bills?"

"It wouldn't be the first time the media has misconstrued the evidence."

Quinn steps forward and tries to protect his boss. "Michael," he says, "I'm not sure why you're so intent on lambasting us for attempting to settle a difficult case and for conducting some legitimate financial transfers. If that's all you have, we'll call it a night and see you in court in the morning."

I can't back down now. "I think you were more concerned about the O'Connell case than you've admitted. That's why you authorized a five-million-dollar transfer to the trust account at Shanahan, Gallagher and O'Rourke."

"That's nonsense, Michael. We had several cases in settlement negotiations, and we wanted to have enough funds on hand to resolve all of them."

"Why did you need a cashier's check?"

"We wanted readily available funds."

"Ms. Concepcion wouldn't accept a check written on the account of the archdiocese?"

"Ms. Concepcion was not acting rationally. She erroneously believed we had reneged on a settlement of an earlier case and was insisting on a cashier's check."

"Perhaps you had the money issued in the form of a cashier's check to make the funds more difficult to trace," I say.

"Obviously, that ploy didn't work. I think we're done."

No, we aren't. "I believe Ms. Concepcion rejected Mr. Peterson's offer when they spoke at nine-fifteen last Monday." I look at Shanahan and Quinn in turn and say, "He reported on his discussion to both of you, and you discussed it with each other." I turn to Peterson and say, "That's true, isn't it?"

"Yes."

Quinn says, "He was just doing his job. We're the attorneys for the archdiocese."

"Then you called her again at nine forty-five and told her you were going to make one last offer to settle—I don't know what the amount was, but I'd guess maybe a million bucks. She turned you down flat, and that was supposed to be the end of it."

"That *was* the end of it," Quinn insists.

"If I were a betting man, I'd guess that you talked to each other again after Ms. Concepcion rejected your offer, didn't you?"

Quinn doesn't deny it. "I called John to inform him that he needed to get ready for trial."

Shanahan doesn't say anything.

"You talked about more than that, didn't you?" I say. "You guys must have spent a few minutes strategizing."

"We did."

"And you even talked about what it might take to settle the case, didn't you?"

"Of course."

"And like all good lawyers you discussed the upper and lower limits on what might be a suitable resolution for this case, didn't you?"

"That's what good lawyers do, Michael."

It's true. Here goes. "And you decided to approach Ms. Concepcion with one final offer—one magnanimous gesture to try to avoid protracted litigation and severe embarrassment to the archdiocese—something you were going to have trouble explaining to the archbishop."

Quinn shakes his head violently and says, "No, Michael."

"Coincidentally, you happened to have a five-million-dollar cashier's check sitting around just waiting to be handed over to Ms. Concepcion to make all of your problems go away once and for all. You'd already discussed the limits on what you were willing to pay to make this case disappear. It was a five-million-dollar insurance policy. You knew you could sell it to Archbishop Keane—you've always done so in the past, and you would have looked like heroes on the eve of trial."

"No, Michael."

I didn't expect him to budge. I point at Shanahan and say, "You went over to Ms. Concepcion's apartment at a quarter to one to make your final offer. You parked in the alley behind her apartment and went inside to talk to her, and she was still very much alive at the time. You offered her the five million dollars. It was the ultimate win-win-win situation—you were going to settle a contentious and potentially devastating case, Ms. Concepcion would get a bundle of dough for her client and the archdiocese would avoid the public humiliation of having a renegade priest's record held up for public inspection."

"That's preposterous," Shanahan says. He picks up his briefcase and adds, "And utterly insulting."

I'm not finished. "Everything went wrong because you overestimated your ability to persuade her to settle and you underestimated her principles. Unlike most lawyers you've faced, you couldn't buy her off. She turned you down and sent you packing."

"You're crazy."

"You had a high-profile case you couldn't win. You knew the archbishop would be unhappy—perhaps so unhappy that he would have sent his business to another firm. You knew your cozy little financial arrangement with the archdiocese would become a matter of public record—everybody would know that you and Father Quinn had set up a system to pay off witnesses and buy off plaintiffs. Who knows how many other people you've bought off—or tried to. You had a situation that was spinning out of control, and you couldn't let that happen, so you had to go to Plan B. You took matters into your own hands and you knocked her unconscious. You knew very well she had been experiencing emotional problems, and you tried to make it look like a suicide by putting her into the bathtub and slitting her wrists. You even went to the trouble of putting skin cream all over her body. It wasn't a bad plan—especially if you were making it up on the fly. If my guess is correct, you were probably wearing gloves to avoid leaving any fingerprints."

"You're insane," Shanahan says.

"It might have worked, except you left a small bruise on her shoulder that Dr. Beckert correctly identified and you carelessly put her body in the tub facing the wrong direction. This time Dr. Beckert got it right—it wasn't a suicide. You got lucky because Father Aguirre had been to her apartment earlier that evening and he was kind enough to leave his fingerprints all over the bathroom and the murder weapon. They were even able to lift his prints off her body. You were going to be involved in his defense—in fact, you tried to control his defense—until Father Aguirre hired us. You did everything in your power to persuade him to fire us, and if my guess is correct, you tried to intimidate us by hiring a man who was driving a stolen Chevy Impala. Coincidentally, the same car was seen behind the Mitchell Brothers' Theater right after Jane Doe was shot and behind our office on the night that it was set on fire."

"I don't have to listen to this," he says. "If you raise any of this in court, I'll bring you up before the State Bar. I was never anywhere near Ms. Concepcion's apartment that night. You don't have a shred of evidence that any of this fantasy ever happened."

"Yes, I do."

"What are you talking about?"

My eyes bore into his when I say, "You drive a Lexus RX 330, don't you?"

"So what?"

"It was parked in the alley at the rear of Ms. Concepcion's apartment building when you went inside to see her last Monday night."

"No, it wasn't."

"We have a witness, John."

He stops cold.

"A man tried to steal your car while you were inside Ms. Concepcion's apartment. We found him, and he's prepared to testify."

"You'll never be able to prove any of this."

I turn to the back of the cathedral, where Luis Alvarado appears, flanked by Rosie, Pete and Roosevelt. "Do you recognize that man?" I ask.

Shanahan's eyes lock onto Alvarado's. "Of course not," he says.

"Well," I say, "he recognizes you." I turn to the archbishop and say, "Before we leave tonight, you might want to escort Mr. Shanahan to one of the confessional booths. I think you and he will have some interesting things to talk about."

The archbishop turns to his outside counsel and says,

"If any of this is true, John, I am shocked and absolutely appalled."

"It isn't true," he insists.

The archbishop glances at the altar and makes the sign of the cross. He pauses for a moment to recite a silent prayer, then he turns back to Shanahan and says, "We need to talk, John."

The color leaves Shanahan's face and he turns to Peterson. "I want to talk to my lawyer," he says.

Chapter 56

"Life Has Consequences"

Prominent San Francisco attorney John Shanahan has been charged with first-degree murder in connection with the death of Maria Concepcion. District Attorney Nicole Ward is attempting to determine whether charges will also be brought against Father Francis Xavier Quinn. It does not appear that any charges will be filed against Archbishop Albert Keane.

—*San Francisco Chronicle,* Tuesday, December 16

"IT'S NICE TO be home," Ramon whispers. His voice is filled with a combination of relief and exhaustion as we're sitting in the front pew at St. Peter's at eight o'clock the next night. The flickers of the votive candles are reflecting off the ceiling, and I'm reminded that it was less than two weeks ago when our little adventure started. It seems much longer. "It was nice of the children to come out and greet me."

"Yes, it was." There was a makeshift sign on the front steps welcoming Ramon back to the church, and a large gathering in the social hall that was more somber than celebratory. The kids welcomed him with open arms, but the adults were more subdued.

"Things take time," I say. "People forgive."

"But they never forget."

I look up at the murals on the ceiling and think of the

times I came here with my parents when this church was a haven. I remember the comfort it brought me when my brother was lost in Vietnam. I think of the pain when I came to the conclusion that I was ill suited for the priesthood. It's still a sanctuary full of hope and wonder, but it's tempered by a half century of experience. "It's over, Ramon," I say.

"I can't believe John Shanahan killed Maria."

"He probably thought he was going to settle the case and look like a hero to the archbishop. He couldn't buy her off, and he lost his temper. He was trained as a Marine and reacted when he thought he had no other options."

"I guess it goes to show just how far people will go to avoid losing a big case."

"Or to avoid having to give bad news to their meal-ticket client. Who knows what other hanky-panky was going on with the funds in his trust account? It wouldn't surprise me if he was skimming some money off the top as a gratuity."

"Desperate people do desperate things," he says. "He has over three hundred lawyers to feed. A bad result in a big case for the archdiocese would have been a disaster for his firm. A revelation of financial improprieties involving funds belonging to the archdiocese would have put him out of business."

"You're more understanding than I am," I say.

"You learn a lot of humility when you're accused of murder."

"It still doesn't justify Shanahan's actions."

"Of course not, but it may help to explain them."

We watch the dancing lights from the candles. He

turns to me and says, "Are they going to charge Francis Quinn?"

"Probably not. Roosevelt said they think Quinn gave Shanahan authorization to try to settle the case for up to five million dollars, but he didn't tell him to kill her."

"What about the death of Jane Doe?"

"It was a professional job. They're trying to find a connection between the transfer of funds from Shanahan's trust account and several other cases, including the disappearance of another dancer from the Mitchell Brothers' and the fire at our office. So far, they haven't been able to connect the dots."

"Do you think they will?"

"Roosevelt is tenacious."

My old friend turns to me and asks, "Do you think you made the right move?"

"In talking to Shanahan and the archbishop last night?"

"In leaving the Church."

That's a tougher call, and I go with an old standby. "It was the right move for me."

"No regrets?"

"None." I reconsider and say, "Maybe a few."

"Such as?"

"I used to have more time to sit in church and think."

"You still can."

"It isn't the same. I've gotten too old and cynical."

"It's never too late."

"It may be for me."

"You're a good lawyer, Mike."

"Thanks. Do you buy the old line that everything happens for a reason?"

"Most of the time."

"Maybe the reason you became a priest was because you knew Rosie and I would need you, and maybe I became a lawyer because I knew you were going to need me."

"Maybe you became a lawyer because you weren't happy being a priest."

"Maybe you're still a priest because you're more perceptive than I am."

"You lawyers always have to have the last word."

He's right. "What are you going to do next?" I ask.

"I'm going to take some time off."

"Vacation?"

"They're going to make me resign."

"Not necessarily."

"I was charged with murder. I had inappropriate relations with a parishioner. I acted as a sperm donor and lied about it."

"We can fight it," I say.

"I don't think so, Mike."

"You didn't do anything illegal."

"Maybe not, but I did a bunch of stuff that falls somewhere between bad judgment and flat-out immoral."

"That's why we go to confession, Ramon."

"Confession doesn't always wipe the slate completely clean. I try to teach the children that life has consequences. The same standard should apply to me."

"Do you regret trying to help Maria?"

"No. I saw a desperately unhappy woman in need, and I did what I could."

"Are you prepared to accept the consequences even if it means leaving St. Peter's?"

"Yes."

Impressive. "So," I say, "let me ask you again. What are you going to do?"

"I'm not sure. I'm still committed to doing God's work."

"There are a lot of ways to do God's work without being a priest."

"You aren't suggesting that I go to law school, are you?"

"I like to think it's one way of helping our neighbors."

"If it's all the same to you, I think I'll try some other way. Maybe I can find something in the nonprofit sector. I love this community. I've always wanted to put together a business to develop affordable housing."

"You may have some stiff competition from Eduardo Lopez."

"After his testimony yesterday, I think it may be difficult to find anybody who will be willing to do business with him." He turns somber. "I decided to devote myself to doing good works," he says. "I think I can find a way to do that without being a priest—or a lawyer."

"It might open up some new options for you," I say. "Who knows? Maybe you could settle down and get married."

"I don't think that's in the cards," he says. "I'm more interested in spiritual issues. The whole sex thing is vastly overrated, and it always seems to get me into trouble."

Me, too. "Does that mean you'll stop bugging me about getting married again?"

"Not a chance."

CHAPTER 57

A Christmas Carol

Only one more shopping day until Christmas.

—*San Francisco Chronicle*, Wednesday, December 24

MY BROTHER'S COLLAR is turned up as he's sitting in the second row of the otherwise-empty bleachers next to the home bench at the Big Rec baseball field near the Steinhart Aquarium in Golden Gate Park. I pitched on this field when I was on the St. Ignatius varsity, and I once threw a two-hit shutout against Galileo. It brings back good memories. It's three o'clock in the afternoon of Christmas Eve and a blanket of heavy fog is rolling in. "Nice to have a chance to play hooky, Mick," he says.

I zip my ski jacket and pull my knit hat down a little tighter. "Can't we play hooky somewhere inside?" I ask.

"You said you wanted to meet him."

"Can we do it soon?"

"As soon as this inning is over."

I feel the biting wind on my face and ask, "Why are these guys playing in December?"

"It's their last tune-up before a big semipro tournament in Phoenix next week."

"It's forty-four degrees," I say. "It feels like a night game at Candlestick."

"You can go watch them play in Arizona if you want warm weather."

A team called SFPD's Finest is thrashing a bunch of firefighters from Daly City. The cops are led by a good-looking ringer who is at least six-six and a chiseled two hundred forty pounds. The overmatched firemen can't touch his fastball, and he strikes out the side for the third inning in a row. He carefully avoids touching the foul line as he leaves the mound and heads for the dugout.

Pete motions to the pitcher, then he nudges my arm. "Come on, Mick," he says. We walk over to the bench, where the pitcher is donning a down jacket. Pete approaches him cautiously and says, "Hey, Pick."

The behemoth turns around and nods. "Hey, Pete."

A man of few words. Pete gestures toward me and says, "Mike."

Pick nods. "Hey, Mike."

I extend my hand, but he doesn't take it. "Hey, Pick," I say. "Thanks for everything."

"You're welcome." I'm about to lavish praise on him for helping us solve Concepcion's murder when he says, "Gotta get back to work." Without another word, he heads toward the far end of the bench and sits by himself to watch his teammates bat.

Pete turns to me and says, "He liked you, Mick."

"He wouldn't even shake hands with me."

"He doesn't shake hands."

"Why not?"

"He doesn't let anybody touch his pitching hand." My all-knowing younger brother gives me a wry grin and says, "No kidding, Mick. He really liked you."

"How could you tell?"

"He spoke to you."

"He didn't say two words to me."

"If he didn't like you, he wouldn't have said anything at all."

THE HEATER IN my Corolla is trying as hard as it can as I'm driving Pete home. It works better since Preston Fuentes fixed my window. "Can I ask you something?" I say.

"Sure."

"Who's Vince?"

"The catcher on Pick's semipro team."

"Seriously?"

"Yeah. He was at the game. I should have introduced you to him, too."

"Does that mean—"

"Yeah, Mick. He's a cop. We used to work together at Mission Station. We help each other out every once in a while. I figured I'd better have somebody keep an eye on you who knew what he was doing."

"Thanks, Pete."

"You're welcome. I gotta make sure nothing happens to you, Mick. You're my best referral source for nonpaying clients."

"And it doesn't bother him that he's catching a guy who deals in stolen auto parts?"

"It's just baseball, Mick. He was all-conference at Sacred Heart and played in the A's organization for a couple of years."

We drive in silence down Nineteenth Avenue and we turn right onto Kirkham. Pete says, "Did you hear that F. X. Quinn resigned? He's being investigated for using Church funds for payoffs."

Doesn't surprise me.

He gives me a sly grin and says, "What is it with lawyers and priests?"

"Trouble seems to follow us everywhere," I say. I take a deep breath and ask, "What are you up to tonight?"

"Donna and I are going to put up the tree."

"Do you need some help?"

"Nah."

"You want to come over to Rosie's for a while?"

"I think we'll stay home tonight."

We head west toward the bungalow that's been Daley family headquarters since we moved out of the Mission more than forty years ago. Pete is taking better care of it than our mom did. She was battling Alzheimer's for the last few years of her life, and she didn't really have the capacity to deal with it. I pull up in front of the old place, which has a fresh coat of paint and a mountain of memories. Sometimes I think we should sell it, but Pete is attached to it and the mortgage was paid off thirty years ago.

I turn off the ignition and say, "Sure I can't persuade you to come over?"

"Not tonight, Mick."

"You'll be over for Christmas dinner tomorrow, right?"

"Wouldn't miss it."

"And you'll bring Donna?"

"Yeah. She's a little under the weather, but she'll be

there if she's feeling okay." He starts to open the door, and then he stops. "I have some news, Mick," he says. "I was going to tell you about it tomorrow, but I'd better let you know so you'll be prepared."

Uh-oh. I hope this doesn't mean he and Donna are on the outs. "Good news?" I ask.

"Yeah."

I wait.

His tone is even, almost apologetic, when he says, "Donna and I are getting married."

Yes! "That's terrific." I see the ambivalent look on his face and add, "Isn't it?"

"Of course."

Something's up. "You don't seem to be wildly enthusiastic about it."

"It came up kind of suddenly, and I'm still getting used to the idea."

"For what it's worth, I think it's great."

"If you thought it was so great, you and Rosie would have gotten remarried by now."

I don't want to go there. "It didn't work out very well the first time," I say. I quickly shift back to the matters at hand. "Have you set a date?"

"Yes. Are you free next Saturday night?"

Huh? "Do you want me to help you look at a banquet room or check out a band?"

"No, I want to invite you to our wedding."

"Excuse me?"

"You heard me."

"Seems a bit sudden."

"We aren't the most patient people in the world."

Uh-huh. "Where is the wedding going to be held?"

"St. Peter's. Immediate family only. Ramon is going to officiate."

Excellent.

He adds, "It may be his last official duty as a priest for a while."

Or forever.

"There's something else I need to tell you," he says. His face breaks into a sheepish grin. "I'm going to be a daddy."

Whoa. "Really?"

"Yep." He cocks his head to one side and says, "You aren't going to give me any shit about premarital sex, are you?"

"Nope." It's a Daley family tradition. I give him a broad smile and say, "When is the baby due?"

"July."

"Boy or girl?"

"Don't know yet."

"We've got plenty of baby stuff you can have."

"I appreciate it, Mick."

"Is Donna okay?"

"Except for puking every morning, she's just fine."

I give my kid brother a light punch on the shoulder and say, "It's gonna be great, Pete."

"Thanks, Mick."

R OSIE IS LOOKING at the blinking lights of the Christmas tree as she's sitting on the sofa in her living room. "Why are you awake?" I ask.

"I was just trying to organize our new office," she says.

"Are you serious?"

"No. I think I've found some temporary space on Howard Street."

I'm glad we won't be practicing law next to Tommy's playpen for much longer. "Why are you really up?" I ask.

"It's four A.M.," she replies. "Tommy will be up any minute now."

I wink and say, "I talked to him about it. He's giving us the night off."

"I don't think so. He's more reliable than the trains in Switzerland."

"He's giving us an early Christmas present."

"Don't bet on it."

I walk across the room and sit down next to her. "Is everything ready?" I ask.

"I think so. It's Tommy's first Christmas, and I want to be sure it's a memorable one."

"He won't remember anything by this time tomorrow."

She smiles.

"You ought to go to bed," I tell her. "We have a busy day tomorrow."

"It's nice to have a little quiet time. Besides, I'm still getting used to the idea of your brother getting married again."

"I think it's going to work out this time."

"So do I." She yawns and stretches out on the sofa with her head resting in my lap. "You don't think we should revisit our current situation, do you?"

"Not at four o'clock in the morning."

"How about after we get a good night's sleep?"

"I'm willing to consider it."

"I'm serious, Mike."

"So am I."

If past history is any indication, this discussion won't last long.

"At the very least," she says, "I think we should take a little break until the end of the year. We can get back to work in January."

"*You* can take a break," I tell her. "I have a full plate."

"Ramon's case is over," she says. "You aren't planning to represent John Shanahan, are you?"

"Believe it or not, he hasn't asked me."

Another smile.

"Besides," I add, "my other clients are keeping me very busy."

"What other clients?"

"Luis Alvarado came in today. He got his temporary visa and wanted to express his gratitude. And Anna Moreno called. I found her a new job and a new apartment."

"Where is she working?"

"She's a hostess at Lopez's restaurant." I arch an eyebrow and add, "Don't worry—he's adopted a hands-off policy."

"How did you manage that?"

"I told Lopez that if he didn't hire a few of my friends, I was going to bring the mother of all sexual-harassment suits on behalf of Mercedes Trujillo. He promoted her to evening manager, and Anna is working for her."

"You're good, Mike."

"I know."

She gives me a knowing look and says, "You realize we were able to solve Ramon's case because we traded legal services and stolen auto parts for information."

"Good lawyers find practical solutions to real-world problems."

"It doesn't bother you?"

"This isn't figure skating, Rosie. They don't give style points. At the end of the day, we got a good result for Ramon and we found the real killer. That's all that matters."

She gives me a serious look and says, "We didn't get a good result for Jane Doe."

"We can't fix everything, Rosie."

"We can try. Is Roosevelt going to be able to find the killer?"

"I hope so. He's tenacious."

"Do you think it's the same guy who torched our office?"

"Probably."

We sit in silence and look at the blinking lights. Finally, Rosie says, "Tommy was trying to walk yesterday."

"How'd he do?"

"He's starting to get the hang of it." She swallows hard and says, "I want to spend more time with him."

I think about all of the landmark events in Grace's life that we've missed because of commitments to our clients. "So do I."

"Then we're going to have to make a few adjustments."

"What do you have in mind?"

"Job sharing is very trendy nowadays. I can work Monday and Wednesday and you can work Tuesday and Thursday. We can trade off Fridays and cover for each other."

"Can we afford it?"

"Probably not, but we can operate like the state of California—deficit spending."

"Will we be able to afford my apartment?"

"It will be tight."

"You aren't thinking I should move over here, are you?"

"Let's start with job sharing, and then we can work our way to more complicated issues."

Not a bad idea. I touch her cheek and say, "Let's give it a try for a few months and see how it goes."

"And if it doesn't work?"

"We'll make it work."

"We may not be able to take any vacations for a few years."

"I get bored in Hawaii."

"We won't be able to take on any big cases if we're both working part-time."

"If it's all the same to you, I'd like to stay away from big cases for a while."

"Are you prepared to turn down a murder trial if it lands on our doorstep?"

"Yes."

"Promise?"

"I promise. I'd like to watch Tommy grow up, and I'd

like to spend more time with Grace before she becomes a teenager and doesn't want to be seen with me."

"Did I tell you she got invited to a New Year's party next week?"

"You did."

"Did I mention the party is at a boy's house?"

"You didn't."

"Did I mention the boy really likes her?"

And so it begins. "Do you think we should hire Nick the Dick to check him out?"

"It isn't a bad idea."

The crow's-feet at the corners of her eyes crinkle as her smile broadens. "Are you really willing to slow down a bit?" she asks.

"Yes."

She reaches up and gently touches my cheek, then she pulls her face up to mine and kisses me.

"What's that for?" I ask.

"Merry Christmas, Mike." Her lips transform into a warm smile. "Do you hear that?"

The house is completely silent. "Hear what?"

"The sound of quiet at four o'clock in the morning."

I touch a finger to her lips; then I lean over and kiss her softly. "Merry Christmas, Rosie."

Acknowledgments

Writing these stories is a collaborative process for me. I get an enormous amount of help, and I want to take the opportunity once again to thank the kind people who have been so generous with their time.

Thanks to my beautiful wife, Linda, who still reads all of my drafts, keeps me going when I'm stuck and remains supportive when I'm on deadline. Thanks also to our twin sons, Alan and Stephen, who are very understanding when I have to spend time working on my books.

Thanks to Neil Nyren, my patient and perceptive editor and friend, for your comments and unending support. Thanks to the team at Putnam for your hard work, dedication and good humor. I really appreciate it.

Thanks to my extraordinary agent, Margret McBride, and to Donna DeGutis, Renee Vincent and Faye Atchison at the Margret McBride Literary Agency. You're still the best.

Thanks to my teachers, Katherine V. Forrest and Michael Nava, and to the Every Other Thursday Night Writers' Group: Bonnie DeClark, Meg Stiefvater, Anne Maczulak, Liz Hartka, Janet Wallace and Priscilla Royal. I can't do this without you.

Thanks to Inspector Sergeant Thomas Eisenmann and

Officer Jeff Roth of the San Francisco Police Department, and to Inspector Phil Dito of the Alameda County District Attorney's Office, and to Linda Allen of the San Francisco District Attorney's Office and Jack Allen of the Solono County District Attorney's Office. Keep fighting the good fight.

A special thanks to Sister Karen Marie Franks of St. Dominic's Convent in San Francisco for your help with theological issues.

Thanks to my friends and colleagues at Sheppard, Mullin, Richter & Hampton (and your spouses and significant others), for being so supportive through the births of five books. In particular, thanks to Randy and Mary Short, Cheryl Holmes, Chris and Debbie Neils, Bob Thompson, Joan Story and Robert Kidd, Lori Wider and Tim Mangan, Becky and Steve Hlebasko, Donna Andrews, Phil and Wendy Atkins-Pattenson, Julie and Jim Ebert, Geri Freeman and David Nickerson, Kristen Jensen and Allen Carr, Bill and Barbara Manierre, Betsy McDaniel, Ted and Vicki Lindquist, Tom and Beth Nevins, Maria Pracher, Chris and Karen Jaenike, Ron and Rita Ryland, Bob and Elizabeth Stumpf, Kathleen Shugar, John and Judy Sears, Dave Lanferman, Mathilde Kapuano, Jerry Slaby, Guy Halgren, Dick Brunette, Aline Pearl, Steve Winick, Sue Lenzi, Larry Braun and Bob Zuber.

Thanks to my supportive friends at my alma mater, Boalt Law School: Kathleen Vanden Heuvel, Leslie and Dean Bob Berring, Louise Epstein and Dean Herma Hill Kay.

Thanks always to the kind souls who provide comments on the early drafts of my stories: Jerry and Dena Wald, Gary and Marla Goldstein, Ron and Betsy Rooth, Rich and Debby Skobel, Dolly and John Skobel, Alvin and Charlene Saper, Doug and JoAnn Nopar, Dick and Dorothy Nopar, Rex and Fran Beach, Angèle and George Nagy, Polly Dinkel and David Baer, Jean Ryan, Sally Rau, Bill Mandel, Dave and Evie Duncan, Jill Hutchinson and Chuck Odenthal, Joan Lubamersky and Jeff Greendorfer, Tom Bearrows and Holly Hirst, Chris and Audrey Geannopoulos, Julie Hart, Jim and Kathy Janz, Denise and Tom McCarthy, Raoul and Pat Kennedy, Eric Chen and Kathleen Schwallie, Jan Klohonatz, Marv Leon, Ken Freeman, David and Petrita Lipkin, Pamela Swartz, Cori Stockman, Allan and Nancy Zackler, Ted George, Nevins McBride, Marcia Shainsky, Maurice and Sandy Ash, Elaine and Bill Petrocelli, Penny and Tom Warner, Sheila, Alan and Leslie Gordon, Stacy Alesi, Gail Foster, Bert and Amie Keane, Jeff Pick, JoAnn and Ignatius Tsang, Sue and Michael Schwartz and Patty, Jeffrey, Jack and Taylor Norman.

Thanks always to Charlotte, Ben, Michelle, Margaret and Andy Siegel, Ilene Garber, Joe, Jan and Julia Garber, Roger and Sharon Fineberg, Jan Harris Sandler and Matz Sandler, Scott, Michelle, Stephanie, Kim and Sophia Harris, Cathy, Richard and Matthew Falco and Julie Harris and Matthew and Aiden Stewart.

Finally, a big thanks once again to all of my readers, and especially to those of you who have taken the time to write. Your support means more to me than you'll ever imagine, and I am very grateful.